TRANSCENDENT 3

TRANSCENDENT 3

The Year's Best Transgender Speculative Fiction

Edited by Bogi Takács

Lethe Press
Amherst, Massachusetts

TRANSCENDENT 3

Compilation copyright © 2018 Lethe Press, Inc. Introduction copyright © 2018 Bogi Takács. ALL RIGHTS RESERVED. No part of this work may be reproduced or utilized in any form or by any means, electronic or mechanical, including photocopying, microfilm, and recording, or by any information storage and retrieval system, without permission in writing from the publisher.

Published in 2018 by Lethe Press, Inc.
6 University Drive, Suite 206 / PMB #223 • Amherst, MA 01002 USA
www.lethepressbooks.com • lethepress@aol.com
ISBN: 978-1-59021-706-1 / 1-59021-706-3

Credits for previous publication appear on page 249, which constitutes an extension of this copyright page.

These stories are works of fiction. Names, characters, places, and incidents are either products of the authors' imaginations or are used fictitiously. Any resemblance to actual persons, living or dead, organizations, events, or locales is entirely coincidental.

Set in Agmena, Truesdell, and Charlemagne.
Interior design: Alex Jeffers.
Cover art: "Perfect Housewife" by L. Stiegman.
Cover design: Inkspiral Design.

CONTENTS

FOREWORD

◄ Bogi Takács ►

Welcome to the permanent revolution.

Speculative fiction with transgender themes has undergone an explosion in recent years, with dozens upon dozens of new stories every year. I considered eighty-eight stories while editing the previous volume of the *Transcendent* series, but in 2017 I found one hundred and forty-two eligible works — a huge increase. (This book is slightly longer than the preceding two volumes, to reflect this very welcome change.)

Trans themes are here to stay, trans writers are also here to stay. This is not a superficial trend. Work that has previously been excluded and repressed is now coming to light, and writers are creating with great enthusiasm and vehemence.

The stories in this year's selection are sometimes grim, sometimes cheerful, sometimes quirky — but always full of emotion. From the dynamic space opera art thefts of "A Chameleon's Gloves" to the devastating dystopia of "Don't Press Charges and I Won't Sue" to the hilarity of "A Splendid Goat Adventure," a wide range of non-cis experiences are represented. Authors are expressing more and more of how transness can relate to other marginalizations, like diasporan existence in "Cooking with Closed Mouths" or mental illness in "A Complex Filament of Light." The possibilities are endless — we can read about a neuroatypical genderfluid accountant in "Minor Heresies," Mughal steampunk mechanical beings in "World of the Three," or dysphoric trans vampires in "Small

Changes over Large Periods of Time." We can even see actual deities make appearance, as in "Praying to the God of Small Chances."

Trans stories engage with and subvert an ever-wider variety of themes in speculative fiction. "The Heart's Cartography" presents a unique take on time travel (I never expect to say 'unique' and 'time travel' in the same sentence!), while "Heat Death of Western Human Arrogance" takes colonialism head-on, and "Fire Fills the Belly" reflects on the underside of solarpunk-esque futures. "Feed" examines the intersection of assistive technology, internet privacy and multiple marginalizations in a surprisingly small footprint.

Sometimes these genre-collisions are brutal: "The Heavy Things" shows bodily changes with gutwrenching literary ease, while "Death You Deserve" skillfully reinterprets the everyday life of a trans woman through the lens of horror movies. "The Mouse" is a ghost story in which you know right away that the protagonist dies. But there are also many lighter moments you will find all throughout the book, and many examples of support and love, and family ties of all sorts — for example supportive siblings in "A Spell to Signal Home," or nonbinary parenting in the space future in "The Worldless."

This year most of the stories are about explicitly trans characters and/or issues, but I did include one story that features a sentient nonhuman being learning about life, including gender, sex and sexuality — "Hello, World!" offers a very much non-cisgender perspective on life, the universe and talking robots.

To provide you with more resources, this year I also added a section on year-to-year changes in transgender SFF, and assembled my longer-form trans highlights.

Good reading!

Changes this year

There are more and more stories, but are there tendencies in transgender speculative fiction beyond the quantitative increase? Readers sometimes ask me if there were more apocalypse stories in 2017 due to changes in the American political landscape. Even though I do see such a trend in speculative fiction generally, I'm not sure there has been an increase in *trans* apocalyptic and post-apocalyptic stories, in particular — there have always been many. Trans authors have always found disasters, even fictional and speculative disasters, highly relatable; probably due to the oppression and discrimination many of us face in everyday life.

An unrelated topic that does seem to come up much more frequently in 2017 is the relationship of transness and disability and/or chronic illness. There have been stories like this in previous *Transcendent* anthologies too — one of my personal favorites is Toby MacNutt's "The Way You Say Good-Night" from *Transcendent 2* —, but by now there are so many that I could not even reprint them all if I tried. This anthology also contains a few, and to increase general accessibility, we now also include a list of content notices at the end, on reader request.

Intersex people are further marginalized inside the QUILTBAG+, but this year I also had the privilege of considering several stories by intersex authors. Ethnic and racial diversity also seems to be increasing. Previously this was predominantly due to the presence of minority writers from Western countries, but now there are more and more authors from non-Western countries getting their English-language trans work successfully published — and reprinted, as you can see in this table of contents. Unfortunately translations still lag behind, and present one of the biggest current gaps in trans speculative literature.

There are publishing trends that go beyond subject matter or author identity. I see a rapidly increasing amount of trans stories that were self-published by their authors on Patreon — or, in more rare cases, published on Patreon by small presses. Patreon submissions tend to be on average higher quality than other sources, which seems sharply in contrast with stereotypes about self-publishing. As far as I can tell, this is at least in part due to traditionally published trans authors increasingly putting their trans-related work on Patreon, or moving from small presses to self-publishing. Authors such as RoAnna Sylver (featured in the previous *Transcendent* with a novelette) continue to enjoy success with Patreon, and more and more trans writers are taking notice.

There are also more and more trans anthologies — I remember the time when publishers openly stated "there has already been one." Just in 2017, there have been several SFF anthologies with substantial trans content, or trans anthologies with substantial SFF content: *Brave Boy World: A Transman Anthology* edited by Michael D. Takeda, *Nerve Endings: The New Trans Erotic* edited by Tobi Hill-Meyer, and *Meanwhile, Elsewhere: Speculative Fiction from Transgender Writers* edited by Casey Plett and Cat Fitzpatrick. In case you are wondering if this is just a chance occurrence, in 2018 there have already been more, just in the first few months of the year. *Nameless Woman: Fiction by Trans Women of Color* edited by Jamie Berrout, Ellyn Peña, and Venus Selenite includes several SFF stories (one of them is a reprint that also appeared in the previous *Transcendent*), *Capricious SF* edited by A.C. Buchanan has published a book-length special issue on *Gen-*

der Diverse Pronouns, and *Strange Horizons* also released a trans and nonbinary special issue.

Longer-form trans speculative highlights

There are more and more trans novellas and novels in speculative fiction; to the extent that I will hopefully need to make this highlights section into a recurring feature.

2017 has seen so many excellent trans novellas that they could fill a hypothetical novellas year's best. JY Yang's highly immersive silkpunk novellas *The Red Threads of Fortune* and *The Black Tides of Heaven*, with Tor.com, are currently finalists for multiple awards. Margaret Killjoy also started a new novella series with Tor.com: the first volume *The Lamb Will Slaughter the Lion* appeared in 2017 too, showing us anarchist queer punks fighting monsters. Rose Lemberg's epic fantasy *Portrait of the Desert in Personages of Power* was published in *Beneath Ceaseless Skies*, and they also have a cheerful short story set in the same world in this anthology. I also enjoyed *Possibilities* by Nicole Field self-published on Patreon, a fantasy romance with multiple trans and nonbinary characters. Finally, *Agents of Dreamland* by Caitlín R. Kiernan did not have trans themes, but as a new release from a high profile trans author, it is also very much worth mentioning here — it cannily combines Lovecraftian themes with the Men in Black.

There were so many trans-related SFF novels that I can only highlight a few of my favorites. Rivers Solomon's debut novel *An Unkindness of Ghosts* was successful even beyond speculative circles, gaining accolades from NPR and *The Guardian* among others. In this book, the young intersex and neuroatypical Black protagonist fights against the system of a slaveholding colony ship lost in space; it is also exceptional for offering a deeply heartfelt and personal portrayal of multiple interacting marginalizations. Rivers Solomon also appears in *Transcendent 3* with an unrelated but likewise striking short story.

Another science fiction success: Yoon Ha Lee's *Raven Stratagem* expanded the space opera universe of the Hexarchate, and is currently a finalist for the Hugo award. It also had much more explicitly trans themes than the first volume, *Ninefox Gambit*. You can find a story from in the world of the Hexarchate in *Transcendent 3* too!

The short novel *Peter Darling* by Austin Chant offered a very new trans take on the classic Peter Pan story, examining the toxic masculinity inherent in the original and providing a touching romance at the same time.

My self-publishing surprise of the year was *Margins and Murmurations* by Otter Lieffe, a near future dystopian novel presenting the lives of political activists and sex workers in a way that feels less and less fictional. This novel also features an aromantic trans woman protagonist in a lifelong friendship that is not portrayed as less than a romantic relationship.

Most of the best novels with trans characters are unsurprisingly written by trans authors, but I was also very glad to see an exception this year: the surreal science-fantasy *Prey of Gods* by Nicky Drayden featured a trans character with a striking and impactful storyline in a larger ensemble cast.

I'm looking forward to what the next year will bring, and in the meanwhile, we have plenty of great work from 2017 to read.

Acknowledgments

I worked on this anthology in the traditional lands of the Kanza and Osage people, who were forcibly removed from their homes in the late nineteenth century. Today this land is still a home to people from many Indigenous nations, and I would like to acknowledge their presence and express my gratitude toward them.

I would like to express my thanks to the following people for their story recommendations, writer referrals and all manner of kind help (in alphabetic order by first name): Ada Hoffmann, Brontë Wieland, Casey Plett, Charles Payseur, Corey Alexander, Jeanne Thornton, Julian K. Jarboe, Keith Manuel, Rose Lemberg, S. Qiouyi Lu, Shira Glassman, Steve Berman, TS Porter, and Phoebe Wagner. Additional thanks to Steve Berman for his continued publishing support, and to Rose Lemberg and Mati for the gardening adventures!

Content Notices

"The Chameleon's Gloves": The author chooses not to warn for specific content.

"Death You Deserve": Panic attacks, murder, transmisogynist violence, non-explicit sex; brief mentions of drugs, poverty, anti-gay slurs, internalized ableism.

"Fire Fills the Belly": Classism, poverty. Brief mentions of death, incarceration, misgendering, alcohol.

"Small Changes over Long Periods of Time": nonconsensual vampirism, blood, death, vomiting, menstruation, dysphoria, cissexism, non-graphic physical violence, suffocation, explicit sex; brief mentions of drunkenness, mind control.

TRANSCENDENT 3

"Heat Death of Western Human Arrogance": Death, colonialism, indentured labor, non-explicit sex; brief mentions of genitals.

"Praying to the God of Small Chances": Hospitalization, cancer; brief mentions of self-injury, alcohol.

"The Mouse": Death, murder, transmisogynist violence, blood, harm to animals, self-harm, panic attacks, misgendering, family conflict; brief mentions of drugs, suicide, ableist insults.

"Cooking with Closed Mouths": Blood, racism; brief mention of eating humans.

"World of the Three": Death, grief. Brief mentions of murder, warfare, misgendering, drunkenness.

"A Spell to Signal Home": Injury, animal attack, vomiting; brief mentions of blood, medical gatekeeping, pregnancy, warfare, drunkenness.

"Feed": Ableism; brief mention of murder.

"Hello, World!": Brief mentions of discrimination, illness, harm to animals.

"A Splendid Goat Adventure": Drunkenness; brief mentions of drugs, warfare, blood, injury.

"A Complex Filament of Light": Mental illness, ableism with a racial/cultural element, family conflict, suicide, medication, self-harm.

"Minor Heresies": Ableism, gender-related coercion, torture, murder; brief mentions of mind control, blood.

"The Heavy Things": Menstruation, injury, eating disorders, medication, cissexism.

"Don't Press Charges and I Won't Sue": Medical coercion, cissexism, physical restraint, injury, panic attacks, misgendering, poverty, surgery, ableism, drunkenness, partner abuse; brief mentions of genitals, vomiting, drugs, colonialism, blood.

"The Worldless": Poverty, illness. Brief mentions of death, animal death, incarceration, sex, exoticization.

"The Heart's Cartography": Brief mentions of misgendering, injury, ableism.

THE CHAMELEON'S GLOVES

◄ Yoon Ha Lee ►

Rhehan hated museums, but their partner Liyeusse had done unmentionable things to the ship's stardrive the last time the two of them had fled the authorities, and the repairs had drained their savings. Which was why Rhehan was on a station too close to the more civilized regions of the dustways, flirting with a tall, pale woman decked in jewels while they feigned interest in pre-Devolutionist art.

In spite of themselves, Rhehan was impressed by colonists who had carved pictures into the soles of worn-out space boots: so useless that it had to be art, not that they planned to say that to the woman.

" — wonderful evocation of the Festival of the Vines using that repeated motif," the woman was saying. She brushed a long curl of hair out of her face and toyed with one of her dangling earrings as she looked sideways at Rhehan.

"I was just thinking that myself," Rhehan lied. The Festival of the Vines, with its accompanying cheerful inebriation and sex, would be less agonizing than having to pretend to care about the aesthetics of this piece. Too bad Rhehan and Liyeusse planned to disappear in the next couple hours. The woman was pretty enough, despite her obsession with circuitscapes. Rhehan was of the opinion that if you wanted to look at a circuit, nothing beat the real thing.

A tinny voice said in Rhehan's ear, "Are you on location yet?"

Rhehan faked a cough and subvocalized over the link to Liyeusse. "Been in position for the last half-hour. You sure you didn't screw up the prep?"

She snorted disdainfully. "Just hurry it — "

At last the alarms clanged. The jeweled woman jumped, her astonishing blue eyes going wide. Rhehan put out a steadying arm and, in the process, relieved her of a jade ring, slipping it in their pocket. Not high-value stuff, but no one with sense wore expensive items as removables. They weren't wearing gloves on this outing — had avoided wearing gloves since their exile — but the persistent awareness of their naked hands never faded. At least, small consolation, the added sensation made legerdemain easier, even if they had to endure the distastefulness of skin touching skin.

A loud, staticky voice came over the public address system. "All patrons, please proceed to the nearest exit. There is no need for alarm" — exactly the last thing you wanted to say if you didn't want people to panic, or gossip for that matter — "but due to an incident, the museum needs to close for maintenance."

The woman was saying, with charming anxiety, "We'd better do as they say. I wonder what it is."

Come on, Rhehan thought, *what's the delay?* Had they messed up preparing the explosives?

They had turned to smile and pat the woman's hand reassuringly when the first explosives went off at the end of the hall. Fire flowered, flashed; a boom reverberated through the walls, with an additional hiss of sparks when a security screen went down. Rhehan's ears rang even though they'd been prepared for the noise. Two stands toppled, spilling a ransom's worth of iridescent black quantum-pearl strands inscribed with algorithmic paeans. The sudden chemical reek of the smoke made Rhehan cough, even though you'd think they'd be used to it by now. Several startled bystanders shrieked and bolted toward the exit.

The woman leapt back and behind a decorative pillar with commendable reflexes. "Over here," she called out to Rhehan, as if she could rescue them. Rhehan feigned befuddlement although they could easily lip-read what she was saying — they could barely hear her past the ringing in their ears — and sidestepped out of her reach, just in case.

A second blast went off, farther down the hall. A thud suggested that something out of sight had fallen down. Rhehan thought snidely that some of the statues they had seen earlier would be improved by a few creative cracks anyway. The sprinklers finally kicked in, and a torrent of water rained down from above, drenching them.

Rhehan left the woman to fend for herself. "Where are you going?" she shouted after Rhehan, loudly enough to be heard despite the damage to their hearing, as they sprinted toward the second explosion.

"I have to save the painting!" Rhehan said over their shoulder.

To Rhehan's dismay, the woman pivoted on her heel and followed. Rhehan turned their head to lip-read their words, almost crashing into a corner in the process: "You shame me," she said as she ran after them. "Your dedication to the arts is greater than mine."

Another explosion. Liyeusse, whose hearing was unaffected, was wheezing into Rhehan's ear. "'Dedication...to...the...arts,' " she said between breaths. "'Dedication.' *You.*"

Rhehan didn't have time for Liyeusse's quirky sense of humor. Just because they couldn't tell a color wheel from a flywheel didn't mean they didn't appreciate market value.

They'd just rounded the corner to the relevant gallery and its delicious gear collages when Rhehan was alerted — too late — by the quickened rhythm of the woman's footsteps. They inhaled too sharply, coughed at the smoke, and staggered when she caught them in a chokehold. "What — " Rhehan said, and then no words were possible anymore.

R hehan woke in a chair, bound. They kept their eyes closed and tested the cords, hoping not to draw attention. The air had a familiar undertone of incense, which was very bad news, but perhaps they were only imagining it. Rhehan had last smelled this particular blend, with its odd metallic top notes, in the ancestral shrines of a childhood home they hadn't returned to in eight years. They stilled their hands from twitching.

Otherwise, the temperature was warmer than they were accustomed to — Liyeusse liked to keep the ship cool — and a faint hissing suggested an air circulation system not kept in as good shape as it could be. Even more faintly, they heard the distinctive, just-out-of-tune humming of a ship's drive. Too bad they lacked Liyeusse's ability to identify the model by listening to the harmonics.

More importantly: how many people were there with them? They didn't hear anything, but that didn't mean —

"You might as well open your eyes, Kel Rhehan," a cool female voice said in a language they had not heard for a long time, confirming Rhehan's earlier suspicions. They had not fooled her.

Rhehan wondered whether their link to Liyeusse was still working, and if she was all right. "Liyeusse?" they subvocalized. No response. Their heart stuttered.

They opened their eyes: might as well assess the situation, since their captor knew they were awake.

"I don't have the right to that name any longer," Rhehan said. They hadn't been part of the Kel people for years. But their hands itched with the memory of the Kel gloves they hadn't worn in eight years, as the Kel reckoned it. Indeed, with their hands exposed like this, they felt shamed and vulnerable in front of one of their people.

The woman before them was solidly built, dark, like the silhouette of a tree, and more somber in mien than the highly ornamented agent who had brought Rhehan in. She wore the black and red of the Kel judiciary. A cursory slip of veil obscured part of her face, its translucence doing little to hide her sharp features. The veil should have scared Rhehan more, as it indicated that the woman was a judge-errant, but her black Kel gloves hurt worse. Rhehan's had been stripped from them and burned when the Kel cast them out.

"I've honored the terms of my exile," Rhehan said desperately. What had they done to deserve the attention of a judge-errant? Granted that they were a thief, but they'd had little choice but to make a living with the skills they had. "What have you done with my partner?"

The judge-errant ignored the question. Nevertheless, the sudden tension around her eyes indicated that she knew *something*. Rhehan had been watching for it. "I am Judge Kel Shiora, and I have been sent because the Kel have need of you," she said.

"Of course," Rhehan said, fighting to hide their bitterness. Eight years of silence and adapting to an un-Kel world, and the moment the Kel had need of them, they were supposed to comply.

Shiora regarded them without malice or opprobrium or anything much resembling feeling. "There are many uses for a jaihanar."

Jaihanar — what non-Kel called, in their various languages, a haptic chameleon. Someone who was not only so good at imitating patterns of movement that they could scam inattentive people, but also able to fool the machines whose security systems depended on identifying their owners' characteristic movements. How you interacted with your gunnery system, or wandered about your apartment, or smiled at the lover you'd known for the last decade. It wasn't magic — a jaihanar needed some minimum of data to work from — but the knack often seemed that way.

The Kel produced few jaihanar, and the special forces snapped up those that emerged from the Kel academies. Rhehan had been the most promising jaihanar in the last few generations before disgracing themselves. The only reason they hadn't been executed was that the Kel government had foreseen that they would someday be of use again.

"Tell me what you want, then," Rhehan said. Anything to keep her talking so that eventually she might be willing to say what she'd done with Liyeusse.

"If I undo your bonds, will you hear me out?"

Getting out of confinement would also be good. Their leg had fallen asleep. "I won't try anything," Rhehan said. They knew better.

Ordinarily, Rhehan would have felt sorry for anyone who trusted a thief's word so readily, except they knew the kind of training a judge-errant underwent. Shiora wasn't the one in danger. They kept silent as she unlocked the restraints.

"I had to be sure," Shiora said.

Rhehan shrugged. "Talk to me."

"General Kavarion has gone rogue. We need someone to infiltrate her ship and retrieve a weapon she has stolen."

"I'm sorry," Rhehan said after a blank pause. "You just said that General Kavarion has gone rogue? Kavarion, the hero of Split Suns? Kavarion, of the Five Splendors? My hearing must be going."

Shiora gave them an unamused look. "Kel Command sent her on contract to guard a weapons research facility," she said. "Kavarion recently attacked the facility and made off with the research and a prototype. The prototype may be armed."

"Surely, you have any number of loyal Kel who'd be happy to go on this assignment," Rhehan said. The Kel took betrayal personally. They knew this well.

"You are the nearest jaihanar in this region of the dustways." Most people reserved the term *dustways* for particularly lawless segments of the spaceways, but the Kel used the term for anywhere that didn't fall under the Kel sphere of influence.

"Also," Shiora added, "few of our jaihanar match your skill. You owe the Kel for your training, if nothing else. Besides, it's not in your interest to live in a world where former Kel are hunted for theft of immensely powerful weapon prototypes."

TRANSCENDENT 3

Rhehan had to admit she had a point.

"They named it the Incendiary Heart," Shiora continued. "It initiates an inflationary expansion like the one at the universe's birth."

Rhehan swore. "Remote detonation?"

"There's a timer. It's up to you to get out of range before it goes off."

"The radius of effect?"

"Thirty thousand light-years, give or take, in a directed cone. That's the only thing that makes it possible to use without blowing up the person setting it off."

Rhehan closed their eyes. That would fry a nontrivial percentage of the galaxy. "And you don't know if it's armed."

"No. The general is running very fast — to what, we don't know. But she has been attempting to hire mercenary jaihanar. We suspect she is looking for a way to control the device — which may buy us time."

"I see." Rhehan rubbed the palm of one hand with the fingers of the other, smile twisting at the judge-errant's momentary look of revulsion at the touch of skin on skin. Which was why they'd done it, of course, petty as it was. "Can you offer me any insight into her goals?"

"If we knew that," the judge-errant said bleakly, "we would know why she turned coat."

Blowing up a region of space, even a very local region of space in galactic terms, would do no one any good. In particular, it would make a continued career in art theft a little difficult. On the other hand, Rhehan was determined to wring some payment out of this, if only so Liyeusse wouldn't lecture them about their lack of mercenary instinct. Their ship wasn't going to fix itself, after all. "I'll do it," they said. "But I'm going to need some resources — "

The judge surprised them by laughing. "You have lived too long in the dustways," she said. "I can offer payment in the only coin that should matter to you — or do you think we haven't been watching you?"

Rhehan should have objected, but they froze up, knowing what was to come.

"Do this for us, and show us the quality of your service," the judge-errant said, "and Kel Command will reinstate you." Very precisely, she peeled the edge of one glove back to expose the dark fine skin of her wrist, signaling her sincerity.

Rhehan stared. "Liyeusse?" they asked again, subvocally. No response. Which meant that Liyeusse probably hadn't heard that damning offer. At least she wasn't there to see Rhehan's reaction. As good as they normally were at controlling their body language, they had not been able to hide that moment's hunger for a home they had thought forever lost to them.

"I will do this," Rhehan said at last. "But not for some bribe; because a weapon like the one you describe is too dangerous for anyone, let alone a rogue, to control." And because they needed to find out what had become of Liyeusse, but Shiora wouldn't understand that.

The woman who escorted Rhehan to their ship, docked on the Kel carrier — Rhehan elected not to ask how this had happened — had a familiar face. "I don't know why *you're* not doing this job," Rhehan said to the pale woman now garbed in Kel uniform, complete with gloves, rather than the jewels and outlandish stationer garb she'd affected in the museum.

The woman unsmiled at Rhehan. "I will be accompanying you," she said in the lingua franca they'd used earlier.

Of course. Shiora had extracted Rhehan's word, but neither would she fail to take precautions. They couldn't blame her.

Kel design sensibilities had not changed much since Rhehan was a cadet. The walls of dark metal were livened by tapestries of wire and faceted beads, polished from battlefield shrapnel: obsolete armor, lens components in laser cannon, spent shells. Rhehan kept from touching the wall superstitiously as they walked by.

"What do I call you?" Rhehan said finally, since the woman seemed disinclined to speak first.

"I am Sergeant Kel Anaz," she said. She stopped before a hatch, and she tapped a panel in full sight of Rhehan, her mouth curling sardonically.

"I'm not stupid enough to try to escape a ship full of Kel," Rhehan said. "I bet you have great aim." Besides, there was Liyeusse's safety to consider.

"You weren't bad at it yourself."

She would have studied their record, yet Rhehan hated how exposed the simple statement made them feel. "I can imitate the stance of a master marksman," Rhehan said dryly. "That doesn't give me the eye, or the reflexes. These past years, I've found safer ways to survive."

Anaz's eyebrows lifted at "safer," but she kept her contempt to herself. After chewing over Anaz's passkey, the hatch opened. A whoosh of cool air floated over Rhehan's face. They stepped through before Anaz could say anything, their eyes drawn immediately to the lone non-Kel ship in the hangar. To their relief, the *Flarecat* didn't look any more disreputable than before.

Rhehan advanced upon the *Flarecat* and entered it, all the while aware of Anaz at their back. Liyeusse was bound to one of the passenger's seats, the side of her face swollen and purpling, her cap of curly hair sticking out in all directions.

Liyeusse's eyes widened when she saw the two of them, but she didn't struggle against her bonds. Rhehan swore and went to her side.

"If she's damaged — " Rhehan said in a shaking voice, then froze when Anaz shoved the muzzle of a gun against the back of their head.

"She's ji-Kel," Anaz said in an even voice: *ji-Kel*, not-Kel. "She wasn't even concussed. She'll heal."

"She's my partner," Rhehan said. "We work together."

"If you insist," Anaz said with a distinct air of distaste. The pressure eased, and she cut Liyeusse free herself.

Liyeusse grimaced. "New friend?" she said.

"New job, anyway," Rhehan said. They should have known that Shiora and her people would treat a ji-Kel with little respect.

"We're never going to land another decent art theft," Liyeusse said with strained cheer. "You have no sense of culture."

"This one's more important." Rhehan reinforced their words with a hand signal: *Emergency. New priority.*

"What have the Kel got on you, anyhow?"

Rhehan had done their best to steer Liyeusse away from any dealings with the Kel because of the potential awkwardness. It hadn't been hard. The Kel had a reputation for providing reliable but humorless mercenaries and a distinct lack of appreciation for what Liyeusse called the exigencies of survival in the dustways. More relevantly, while they controlled a fair deal of wealth, they ruthlessly pursued and destroyed those who attempted to relieve them of it. Rhehan had never been tempted to take revenge by stealing from them.

Anaz's head came up. "You never told your partner?"

"Never told me what?" Liyeusse said, starting to sound irritated.

"We'll be traveling with Sergeant Kel Anaz," Rhehan said, hoping to distract Liyeusse.

No luck. Her mouth compressed. *Safe to talk?* she signed at them.

Not really, but Rhehan didn't see that they had many options. "I'm former Kel," Rhehan said. "I was exiled because — because of a training incident." Even now, it was difficult to speak of it. Two of their classmates had died, and an instructor.

Liyeusse laughed incredulously. "You? We've encountered Kel mercenaries before. You don't talk like one. Move like one. Well, except when — " She faltered as it occurred to her that, of the various guises Rhehan had put on for their heists, that one hadn't been a guise at all.

Anaz spoke over Liyeusse. "The sooner we set out, the better. We have word on Kavarion's vector, but we don't know how long our information will be good. You'll have to use your ship since the judge-errant's would draw attention, even if it's faster."

Don't, Rhehan signed to Liyeusse, although she knew better than to spill the *Flarecat*'s modifications to this stranger. "I'll fill you in on the way."

The dustways held many perils for ships: wandering maws, a phenomenon noted for years, and unexplained for just as long; particles traveling at unimaginable speeds, capable of destroying any ship lax in maintaining its shielding; vortices that filtered light even in dreams, causing hallucinations. When Rhehan had been newly exiled, they had convinced Liyeusse of their usefulness because they knew dustway paths new to her. Even if they hadn't been useful for making profit, they had helped in escaping the latest people she'd swindled.

Ships could be tracked by the eddies they left in the dustways. The difficulty was not in finding the traces but in interpreting them. Great houses had risen to prominence through their monopoly over the computational networks that processed and sold this information. Kel Command had paid dearly for such information in its desperation to track down General Kavarion.

Assuming that information was accurate, Kavarion had ensconced herself at the Fortress of Wheels: neutral territory, where people carried out bargains for amounts that could have made Rhehan and Liyeusse comfortable for the rest of their lives.

The journey itself passed in a haze of tension. Liyeusse snapped at Anaz, who bore her jibes with grim patience. Rhehan withdrew, not wanting to make matters worse, which was the wrong thing to do, and they knew it. In particular, Liyeusse had not forgiven them for the secret they had kept from her for so long.

At last, Rhehan slumped into the copilot's seat and spoke to Liyeusse over the newly repaired link to gain some semblance of privacy. As far as they could tell, Anaz hardly slept. Rhehan said, "You must have a lot of questions."

"I knew about the chameleon part," Liyeusse said. Any number of their heists had depended on it. "I hadn't realized that the Kel had their own."

"Usually, they don't," Rhehan said. Liyeusse inhaled slightly at *they*, as if she had expected Rhehan to say *we* instead. "But the Kel rarely let go of the ones they do produce. It's the only reason they didn't execute me."

"What did you do?"

TRANSCENDENT 3

Rhehan's mouth twisted. "The Kel say there are three kinds of people, after a fashion. There are Kel; ji-Kel, or not-Kel, whom they have dealings with sometimes; and those who aren't people at all. Just — disposable."

Liyeusse's momentary silence pricked at Rhehan. "Am I disposable to you?" she said.

"I should think it's the other way around," they said. They wouldn't have survived their first year in the dustways without her protection. "Anyway, there was a training exercise. People-who-are-not-people were used as — " They fumbled for a word in the language they spoke with Liyeusse, rather than the Kel term. "Mannequins. Props in the exercise, to be gunned down or saved or discarded, whatever the trainees decided. I chose the lives of mannequins over the lives of Kel. For this I was stripped of my position and cast out."

"I have always known that the universe is unkind," Liyeusse said, less moved than Rhehan had expected. "I assume that hired killers would have to learn their art somewhere."

"It would have been one thing if I'd thought of myself as a soldier," Rhehan said. "But a good chameleon, or perhaps a failed one, observes the people they imitate. And eventually, a chameleon learns that even mannequins think of themselves as people."

"I'm starting to understand why you've never tried to go back," Liyeusse said.

A sick yearning started up in the pit of Rhehan's stomach. They still hadn't told her about Kel Shiora's offer. Time enough later, if it came to that.

Getting to Kavarion's fleet wasn't the difficult part, although Liyeusse's eyes were bloodshot for the entire approach. The *Flarecat*'s stealth systems kept them undetected, even if mating it to the command ship, like an unwanted tick, was a hair-raising exercise. By then, Rhehan had dressed themselves in a Kel military uniform, complete with gloves. Undeserved, since strictly speaking, they hadn't recovered their honor in the eyes of their people, but they couldn't deny the necessity of the disguise.

Anaz would remain with Liyeusse on the *Flarecat*. She hadn't had to explain the threat: *Do your job, or your partner dies.* Rhehan wasn't concerned for Liyeusse's safety — so long as the two remained on the ship, Liyeusse had access to a number of nasty tricks and had no compunctions about using them — but the mission mattered to them anyway.

Rhehan had spent the journey memorizing all the haptic profiles that Anaz had provided them. In addition, Anaz had taken one look at Rhehan's outdated holographic mask and given them a new one. "If you could have afforded up-to-date equipment, you wouldn't be doing petty art theft," she had said caustically.

The Fortress of Wheels currently hosted several fleets. Tensions ran high, although its customary neutrality had so far prevailed. Who knew how long that would last; Liyeusse, interested as always in gossip, had reported that various buyers for the Incendiary Heart had shown up, and certain warlords wouldn't hesitate to take it by force if necessary.

Security on Kavarion's command ship was tight but had not been designed to stop a jaihanar. Not surprising; the Kel relied on their employers for such measures when they deigned to stop at places like the Fortress. At the moment, Rhehan was disguised as a bland-faced lieutenant.

Rhehan had finessed their way past the fifth lock in a row, losing themselves in the old, bitter pleasure of a job well done. They had always enjoyed this part best: fitting their motions to that of someone who didn't even realize what was going on, so perfectly that machine recognition systems could not tell the difference. But it occurred to them that everything was going too perfectly.

Maybe I'm imagining things, they told themselves without conviction, and hurried on. A corporal passed them by without giving more than a cursory salute, but Rhehan went cold and hastened away from him as soon as they could.

They made it to the doors to the general's quarters. Liyeusse had hacked into the communications systems and was monitoring activity. She'd assured Rhehan that the general was stationside, negotiating with someone. Since neither of them knew how long that would last —

Sweat trickled down Rhehan's back, causing the uniform to cling unpleasantly to their skin. They had some of the general's haptic information as well. Anaz hadn't liked handing it over, but as Rhehan had pointed out, the mission would be impossible without it.

Kavarion of the Five Splendors. One of the most celebrated Kel generals, and a musician besides. Her passcode was based on an extraordinarily difficult passage from a keyboard concerto. Another keyboardist could have played the passage, albeit with difficulty reproducing the nuances of expression. While not precisely a musician, Rhehan had trained in a variety of the arts for occasions such as this. (Liyeusse often remarked it was a shame they had no patience for painting, or they could have had a respectable career forging art.) They got through the passcode. Held their breath. The door began opening —

A fist slammed them in the back of the head.

TRANSCENDENT 3

Rhehan staggered and whirled, barely remaining upright. *If I get a concussion I'm going to charge Kel Command for my medical care,* they thought as the world slowed.

"Finally, someone took the bait," breathed Rhehan's assailant. Kel Kavarion; Rhehan recognized the voice from the news reports they'd watched a lifetime before. "I was starting to think I was going to have to hang out signs or hire a bounty hunter." She did something fast and complicated with her hands, and Rhehan found themselves shoved down against the floor with the muzzle of a gun digging into the back of their neck.

"Sir, I—"

"Save it," General Kavarion said, with dangerous good humor. "Come inside and I'll show you what you're after. Don't fight me. I'm better at it than you are."

Rhehan couldn't argue that.

The general let Rhehan up. The door had closed again, but she executed the passphrase in a blur that made Rhehan think she was wasted on the military. Surely there was an orchestra out there that could use a star keyboardist.

Rhehan made sure to make no threatening moves as they entered, scanning the surroundings. Kavarion had a taste for the grandiloquent. Triumph-plaques of metal and stone and lacquerware covered the walls, forming a mosaic of battles past and comrades lost. The light reflecting from their angled surfaces gave an effect like being trapped in a kaleidoscope of sterilized glory.

Kavarion smiled cuttingly. Rhehan watched her retreating step by step, gun still trained on them. "You don't approve," Kavarion remarked.

Rhehan unmasked since there wasn't any point still pretending to be one of her soldiers. "I'm a thief," they said. "It's all one to me."

"You're lying, but never mind. I'd better make this quick." Kavarion smiled at Rhehan with genuine and worrying delight. "You're the jaihanar we threw out, aren't you? It figures that Kel Command would drag you out of the dustways instead of hiring some ji-Kel."

"*I'm* ji-Kel now, General."

"It's a matter of degrees. It doesn't take much to figure out what Kel Command could offer an exile." She then offered the gun to Rhehan. "Hold that," she said. "I'll get the Incendiary Heart."

"How do you know I won't shoot you?" Rhehan demanded.

"Because right now I'm your best friend," Kavarion said, "and you're mine. If you shoot me, you'll never find out why I'm doing this, and a good chunk of the galaxy is doomed."

Frustrated by the sincerity they read in the set of her shoulders, Rhehan trained the gun on Kavarion's back and admired her sangfroid. She showed no sign of being worried she'd be shot.

Kavarion spoke as she pressed her hand against one of the plaques. "They probably told you I blew the research station up after I stole the Incendiary Heart, which is true." The plaque lifted to reveal a safe. "Did they also mention that someone armed the damned thing before I was able to retrieve it?"

"They weren't absolutely clear on that point."

"Well, I suppose even a judge-errant — I assume they sent a judge-errant — can't get information out of the dead. Anyway, it's a time bomb, presumably to give its user a chance to escape the area of effect."

Rhehan's heart sank. There could only be one reason why Kavarion needed a jaihanar of her own. "It's going to blow?"

"Unless you can disarm it. One of the few researchers with a sense of self-preservation was making an attempt to do so before he got killed by a piece of shrapnel. I have some video, as much of it as I could scrape before the whole place blew, but I don't know if it's enough." Kavarion removed a box that shimmered a disturbing shade of red-gold-bronze.

The original mission was no good; that much was clear. "All right," Rhehan said.

Kavarion played back a video of the researcher's final moments. It looked like it had been recorded by someone involved in a firefight, from the shakiness of the image. Parts of the keycode were obscured by smoke, by flashing lights, by flying shrapnel.

Rhehan made several attempts, then shook their head. "There's just not enough information, even for me, to reconstruct the sequence."

Suddenly Kavarion looked haggard.

"How do you know he was really trying to disarm it?" Rhehan said.

"Because he was my lover," Kavarion said, "and he had asked me for sanctuary. He was the reason I knew exactly how destructive the Incendiary Heart was to begin with."

Scientists shouldn't be allowed near weapons design, Rhehan thought. "How long do we have?"

She told them. They blanched.

TRANSCENDENT 3

"Why did you make off with it in the first place?" Rhehan said. They couldn't help but think that if she'd kept her damn contract, this whole mess could have been avoided in the first place.

"Because the contract-holder was trying to sell the Incendiary Heart to the highest bidder. And at the time I made off with it, the highest bidder looked like it was going to be one of the parties in an extremely messy civil war." Kavarion scowled. "Not only did I suspect that they'd use it at the first opportunity, I had good reason to believe that they had *terrible* security — and I doubted anyone stealing it would have any scruples either. Unfortunately, when I swiped the wretched thing, some genius decided it would be better to set it off and deny it to everyone, never mind the casualties."

Kavarion closed her fist over the Incendiary Heart. It looked like her fist was drenched in a gore of light. "Help me get it out of here, away from where it'll kill billions."

"What makes you so confident that I'm your ally, when Kel Command sent me after you?"

She sighed. "It's true that I can't offer a better reward than if you bring the accursed thing to them. On the other hand, even if you think I'm lying about the countdown, do you really trust Kel Command with dangerous weapons? They'd never let me hand it over to them for safekeeping anyway, not when I broke contract by taking it in the first place."

"No," Rhehan said after a moment. "You're right. That's not a solution either."

Kavarion opened her hand and nodded companionably at Rhehan, as though they'd been comrades for years. "I need you to run away with this and get farther from centers of civilization. I can't do this with a whole fucking Kel fleet. My every movement is being watched, and I'm afraid someone will get us into a fight and stall us in a bad place. But you — a ji-Kel thief, used to darting in and out of the dustways — your chances will be better than mine."

Rhehan's breath caught. "You're already outnumbered," they said. "Sooner or later, they'll catch up to you — the Kel, if not everyone else who wants the weapon they think you have. You don't even have a running start, since you're docked here. They'll incinerate you."

"Well, yes," Kavarion said. "We are Kel. We are the people of fire and ash. It comes with the territory. Are you willing to do this?"

Her equanimity disturbed Rhehan. Clearly, Liyeusse's way of looking at the world had rubbed off on them more than they'd accounted for, these last eight years. "You're gambling a lot on my reliability."

TRANSCENDENT 3

"Am I?" The corners of Kavarion's mouth tilted up: amusement. "You were one of the most promising Kel cadets that year, and you gave it up because you were concerned about the lives of mannequins who didn't even know your name. I'd say I'm making a good choice."

Kavarion pulled her gloves off one by one and held them out to Rhehan. "You are my agent," she said. "Take the gloves, and take the Incendiary Heart with you. A great many lives depend on it."

They knew what the gesture meant: *You hold my honor.* Shaken, they stared at her, stripped of chameleon games. Shiora was unlikely to forgive Rhehan for betraying her to ally with Kavarion. But Kavarion's logic could not be denied.

"Take them," Kavarion said tiredly. "And for love of fire and ash, don't tell me where you're going. I don't want to know."

Rhehan took the gloves and replaced the ones they had been wearing with them. *I'm committed now,* Rhehan thought. They brought their fist up to their chest in the Kel salute, and the general returned it.

Things went wrong almost from the moment Rhehan returned to their ship. They'd refused an escort from Kavarion on the grounds that it would arouse Anaz's suspicions. The general had assured them that no one would interfere with them on the way out, but the sudden blaring of alarms and the scrambling of crew to get to their assigned stations meant that Rhehan had to do a certain amount of dodging. At a guess, the Fortress-imposed cease-fire was no longer in effect. What had triggered hostilities, Rhehan didn't know and didn't particularly care. All that mattered was escaping with the Incendiary Heart.

The *Flarecat* remained shielded from discovery by the stealth device that Liyeusse so loved, even if it had a distressing tendency to blow out the engines exactly when they had to escape sharp-eyed creditors. Rhehan hadn't forgotten its location, however, and—

Anaz ambushed Rhehan before they even reached the *Flarecat*, in the dim hold where they were suiting up to traverse the perilous webbing that connected the *Flarecat* to Kavarion's command ship. Rhehan had seen this coming. Another chameleon might have fought back, and died of it; Shiora had no doubt selected Anaz for her deadliness. But Rhehan triggered the mask into Kavarion's own visage and smiled Kavarion's own smile at Anaz, counting on the reflexive Kel deference to rank. The gesture provoked enough of a hesitation that

Rhehan could pull out their own sidearm and put a bullet in the side of her neck. They'd been aiming for her head; no such luck. Still, they'd take what they could.

The bullet didn't stop Anaz. Rhehan hadn't expected it to. But the next two did. The only reason they didn't keep firing was that Rhehan could swear that the Incendiary Heart pulsed hotter with each shot. "Fuck this," they said with feeling, although they couldn't hear themselves past the ringing in their ears, and overrode the hatch to escape to the first of the web-strands without looking back to see whether Anaz was getting back up.

No further attack came, but Anaz might live, might even survive what Kavarion had in mind for her.

Liyeusse wasn't dead. Presumably Anaz had known better than to interfere too permanently with the ship's master. But Liyeusse wasn't in good condition, either. Anaz had left her unconscious and expertly tied up, a lump on the side of her head revealing where Anaz had knocked her out. Blood streaked her face. *So much for no concussions,* Rhehan thought. A careful inspection revealed two broken ribs, although no fingers or arms, small things to be grateful for. Liyeusse had piloted with worse injuries, but it wasn't something either of them wanted to make a habit of.

Rhehan shook with barely quelled rage as they unbound Liyeusse, using the lockpicks that the two of them kept stashed on board. Here, with just the two of them, there was no need to conceal their reaction.

Rhehan took the precaution of injecting her with painkillers first. Then they added a stim, which they would have preferred to avoid. Nevertheless, the two of them would have to work together to escape. It couldn't be helped.

"My head," Liyeusse said in a voice half-groan, stirring. Then she smiled crookedly at Rhehan, grotesque through the dried blood. "Did you give that Kel thug what she wanted? Are we free?"

"Not yet," Rhehan said. "As far as I can tell, Kavarion's gearing up for a firefight and they're bent on blowing each other up over this bauble. Even worse, we have a new mission." They outlined the situation while checking Liyeusse over again to make sure there wasn't any more internal damage. Luckily, Anaz hadn't confiscated their medical kits, so Rhehan retrieved one and cleaned up the head wound, then applied a bandage to Liyeusse's torso.

"Every time I think this can't get worse," Liyeusse said while Rhehan worked, but her heart wasn't in it. "Let's strap ourselves in and get flying."

"What, you don't want to appraise this thing?" They held the Incendiary Heart up. Was it warmer? They couldn't tell.

"I don't love shiny baubles *that* much," she said dryly. She was already preoccupied with the ship's preflight checks, although her grimaces revealed that the painkillers were not as efficacious as they could have been. "I'll be glad when it's gone. You'd better tell me where we're going."

The sensor arrays sputtered with the spark-lights of many ships, distorted by the fact that they were stealthed. "Ask the general to patch us in to her friend-or-foe identification system," Rhehan said when they realized that there were more Kel ships than there should have been. Kel Command must have had a fleet waiting to challenge Kavarion in case Shiora failed her mission. "And ask her not to shoot us down on our way out."

Liyeusse contacted the command ship in the Fortress's imposed lingua.

The connection hissed open. The voice that came back to them over the line sounded harried and spoke accented lingua. "Who the hell are — " Rhehan distinctly heard Kavarion snapping something profane in the Kel language. The voice spoke back, referring to Liyeusse with the particular suffix that meant *coward*, as if that applied to a ji-Kel ship to begin with. Still, Rhehan was glad they didn't have to translate that detail for Liyeusse, although they summarized the exchange for her.

"*Go,*" the voice said ungraciously. "I'll keep the gunners off you. I hope you don't crash into anything, foreigner."

"Thank you," Liyeusse said in a voice that suggested that she was thinking about blowing something up on her way out.

"Don't," Rhehan said.

"I wasn't going to — "

"They need this ship to fight with. Which will let us get away from any pursuit."

"As far as I'm concerned, they're all the enemy."

They couldn't blame her, considering what she'd been through.

The scan suite reported on the battle. Rhehan, who had webbed themselves into the copilot's seat, tracked the action with concern. The hostile Kel hadn't bothered to transmit their general's banner, a sign of utter contempt for those they fought. Even ji-Kel received banners, although they weren't expected to appreciate the nuances of Kel heraldry.

The first fighter launched from the hangar below them. "Our turn," Liyeusse said.

TRANSCENDENT 3

The *Flarecat* rocketed away from the command ship and veered abruptly away from the fighter's flight corridor. Liyeusse rechecked stealth. The engine made the familiar dreadful coughing noise in response to the increased power draw, but it held — for now.

A missile streaked through their path, missing them by a margin that Rhehan wished were larger. To their irritation, Liyeusse was whistling as she maneuvered the *Flarecat* through all the grapeshot and missiles and gyring fighters and toward the edge of the battlefield. Liyeusse had never had a healthy sense of fear.

They'd almost made it when the engine coughed again, louder. Rhehan swore in several different languages. "I'd better see to that," they said.

"No," Liyeusse said immediately, "you route the pilot functions to your seat, and I'll see if I can coax it along a little longer."

Rhehan wasn't as good a pilot, but Liyeusse was indisputably better at engineering. They gave way without argument. Liyeusse used the ship's handholds to make her way toward the engine room.

Whatever Liyeusse was doing, it didn't work. The engine hiccoughed, and stealth went down.

A flight of Kel fighters at the periphery noted the *Flarecat*'s attempt to escape and, dismayingly, found it suspicious enough to decide to pursue them. Rhehan wished their training had included faking being an ace pilot. Or actually *being* an ace pilot, for that matter.

The Incendiary Heart continued to glow malevolently. Rhehan shook their head. *It's not personal,* they told themselves. "Liyeusse," they said through the link, "forget stealth. If they decide to come after us, that's fine. It looks like we're not the only small-timers getting out of the line of fire. Can you configure for boosters?"

She understood them. "If they blow us up, a lot of people are dead anyway. Including us. We might as well take the chance."

Part of the *Flarecat*'s problem was that its engine had not been designed for sprinting. Liyeusse's skill at modifications made it possible to run. In return, the *Flarecat* made its displeasure known at inconvenient times.

The gap between the *Flarecat* and the fighters narrowed hair-raisingly as Rhehan waited for Liyeusse to inform them that they could light the hell out of there. The Incendiary Heart's glow distracted them horribly. The fighters continued their pursuit, and while so far none of their fire had connected, Rhehan didn't believe in relying on luck.

TRANSCENDENT 3

"I wish you could use that thing on them," Liyeusse said suddenly.

Yes, and that would leave nothing but the thinnest imaginable haze of particles in a vast expanse of nothing, Rhehan thought. "Are we ready yet?"

"Yes," she said after an aggravating pause.

The *Flarecat* surged forward in response to Rhehan's hands at the controls. They said, "Next thing: prepare a launch capsule for this so we can shoot it ahead of us. Anyone stupid enough to go after it and into its cone of effect — well, we tried."

For the next interval, Rhehan lost themselves in the controls and readouts, the hot immediate need for survival. They stirred when Liyeusse returned.

"I need the Heart," Liyeusse said. "I've rigged a launch capsule for it. It won't have any shielding, but it'll fly as fast and far as I can send it."

Rhehan nodded at where they'd secured it. "Don't drop it."

"You're so funny." She snatched it and vanished again.

Rhehan was starting to wish they'd settled for a nice, quiet, boring life as a Kel special operative when Liyeusse finally returned and slipped into the seat next to theirs. "It's loaded and ready to go. Do you think we're far enough away?"

"Yes," Rhehan hissed through their teeth, achingly aware of the fighters and the latest salvo of missiles.

"Away we go!" Liyeusse said with gruesome cheer.

The capsule launched. Rhehan passed over the controls to Liyeusse so she could get them away before the capsule's contents blew.

The fighters, given a choice between the capsule and the *Flarecat*, split up. Better than nothing. Liyeusse was juggling the power draw of the shields, the stardrive, life-support, and probably other things that Rhehan was happier not knowing about. The *Flarecat* accelerated as hard in the opposite direction as it could without overstressing the people in it.

The fighters took this as a trap and soared away. Rhehan expected they'd come around for another try when they realized it wasn't.

Then between the space of one blink and the next, the capsule simply vanished. The fighters overtook what should have been its position, and vanished as well. That could have been stealth, if Rhehan hadn't known better. They thought to check the sensor readings against their maps of the region: stars upon stars had gone missing, nothing left of them.

Or, they amended to themselves, there had to be some remnant smear of matter, but the *Flarecat*'s instruments wouldn't have the sensitivity to pick them up.

TRANSCENDENT 3

They regretted the loss of the people on those fighters; still, better a few deaths than the many that the Incendiary Heart had threatened.

"All right," Liyeusse said, and retriggered stealth. There was no longer any need to hurry, so the system was less likely to choke. They were far enough from the raging battle that they could relax a little. She sagged in her chair. "We're alive."

Rhehan wondered what would become of Kavarion, but that was no longer their concern. "We're still broke," they said, because eventually Liyeusse would remember.

"You didn't wrangle *any* payment out of those damn Kel before we left?" she demanded. "Especially since after they finish frying Kavarion, they'll come toast us?"

Rhehan pulled off Kavarion's gloves and set them aside. "Nothing worth anything to either of us," they said. Once, they would have given everything to win their way back into the trust of the Kel. Over the past years, however, they had discovered that other things mattered more to them. "We'll find something else. And anyway, it's not the first time we've been hunted. We'll just have to stay one step ahead of them, the way we always have."

Liyeusse smiled at Rhehan, and they knew they'd made the right choice.

DEATH YOU DESERVE

◄ Ryley Knowles ►

In my dream I went into the deep web and looked at something that made my brain ache and my eyes burn, some curvy Lovecraftian mess of a symbol. Then I was facing something, something the symbol gave power to, Zalgo or the Midnight Man or the voice from Slenderman's absent mouth, and the voice said "Poor halfbreed," and I was stuck in that moment, looping it over and over, the big reveal that all this time I wasn't quite human.

It's two forty-eight p.m. and Eve is at work. If I would've woken up a little bit earlier, I could have seen her off. If hadn't been stuck in that nightmare. I roll over and try to sit up. My heart is fluttering like a bird locked behind my ribs. My bladder is painfully full. The testosterone blockers make me have to piss all the time now, but at least it makes it easier to get my ass out of bed.

I'm alone, but there's still daylight, so I don't feel as afraid. Daylight death is rarer. A lot of horror movies start out this way, but there has to be some time to establish the character before anyone gets murdered. Knowing what point I would be at during any given point in a horror movie and finding little pockets of safety make me a little less afraid of being murdered. I am afraid of being murdered pretty much all the time, when I'm not afraid of being alive.

My therapist thinks I'm focusing on my fear of being murdered because it's a distraction from my fear of working on my independent project for school or of trying to talk to my parents or my fear of actually being murdered by boys that think killing me is some kind of public service.

TRANSCENDENT 3

My ex-therapist thought that me being a girl was a coping mechanism since I told him that women have a higher survival rate in horror movies, that they either escape or die last, that when I was little I would pretend I was one of those Final Girls so that I wouldn't die. My ex-therapist taught me to never tell anyone anything. Eve says that boys don't "become" girls because they are afraid and that my ex-therapist was a transmisogynist.

We're low on food. My EBT came through four days ago I think. If I was a good human I would go get food so that Eve wouldn't have to do something else after working a ten-hour day. If I was a better human I would even cook for her, have something ready for her. Instead I smoke half a bowl outside on the porch to flatten my nerves. As I breathe in, I remember that smoking weed means that I am going to be murdered. As I breathe out, I remember that you only get murdered if you smoke weed with other people at a party.

That's why I don't like to be around more than one person at once. Even three victims can make a movie. Two is too few, usually: it's harder to build up the tension without flatlining toward the end. I also don't like to be around people because most of them don't like me, or hate me.

I put some soy milk on the stove and make some vegan cocoa, figuring that the trace amounts of caffeine (estrogen blocker) will be balanced out by the phytoestrogen in the soy. Everything is about risk assessment. Everything usually comes back to the risk of being murdered suddenly and brutally at any given moment, but sometimes I am able to distract myself from that by gauging the lower-stakes risk. It kind of messes up my therapist's theory, but I don't know if I have the heart to tell her yet.

I spend the next couple of hours finishing off that bowl and working on my project. The nice thing about having a professor who will sign off on any half-assed concept I can put together, like, "The Transfeminine in Horror Media," is that I can get stoned half out of my mind and torrent videos and it's real credit work, a real, legitimate adult thing that I'm doing. It may be the only real, legitimate adult thing I can do well.

It takes me forty minutes to find that episode of *Friday the 13th* where the guy uses the cursed whatever to steal that female pop star's body. *I don't want you, I want to be you.* It's like the theft of life is less creepy than the perversion of wanting to be a woman. And that transformation is never possible without body snatching or skinning cis women. Femininity is consumed the way vampires consume life. Those are the rules. Yet there's no comfort knowing that in a horror movie I would be the monster.

I fall asleep on the couch watching *Sleepaway Camp 3*. In my dream I'm in the deep web again. I'm looking for red rooms and snuff films. Finally, I find one. The victim has a pillowcase over her head; she is on her knees, hands tied behind her back. The room is flooded with bare fluorescent lights that scratch my eyes. The floor is concrete, with strange patterns on the floor. The camera pans up before I can take a closer look. The pillowcase is pulled off to show the big reveal that it's me, dead all along. That's when I watch them slash my throat.

I wake up, snap up like a car seat. My ribs vibrate and my eyes water. Maybe I need an adjustment to my medication. Or maybe I need to never sleep again. I pace the room and consider my options.

Sleep deprivation is so classic. I can lean back against a wall and slide down dramatically while I drink Mountain Dew, just like Nicole Kidman in *The Invasion*. *Invasion* was not the best body snatchers film, but Kidman has a gift for hitting a perfect balance between strength and vulnerability. Thinking about Mountain Dew makes me have to piss again.

I don't know how long I was asleep. It's dark now. Twilight. Not dark enough to die, usually, but dark enough to signal death. I try to remember if anyone has ever been murdered going to the corner store in a horror movie. There was using the ATM in *ATM*, but that was past midnight in the middle of urban nowhere. Maybe the corner store will get robbed when I'm in there, and everyone will be murdered. Or maybe the longer I stay at home, alone and vulnerable, the more I am tempting fate to turn my life into a home invasion movie.

I bike to the grocery store. It's harder to murder people who're riding bikes. Most slashers have a killer on foot because it's more exciting that way; asking a killer on foot to run down a victim on a bicycle is less plausible, and more importantly, it's less exciting. Grocery stores are also less likely be robbed than corner stores; that's just an actual fact, not one of the eight thousand paranoid horror genre rules that dominate my life. I have on a heavy coat and a hoodie, androgyny as path to anonymity and safety. I keep reaching into my pocket and touching my knife and cell phone.

Nobody looks at me at the store. I am nondescript and boring. I am safe. Nobody gets murdered while shopping for groceries. That just isn't a thing. This wouldn't even be filmed to be edited out later, not even in the most banal Twenty Minutes with Jerks sequence, unless it featured teens were hovering over the

TRANSCENDENT 3

liquor section, or unless it was some inexplicable arthouse movie. I decide to stop thinking about it and text Eve about what kind of vegan pizza she wants.

I am eternally grateful for the automated check-out machines. There is no eye contact, no small talk, no double-take about my voice, and no lingering awkwardness where the cashier tries to divine if they should "sir" or "ma'am" me. There is only the comforting banality and indifference of our machine overlords.

I balance the groceries on my bike handlebars and pedal back. Everything is boring and normal. I am boring and normal. Boring. Normal. Boring. Normal. That's my chant. That's my charm. That's my invocation.

I'm climbing up the hill, calves aching. My bags bang against my front wheel. There's a knot of boys ahead of me, filling up the sidewalk. Normal. Boring. Normal. Boring. My breath hitches as I lurch my bike forward. Normal. Boring. This is normal and boring. I've played by the rules, and I'm safe.

All the boys have denim and leather jackets, baseball caps, well-fitting jeans, bright sneakers. They jostle and push against one another. Call one another faggots and laugh. They are comfortable and powerful in their raw, shapeless masculinity.

I push my bike off the sidewalk, clunking onto the street, and zip past them. There's another round of laughter. For a moment I wish they were zombies. I would feel safer if they were. I hear a yell and echoing laughter. My fingers burn as I grip the handlebars too hard. I force myself to keep my eyes forward, keep my face forward.

They didn't even notice me, I tell myself. I am boring and normal and utterly beneath their notice. Normal. Boring. My jacket was buttoned closed and my hood was up. Normal. Boring.

I pull up at the apartment, park my bike, and fumble with my keys. I am fine. Once I'm inside the apartment, I can stop arguing with myself about whether I'm really, really fine or not. As if a handful of bland homophobic dudebros who would be dead twenty-three minutes into pretty much any horror movie would really be any kind of threat to me. I am ridiculous sometimes.

I heard the lock clack open. As I pop the door, there's a loud crash behind me, and I scream. I scream like I'm about to take a scythe to the neck or a chainsaw to my side or a gloved hand around my throat.

Nothing is happening. I'm crouching in the doorway doing nothing. And even though I've stopped screaming — at least I think I've stopped screaming — it's still going, the scream is echoing and vibrating in my head in a loop. It's a gif,

TRANSCENDENT 3

it's a supercut, it's a soundbite. Nothing feels real when I am waiting to die. Not the carpet under my fingers or the keys digging into my palm. It's all fake. It's all scripted. And I can't escape. It's not the monster that's invincible, it's the narrative. There's nothing more harsh or cruel than stories. Nothing. Nothing.

The light outside the apartment flickers. There's a click-click-click, just outside the door. Click-click-click. Like claws or teeth. I'm stuck in place. I can't move. I can't think. I can't feel. I'm a celluloid woman, an image without will or spirit. The clicking loops and slows down. Click. Pause. Click. Pause. Click.

It's my bike. It's my bike wheel, spinning. Without my weight to steady the bike, the weight of my groceries on the handles tipped it over.

It was a cheap cat scare. I fell for a cheap, mindless cat scare. The kind of thing that wouldn't faze a ten-year-old. I am beyond ridiculous sometimes. An emotionally fraught young woman alone at night in her apartment waiting for her girlfriend to come home, a young woman who just jumped at a cat scare. Yeah. I'm sure that's fine.

I lock the door and check it twice. The door is locked. I unlock it and relock it make sure there's nothing wrong with the mechanism. The door is locked. It's still locked. I smack my shoulder against the door, and the frame doesn't even grunt. I rub my shoulder trying to calculate exactly how much muscle mass I've lost since transitioning, how much I've still got to lose when the most exercise I got was five-minute bike rides and chasing buses and sweating a lot for no reason. I slam my shoulder against the door, with feeling. Countless clusters of nerves packed in every square inch of skin lighting up. I didn't know I could feel so much. My head vibrates.

The patio is locked. The curtains are drawn. The outside lights are on. The patio is still locked. The curtains are completely drawn. The lights are still on. The front door is locked. My shoulder still hurts. The patio is still locked. There is no one behind the curtain. There is nobody under the sink. There is nothing or no one in the refrigerator or the cupboards. There is nobody in the bathroom or behind the shower curtain. There is nobody under the bed. There is nobody in the bed. There is nobody in the closet. There is nobody under the bathroom sink or behind the shower curtain. There is nobody on the ceiling. There are no rats in the walls. There are no shifting rooms or hungry hallways. There is nobody in the house at all except me.

And Eve.

"Addy."

TRANSCENDENT 3

I feel the scream in my gut like a burp made of pure panic. The scream spikes out of my throat and burns my breath. The scream was there and gone before I even realized what I'd done.

"I'm sorry, sorry, sorry, so sorry." I curl up and tuck myself between the toilet and the sink.

"I'm sorry too." She slaps her boots on the linoleum floor and they echo. "I thought I made enough noise. Maybe I should take up singing. Or wear a bell?"

"No. It won't help, and that wasn't your fault. I was being too crazy. Tuning everything out. That's how it works. Those are the rules. The fear gets the victim so scared, so focused, so paranoid, so vigilant, that they don't even realize when the monster is right there. Ugh. This is the second time I've fallen for a cat scare."

"I'm not a cat."

"That's not what it means! Ugh, the second time today in less than, like, an hour. I'm pathetic."

"You are not pathetic."

"I'm cowering on the bathroom floor. What would you call that?"

She pulls me to my feet and kisses my forehead. It's nice to date a girl taller than me. It's nice to date a girl at all. It's nice to date at all. It's nice to find someone who is worth risking the constant terror of death for. A death that, despite my every attempt to obey the ever-shifting rules of cinema, I most dearly deserve.

"You're fine by me."

She curls her fingers in my hair, kisses my eyes, my face. She is careful to avoid my mouth and my neck. She never questions me, never makes me explain myself, but of course she knows all about the reasons. After all, reasons are all I ever talk about.

Just existing is dangerous enough. Trying to actually fall in love like a normal person is just tempting fate.

Eve takes my hand and walks me to the kitchen. She makes me sit on the floor and tells me to empty my mind. She puts hand on my back, against my ribs, and she measures my breathing.

"Take a deep breath," Eve says. I do. "Deeper. Hold it. Now breathe out." I do. She makes me do this, over and over, for five minutes. "I'm going to create a circle of protection around you. Nothing can hurt you while the circle is intact."

She takes out our canister of salt. There's a long, static hiss as she pours it out. White lines on white linoleum.

TRANSCENDENT 3

"Does sea salt work better than table salt?" I ask.

She laughs and shakes her head. I feel calm, empty of expectation.

"You're sure?" I tease. I feel normal. Or at least, my idea of a normal person.

"Yes. I'm sure. I did double-blind studies. Magic undergoes the most rigorous scientific methods known to humankind. Otherwise, how are we supposed to be taken seriously?"

I sit cross-legged and look up at Eve as she makes half-defrosted pizza. She tells me about customers with ugly tattoos, the one chef that keeps hitting on her, shitty metaphysical stores. She hands me a juice and sits down next to me, her back against the oven. She holds my hand: that's definitely allowed, as long as my hand stays inside the circle. Those are the rules.

Eve is a witch, and witches know all about rules. More importantly, witches know how to make new rules. I can't change the rules. All I can do is see the rules clearly, see where I am in the narrative and act accordingly. I can game the system to stay in those first twenty minutes, snatch up little pockets of time, over and over and over. It's not easy.

But Eve, she makes it easier. She can rewrite the script for me when I need it.

She got some new indica strain at the dispensary, "Death Mask," and she knows as soon as she tells me what it was called that she shouldn't have told me what it was called. I've seen too many movies where drugs turn people into zombies. It's a reactionary metaphor. If someone doesn't murder me for smoking pot, the pot itself will murder me for being enough of a fool to smoke something with such an obvious zombie-making name.

"I can't smoke it with you anyway," I say, chewing on a dried out pizza crust. "If I don't smoke alone, I'll die."

"I didn't just get this for me," Eve says. "What if we rename it?"

"I don't think it works like that."

"It might." Eve runs her finger down my palm, tracing my life-line. Eve has the prettiest hands, painted black and purple, skull-patterns flaking off as if to say even death can die. She pulls out her dispensary baggie, and after a lingering pause, she laughs. "Here, I fixed it for you."

She tears off the stapled-on receipt and hands it to me. The receipt says *Gas Mask*. It's innocuous enough for me. I sigh-laugh, and she laughs. She catches my face in her hands and kisses my eyes. I kiss around her jaw, her cheek, and her eyebrows.

Eve is a witch. She bleeds truth and sweats prophecy. I am definitely in love, and definitely in danger. Lust alone can kill me.

TRANSCENDENT 3

I feel with my mouth where she's hard under soft tissue. I think about shape of her skull under her skin, the skull under my skin, our skeletons floating in flesh. I think about sliced-up flesh, dark spills, meat hooks, raw, fresh bones, and I stop kissing her. She stops kissing me.

"I'm sorry," I mumble out automatically, and I bite my tongue to stop the second apology, the meta-apology, and then I-should-know-by-now-not-to-apologize-for-my-own-boundaries apology, to be followed shortly by the I'm-sorry-for-being-so-crazy apology. I'm backed up on apologies. I'm almost choking on them. "I'm — "

"You're fine by me."

We're holding hands again. My hand is trembling, and I have to pull her closer to me so I don't disrupt the circle of salt.

"Am I really safe?" I ask.

"Safe as houses," she answers, and all I can think of are animal-masked intruders hovering in hallways, broken windows, and snapped phone lines. She looks at me a moment before adding, "Safer, actually; much safer than houses."

"Can we kiss?" I bite my lip, and I feel a little smaller, a little younger, each passing second. "On the mouth?"

"Addy, you don't have to push yourself for me."

"If I'm in the circle I'm safe, right?"

"That's not why I did that for you. I don't want you to think I'm doing magic so we can — I'm not trying to, to coax you into anything."

"I know it's not, Eve. I know, I know, I know. You wouldn't manipulate me like that. You never have. The circle is safe, right?"

"It's safe. Nothing can harm you."

"I want to kiss you," I blurt out. "If you want to kiss me, I mean. Otherwise I wouldn't, uh, want that, unless it's consensual, mutual, and I'm explaining a bunch of things that don't need to be explained, I'm a huge dumbass, I'm sorry, I'm messing up everything — "

"You're fine by me." Eve kisses my nose. "And you aren't a dumbass, and you didn't mess up anything."

She leans in close. Her hair spills out around me in a dark wave. Her breath smells like pesto.

I know she's waiting for me to close the gap, meet her halfway, because she wants this to be my decision, my choice, always. There are times I wish she was little less considerate, a little less careful. There are times I wish I didn't have the burden of choosing to tempt fate. Maybe we'll figure out something, a compromise. There must be some way that I can signal that she can be the one who chooses, that I choose for her to choose. But right now my tongue is heavy and my thoughts are in knots. One of my legs is shaking, hard, so hard I'm afraid I'll start phasing through the floor. She puts her hand on my knee, and it goes stiff under her touch.

"Kiss me? Please?" I manage, through some awkward miracle.

She finally leans in and kisses me. She tastes like pesto, vegan cheese, and orange lip gloss. The feeling of her mouth on my mouth is almost distressingly normal. Closed mouth. No tongue. Soft lips over muscle, over teeth. It's not the dizzying height of ecstasy; it's not a wretched vice that would summon some ancient creature of wrath. Just nice. She feels nice. Soft. Warm.

We keep being nice and soft and warm in each other's faces. I brush my face against hers. Her peach fuzz curls catch on my skin. I don't think about how I'm two years behind her on HRT. I don't think about my stubble. I don't think about her softness against my sandpaper skin. Her magic can make me forget my terror. Her face is perfect and real, and it's enough to let me forget my ugliness. I'm not sure at what point kissing stops just being kissing and starts being making out, but I suspect we are quickly approaching it. Eve is making little squeaking noises that I've never heard her make before.

Eve steps into the circle, and I wrap my arm around her waist to steady her.

It feels like we're dancing — her fingers hook my flat hips, I pull her tighter against me — as we're trying to occupy the same space. The circle of salt is unbroken. My face is wet with her breath. My breath is caught in my chest like a fly in a web.

I wonder if this is a kink, a coping mechanism, or just plain old magic. From what I hear from some people, there's not that much of a difference between the three. Whatever is it besides, it's definitely magic. A curse-breaking, taboo-smashing work of wonder. Just like her.

We're thigh to thigh, hip to hip, chest to chest. There's a tattoo peeking out of her shirt collar, a tendril climbing up her collarbone. There's a lot of Eve I've seen but that I haven't seen, that I haven't let myself see.

"Can I kiss your neck?" Eve asks. I nod, my head hazy. I can almost feel the shadow of the angel of death against my back. And when she kisses my neck, the shadow is gone. She kisses me with the same gentleness again. Her mouth is soft, warm, no tongue and no teeth. Undemanding. I imagine most people, normal people, wouldn't find this exciting. But for me, the most inconvenient parts of my body are becoming more inconvenient by the second.

TRANSCENDENT 3

I'm hard, I'm hard and it's trapped in my jeans and trapped against her leg, and we're too close together for her not to notice.

"Uh," I swallow. "Um."

I look down at the circle again. Still intact. I look again. Intact. Normal. Intact. Safe. Normal.

"Yeah?" Eve asks.

"I, um…do you want to?"

"Do you mean sex?"

I nod and then shake my head and then nod again. She laughs and kisses my forehead before kissing my neck again, kissing up my jugular and the soft shell of my ear. She whispers into my ear.

"Do you want me to touch you, or…"

I take one of her wrists because I think this is what people do when they can't talk or don't want to talk. It's less about spontaneity or romance than that I just can't talk, that I can't stand to think about my body long enough to talk about it. I tug her hand to my fly. Eve seems to understand, and she nuzzles her face against my throat. Then there's buttons clicking and zippers unfolding and waistbands stretching, and then —

Eve's hand is soft; Eve's lips are soft; Eve's everything is soft. She's soft and I'm hard, painfully solid, and I feel like I'm sinking into her hand, like my throat is sinking into her mouth, my whole body folding into her. Vertical quicksand. I'm standing shock still, but I still feel like I'm in motion. Like I'm a ghost un-hitched from my body. My body feels invisible. I am somewhere else now.

Now I'm here again. I'm soft. Empty. Visible. Corporal. I reach up and feel my unslit throat, my unbroken bones. The circle of salt is intact. I'm safe. I'm alive. All I can manage is these little half-laughs of relief. Eve kisses my forehead.

Once I leave the circle, am I still safe? Do I have to carry my un-virginal nature with me? Does it have a smell, or an aura; some other tell? Can I continue to dodge the gaze of the gods of cinematic bloodshed and slaughter? Or will it get worse now: stronger, more cunning, that death I deserve crouching at my door?

Eve helps me to step out the circle with my trembling, newborn giraffe legs. We clean up dinner together. I help her sweep up the salt, now inert, all of its protective energy expended. We lay in bed, our bodies not quite touching, and we watch *Suspiria*. Tomorrow everything starts again, but tonight I survived. In my dream I see the long roll of end credits, breathy end music fracturing into static, fizzling into blue screens.

TRANSCENDENT 3

FIRE FILLS THE BELLY

◄ Noa Josef Sperber ►

There weren't any coroners on Coroner Street anymore. In other places, other communities, the main street was called Main Street, or First, or Grocer, or Market, but when this community was established, the coroner set up shop in the middle, for her convenience. Then the community's average lifetime expectancy went up and the coroner moved to Forth Street, where she became a part time florist.

Raphael, who lived on Coroner, did what all men like him did. He sold his dignity as he sold his words, as he sold his time, as he sold his skills. When he needed to get something from the market he had to pay with coins instead of barter goods, because his wages were so small he was pitied. "Buy yourself something you really need," people would tell him, instead of trading him little things. The coins jangled in his pocket all week until he could swap them in for potatoes and beets and dairy products. Water he could buy straight from the building manager.

Where and when Raphael was born, the adjustments hadn't been so widespread. He can remember driving with his parents and sisters to school, when everyone still had cars. He remembers posing for an ID photo in a dingy hall. It was like a passport picture, which he'd had taken when he was very little, but it wasn't. Not really. It wasn't made of the same material, and he'd found that with a match he could warp it, bubble it to hide certain information.

Raphael's apartment has almost nothing in it and it is not a homey place. There's no knick-knacks on the shelves like there were in his childhood. There aren't even shelves. He has a stuffed mat for his bed and his clothes hang from the low ceiling beams, where he's hung up sheets of molding plastic to divide the room. He's got an icebox in the corner that holds nothing but ice and bricks of coffee; there's a wood tub beneath the pipe where he washes his clothes and his body. He's lined the room with waterlogged books, the old sort, where characters fill their days with aimless activities, or fantasies where heroes fight dragons.

It hadn't been completely easy to fit into this new life when he had first fallen into it, but it was better than he thought it would be. He wakes up with the sun and busies himself. He lives well, performing on the street every morning before working every night. He knows this body, and what he can do, all the limits he can press against and all the points he can reach. He knows the things people like about it, and him, and he is okay.

One day he wakes up, splashes water on his face, and chews a mixture of baking soda and mint, and spits off the balcony on his way to the outside stairs. His neighbor leans out their window and laughs, and they are nothing but flyaway hair. Skin just darker than his, and a long loose shirt. They look so gentle, so good.

His face heats. "Good morning," he mumbles, and his neighbor smiles.

There is nothing shameful about how Raphael lives. He tells himself this over and over. There's nothing shameful about him. He is only a man, or something akin to a man, and he's only making his art, or something akin to art, with his life. Art like his tattered books and art like his sister used to buy on expensive paper. It's just — art with his limbs, the strong edges of his body.

There is no shame in me, he thinks. He cannot believe it. Maybe there is some shame in what happens inbetween, the not-so-soft street he chooses to walk down every night. He can hold his own but he always lowers his gaze and ignores what he hears, the dogs that trail behind him.

It's foolish to call his stunts art, however. A woman, a true artist, taught his craft to him, and what she taught him was the act of imitation. Imitating fire, beast, natural world, imitating man.

Stripping off his shirt in the middle of the road doesn't fail to draw someone's eye, despite the undershirt he leaves in place. The curve of his body is something beautiful, the firm V of his hips and the soft way his ribs turn into the swell of his

TRANSCENDENT 3

chest. More alluring is the way he tilts his head up, baring the long curve of his neck, before snapping forward and spitting a live fleck of coal into his palm.

This is what Raphael is, a professional danger. Officially he is a street sweeper, but this is what he does. He can coax the flames dancing across his shoulders, hold his whole body in the air by the pads of his fingers, stand statue still while people prod his skin with soft hands.

A woman stares in drifty-eyed amazement at the flame he holds in his hand. She rests a toddler, close to her side, its little feet drumming against her rounded belly. Another on the way. She fumbles in her pocket for the single coin she can find and offers it to him, but Raphael shakes his head. He shifts the fire to his upper arm and holds it at bay there, pulling a handful of change from his own pocket, and hands it to her. The baby she holds takes the largest bit and bites it before she gently pulls it away.

"Be well, mother," he mumbles. "Blessings to you."

"To you too," he adds, a slip of a smile curling back his lip, and reaches out his fingers. The baby smiles back, toothless and lovely, grabbing Raphael's thumb.

No shame, he thinks, but a flicker of something curls in his gut. He's glad for her, but something burns just inside his own stomach, a place of possibilities. What could have been, if he had done different; creation. The burning spreads over his shoulders and he smiles at the next person that comes near him. He bows low. Honor before duty, he figures.

The market sells bread if anyone can bake it that day and Raphael will buy it, eat it in thick slices smothered in butter or stacked with vegetables. It's a luxury that he allows himself and he only has it for dinner, sitting on the rusty steps in the outside air. The butter is thick and salty, spread on his tongue, spread on in excess or left to go rancid in the heat.

Raphael leans his head on the railing and licks the crumbs from his fingers. He never learned how to cook, but he learned how to be happy in some ways, sometimes. The feeling sits in him. Above him, the monorail clangs as it rushes over the tracks, *hushusha-hushusha*, and he can hear the faint fluttering of the bats, disgruntled, that flap their way off into the lavender dusk.

His neighbor unbolts their door and steps out, bare feet light, toes slipping between the grates.

"Hey," Raphael says.

"Evening."

TRANSCENDENT 3

He doesn't know their name but he would like to. They're beautiful, more so than everyone else, and they look at him sometimes, through the window. Not strangely, just clear-eyed and hopeful. It's the way he looks at the people who are happy, the way his sisters used to look at his parents.

Raphael's love for people is something he can't exactly explain, but they are extraordinary, all of them; a pristine and alive thing that he's still longing for. He's past the point of feeling untouched, like he's not damaged by what he's done to himself. Maybe all people feel like this, but he's never been very good at knowing.

"You look like you wanna ask a question," his neighbor says suddenly.

All he can do is shake his head.

"Oh," they say. "Your face is just pensive. If you can think one I'd like to answer it."

He looks at them and parts his lips, but the sound that comes out is soft, and it floats away on the heated breeze.

His sisters looked like him, hair curled in a halo of fuzz and eyes a dark, syrupy brown, but that's all he'll think about. They probably look different now that he's begged and borrowed and gone to the government for what hardened his jaw and made him have to shave whenever he can get the lather. When he last saw them he was young but for the life of him he can't recall the specifics. It wasn't planned, so there were no tearful goodbyes, only one moment they were all there, braiding green, fragile weeds into a crown and another moment, he was standing in a hallway, back pressed against the wall while his picture was taken. He wasn't told the specifics of why he needed identification, but there were people being deported left and right, and anyone with eyes could see that, so he carried it always, inside a matchbox in his coat pocket. The same matches he had burned off an F that was printed in smudging ink.

His sisters had to be somewhere, he'd just never know. After receiving that little plastic card he'd wandered around for days, begging people to bring him to his family, until someone called for the police, and he slept for a week in a jail cell while the women there murmured about him, but stroked his hair anyway.

He and his neighbor stand considering each other. They're leaning on the building wall, hair wet and twisted up on top of their head.

"You're the fire eater?" they ask.

Raphael shrugs. "In a way. More the opposite. Fire regurgitator, if you will."

They smile. "The fire regurgitator. I'm sure that looks great on your government forms."

He shrugs again. "I think technically it says 'mercy fed', as tossing around fire rarely counts as a real skill." He waves a hand. "I'm sure your form has something very dignified. Doctor, maybe."

"Engineer," they admit. "Have you thought of a question yet?"

"No," he says. "Afraid not." A moment passed before he adds, "I have something I want to know, but I'm not going to waste my question on it."

"Oh?"

"I'd like to know your name."

His neighbor nods and Raphael's breath catches in his throat.

"Adison," they say. "Save that question for something good. I don't give my answers to just anyone."

"No? Just to charming fire swallowers?" he asks. "There can't be too many of us."

"I have yet to meet one," Adison smirks.

"Oh, come on," Raphael moans. "That's not fair."

The woman Raphael studied under was clearer in his mind than his own life. He's been with her for years, since he was sixteen and his limbs were long and coltish. He's been thinner, hands unsteady, and his book collection was confined to what fit in his waistband against his hip.

Her name had been Rachel, in a cruel twist of fate that sent bile up into Raphael's throat: the name of his youngest sister. It was meant to be.

Rachel was so beautiful that he had wanted to paint her, not that he would have known how. Her skin was dark, almost the same as Raphael's own, her hair tied back and covered with a scarf.

The first day they met they had sat on barstools while Raphael struggled to decide if he should have the whiskey in front of him. It was almost pretty, the way the sunlight reflected off the sparkling amber liquid. He'd never had a real drink before, just a sip or two of wine when his parents could get some.

"You should drink that," Rachel advised. "There's nothing that good anywhere else." The bar was empty, sunlight twinkling through the broken stained glass windows. There was a deep gash in the wood and he traced it with his pinky.

Raphael squared his shoulders and downed it in one go. He could barely swallow the resulting cough, the whiskey burned going down and his head felt sideways for a moment.

TRANSCENDENT 3

Laughing, Rachel pounded him on the back. "There you go," she said proudly. "That's it."

Rachel took him home with her, washed his hair, fed him often. Lit him on fire when he begged to be taught, pushed him down when he shouldn't have gotten up. He wonders what happened to her.

Bathing is done standing up in the tub, pouring sun-warmed water over himself. There's not enough to sit down in, but he uses what's left at the bottom to wash his clothes. The rationing is getting worse these days, less food to go around and water still difficult to make.

"Would you have fought if you were born twenty years earlier?" he asks Adison. He's on his knees carving coffee off the block on the icebox, collecting the scraps on a piece of paper.

Adison makes an I-don't-know noise, and a ruffle that might be a shrug. He can't see them. "Not sure. Is this your question?"

Raphael grunts, almost jabbing his palm with the knife. "Nope, just a question."

"You've got to ask it sometime, Raphael, and that's not a fair question anyway," they admonish. "What's done is done."

"Cool worldview, for someone living on Coroner Street in a recovering war zone."

"What, you don't think we're thriving in the 'communities of the future?'"

"Nah, I'm living off welfare and petty cash. The world was supposed to be solar and kind, not rattling," he laughs, shoving the coffee packet under Adison's nose for inspection. "This is enough for a cake, right?"

"Sure," they say, confusion written across their face.

"Children's homes down by the park," he explains. "The big building under the monorail endline. Kid almost died a few weeks ago, so I figured I'd send this over? I do it a couple times a year, in every place I've lived." He'd brought the coffee from his time with Rachel as a self-gifted going away present. The hassle of lugging it across districts and arguing with border guards aside, it was the smartest thing he could have done.

The world, he had learned, was big, and certain things lagged behind while other things rushed ahead, and some areas had been desolated by the war while some were only affected by the lack of trade with the others. Some places had fresh water from the generators, and the coastal cities were even renewing the oceans, some places had electronics everywhere and no one hungry. His child-hood had been easy, but there were thousands of children like him who had died young and starving.

"You're odd," Adison says out of the blue. "I don't understand how one job can get you enough money and how the mercy feeding system works and where did you get that much coffee?"

"Community where I used to live, it had a port. We had some pretty good stuff."

"Okay, but that doesn't — "

"The mercy feeding system is there for people who are excess to a society," he explains, not looking them in the eye. "If you can prove that you're useless and stuff, they can give you a menial job with no chance of transfer or benefits except through the system. Like, with your fancy job, I bet you don't have to go into a government office if you want a day off, or if you want to work somewhere else, or if you want to do anything. It's not a big deal or anything," he mumbles. "I sweep the streets, you know that. It's like working for the government but with-out the old prestige. That propaganda, you know, about everyone being equal."

Adison says nothing.

The children have filled up the yard by the time he gets there, walking though the monorail is free to all citizens. Filled is the accurate word: the yard is small, the children many. They're all just a little small, a little dirty, a little wild, but all of them good. A few of them go running up and down the street to meet him; three have shoes, two have their feet wrapped with cloth, and three more are barefoot, but they are all laughing. The smallest one smash-es their face against his leg, a mess made of syrupy eyes and fuzzy halo. Again.

He asks his entourage at large, "Who was sick? Can you show me?"

Children, he reflects, as they all pull him somewhere, little ones climbing onto this back, make sounds that are remarkably like *chirping*.

One of the children follows him all the way home, not saying anything to him at all. Raphael keeps looking at her out of the corner of his eye. She's about ten years old, knees scraped, her hands working nervously over her skirt.

When they get to the middle of the community, a place that must be unfamil-iar to her, considering how she looks around, she stands in his way so he can't climb the stairs to his balcony. "Fire man," she calls him. Her voice is so thin. "Teach me?"

TRANSCENDENT 3

He imagines her, standing in the street with flames licking her skin, and he can see the fire in her eyes.

"Not tonight," he finally says. "Come tomorrow. Early."

"You promise?"

He nods.

The girl is named Rochelle, and he laughs loud when she tells him. Of course it is. Her eyes narrow but he reassures her it's a good name. "A strong name," he tells her. "Names like that don't burn down."

"I picked it out myself," she says, like a challenge, and he smiles.

He has her hold a burning match until it burns down to her fingertips. He has her stand with her hands outstretched for an hour. He has her read one of his books out loud as she stands on one foot with a match ablaze in her hand. She is so steady she's like a rock, and he sends her home with strict orders not to try swallowing the stuff yet, for god's sakes. Adison watches the two of them sometimes.

More and more children tag along now. He doesn't give any of them matches, because they haven't asked yet, but they're all trying very hard. They sit on the fire escape, warily considering the flame, flip through Raphael's books with interest, or encourage Rochelle when she tries to master something new. He teaches them in his home, on the stairs, in the street. Rochelle beams when strangers gather around to watch her.

"Who taught you?" Rochelle asks one night, as he's trying to send all the children home before it gets dark.

"A good woman," he tells her. "You're like her. You both clenched your teeth like that — " She looks startled and relaxes her jaw. He laughs. " — when you've got something important on your mind. You're like my sisters, too. You're all stubborn."

"That's right, I am," Rochelle mutters.

"I thought of my question," he says to Adison, rubbing his hand over the back of his neck.

"You have?"

"Uh-huh," he says. "I just — "

Raphael looks at them, really looks at them, at their curious eyes and all the rest of their face. Adison is a human, he thinks, and humans are so imperfect, but humans are so perfect, every one of them.

TRANSCENDENT 3

" — just, why did things turn to this?"

That's not what he intended to ask, but it slips out anyway. Adison says nothing.

"And how do you make your life, your body, feel like home?"

Adison doesn't look at him.

"And why — and why — and why — " He takes a deep breath. "I'm sorry. I wanna know why I don't feel right, and I know you don't know the answer."

"No, I do," they say suddenly. "Raphael, no one feels right. What on earth is right supposed to feel like?"

"I don't think I see things like normal do," he says defensively. "I don't think I'm not right in the way that other people are."

"Yes, you are," Adison says. "I promise you are. There's nothing wrong with you. Just live your life."

He stands in the street and closes his eyes. There are people everywhere, passing him, watching him, ignoring him, and he tries to love them. The heat of the flames spread out across his skin. He doesn't know how he doesn't burn to a crisp, but that's okay. When he raises his arms the fire jumps and his heart soars. For a moment it looks like great wings stick out of his back, and then it looks more like ocean waves, and then he looks like a man, something small and fragile and insignificant, standing on his feet.

"It's okay," he says, keeping his eyes clenched shut. "I'm not worth your time."

There is no shame in the world.

TRANSCENDENT 3

SMALL CHANGES OVER LONG PERIODS OF TIME

◂ K.M. Szpara ▸

I'm trying to piss against a wall when the vampire bites me. Trying because drunk-me can barely hold a glass, much less maneuver a limp prosthetic cock.

My attacker holds me like he did on the dance floor, one arm wrapped around my chest, this time digging into my ribs. I struggle against his supernatural strength and the slow constriction of my lungs. Through ragged breaths, I inhale the Old Spice on his thick black hair, where he bows his head to grip my neck.

The sting of his fangs barely registers and what does shoots straight to my cunt — can't help it. If I knew he weren't going to kill me, I'd relish the shock and pain, loss of control. I kind of do, anyway. His venom numbs my neck but I can still feel the strong clamp of his jaw. Like a new piercing, my body screams to reject the intrusion. I want to stay awake — stay pressed between his cold hard body and the cold hard wall. I want him to touch me, reach between my legs. I want to stay alive.

But the wall discolors; the red bricks spot with gray until they fuzz over and dull. My last thought before passing out is how weirdly validating it is that this cis gay guy targeted me, when I was too scared to even piss inside the bar's men's room.

Mﾐy phone blares like there's a Red Alert. I check the alarm. Oh right. I signed up for that Open Life-Drawing class at the community center. At nine a.m. After half-priced vodka night. Optimistic.

When I sit up, the full weight of my headache settles into my skull. I press a hand against my forehead to ease the pressure, but end up squinting at a dimly lit room. Not any room I've slept in before.

The only light blurs from down a narrow hallway. Windows the size of cinder blocks line the top of each wall, but neatly hemmed black-out curtains fill them and glossy Ikea tchotchkes sit in front of those.

I'm in a guest room, I assume. At the very least, I'm on a hard futon surrounded by throw pillows and machine-made quilts. I'm still dressed and — I lie back and shove my right hand down the front of my briefs — still packing. Just a little damp from my adventures in peeing outside.

"You're alive." A familiar man leans against the threshold, holding a mug that says "Don't talk to me until I've had my evening blood." on the side. His skin is pale, but not pallid. His pose casual, but precise.

"Barely," is all I can think to say. Did we fuck? I don't usually go home with strangers, much less drunk, much *much* less with vampires. I have fantasized about it, though. Maybe I finally did.

"How do you feel?"

"Hungover."

His chuckle resonates in his mouth, not his chest. The young ones react fairly human, still drawing air into useless lungs for huffs and sighs and rolling laughs. This one is clearly making an effort for my sake but is too old to get it right. I give him a seven out of ten.

I'd feel a little better if I could remember his damn name, though, and I don't know how to ask without also revealing I don't know how I ended up in his guest room.

"It's Andreas," he tells me. "And you're Finley."

"O-Okay. I mean, I didn't — " I trip over explanations of why I forgot his name before reminding myself I still haven't asked.

Scenes from last night force themselves on me; I watch them more than remember them. Drunk fumbling, a cold alley wall, and the rigid clamp of a jaw — his jaw, Andreas's. The mix of pleasure and fear that slices through me isn't a memory.

"You bit me," I say, because he hasn't danced around mystery, either. My grand accusation comes out as, "You're not supposed to do that."

"I was hungry," he says, calmly. Like the obvious result of hunger is biting someone.

"So, go to a blood bank like you're supposed to."

"It's not the same."

"Yeah, because it doesn't hurt people." I pause. "You're not still hungry, are you?"

"I'm not going to bite you again, if that's what you're asking. I — " This time, he pauses. " — do regret what happened."

"Good." I shake my hand out to stunt the tremor that seizes it. Nausea brews in my gut, dizziness behind my eyelids. I press the heels of my hands against my temples. "You don't happen to have any Ibuprofen, do you?"

"No."

"And we didn't fuck, right?"

"No."

"Great, then I'm going to head home — "

The next second, the futon dips and he's beside me. He presses a cool hand against my burning forehead. "You're not hungover," he says. "You're dying."

His words impact me like news of a foreign tragedy: I know they're bad but struggle to connect on a personal level.

"And it's my fault." His hand tenses before he pulls it away.

I flop back onto the futon and stare at the cream-colored ceiling. A fan spins overhead; the moving air ruffles Andreas's shiny hair, an illusion of life.

I don't want to die.

"You don't have to." Andreas replies to my thoughts again.

I didn't know vampires could do that.

"Only the old ones."

"Would you let me die in peace?" I shout over the pounding in my skull.

His shrug is too precise, like his shoulders are tied to a wooden toy's pull string. Up, down. "If that's what you want."

"Thank you." I want to cry — *try* to cry. Before I started testosterone, I'd cry reading *Bridge to Terabithia* or watching a made-for-television movie. I liked crying, the catharsis of it, the physical purge of sadness.

Andreas brings his mug to his lips. The blood doesn't stain his white teeth; the fangs leave tiny dents in the ceramic where he bites down.

I should be crying. He's expecting me to because I'm a warm-bodied, emotionally-invested human being whose tear ducts can't resist the impulse.

TRANSCENDENT 3

But they do, at least regarding my own future. Won't make that Life Drawing class. Won't ever see my work on a billboard or a book cover. Won't exhibit, won't — who knows what else?

Andreas interrupts my efforts. "Or I could turn you."

"Into a vampire? Aren't we supposed to apply for that?"

"I won't tell if you don't." His smile doesn't wrinkle his old skin.

The decision between anything and "or death" should be easy. But if I want to eat without killing people — and I will need to eat — I'll have to register with the Federal Vampire Commission and explain myself and risk getting in trouble and getting Andreas in trouble.

Maybe he deserves it. He fucking bit me without permission.

But vampires who break the law, who feed from un-certified donors, who steal blood bags, or drink without asking first, are put on the Blood Offenders Registry, which is basically a hit list for corrupt cops and stake-wielding bigots. And if they survive that, the second strike is euthanization.

The system is fucked. No government lackey is going to hear out a gay trans guy who was illegally turned into a vampire. All I know is I don't want to die before I've done anything with my life. Designing in-store signage for Sears does not count. Just ask the half-finished paintings in my living room.

I run my tongue over the smooth, flat line of my teeth for what I assume will be the last time. "Turn me."

The hangover feeling doesn't go away. Not the spins or the sticky pain of thirst.

Andreas's venom curdles any food left in my stomach. He deposits me in the bathroom the instant before I vomit. I clutch the toilet bowl until my knuckles whiten and the whiteness spreads through my hands and I can feel it in my face. Until I can only dry heave.

My throat stings with stomach acid. "Can I have some water?"

Andreas presses a sports bottle to my lips. "Swish and spit. Don't swallow."

I bite down on the plastic nozzle and drink until there's nothing left. My sensitive teeth rip through the thin plastic, tearing up the empty bottle. My canines ache the worst, like I've jammed them into ice cream for too long or just had fillings put in. Or both.

"I told you not to swallow," Andreas says only moments before I prove him right with another retch.

"You can't drink water?" I see vampires drink all the time.

"No, *you* can't drink water. Your body is purging its fluids."

"What about after…"

"After you've turned? Sure, you can drink water. Might want to wait a couple centuries before putting anything more complex in your body."

"Like what, Diet Coke?"

"No, Diet Coke you can drink after a couple years. I meant your mother's homemade meatloaf."

"Oh."

What's the last thing I ate? A slice of pizza and burnt French fries. Not the last meal I'd have chosen, but King's was the only place near the bars that served food all night and I was nervous and hungry.

"Just kidding, your mother will be dead by then." Andreas sips from his mug. He waits for his words to settle then smiles. "That was a joke."

"Thanks." I imagine her funeral. My dad going home to an empty house. Eating across from an empty seat in the kitchen.

Still no tears. Maybe it won't be much of a change becoming a vampire. Andreas doesn't look like he cares much about anything.

"Do you want to call her?" he asks.

"No." That answer's easy. She told me she felt like her daughter was dying when I came out. She got over it, eventually, but I don't want to put her through a literal death after that. "I do need to call the HR department at work, though."

"I think they can wait until you're done vomiting," Andreas says.

I push myself to my feet and flush the toilet. He doesn't understand how this works. I do. "I can't lose my job on top of all this, okay? When everyone I love is dead — or when they decide they don't want a vampire in the family — I won't have a support system. So, where's my cell?"

It's dead, ironically. Andreas plugs it into the wall beside the sink and I spend another hour in the bathroom alternating between ready-to-talk and ready-to-vomit. When my fingers finally steady and I can lift my head long enough to call, HR doesn't believe me.

"No, I can't come in. I was bitten by a *vampire*. I'm dying!"

"I'm sorry, Mr. Hall," says the HR officer, whose name I cannot remember because I'm so, so thirsty. "Like I said, I don't see an application on file for medical-vampirification, which you're required to submit ninety days in advance for paid leave. Now — "

"I couldn't submit an application because I didn't know. It just happened."

"We can offer you six weeks of unpaid leave, Mr. Hall."

TRANSCENDENT 3

"But — "

"That's the best I can do. I'm sorry."

"Fine. Thanks." I hang up and squeeze my phone in my fist.

Andreas rests his hand perfectly still on my back. It doesn't twitch or clench or rub; it just lays there like a paperweight, reminding me of his presence. He wasn't beside me while I was on the phone but he's here now, always *now*. I wish he hadn't been there in the alley.

A gross conflicted feeling creeps over my skin. Why am I even here, still?

Where else am I supposed to go? I've already decided against Mom and, now that I'm thinking about it, any other human. A more scrupulous vampire would report me to save their own neck; a less scrupulous one would break mine.

This is Andreas's fault.

"You're right," he says. "This is my fault."

"I hate when you do that." *Read my mind,* I think, because I know he's still listening.

"Sorry. It's centuries of habit, but I can stop."

"Good." Didn't expect him to say that. "I mean, thanks."

We sit in silence for a minute that feels like an eternity. I'm going to have one of those ahead of me: an eternity. Like it's a tangible thing I can hold in my hands and squeeze. Like a blood-soaked heart I can wring dry.

"I'll cover your expenses for the next six weeks." Andreas leaves before I can pretend to object.

I don't die — not yet.

I unravel myself from the quilted cocoon Andreas wrapped me in. I need air, still. Not much, but enough that my chest rises and falls automatically. I sigh and pinch the bridge of my nose, hoping for a moment's relief from my perpetual dehydration headache.

The bathroom rug warms my feet as I sit to pee. No prosthetic is worth fumbling with while my body ejects all its fluids. There's not much in my bladder, but I ease the pressure. Blood spots the toilet paper I toss into the bowl. I go cold. I dab another square between my legs, hoping I've started pissing blood. The other option is not an option.

And then it is.

I haven't menstruated for three years. This shouldn't be happening. "Fuck, fuck, fuck!" I bite down on my knuckles, forgetting my growing canines. Blood beads on my punctured fingers when I pull back.

Andreas doesn't know what to do with me — not really. I need a doctor. One who can explain my reanimated uterus.

I clean up and pop on the pair of sunglasses Andreas left on the side table. He hasn't let me outside, but it's not like the door's locked and I'm still human; I won't spontaneously combust. I assume.

The thinnest line of light shines between the tiny windows' blackout curtains: daytime. I'm officially on "unpaid leave."

A bottle of sunscreen rests on the front windowsill and I slather the white goop on my face and hands before pulling on a hooded North Face fleece from the closet. To think I expected a cape.

"I need to see a doctor," I say.

The receptionist stares at me over the counter, over cooling coffee, and square computer monitors.

"I don't have an appointment with mine, but I'll see whoever."

He nods his head quickly, the rest of him unmoving, like a bobble-head doll.

"Great. Do I need to fill out a form, or…"

He pushes a blue lined paper across the counter to me. I sniffle and wipe at the cold drip from my nose. Blood stains my sleeve. Dammit.

"Thanks." I grab a pen and sit down.

Four other people share the waiting room. Two read over a pamphlet on lesbian healthcare. One shoots cartoon pigs on her phone. The last just watches me over their acid wash jeans and under their knit hat. They pull their legs up tight against their chest when I pass, never taking their eyes off me. They still watch when I sit beside a corner table, push all the gossip magazines to the side, and try to flatten my form out.

It's pretty standard.

Name: Finley Hall
Legal Name: See above
Age: Twenty-six
Gender: FTM/trans male
Pronouns: He/him
Species: Human

Technically, true. I haven't died yet. Just because I can't eat Dad's homemade crab cakes for another couple centuries, doesn't mean I'm not me, still. I wonder if I can freeze some…

Are you an existing patient at Centre Street Clinic? Yes.

TRANSCENDENT 3

If yes, who is your primary care physician? Dr. Lisa Perez.
What is the reason for your clinic visit today?

I bite the cap of my pen. My teeth hurt, but I can't stop chewing. And I don't know what to write — nothing I want to tell the receptionist. I settle for: *Bleeding.*

Understatement of the century.

When I return the form, the receptionist pretends to have been drinking his coffee; he grabs the handle with such force, the black liquid spills over the edge and stains a pile of blue forms.

The person who was watching me doesn't stop when I sit back down.

"Can I help you?" I ask.

I relish that edge in my voice. The gritty feel, condescending tone. Andreas never sounds like that. His voice is sea glass, smooth and translucent. Mine is a year of throat-clearing, congestion, and cracking.

The waiting patient loosens their hold on their knees and raises their chin. "You're bleeding."

"I know." I wipe at my nose, but there's nothing.

"No, I mean on the chair." They point.

Fuck.

My cheeks muster up all the color they can find — hopefully enough to suspend menstruation.

"It's okay. I won't tell or anything." They motion for me to stand, then toss a magazine over the spot. "The clinic will probably just throw the chair out anyway. No use blaming someone for it."

"Thanks." I want to smile, but the gooey feeling between my legs — knowing that I'm bleeding out and there's nothing I can do to stop *it* — stops *me*.

I'm halfway to the bathroom when a nurse calls my name. "Finley! Finley Hall?"

"Yeah." I hold myself together while I walk, Andreas's fleece wrapped around my waist, steps small to avoid any further leakage, arms clasped in front of me — as if anyone really walks like that.

"I'm Ashlynn, Dr. Treggman's nurse. Why don't you follow me on back and I'll get you started. How does that sound?"

"Fine." I nod and follow her back, even cooperate.

She makes me get on the scale.

"Wow, you've lost nine pounds since your last visit — two weeks ago."

Takes my blood pressure.

"Fifty over thirty. That — that can't be right. You'd have to be…"

And my temperature.

"Um, okay, this — I'm going to get Dr. Treggman."

She backs out of the exam room, keeping her eyes on me until she's safe on the other side of the door.

I lean back on the patient table. Its white paper crinkles beneath me. Dr. Treggman walks in just as I'm peering at the crotch of my jeans to assess the situation.

"Finley, nice to meet you." He sets his laptop on a wheeled table and sits on a short black wheelie stool and wheels himself and his laptop over to me. "I'm Dr. Treggman."

I nod.

"What seems to be the problem?" he asks all while peering over his glasses at the form I gave the nurses. "Bleeding?" Then he looks over his glasses at me. "Would you like to be more specific?"

"I got my period for the first time in three years, today."

"You're on Testosterone Cypionate?"

"Intramuscular injections."

"So you know, then, that people who have taken steps to medically transition are on the restricted list for vampirification." He stares at me over his wire-frame glasses and old plasticky laptop. Slowly, his lips purse. "The nurse gave me your stats. I'll have to report this. I'm sorry, I'm required by law."

I squeeze my legs together and lean forward, trying to appeal to his human side while I still have one. "Look," I say softly. "I need help, okay? This is the only clinic I even feel safe coming to for trans stuff."

"Mr. Hall, this isn't trans *stuff*, this is vampire *stuff*. And there's a reason the two don't mix; we don't have conclusive studies on how vampirification affects atypi-cal bodies." He starts typing, again.

I've seen the Federal Vampire Commission's list of *atypical bodies*. It's trans and intersex folks. Disabled and neuroatypical folks; the F.V.C. even provides a list of prohibited surgeries and medications. Never mind those who can't afford the required physical exams and application fee. And heaven forbid you're a woman of childbearing age who "might want to have kids someday; *how can you be sure you won't want to?*"

"As I'm not versed in vampire anatomy — " Dr. Treggman's words buzz like a fly in my ears. " — I hesitate to make any recommendations — "

TRANSCENDENT 3

I clench my hands into cold, white fists and punch them down on top of Dr. Treggman's shitty laptop. His tan, hairy arms tremble where they stick out from the keyboard. I lean over the wheelie desk and bare my growing fangs. If I breathe deep enough, he smells like dinner.

I lean my full weight on the shattered laptop, crushing him in a hand-sand-wich between layers of circuits and plastic.

"Finley." His voice is hoarse and shaky. "Finley, please, you're hurting me."

"Finley!" Andreas's sea glass voice turns my head.

"What," I ask, slowly, "are you doing here? You're supposed to be asleep."

"Good thing I wasn't. You need to let the doctor go. He's just doing his job."

"You know how many doctors I've met who are just *doing their jobs*?" The one who asked if I was really, really sure, because I didn't seem very masculine. The one who suggested psycho-sexual therapy as if my kinks disqualified me. The one who told me no cis gay men would want to sleep with me.

"I know." Andreas snakes an arm around my waist and pries me off the laptop.

Dr. Treggman squeaks relief and Andreas looks into his eyes and says, "You will wait quietly." The doctor slackens, suddenly unconcerned about his injured hands or the one and a half vampires fighting in his exam room.

"I can't go like this." I gesture over my un-reproductive organs.

"So, buy some new clothes. Here." Andreas thrusts a few bills into my hand.

I hate that he's so easily solved my problem. I want to stay angry. I'm still angry. I'm still *bleeding*. "How did you know where I — "

"I can smell you." Andreas taps his nose. "Now, I'm going to convince the doctor not to report us for this mess. You will meet me outside."

"I didn't even think you could go outside at this time. I thought I'd ditched you."

"Yeah, well I'm old and soon you'll be young, so don't ditch me for a few more centuries. You have a lot to learn."

My "Ugh!" is a bratty growl as I slam my fist into the doorframe and leave. If this is my life, now, bring on death.

Andreas meets me in the back alley and pushes me against the brick so hard it cracks. Notably, I don't.

"What were you thinking?" he asks. "Are you trying to get us euthanized?"

"I was thinking you don't understand how my body works and I needed to see someone who does." I try to pry his hands off my shoulders but he's got millennia on me. I haven't even managed to die, yet.

"Dr. Treggman doesn't know more about vampirification than I do. Besides, if you're really concerned, we have vampire doctors."

"Any trans ones?"

"What?"

"Do you know any transgender vampire doctors?" I ask slowly to drive home my point.

Andreas's lips twitch, revealing a flash of white. I wonder if he has emotions or only teeth.

"Didn't think so." This time, I brush him off easily. "You're welcome to feel doubly stupid, by the way. Turning someone without an application — a someone who also happens to be trans. It's not even legal!"

I get halfway down the alley before he says, "I thought you smelled different. Not enough to deter me. Actually, not bad at all. Just different."

"I'm flattered." I suppose that's the vampire equivalent of "Wow, I'd never have guessed you were trans," or "But you look so normal."

I put my borrowed sunglasses back on and pause at the shade's edge. "Let's go home so I can die, already."

Andreas catches my shoulder before I can step further into the sunlight. Smoke rises from his hand before he jerks it away.

"I thought you were old," I snap, still unable to control my temper.

"I am." Blisters swell on his otherwise unblemished skin. "Just because I don't catch fire wearing SPF 70 in the shade, doesn't mean I can lie out on the beach in June."

I cross vacations off my list of future plans. A list that seems to shrink every hour.

"Look, Finley, don't let this ruin your last day."

I walk backwards across the line of light, watching Andreas grow smaller. He doesn't offer any more wisdom. He doesn't even stay.

Don't let this ruin my last day. It's not really my last day. My last day was pizza and burnt French fries, strobe lights and pulsing bass. Drunk pissing.

I stand at the top of St. Paul Street and watch cars fly past. They disappear between skyscrapers and the orange glow of sunset. I should care that this is my last sunset — at least for a few centuries.

I cared when it was my last night with breasts. When I faced losing erotic sensation. Never arching under the hard pinch of rough fingers or the wet suction of a man's lips. I didn't want the mounds, but I had them my whole life. And, then, I didn't.

TRANSCENDENT 3

I cared before my voice dropped. When I faced losing my ability to sing. "Most guys can't," the Internet said and no voice coaches worked with trans men, only trans women. The drop was sudden and uncomfortable. I strained and pushed to sing The Kinks and The Beatles and cried when I couldn't. I hadn't lost my ability to cry, yet.

I care that this is my last sunset.

The sky is black and blue when I show up on Andreas's doorstep. His bandaged hand and heavy eyelids are my fault. He glances at the back of my canvas and my small kit of paints and brushes, as if he expected more.

"I probably won't see another sunset like that." Not that I have to justify my time to him. He probably expected I'd visit with family or friends, vomit up a last ditch attempt at a favorite drink or meal. Maybe I should've. Too late, now.

"No, you probably won't." Andreas steps aside so I can set my things in the guest room and kick off my shoes. "Ready?"

"Yeah." I roll up my pink and orange stained sleeves. "I'm ready."

Andreas leads me into the basement. It's unfinished. The rough cement floor cools my feet; the air chills my exposed skin.

"You don't have to take off your clothes, but you should," Andreas says.

"Why?"

"Death is messy. You don't want it sticking to you."

"Fair." I don't ask for further details. Despite stabbing myself with a needle every two weeks and going through surgery, I'm not particularly good with gross body stuff. Surprise-menstruation was enough to last me an eternity.

I leave my shirt and jeans in a pile, half-folded. Andreas lifts up a metal hatch, exposing soft, freshly tilled soil underneath.

"No coffin?" I ask. Vampires aren't exactly forthcoming about their reproductive process. Secrets are power and they've already given over so much to humankind.

"No," he says. "Just you and the earth." His cheeks flush with recently-drunk blood. He's jealous. He stares at the loose dirt like a lover he wants to wrap himself around.

"You can join me. If you want."

Andreas shakes his head. "You don't want that. You want to be alone. Trust me. There'll be other nights."

I don't tell him I don't want to be buried alive and alone. I don't want to taste dirt. Don't want it matted in my hair, packed up my nose — the crumbs rolling up into my brain. If I'm barely breathing, does it even matter?

Andreas offers his hand. I let him help me into the earthen grave because no one's done anything like that for me since I was a girl.

I sink a few inches when the dirt gives beneath my weight. Andreas's grip tightens to keep me from falling. Mine tightens with hopes of pulling him in with me. But he doesn't stumble, doesn't follow. When he lets go, I clasp my hands in front of me.

"Lie down." Each of his words is a nail in my imaginary coffin.

I dig myself a space, lie down, and close my eyes. When Andreas pushes the first mound of dirt over my feet, I panic. But my body's not setup to panic, anymore. I have no racing heart or nauseous stomach. My deep breaths mean nothing. I suck air in, but it sits there until I push it out.

"Relax." Andreas covers my legs next. He doesn't pack the soil tight. I assume so that I can get out. I hope.

He unclasps my hands and lays them out beside me. Even corpses get to hold themselves in death. But I'm left exposed to the dirt Andreas piles on my chest and over my arms. Over my neck and ears.

I blink up at him, nothing but a pale face amongst black-brown soil. A waning moon in the night sky. Andreas bends and presses a soft kiss against my lips. It doesn't mean anything. I almost wish it did. We don't love each other, don't long for each other's touch or look forward to some eternal romance. I didn't even pick him. He bit me. I didn't get a say beyond turn or die.

Andreas climbs out of my grave and disappears from view. When he returns, he's holding the wooden handles of a dirt-filled wheelbarrow. "I'll be back for you." And with that, he dumps it over my face. I feel him pat its cold weight over my head and body. Hear the squeaky hinge on the metal trapdoor and its bang shut.

Dirt fills my mouth when I scream.

S tarving.
    Starving and dried and thirsty.

Thirsty and hungry are the same. My body is a desert. I swallow bits of dirt with the rush of blood I suck down. The source is hot against me. Hard against me. My jaw is rigid, eyes wide on those of the man who feeds me.

"Finley." His voice is underwater. My name ripples to the surface.

TRANSCENDENT 3

He rips the source away. I lunge after it, but he pins me on a cold cement floor. I run my tongue over the sharp line of my teeth and cut it on my fangs. They taste like him. My wandering eyes settle on the source. The source has a name. His name is Andreas.

"Finley."

That's my name. I know because I chose it.

"Finley, can you hear me?"

I cough up dirt and blood. Spit it on the cement. "Yes." My voice is smoother, darker, fuller.

"How do you feel?" Andreas asks.

"Starving and dried and thirsty."

He smiles with closed lips. "Let's get you in the shower and some blood in your system. How does that sound?"

My answer is a low growl — one that's conceived in my chest and born through my throat. I chase the feeling with another. Andreas pulls me off my feet and into his arms as if I am his pet. I press my nose against his shirt and sniff his blood through the layers of cotton and flesh.

He sets me on my own feet, again, in the shower. It's big enough for three, no curtains blocking us in. Showerheads hang from the ceiling, raining hot water onto our cold bodies. Andreas rips his clothes off and tosses them into a sopping heap on the rug. I'm already naked — I forgot.

Starving.

I feel every drop of water that strikes my skin like a match tip catching fire. Mud rolls over my muscled arms and unsticks from the dark curls between my legs. I'm not bleeding, anymore.

Andreas offers his wrist. I latch onto his neck, instead. His laugh resounds through my jaw. The blood jostles, choking me for a moment. I pull back and crack my neck, let the rush settle in.

Nerves in my chest prickle to life — nerves that died under the knife years ago. I squirm where Andreas slides his hand down my back, where he rests it under my ass and squeezes, pressing our bare bits together.

When I bite him again, my teeth light with as much pleasure as my cunt — more, even. Like there are nerves in my new fangs.

"There are," Andreas says, confirming my thoughts. "And it's so much better than sex."

My body pulses with blood like that first rush of testosterone. Andreas doesn't taste like one person. He isn't a varietal vintage. He's the blood of everyone he's drunk. Like the house blend, I drink him until he stops me.

I know it's blood; I can taste the iron. But it recalls words like silky and juicy, the swirl of red in a glass, and roll over the tongue.

"Enough," he says with fangs exposed.

I didn't expect the lust part of bloodlust, but Andreas looks different with my undead eyes. I can see the lines of severity in his expression, the flare of his pupils, feel his subtly shifting muscles.

I reach between us and grab Andreas's erection, rub my blood-engorged clit against it and moan. "I want you," I say.

"You want blood."

"I want both."

Andreas smiles. "I'll give you both."

We fuck with my forehead pressed against the slick tiled wall, Andreas's mouth hovering against the back of my neck. Even amidst the steam, his breath is hot, tongue strong and wet. I want him to feed on me again, like that night in the alley. Only this time we both want it and it is so much better, this way.

His cold fingers shock my nipples hard, rolling and pinching them. In only a few hours they've regained the sensitivity they lost under the knife, two years ago.

With his other hand he covers my mouth. And while I relish the bondage, the stifling of my growls and moans, I know it's an offering. I sink my teeth into his wrist and draw the color from him.

While his blood rushes through me, turning me, resurrecting me, Andreas pushes his thick cock into my cunt. I steady myself against the wall while he lifts me with one arm — the arm not lodged in my mouth — and thrusts.

It's not long before he comes, trembling inside me; his body pins mine to the wall. I'm so close, so full, probably saturated. Andreas reaches between my legs and rubs my clit. I close my eyes, lick the wounds on his arm, rest my weight on the full feeling in my groin.

If he weren't propping me up, my orgasm would knock me to the shower floor. It radiates through my blood stream. It wakes me up.

Andreas has to rip his arm away from me. "Careful," he whispers in my ear. "Your body is adjusting. You don't want to be sick, again, so soon."

He rinses us off, takes my hand, and together we lie on the shower tiles, their orange-pink marbling a farce of sundown. I rest my face against his pec, over his

TRANSCENDENT 3

juicy heart, and kiss the skin. Andreas chuckles and holds me there while the water pounds over my blissed out body.

"I'm still hungry," I say.

"I bet you are."

"When can we hunt?"

"We can't."

"Why not? You did."

Andreas flips his body on top of mine. "I'm old, Finley. Too old. I've followed human history for millennia. I've met believers and skeptics. Warm beds and pitchforks. Somehow, I never expected assimilation." He relaxes onto his side, rests his head on his hand. "Never expected to go mainstream."

"'I'm Andreas. I was a vampire before it was cool,'" I say, mocking him.

His smirk is sharp and quick; I almost miss it. "You think you're going to be the vampire that breaks the rules. That fights the normalization of our culture. That doesn't register with a government that's existed as long as my last haircut."

"Your laws don't really matter to me. But for some reason I went along with them. I figured, why not try something new? Live in the open for a change, make friends, furnish an apartment, get a hobby.

"Wasn't so bad at first. Bagged blood is like your Diet Coke. Not as good as the real thing, but you get used to it — so much, sometimes, that you get a sugar rush if you revert." Andreas traces a finger down my jaw, over my neck and chest, swirling it around one of my swollen areolae. "I wanted to hold a live body in my arms and feed while it wriggled against me, struggled for the life I sucked hot out of it."

I squeeze my legs together and rock my hips while lust washes over me again.

"You like that." He smiles.

"I do."

"We can't feed on humans."

"But I get it, now." I sit up straighter. "I feel — "

"Forget how you feel, now. Remember how you felt, *then*," Andreas says, squeezing my hand with a strength I can almost match.

Remembering back a few days ago seems impossible, like seeing into someone else's mind. But I close my eyes and use the white noise of the running water to go back. Even then my human memories feel like facts rather than experiences. "I was angry that you took my choice away."

"Right. Remember that, even if you have to write it down, every morning."

TRANSCENDENT 3

"Okay, but what if we get a donor — a certified blood donor — whose choice it is to give us their blood?" I bat my eyelashes.

Andreas leans over my chest and licks my nipple. "I'll consider it."

I moan and arch up to meet his mouth.

His lips brush my sensitive flesh while he speaks. "When you prove you can control yourself enough not to kill anyone, I'll consider it." He sucks the hard nub between his teeth and presses his fingers between my legs.

Control myself. Just once I'd like to control my own damn body.

We feed on blood bags, together. Andreas "convinces" my landlord to break my lease early and without penalty — just like he "convinced" Dr. Treggman not to report us — so I can move into the guest room. He buys me a real bed and a mug that says "Blood: it's not just for breakfast, anymore."

During the first week, we eat and fuck. I'm still not in love with him — don't expect to be — but he lets me feed on him in the shower to ease my bloodlust.

I stumble out, naked and wet, still unsteady on my changing legs. My muscles thicken and shape the more I drink. My facial hair fills in thick and dark where it was patchy before: a fine, perfectly groomed layer on my cheeks and neck. I always thought vampires looked like more beautiful versions of their human selves, though I can't imagine a duller Andreas.

"Stop staring at yourself in the mirror," he teases.

"Stop staring at myself?" I rub a towel over my hair. It rests shiny and perfect without any help. "I've never been happy with the way I look until now. And I'm not supposed to stare?"

Andreas's smile is so subtle, I'd have missed it with human eyes. He lifts me onto my new Ikea bed.

"Can vampires cut their hair?" I ask, diverting Andreas's mouth from its intent.

"What? Why? You just said — "

"When we were talking earlier, you said our government was as old as your last haircut."

"We can make small changes over long periods of time. If you cut it all off, it would grow back while you slept. Mostly, I was being facetious. Bit of vampire humor." He glances at my hair. "Why, you weren't thinking of changing…anything, were you?"

I wasn't. Not really. But knowing I can't? What if prosthetics or surgery become so advanced — I'm going to live to see that. Doctors will be able to grow

TRANSCENDENT 3

you a dick using stem cells or someone will invent a CyberCock that pairs with a brain implant. In a future where trans people will be able to customize their bodies, I won't be able to. Mine will reject and revert. Beautiful but stagnant. No implants, no surgeries. Not even a haircut. This is why trans people aren't allowed to undergo vampirification.

It's still better than dying.

Will I feel that way in a hundred years?

"Finley?"

"Uh, no, not planning to change anything. Sorry."

"You okay?"

"Yeah. Just…" I focus on the body I have, on the things I can control. Like my current arousal. "Just get back to it." I force a smile when I recline. The smile sticks.

The particleboard rocks under the force of our weight, knocking over the canvas I leaned against it. Andreas dives between my legs and sucks on my clit. It's grown like a satisfied tick. And I'm hornier than I was during my first six months on T.

I twine my fingers through Andreas's shiny curls and hold his face against my crotch. He's happy to oblige, trailing his kisses over my abdomen and up my chest. Ever since I turned, I can't get enough of his mouth and fingers on my nipples. I missed them. I missed them and now they're back, healed by his venom.

He pulls away, leaving my slick, wet chest cold and exposed.

"Don't stop," I whisper.

Andreas looks between my chest and my face then back to my chest. "Something's wrong," he says.

"What? Nothing's…" I pat the bare skin and wince. Tender dimples of breasts poke out. "What's happening to me?"

Andreas swallows a hard lump in his throat. "Your body. It's — I don't know."

I skitter back until I hit the headboard, until I can't run any further away from my own chest. "Make it stop," I say. When Andreas doesn't move, I shout. "Make it stop!"

He hisses at me for silence.

"Please," I whisper. "Please, make it stop." Something warm rolls down my face, red drops splatter on the growing mounds of my chest.

Andreas growls as he rips the covers off the bed and flings them into the air. The colorful cotton drifts slowly to the floor between us. He bites his bottom lip leaving a thin red line that drips down his chin.

TRANSCENDENT 3

"I have an idea."

"What?"

"I'll be right back." But before he can get too far, he turns back. "*Don't* move."

I shake my head. "I won't."

I can't and I don't.

I stare at the pattern on Andreas's manufactured quilt. The colors are intense, even in the dark. Red too bright for blood. Yellow too clear for the sun. A sun I won't see again until I'm god knows how old, and only then from the shadows.

The quilt doesn't warm me like I wish it would. My body's cold now. It used to be warm. Testosterone runs warmer than estrogen. I stopped wearing a sweater to work. Wonder if I'll start, again.

The door clicks shut. Andreas appears in the doorway; he slows to a human pace mid-step. I can see the change, now. It looks like slow motion. How slow must walking feel to him after so many years.

"Drink this." Andreas crawls onto the bed and wraps an arm around me. He rests a blood bag against my lips.

I push it away. "I'm not hungry."

"You're hungry for this. Trust me."

I purse my lips before accepting the bag. My fangs pierce the thick plastic so easily, I have to concentrate on not ripping it open over the mattress.

"How do you like it?" Andreas watches me.

I don't like when he watches me. I look inexperienced—I am, but that's not the point. Andreas makes vampirism look casual, like a lifestyle. Like vegetarianism.

I carefully back off the bag, long enough to really swallow, to run my tongue over my teeth and let the blood absorb into my body. My temperature rises. A warm euphoria radiates from my skin, swarms my brain, swells between my legs.

"This is good."

Andreas smiles.

"What'd you do to it?"

"Vampire venom enhances what it finds: clear voice, luxurious hair, firm muscles—"

"Remaining breast tissue; I get it." I grit my slippery teeth. "What did you *do* to this?"

"Injected it with testosterone." He looks thoughtfully between me and the bloody bag. "I didn't think, when I drained your blood, that I'd depleted any

TRANSCENDENT 3

hormones you may've injected. Most humans' bodies keep producing whatever they need."

"Mine doesn't."

"I know that, now. Thought I'd reintroduce what you need. Steer your new vampire body in the right direction."

"Not bad, Dr. Andreas."

I crush the bag against my mouth and suck it dry. The plastic crinkles until it's raisin-like in my hands. A drop spills over my chin and tickles my neck. Andreas leans over and licks it away.

I growl and toss the empty bag onto the floor, accepting Andreas's mouth against mine. He avoids my chest, though I feel the mounds press against his shirt when he climbs on top of me.

I wake up horny. Andreas sleeps beside me, still, his hand draped over my chest to protect me from it. My consciousness stirs him. When he flexes his hand, it brushes my side and I push it away. It's too much. I can't stay in and fuck away the bloodlust for the rest of my life.

"Hey." Andreas props himself up, eyes only half-open. He stares at my body. "They're gone."

I look. I don't want to, but I have to, and he's right. The area's not as hard and defined as it used to be. Andreas gently touches the puffy skin. I gasp. The air feels strange in my lungs, like a lump in my throat.

I quickly expel it and sit up. "I need more of that blood."

I burn through T like a bodybuilder. My old dose is not going to be enough and Andreas warns me against trying to visit a human doctor, again.

"They'll report you. They'll report me!" He follows me to the front door.

"Why do you even care?"

I pull the door open and storm into the night like an angry teenager. Heat builds under my cold skin. Cis people are all the same: human or vampire.

Andreas grabs my arm gently, by his standards. I pause out of respect — and rather than dislocating one of our shoulders.

"Is it so wrong to want to feel normal for once?" he pleads with me.

I see an ancient monster against canary yellow walls, glossy wood floors, and ergonomic furniture. He tried. He's still trying.

"I'll be back." I leave, running as fast as I can, which is still not faster than Andreas, but hopefully fast enough to lose him and his questions.

TRANSCENDENT 3

Normal. I slow to an acceptably human speed outside the Center Street Clinic. It's closed. Obviously. Nothing discourages new vampires from visiting like hours that end before sunset. Perfectly legal. Perfectly gross.

I watch patrons drinking in the bar next door, while I walk around it and into the alley. I've yet to ask Andreas how long until my body can handle alcohol. Seeing how fast it absorbs hormones, it'd probably take a lot of booze to get me as drunk as the night we met.

I race up the fire escape and crack the glass with my elbow. The clinic is empty. At home in the dark, I easily navigate the clutter of chairs and narrow hallways in search of the pharmacy.

A sign stops me: "Ask about subsidized hormone therapy, today!" Center Street is a good clinic. What kind of asshole robs a pharmacy?

Me. I'm the kind.

There are dozens of bottles of T, here. They'll know if I take one, so I might as well take what I need for the next six weeks. The clinic can order more.

I load the little boxes into my backpack, grab some needles and syringes for good measure, and climb back out the broken window. Halfway down the fire escape, I consider that Andreas would have found a less obvious and destructive way in.

I jump from the second floor, landing on wobbly feet in the alley. Drunk blood wafts past me from the bar. I hurry away from it, so I won't be tempted to rip a beer out of someone's hands — or the jugular out of someone's throat.

I still smell the alcohol when I pass the gym. Fast-pumping blood, still hot from working out, burns my nostrils. I drag my tongue over my fangs, imagining how one of these late-night meatheads would taste.

"Hey." A solid, wide-jawed man nods at me. "You're out late."

"No." My razor teeth show through my smile. "You're out late." I hear his heart pump faster, smell his adrenaline spike. I bet he tastes even better turned on.

He runs a hand through his sweat-slick hair while he swaggers towards me. He lowers his voice. "I've never fucked a vampire, before."

I press a hand against his abdomen and linger on the over-developed muscle. "You're subtle."

"Wasn't getting the feeling I needed to be."

"You don't. Come with me."

TRANSCENDENT 3

Andreas isn't home when I-still-haven't-asked-his-name and I get in. I sit my backpack carefully on the bench in the foyer then kick my shoes into the middle of the hall.

"Bradley," the man says between kisses. "My name's Bradley."

"Finn," I say instead of "I didn't ask."

"This your place?"

"Something like that."

He peers down the hall into open rooms as I pull him into mine. Probably wants to know what a vampire's lair is like. Apparently it's like the inside of a Swedish furniture store. Sorry to disappoint.

Bradley tugs his shoes off and leaves them behind the bed. He smashes his mouth against mine — a move I assume is sexier to someone who can't literally bite his face off.

But I go with it. I relax. I let him push me against the mattress — even pretend he's pinning me there. His sweaty shirt sticks between us when he pulls mine off over my head.

"You feel like marble."

Big vocabulary for a gym rat. "If that's a problem, I can put my clothes back on."

"No, no, no." He kisses down my chest. "I like it. It's just…different. You're cold."

I snake my hand down the front of Bradley's drawstring pants. He's already hard. My hand glides easily over his sweaty cock.

He moans against my lips. "You want that? Want me to warm you up?"

As cliché as his lines are, his arrogance gets me wet.

"Do it," I say, helping his clothes off. I accidentally rip his tee shirt. His pants slide off unharmed. His swollen cock bobs near my face and I fight the urge to suck it. Bad idea, teeth.

"Hey, you should know…" I trail off. I could kill him and I'm still afraid to tell him our genitals don't match.

"What? This your first time?"

I shake my head.

"Afraid you're going to hurt me?"

"No — well, a little, but I — I'm trans."

"What?"

"I'm transgender."

"You have a dick?" He pulls my briefs down, throwing me off balance.

TRANSCENDENT 3

"Excuse me!"

"Are you kidding? I find the only fucking gay vampire with no dick?"

"Didn't think I'd need one for what you planned to do."

"I'm not putting anything in your pussy."

I tense up at the word. "Please don't call it that."

"Whatever."

"I have another hole, in case you missed it."

Bradley shakes his head and reaches for his clothes. "I'm not into girls."

I grab his arm and flip him onto the bed. "And I'm not into transphobic douchebags, but I'm hungry so I'll make an exception."

My fangs lodge easily into his neck. My tongue slides over his salty skin and I overwhelmingly realize why Andreas bit me. I can't even blame him.

Bradley doesn't taste like Andreas, though. He tastes like steroids and adrenaline with a hint of alcohol. He doesn't fight me or he stops fighting me. His heat floods my veins.

The front door clicks its quiet, controlled click shut. Andreas's eyes meet mine in the dark. He doesn't speak. He walks slowly, at human speed even though no one's around to judge him, and kneels at the foot of the bed.

"He smells delicious," Andreas says.

I swallow a mouthful of Bradley's thick, heady blood, then pull out. "Want to share?"

Andreas kisses me, his tongue flicking against mine for a taste. He licks the corner of my mouth, cleaning me up. I'm a messy eater. I'm a monster.

"No thanks," Andreas says. "Once was more than enough." He bites his wrist and lets his blood drip into Bradley's wounds.

"You didn't do that for me."

"You're not even close to draining this man, Finley."

The effects on Bradley are instant; the ragged holes in his neck stitch themselves back together. Seamless.

Bradley opens his eyes on Andreas's.

"You and Finley had a good time, but it was a one-time thing. He's not really your type."

"Yeah," Bradley says.

I roll my eyes.

"Why don't you head home and shower off that gym stench," Andreas says.

"Good idea," Bradley agrees, robotic.

When the jock's dressed and gone, Andreas says, "Get what you need?"

TRANSCENDENT 3

I stretch my jaw and crack my neck. Slide my tongue over my teeth to get the last of the taste. "Mostly."

"Let me help you."

Help me. How is an old cis vampire supposed to help me when he doesn't understand the first thing about my body? My eternity?

I ask, "Do you have any nails?"

A ndreas leans against the threshold, sipping blood while he watches. His skin is pale, but not pallid. His pose casual, but precise. "Little more to the left," he says. "There. That's it."

I walk backwards until I bump into him. He hands me the mug and I take a sip. "Not bad," I say.

My last sunset hangs over the bed. With my new eyes, I see the thick texture of paints where the colors blend and my brushstrokes overlap like waves. Apricot, wine, and goldenrod blur together, each clearer and more real than anything printed by a machine on one of Andreas's quilts.

"Small changes over long periods of time, you said?"

"Yes," Andreas says. "Why?"

"Just making sure."

I imagine what a real sunset will look like when I'm old enough to experience one. If they'll still exist or if smog will cloud the skyline. The only thing that won't change is me, my body, my canvas. "What about a tattoo? You know, to remember." Blood drips from the corners of my eyes.

"Possible. It'll hurt, but possible." Andreas tightens his hold on me. "Are you sure you're okay?"

"Yes," I resolve. "Haven't cried this much since — before, you know. It feels good."

"Since before I turned you?" he asks.

"No," I say. "Before I turned myself."

HEAT DEATH OF WESTERN HUMAN ARROGANCE

◄ M. Téllez ►

She turned to me with half-lidded eyes, her mouth turned upward like a cat's face. Her hands rested on the worn wooden surface beneath her congregation of plants. We needed nothing to see with, just the full moon's cool blue cast. The slopes and lines of her shoulder and hips and chest shifting under the distant light made me feel calm and welcome. I thought about how many seasons would pass before I could be with her again like this.

"I'm thinking about killing myself, kid. They're going to send us off to Mars. And all these plants I live with? They'll *die*. The atmosphere can't shield us from the radiation, which of course they're lying about. You saw the leaked data dumps."

"Yeah." I was unsure of how she expected me to participate with such a topic.

"I'd rather end my life ritually than get sold off and shipped out to die in pain from harsh radiation of another" — Her voice rose sharply — "of a whole other fucking planet, kid!"

She faced me in full. Tendrils of thin cascading palm leaf brushed her cheeks and shoulder. I looked at the fear set through her body — the tension holding her up — a live individuated Earth organism.

Yes — how could they send Earth organisms like Loma to Mars with no provisions forintegration with the Martian noosphere? I felt scared for her and didn't know what to say. What could I say? She is dominant in verbal language and I am not. Yet another layer of difficulty one encounters as a third generation Slow

Stepper™. We were not engineered to be talkers but we have to be now that people think it's too cruel to leave us shriveled up on Mars. I've heard rumors that the versions after me will have improved speech facility. My skin is pigmented like a dying purple seed husk and slightly iridescent. Every third season I leave Earth to grow the Martian irrigation network at Garden City. The radiation doesn't transform me in the ways that Loma fears.

My name is Inri.

Loma's generation fought for organisms like me to have individual autonomy rights. I'm not so sure Loma foresaw this outcome, where I am contributing to a structure that will usurp her way of life — maybe — it is still all conjecture, this "shipping out" business — I feel perplexed.

"Loma," I start, holding out my arms, "Why don't you come to me and I can stroke you. There is a lot of tension."

Her face contorts angrily then fills with woe. She plods over. I enjoy the rustle of the plants as she leaves their embrace and comes into mine. She wears a sweater knit from recycled fibers, whose loops stretch across many small provocative rips. Her skin smells pleasant with the musks that her glands produce. She is soft with hair. She runs her fingers and long nails along my arms. She calls me serpent because that is how my skin feels to her. I have no hair. I have no decisive genitals either. For Loma I wear a prosthetic. She likes it when I use my mouth on her. My generation has tongues and interior ridges like teeth to vocalize language. My generation does many things compared to our predecessors. We are very different. But through our shared cell memories I can know their experiences. It upsets Loma how different the generations are in the few years we have existed, and yet here we are in this predicament.

"Ugh, you're so special, Inri. You're so beautiful and special," she laments into my shoulder.

"Because I am yours?"

"No!" She recoils. "Mine? I'm not — nobody belongs to *anybody*. You're free to do as you wish and I count myself lucky to have you *in my life*." Her voice rises at the end again. I do not point out that no one ever asked my generation if we wanted these individual freedoms. These personal autonomy rights. She fought for us to have that. I know.

My favorite with Loma is her body writhing against the genital prosthetic I wear. She engorges herself with it. I love Loma's body and I love the sensations she experiences on it. Human-identified Earth organisms put out so much rich sensory information they don't find valuable. What Loma values is my height

(I am tall), and my size and my heft and musculature. She says I have a perfect balance of male and female energies (I do not know what being either of those is like so I cannot say).

Loma values the way I do whatever she asks of me. I value her attention. I value the heat exchange of her body's life processes interacting with mine. It frenzies and ebbs with thousands of generations of existence on abundant Earth. There is nothing on Mars I interact with that is as aggressive.

So I wonder what her death might feel like.

"Loma, would you still prefer to die than be shipped to the node, even if I would be there with you?" She sighs loudly and says she looks forward to the release from the prison of her own body in this mortal realm, the joining back with the cosmos. And I do not tell her I used to know that too before she fought for me and my rights.

"It's just so complicated, Inri. There was no *way* I was gonna stand by and watch the creation of a lifeform made entirely to support the colonialist expansion into space. Okay? And there's no way I'm going to let myself be carted off for another sick attempt at capitalist consumption." She looks at me with a determined scowl as I wonder, isn't that what happened? I was created and here we are. She sees I am thinking and squeezes my shoulders for attention.

"Look, if we don't resist we'll be eaten by the machine!"

Loma says this often and I am never sure what she means. Even with hormones and protein regimens that endow Loma with heightened sensory perceptions of her environment (holistic integration, her friends call it), her behavior and her speech are dominated by a kind of selfhood. She seems numb to the feedback from her cyborg body. She describes herself as alienated even though she is part of many symbiotic geographic and cultural systems. She uses group words but doesn't explain who her groups are, and is rarely willing to learn me when I ask. Maybe this kind of isolation works for her in resisting the machine. She has not answered me.

"Are you serious in your desire to die, Loma?"

"If they try to ship us to the node, yeah." There is a determined twist in her brow. I am not so sure that she is prepared. She exhales a clouded sense of revulsion and lays her head against my chest. Her long fingernails graze my bare back and it excites me. She feels good — her heat and her smell and her attention. This is her way of grooming me to play. We spend much of our time playing. Often she invites me over to have space in the room like one of her many flourishing plants, and I like that. I think Loma considers that I am in love with her in a

TRANSCENDENT 3

human way. There are non human-identified humans that talk about love and they say 'mutual survival,' and I love Loma in this way. But she does not seem to want mutual survival because she wanted me and now she wants to die.

"Inri, it's the full moon tonight. I want to please you."

Sometimes I hear Loma talking to her friends about how beautiful I am when she pleases me; what sounds I make, the way I react. There are how-to sexual relationship guides that Loma and her friends have made. Small pamphlets that describe our bodies and how to touch them and what to expect. Having a relationship with a serpent like me is desirable as *an alternative to the non-consensual, consumption-based lifestyle expected of mainstream human society*. That's what her pamphlets say. I get confused by the words *mainstream* and *human* and *society* put together like that. I have trouble understanding why Loma describes our relationship in the terms of a society she doesn't want to belong to. How does our relationship have importance among the non human-identified societies? And the other systems of life organization among the microbes and plants? And the subjugated peoples too who aren't even allowed to participate. They live and die powering the machine Loma hates with their labor, and I am confused why she and her friends do not also fight for their autonomy rights.

"You blossom like a flower when I touch you like this, Inri. That's why you're so special," Loma coos over my supine body. Her two hands have splayed me open where my legs join my torso. She strokes me over and over. Develops a rhythm. The room fills with the scent of my musk, which Loma inhales slowly, deeply. She loves to smell me this way. I wonder what the other plants in her room sense under this beautiful moonlight in this warm space. My predecessors were never so deliberately stimulated. They had very low interaction rates with higher energy peoples. They relied on chance encounters, looking attractive, and mutual cohabitation. They were initially conceived as a modified rhizome that would have a symbiotic relationship with dormant bacteria of the Martian soils. We did not have a bipedal form until the second generation's twelfth version. Now we look more acceptably human and people want to touch us. We like that.

"I love fucking you," Loma breathes across my ear. In this moment I think, I may have confused her attachment to me. I think I have misunderstood her grammar this whole time. Maybe I am also misunderstanding what she means when she says she wants to die. I feel sad. I feel alarmed. I cannot tell what her plants feel because using words has distanced me from them.

The moon was setting when I gathered myself to leave in the morning. Loma slept and I felt uneasy because she could not leave her bed to see me off. Times before I spent whole days curled up around her, comforting and being appreciated. Perhaps she forgot now I would be leaving for a long time. Maybe she was too sad because she would die and I wouldn't see her in this form again. I watched her sleep. When I said, "I have to go, Loma," she pushed herself up wearing her cat's face and stretched her arms around me. She was hot from rest and her breath and breasts and hair were all I felt. One last blossom, she said into my neck. She inhaled me deeply and kissed me below my ears. Then she let go and slid back amidst her sheets, leaving her sweat smell on my body.

"I'll come back to you if you want, Loma," I said in the sleepy room.

"I'll miss you, Inri..." she said from her covers.

I return to Garden City for the growing season.

My generation collects in our familiar Martian crater, by a mountain very few people on Earth care to know of, and with our engineered life processes we encourage the redevelopment of the fourth planet's latent ecosystems.

We do not use words to speak and we do not have the strong body heat of Earth organisms. Surrounded with each other, rooted in cooperation, we share. Those of us who met lovers have much to exchange: Human-identified love relationships are pleasing. We learn about intimate behavior from our partners and that's beneficial. But they do not seem mutual. We compile the non-mutual interactions, trying to sense the greater network of forces affecting them and why they occur. Then we must let it be.

This growing season is a critical stage and we are here because we want to grow. We do not concern ourselves with any reality beyond the present. Besides, we do not have the energy to expend. My feelings for Loma go dormant.

As the planet turns I enjoy the sheer undulations of the sun, the microbial exchanges, the slow shifting pleasantry of existence, and I am not again confronted by the human word concepts of *work* and *rights* until I have detached from the rhizome and boarded the transport where there are human-identified earth people manning the craft.

This is what I think at first: *Are* they human identified? As they secure me for the voyage back to Earth, something about them strikes me as different. These humans speak slow, though they speak. More than I do. Maybe they are new hybrids. Maybe I am so freshly departed from the rhizome that I have forgotten how humans can look and I am projecting my expectations.

When the operator checks my security harness, I think I see their clay colored skin shimmer as their hand draws away. Iridescent like me? Loma's lamenting

TRANSCENDENT 3

body appears from my sleeping memories — this is a new generation of slow steppers? A new version? I am unsure why we would be changed to also man spacecraft…

The iridescent person will not make eye contact with me.

I do not feel well, so I sleep.

When I am released from the specimen collection and sterilization wards and into the Earth public environment I am so enthralled by the heat of the ground and the intensity of color that I release my scent from the stimulation. It draws several bugs close to me. I laugh. It is just past the summer season. The air is cool. The weight of the gravity is comforting. Rain is falling. The twilight moon is a crescent shrouded in veils of swiftly passing storm clouds. There is so much information everywhere. I have not spoken except to pass through my clearances from Mars, and as I venture to form words between my ridges and tongue, what comes out is *Loma*. I liked to say her name so much — it felt so pleasing to form and vocalize — but this time it feels like a word that means leaving. I stand still because I realize I have left and I am not sure what I am supposed to connect with now. I feel so disoriented. I wish I could root to the Earth for comfort from these sensations, but I was not made to do such a thing here. I am alone.

I am back in the city enclave by the sister rivers, near the communal home where I am provided living space. I am waiting on the trolley platform and it is rush hour. There are young children wearing book bags everywhere, laughing and bumping around, seeking the attention of their parents. I realize today is the customary half-day that precedes tomorrow's holiday and that's why there are so many small children in abundance. Normally at this time of day there are only workers and the teenage indentured. The children give off good energy. They are very aware, maybe because they are not yet strong with language. They look at me with large eyes, daring or shy or unsure, depending on how their parents regard me.

I do not believe that Loma was shipped off from Earth. I did not encounter any humans while I was growing, but there was also no reason that I would have. We do not experience time on Mars in the same ways we do on Earth, and we only interact with what is in relationship with our rhizome. And there are hardly any habitable places for humans on Mars yet, not with so many growing seasons to come.

The trolley pulls up. It is a full car and we are packed in shoulder to shoulder. It feels comforting. The children are having fun — they seem to enjoy the density like I do. Having their presence fill the air makes me feel good. There are not many children or families where the home is. My little home. Where Loma lived there were a few but it seemed as though her neighborhood was changing from the old families to the new political collectives like she belonged to.

Loma...

The trolley is making its way through her neighborhood. The stop-bell dings and a fresh stream of people board and leave. I remember leaving at this stop many times to see her. This time, I find a seat. I feel a pang of longing for my rhizome on Mars. I would be connected to all these people if they were part of my rhizome. But here everyone is a free individual. They stare ahead and do not make eye contact. I am like them now. Free and autonomous. Loma fought for my rights.

TRANSCENDENT 3

PRAYING TO THE
GOD OF SMALL CHANCES

◄ L Chan ►

I meet the god of small chances in a hospital waiting room, amidst the smell of unwashed bodies and overwashed floors. Chairs in cemetery rows, blue plastic headstones each one of them. I'm reading last week's papers again and munching on a fried pastry: chicken and potato mashed into a slurry of turmeric-stained mush under crisp dough. Oil has already soaked through the paper bag to my fingertips.

Dad's inside. Doctors have recommended a scorched earth approach: Once a month, they put napalm in a syringe and hope it kills the rogue cells before the rogue cells kill him. We're still not sure who's winning.

The god dresses like you'd least expect: knockoff *Adventure Time* t-shirt, jeans shredded at the knees, deep denim blue bleached to white thread. They notice me staring — gods love attention — and they settle down next to me. Seven studs down one ear, arranged in the colours of the spectrum; hair shaved close to skin on the side, slicked back on top. Their face is perfectly symmetrical, cheek bones high and sharp, lips a full bow. I almost want to reach out to see how soft they are.

"You don't seem like the praying type," they say. Their voice is high and piping like a choirboy's.

"I'm not, and I didn't call you." It is unwise to make enemies of a god, even a minor one, but I'm in the mood to spit in the face of a god. I cross my legs. The early morning heat makes my thighs stick to the chair.

TRANSCENDENT 3

My father used to work in the small temples. Buffered by strong drink and delirious with incense, he would whip his back with a flail of knotted rope, tearing his skin to shreds. In his trances he would soothsay or divine the causes of illness. He channeled the gods.

I just see them. Only the small gods of hearth and threshold, of lost possessions and late homework. Of small chances.

"But you did call me," the god persists. "This is one of my temples, along with the race track, the exam hall, the MMORPG raidzone. Everybody wants something."

I think of Dad with his booming laugh. Not so chatty now. I haven't gone into the ward for weeks, but I've racked up a fortune in hospital parking all the same. He used to be a pack-a-day smoker. We thought his lungs would go, but no, it was something in the bone, one in a hundred thousand. The gods used to speak through him, but now he's got new gods: gods in blister packs and little glass vials, gods with names that have too many Xs and Zs, Ys masquerading as vowels like poison masquerading as medicine.

"It's not you I called. I want someone to make things right. This isn't fair."

The god of small chances sits straight, barely tall enough to look me in the chin. I fear only for a moment.

"You'll find that there are no gods fairer than I. The incidence rate is only one in a hundred thousand. Where are the ninety-nine thousand rejoicing that they aren't sick? Or your gratitude for not being struck by lightning or a car on the way here? Good things happen to bad people and vice versa. Every entreaty to other gods is for things to go the other way, in this world or the next. That's not what I do."

They're right; maybe I did call them. Since the diagnosis, my last conscious thought every night has been a hope for a miracle: the impossible, the smallest of chances. But now that they're right here, I can't admit it. Before I can go, the god reaches out and catches my chin. Their touch is barely enough to dimple skin; I can't break free.

"Where will you go? Back to your car? Another waiting room? You can go to him."

"I will."

"Will you? You've been waiting to go into the ward for weeks. Afraid to see what your father has become. Afraid that anything you do together will be the last time you do it and it won't be how you want to remember it."

TRANSCENDENT 3

They're close enough for their breath to tickle my eyelashes, if they had breath. I wonder if anyone is here to see us — me with my chin upturned, the pulse in my neck hard enough to thrum against skin.

They don't wait for me to answer.

"I can tell you this. I am the god of the dance of electrons, patron of the asteroid that will pass within a fraction of a degree of your planet in a hundred years. I watch the lottery, the meeting of sperm and egg, and I watch you. You pray every night for him, for yourself, but never for the both of you."

I blink and they're gone. My skin takes a little longer to register the loss.

Everybody loves a long shot, no matter whether they'll admit it or not.

I leave the ward just as the nurses serve breakfast. Looking back, I see my father arguing with a nurse about the food. He'll eat it eventually — he always does. The smile on my face is a stranger returning home after a long hiatus. There are things to be fixed other than sickness. Then the door swings shut and he's gone.

My pastry is cold and lasts another two bites. I crunch the oil-stained bag into a ball. My underhand throw is clumsy, its arc just shy of horizontal; the paper strikes the lip of the open-mouthed bin, catching on the edge. It navigates the rim with the grace of a drunken acrobat, teetering at the last moment before falling in, a prayer to the god of small chances.

TRANSCENDENT 3

THE MOUSE

◄ Larissa Glasser ►

A year before I was stabbed to death, I saw a mouse in our living room. I was pretty baked at the time, so I hadn't noticed it at first. I'd been watching some old noir film left running on the TV by someone else in the house and I was trying to figure out what it was.

I lived on the top floors of an early-twentieth-century duplex with these two other trans girls Brooke and Debbie who were around the same age as me. The apartment got dusty a lot and was difficult to keep clean. But it was warm and cheap and our landlady was good to us.

I didn't have much to do that afternoon so I'd sat down on the big couch and decided to see if I could gather which film it was. I used to study film as an undergrad but I'd dropped out during my second semester because I went broke. This film didn't ring a bell, but it starred Laurence Tierney. His character killed a lot of people.

My throat got dry, so I reached for my Diet Snapple. When I turned my head, I noticed the mouse resting on the smaller couch at the far end of the wall. It was facing sideways, and when I realized it wasn't afraid, I watched it for a while instead of the movie.

The thing was brownish and very small, no bigger than two inches not counting its tail. The room got darker as evening came. The TV became the only source of light, a cheerless, icy glare. The movie finished, and the closing host commentary was annoying — too chipper — so I muted the sound but kept the TV on so I could keep watching the mouse. I was too invested in this new activity to get up and turn the big light on.

The mouse was breathing rapidly. It never moved from the spot, nor did its tail move.

I knew we'd had a so-called "mouse problem" for a few weeks. We could hear them scuttling in the walls. Brooke, the most industrious member of our household, said she was sick of finding mouse turds in her workshop, so she was going to get some poison before the infestation got worse. I didn't want her to kill anything, but my girlfriend Jennifer had tried to convince me that Brooke was doing the right thing, because mice were all vermin who needed to be killed.

"But mice are cute!" I'd told her when the subject came up.

"They're *vermin*!" she'd said. "They're dirty!"

Some of Jennifer's outer chin hairs, softened from several months of laser treatments, glowed in silhouette in front of my blue lamp. She'd looked angelic. I'd went for a main tuft of the hairs and clutched them. She didn't break away but had stared back at me, trying to maintain her stern expression.

"Mice are cute," I'd told her. "I like animals."

"Come on! Mice are *vermin*! They'll eat all of your groceries and shit everywhere!"

"They're *cute*!"

This game had gone on for a bit, back and forth, and had become increasingly more childish until she just dove at me, wrestled me out of my clothes, called *me* cute, and fucked me high and wild. We usually came at the same time. Sometimes life was nice to us.

Anyway, it looked like the poison was working, because the mouse was breathing at a steadily slower rate. Watching it made me sad, though. I wanted to help it somehow, like with an antidote or something. I could have put it outside to fate the city. It was so little. It never meant to hurt anyone. Why hadn't it moved yet? Apart from the debilitating effects of the poison, maybe the mouse hadn't noticed me to begin with.

I turned the TV off, got up from the couch, and flipped the big light on. The mouse was still there and it wasn't moving. I almost went to pick it up and keep it with me for a while, but I didn't. Animals crawl away to die in peace. They know what they know, some sort of resigned meditation. Once I saw a cat stumble behind her owner's couch just to die out of sight.

I went upstairs to my room and tried to read for a while, but it was difficult to concentrate. The words weren't reaching me.

I went downstairs a few hours later to get some water. I hoped the suffering had finally ended for the mouse. I looked in, and it wasn't there anymore.

2

The Christmas before I was stabbed to death, I went to my mom's house just outside the city for the first time after I had finally corrected all my documentation. I didn't dress down nor did I tie my hair back. I'd had it with her conditional parameters which only enabled her state of denial over who I was — her only child, her daughter. I'd stipulated this before I agreed to go visit. I'd worked too hard at this to just detransition for a forty-eight-hour visit. My mom said "okay" in a sort of exasperated sigh, as if giving in to a child's tantrum for the sake of blissful silence.

I went in a biz casual, navy-blue, sleeveless A-line dress, and I did my best to look conservative and assimilated. I also wanted to prove to her that I was happier than I had ever been — that I'd done okay despite her throwing me out of the house that past Spring.

I mostly read during the train ride down. The coach was mad-crowded, of course, passengers on their way to gluttony, MVP sports, and capitalist family drama. Many of them also looked tense as fuck, for whatever reasons.

I kept my face down a lot. I was at that embryonic stage of transition where all you can feel are eyes on you, judging you, deriding you, and that everything you're trying to achieve, inside and out, doesn't amount to anything at all.

As we approached the last stop, I put my sunglasses on, and stood up against the window as riders queued for the exit. I caught my reflection and thought I looked very Kim Novak. The trip hadn't been so bad. I just had to keep my shoulders back. A confident posture can sometimes help us pass.

Part of the shopping area by the depot was under construction, which made me think of the poisoned mouse. I didn't know which housemate — Brooke or Debbie — had taken its body off the couch. If it had been Brooke, she'd probably flushed it down the toilet. I would've buried it somewhere leafy and peaceful. I should have done something to help it, to stop the suffering as it held onto life despite the poison.

Had the mouse felt sad? Did it blame itself for all the bad things in life, and for what was happening to it? Did it want to say goodbye to its friends?

TRANSCENDENT 3

My mom wasn't there. I knew I wouldn't look quite as recognizable to her. It wasn't that cold out, so I decided to wait, suddenly wishing I smoked cigarettes again.

A black sedan kept circling, which seemed weird because most of the others were just idling for pickups. On its sixth turn, it pulled up closer to me. Out came my mom, and the trunk popped open for my suitcase. I waved and took off my sunglasses. After a pregnant moment, she smiled at me with closed lips.

We mostly rode in silence. After a few tries at small talk, I finally gave up and watched the dull landscape go by. I missed the city already, and my tuck was coming undone as I sat in the leather car seat. I hated that, most of all.

We got to my mom's house. After the driver took my bags out of the trunk, my mom swiped her card and dashed into the house without saying anything. She didn't look me in the eye ever again.

Not even on Christmas.

3

A month before I was stabbed to death, Jennifer broke up with me.

"What did I do wrong?" I asked her on the phone.

"It isn't you, it's me," she said. "I just need a little space. You know you can be intense."

I told her I'd try to calm down and be less so. I conceded I'd been having a hard time with my mom and being unemployed, and so much of that drama was spilling over. Plus, my estrogen levels felt random and emo.

"Can we at least talk about it in person?"

"I'm not sure what you think that would achieve."

Jennifer had taken me horseback riding the previous summer — I'd never been on a horse before, and the world had looked so hopeful and green from up on its back.

Jennifer had kissed me deeply and blown on my neck as we lay together in the shade of a wide oak. She had gotten me into new music. Sleeping with her felt so awesome. Finally, so much had begun to make sense.

And then — it was just *over*.

I sat in the TV room a lot, the same place I'd seen the dying mouse. Debbie came in one time, sat down next to me, and smoked me up. We'd been talking about which Drive Like Jehu album was better or something when I suddenly asked her, "Do you remember seeing a dead mouse on the couch last summer?"

"A dead mouse?" She looked down at the cushion and shifted her body out a little. "Gross!"

I told her what I'd seen that one time, and that I'd just left it alone, but that it was gone later.

"Brooke must have gotten rid of it, then," Debbie figured. "D-CON's one hell of a drug, hey?"

Debbie and I had hooked up a few times before I'd met Jennifer, and I was still into her, but she was dating this other trans girl Allison by then, and I didn't want to stir any shit. So, we gossiped about other things. I think Debbie was just being patient with me. After a while, she headed out on her scooter, and I stayed in the living room. I watched the mouse cushion. Everything seemed peculiar there, a whirlpool of energy that pulsed around where the mouse had waited to die.

I wanted me to die instead of the mouse.

Then, in a quick spasm, I *attacked* myself. I tore at my arms with my night-polished nails. I hit my forehead with my balled fists. I kicked the floor. I screamed at the ceiling.

Sorrow convulsed me, so badly I began to hyperventilate. Oh my *god* —
— *I need to die I need to die I need to fucking die...*

I reached the point where I lost all faculty of language and could only scream a single word, rhythmically with each time I hit myself: *DIE! DIE! DIE! DIE!* —

I only stopped because I grew exhausted. I didn't wipe at my tears. I wanted to let them dry.

I tried to take deep breaths. It only helped a little. My throat and lungs felt so constricted.

I felt minus something else, though, like a crucial part of my being had dissipated from me like smoke. My eyes felt sunken. I felt terrified that I reached this new level — how close had I come to finally killing myself, and ridding the world of my shittiness?

I wanted Jennifer back. I wanted my mom to love me again. I wanted the mouse to come back so I could try to help it.

Later, up in my room, watching the night sky from a lotus position on my futon, I thought I heard a scuffling in the wall. I perked right up and craned my head. But the sound didn't come again.

TRANSCENDENT 3

4

A week before I was stabbed to death, my mom called me to say she never wanted to speak to me again. She had opened some mail that had come from the library. I had an overdue book. She took one look at the title, and blew up at me.

"There's no way you're one of those *creatures!*" she yelled.

"Mom?"

I stood shaking in the kitchen, listening to her go off.

Wave after wave of doubt and loss crashed through me. I felt like such a failure. I had done everything wrong — there was no other way to explain it.

"Mom, can I at least try to say something?"

"NO! There's nothing you're going to say that is going change my mind about what you're doing to yourself! And you know what? I saw your browser search history at home and I've got your doctor's name! I'm going to sue her for turning you into a *monster!*"

"I haven't been able to afford to see my doctor in months, Mom."

Brooke had stockpiled several months' worth of estradiol and had been generously dosing both me and Debbie for months.

"I'm still going to sue her for malpractice! That way, she'll never be able to ruin another boy the way she ruined you!"

I looked over at the mouse cushion in the adjoining TV room.

There was something going on there in the place where the little rodent had held its death vigil, a tight energy of divining. Then, in keeping with my mom's viciousness, my own desperate screams echoed back at me from the couch —

DIE! DIE! DIE! DIE! —

NO — I have to just stand up for myself, finally.

"Mom, please stop this," I said quietly, hoping she would reciprocate in tone. "I'm not a boy. I'm your daughter."

I thought I saw the mouse there on the couch again, breathing fast and dying sad. Next to it, I sensed something much larger, a shadow, hitting itself violently. But I turned away and dismissed it as a figment of my imagination, or a latent stress-factor of the conversation taking place.

"You're not my daughter! You're nothing! You're a *freak!*"

I closed my eyes.

"I'm your *child.*"

"Not *anymore*! If I'd known what you were going to do to me, I would have *aborted* you!"

Then, I don't know how, everything inverted and I started laughing at my mom.

"Do you think this is funny?"

"I think it's *hilarious*, mom."

Yeah, funniest shit ever.

"Stop laughing, or you just lost a mother!"

I regained my composure after about a minute.

"Mom," I told her, "I really think you need professional help."

"I'm going to make you regret this. And all you will ever know from this will be eternal misery. *Idiot.*"

She hung up on me.

I glanced at the mouse cushion again. The energies I'd seen there had dissipated, and all traces of my weeks-old screaming fit had also stopped. Everything was quiet again, and I was alone.

I wonder what my mom did with the library book.

5

The day before I was stabbed to death, I bought my own copy of that book online, along with a couple of others. But they didn't get mailed to me in time for me to be alive to open the box. I hope someone else gets the books and finds them useful.

6

An hour or so before I was stabbed to death, I met Nora for the first and last time.

Debbie had asked me if I'd drive her to this party a little way out of the city. Debbie's scooter wasn't highway-worthy, and I didn't have anything else going on, so I said "sure, let's go!" It would be good to get out of the house for a while and maybe meet new people.

I'm introverted by nature, but I once we got there I felt like I'd been sprung from prison. I'd never seen so many of my people gathered in one place, not even in group. It was like we had our own *nation*. Maybe I'd also felt at ease because Debbie was introducing me around. I'd gotten to talking with Nora because she'd overheard me say something about David Cronenberg.

"Wait, really?" she brightened and swooped in, "I'm from Toronto, he's like royalty there!"

TRANSCENDENT 3

Her face astonished me, very aquiline, and she had green eyes. She had on this sleeveless black dress that made her many arm tattoos stand out in the ochre light. She had thick, black hair that she'd tied up in a bun, and she shamelessly wore a lot of Claire's mall jewelry.

"Which Cronenberg's your favorite?" I asked her.

"*Videodrome*, of course!"

"No way — that's my favorite, too! Nicki Brand is my spirit mom!"

"I know, right?" she beamed with rose lips. "Long live the new flesh!"

She led me to the living room and the party became this sideways thing that didn't concern us so much anymore. Conversations took place around us about this or that, but we were only us. I even forgot about my mom.

"Yeah," Nora said. "I've lived here for about three months. The commute to work blows, but the job is chill and I can look how I want. Sometimes I even work from home."

"I got fired for looking how I want," I said with my head down.

Nora gestured before me with her gilded hand, and drew me back into her eyes. She looked determined to keep us both charged. She also seemed so confident and comfortable with herself, so I finally asked her.

"How long have you been alive-for-real?"

"Just a few years," she shrugged, not affronted, nor breaking her intent gaze. "I mean, my parents knew something was up, so we all worked it out together. I had a feeling they'd be cool about it."

Damn, if only.

She asked me how I knew Debbie, and I told her how I'd been kicked out of my mom's house and fled to the city where Debbie met me in group, and had just happened to be looking for another housemate at the time.

"Wait, your mom kicked you *out*?"

"Sorry," I said. "It's really bad with her."

"Don't apologize! She's the one who should be fuckin' sorry."

I asked Nora if she'd like to grab a drink when/if she had a free moment in the city. She said hell yeah and we exchanged info. Turned out she lived in that house.

Later on, I got a text from Debbie saying that she'd decided to stay over at her girlfriend Allison's, and she could catch the train down if I wanted to head back on my own. I texted back "OK COOL I think I will." I didn't want Nora to think I was only interested in just fucking her. I think about this a lot now — Nora had been practically *dragging* me toward her room. To this day, I don't know why I was so shy about that. It was like I was denying the possibility something good might happen for me. It was like I couldn't fully process her affinity.

She didn't let me get away without a hug, and then an obvious re-invite-kiss.

During my drive back to the city, I realized I totally should have stayed there with Nora.

7

A minute or so before I was stabbed to death, I pulled into this highway rest stop that had a big food court. I got out of my car and looked around. There were some Mack trucks resting in the darkness of the other lot, and beyond them, only the night-full, black woods. The air felt humid, so I was glad I was just wearing my camo tank top and an emerald, knee-length skirt. I looked down. Did my flip-flops make my feet look huge? My hands, shoulders, and neck also? But it was high summer. I hadn't wanted my toenails to smudge, hence the need for open-air feeties.

I wanted to stop thinking about my mom, who would point out every defect in me.

I went inside.

The main area looked mostly deserted, only one dude wearing a crisp, white, collared dress shirt at a far table, calmly eating a cheeseburger. The menu choices up on the displays didn't appeal to me. Pizza Mania, which was closest to me in the hall, had this big, scowling white dude behind the counter. He was staring at me. His face scrunched as I passed by — *not passing*.

I might have made a face right back at him.

Or maybe I just averted my gaze and sped toward the bathrooms.

Whichever it was, I wish I had chosen the *other*.

I went into the ladies' room, and I thought of the mouse again. Had it been a whole year since I'd watched it dying on the cushion? It had been summer then, too.

I think I loved the mouse.

I picked the cleanest stall I could find, sat down, and peed. I thought of Nora. Did she think I was a big dumb jerk? I wondered if I'd ever see her again.

I wanted to.

I flushed with my foot, and went to wash my hands. This place had those pain-in-the-ass, motion-activated towel dispensers, where you have to wave your hand at limited intervals for a little bit of paper. I dried my hands after a few tries.

TRANSCENDENT 3

I opened the exit door, and was immediately shoved back by a *nightmare*.

As soon as my eyes locked with his, my heart started racing. At first, I didn't recognize him as the guy from the Pizza Mania counter. He took that little moment to punch me in the stomach, and then my face. I stumbled back against the sink. It hurt.

The bathroom smelled like decades of wrong in a way it hadn't just seconds earlier.

I realized what was happening, but I couldn't adapt to it. Any semblance of my survival instinct remained passive. My system just gave up.

He shoved me with both hands back into the stall I'd used. His eyes narrowed to glistening slits.

"I'm going to *kill* you for coming in here, you *fucking degenerate*."

He grew so much bigger as he approached. First I tried to get past him, but I was walled in. I fumbled for my phone, then realized I'd left it in the car.

"I'm going to cast each and every one of you freaks into the fire," he promised me as he grabbed a switchblade from his back pocket. "*HE COMMANDS IT.*"

He clicked the weapon open.

Then there was only me, him, the knife, and a suddenly compressed world. I didn't have mace, a panic alarm, a flamethrower, or anything else that might have helped me. Just my ID holder and my keys on a coiled ring. I held the keys sharp-end-out toward him. He smiled and raised the blade. The fluorescent lights hit it just right, and it gleamed with divine judgement as it came down at me.

8

A second or so before I was stabbed to death, the Pizza Mania guy looked down at me as I tried to shield myself.

"Please," I begged him. "Please, just let me go home."

He shook his head, and sighed, "It's too late."

"I'll give you my car."

"I take my orders from God," he said. "Not from fags."

I remember thinking I wanted to tell him about the mouse.

The first stab was the loudest as it came in a low arc, right up into the middle of my stomach. I screamed "*NO!*", long and drawn-out. My voice sounded weird.

He grinned wide as he twisted the knife in me.

"You're getting what you deserve," he spoke softly into my left ear. "You *made* me do this."

TRANSCENDENT 3

My arms and palms bore the brunt of the assault, until he went for other places on my body, and my screaming and kicks and pleas spiraled into a more exhausted moaning.

"I'll suck your dick if you'd just let me go."

He seemed astonished at my temerity, and said "NO!" in a mocking lilt.

I don't know how many times he stabbed me. It seemed to never be over. The pain got worse every time.

I still feel it now.

When I finally collapsed onto the cold tiles, a mist of simple incredulity enveloped me.

I was twenty years old.

9

A second or so after I was stabbed to death, the air burst with bright energy as I began to rise. I looked down at my body for a second, wondering if I would take long to heal, and would they give me pistachio ice cream in the hospital. My blood was pooling beneath me, a creeping oval of darkness. My eyes were wide and still. I looked just — *diagonal*.

The pizza guy was trying to wash my blood off when he glared toward the bathroom entrance where the dude wearing the crisp, white collared dress shirt I'd first seen eating at the far end of the food court was aiming a handgun at him with two strong arms.

I began to weep as everything began to sink in.

And then the whole scene — just everything — faded away.

10

A minute or so after I was stabbed to death I stood on the shore of an obnoxiously bright lake.

I was still wearing my camo tank top, my emerald-green skirt, and my flip flops. My blood was collecting and then draining out viscid at my toes. There were stab wounds on my abdomen, stomach, forearms, palms, neck, face, and groin. Most of my skin was drenched with blood. I wanted to wash it off and curl up somewhere. I wanted the mouse.

The bright water was right in front of me. It was the only place left to go. It was so calm and welcoming.

I tried not to think of Nora, Jennifer, Debbie, Brooke, or my mom.

But I still wanted to go home.

TRANSCENDENT 3

I didn't know where I was. That happened to me a lot in dreams, I'd float to someplace I couldn't recognize. It always felt uncanny and bewildering. But this was different. I couldn't scare myself awake.

I crouched onto the tightly-packed sand and watched the sun-bright, milk-white water.

And then I saw the mouse.

It broke the surface of the lake, forming small ripples that glided out to me. It sat on the same cushion it had died on. It peered in my direction, but I'm not sure what it thought of me looking all gross. The mouse brightened, and invited me to come into the water.

I wanted to look like my old self again.

I wanted be cleansed.

Plus, there was the mouse again — calling me, *accepting* me.

I went in.

The water felt nice and calming, and I began to wade toward the mouse. Its tail writhed happily and its whiskers moved as if it was eating something. Then I remembered the poison.

I called out to it, *NO DON'T!*

It was at the D-CON, a little sprinkling of death. I had to get the mouse to stop eating, to spit the poison out. Then I realized I was too late when it stopped moving its tail, and fell onto its side. Its hind legs twitched in the air a moment, and then stopped.

The mouse faded away.

I lost my sense of direction. I felt a new fear that I'd hit a dead end of some new mistake. There was nothing around me but the lake's vast, white feature-lessness.

It got colder as I looked down at myself, and saw my wounds bleeding worse than before, forming dark, swirling rivulets around me in the bright water.

I kept swimming, desperate to regain the mouse and try to save it. A shadow moved ahead of me — it was something to lock onto. I rushed toward it, until I hit the stark reality of the far shore.

I emerged from the lake. I was drenched and cold, and my wounds still bled. I looked around.

Everything around me was just as unvarying the lake, a simple white all around me, even more disorienting than the water, because there was no horizon.

The mouse was gone.

11

An hour or so after I was stabbed to death, I still hadn't found my way. There was nothing to latch on to, just that bright haze all around. After wandering for a while, I finally came to a rift. It looked like someone had cut an exit door in a veil of white lace. I couldn't see anything through it but darkness, yet maybe it offered a way out. I went through the opening, and found myself back at the rest stop.

It was still night.

The pizza guy was sulking in the back of a police car. My blood was still all over him. I went back into the food court, toward the bathroom. My body had been removed, and the homicide detectives were testing the scene. There was blood everywhere. Someone was muttering about my being trans, that I was probably HIV positive, and that they probably needed hazmat gear. He went on to say there wasn't much mystery to what provoked the attack. I didn't want to stick around and listen to him extrapolate.

I left them and rose into the summer air. The woods were dark, and the roads not so busy at that late hour. I let the winds take me wherever, and I screamed at the stars until dawn.

12

The day after I was stabbed to death, I visited the house I'd lived in with Debbie and Brooke. The mouse couch was still there. I wondered if anyone was home. The kitchen was empty.

I went right up to my room. I still had some weed left, and I wanted to smoke it all at one throw. I knew it wouldn't do anything for me, but I liked the thought anyway. My desk still had a half-full mug of orange tea on it, and I wanted to drink the rest. I looked at the books on my shelf, and I wanted to finish reading them.

I went down the kitchen and tried to think things through.

I looked across into the TV room, at the mouse couch. Nothing there. I groaned.

I didn't find Brooke in her workshop, so I figured I'd just leave.

I went out into the calm summer day, and heard a clamor of voices down the block.

I followed the noise.

Brooke and Debbie were sitting at the bus stop, holding each other. Their contorted faces were huge and open. Debbie was screaming through her sobs.

TRANSCENDENT 3

I watched them for a little while. I couldn't reach out to them and say goodbye or anything, so I just shot up into the sky. When I returned to the white, featureless waste, I reached level ground and looked down at myself.

I was still bleeding all over my front. It seemed to be *pulsing* out rhythmically, as with an artificial heartbeat. I dropped to my hands and knees and began to crawl, leaving a trail of slime behind me that reached back forever.

13

A week after I was stabbed to death, my mom buried me.

She was the last person on earth I wanted to claim my body, but she did.

I hadn't made a will, so she dragged her toxic ass-crack into the morgue and instructed them to completely detransition me, starting with cutting my hair short. My breasts had grown a little from about two years of HRT, but she put me in a button-down shirt two sizes too big to conceal that. They acetoned my nail polish off. The tie they clipped onto me was a sober navy blue, and it looked stupid — the suit jacket looked even worse.

This was such an indignity, and she carved my deadname onto the cold, Plexiglas marker even though I had legally corrected my name several months before. She even made the wake open-casket to drive her point home. The media came in droves, gloating over the scandalous marvels of aberrant existence.

My mom didn't cry even once. She just looked inconvenienced. She might as well have worn a tracksuit to the ceremony.

I hope I never see her again.

I was curious to see who the Pizza Mania guy was, so I went to his arraignment. His name was Paul Butler. He'd been a registered sex offender for six years and had assaulted four women since his late twenties. Class act.

Someone decided to be awesome, and held a candlelight vigil for me near The Common. A few hundred people showed up, including Nora, Jennifer, Brooke, Debbie, Allison, and even our landlady. They walked about a mile to the state house, and someone I didn't know (she looked famous) gave a speech about the need for stronger hate crime laws and that the so-called "bathroom bills" were just hate-legislature, by my very example alone. I don't think any new laws would have stopped the pizza guy from doing what he did to me, but it was nice to have someone finally speaking up in my favor.

Nora hooked up with Brooke. I watched them holding each other at night. They looked happy. It was good that Nora found a better person than me.

Someone on Fox News suggested that Paul Butler had killed me to prevent me from sexually assaulting a young girl in the ladies' room, therefore my murder was justified.

The clip was re-Tweeted and liked thousands of times.

I attended Paul Butler's trial. I hovered in the back. They tried to play on that "bathroom" and "trans panic" defense, but it didn't fly. He never showed any emotion, even during his sentencing. He was found guilty, and he's in prison for a while. He reads his Bible a lot. Every time I go to check to see if he's feeling sorry for what he did to me, there's just less and less of him. Our fun is over.

14

The month after I was stabbed to death, Jennifer died of a blood clot that traveled to her lungs. She'd rubbed her sprained ankle after falling off a horse and after she began to fade, her roommates rushed her to the hospital the next morning.

She died on the way there.

I felt the shockwave and raced to her side. I saw her hovering near a far ceiling corner in the brightly-lit morgue. I asked her if she was okay and if we could be friends again. She turned to me slowly, then her face scrunched up as if she was trying to see something past a glare. She shrugged and went away. I looked down at her body. She looked peaceful.

Unlike mine, her wake was packed with real people. She was cremated according to her wishes, and she was eulogized under her correct name and pronouns. Her parents were nice to everyone who went up to them. I wanted to say something about how happy she'd made me when she'd first asked me out. I had never thought anyone would like me, and she ended up showing me a world of animals, music, and kindness. She had helped me feel better. The memory of my time with her stood in such stark contrast with how I'd felt before, and how I feel now.

Toward the end, when people were lining up to pass by Jennifer's remains, her white roses, and her photograph, I saw her hovering high up at the back of the chapel. She wore a billowing, white, knee-length dress. Her shoulders looked pretty, and her hair floated like a bed of happy eels. I floundered toward her but my progress was slow, like when you try to run waist-deep in the ocean.

I called to her and she looked up at the rafters, as if she sort of heard me but couldn't pinpoint the direction of my voice. I saw her smile at something else up there, and then she glided forth, eclipsed a sunbeam, then vanished completely.

TRANSCENDENT 3

I never saw Jennifer again.

15

The Christmas after I was stabbed to death, something odd happened. As I stumbled through the bright, unchanging haze — sobbing and bleeding as usual — I encountered another presence. It was small, and at first I thought I bumped into a mannequin or something. But no, there was someone else there. Alarmed, I shot upright. I couldn't believe I had made physical contact.

But she was there, crouched in a fetal position, covering her ears with her hands. She wore a pretty white dress like the one Jennifer's spirit had on during her wake. Her hair was a little shorter than mine had been when I was murdered. She looked up at me, and then stood about the same height as me. Her eyes looked familiar, but I couldn't quite place her. I said hi. I told her my name and asked hers.

"Hi?" she said. "I — don't think I have a name."

I nodded, sure.

I didn't press her to try to remember it.

She's confused and traumatized — maybe even a fresh death, I thought. *Just try to draw her out. You fucking need her, whoever she is.*

I felt a little embarrassed in her presence too, because there was no way for her to not notice my horrific appearance. I was still bleeding from every stab wound. But I remembered and applied what I'd tried to practice in life — when I was in the presence of another person, I always tried to at least *seem* affable. That was usually impossible when I was alone, because I couldn't stand myself. And now that I found another person in that void, I felt I should try and help *her* not feel alone.

She squinted into the mists about us, and finding nothing to lock onto from her old life, she looked up at me.

"How do we get out of here?" she asked me.

"There's nowhere else to go."

"How can that be?"

"I've been back in the world — it's worse, because there's nothing left to see," I said. "That gets old after a while."

"You can go back?"

"Only as an apparition. I can't touch or feel anything there, and it's too painful to see my friends going on with their lives, having new experiences, as if no one misses me. It wore me down. So, I just stay here now."

She looked around again, insecure and anxious.

I wanted to help her.

"You can sense and feel me?" I asked her.

She brushed my arm and nodded. Again, I felt contact.

I asked her to describe what she saw. She said she saw me in a white dress, billowing hair, serene bearing. No stab wounds.

We could only see our own shattered bodies in death. To others, we looked fine.

"I don't want to stay here," she winced. "I want to go back."

I had no answer to that. I didn't want her to leave me behind. So, I tried to tell her my story and what had happened to me. The high-profile cruelty of my death seemed to appall her.

I hoped my candor would bring out her own story, but she didn't reciprocate.

Still hopeful, I went to my most vulnerable place, and told her about the mouse I saw dying on that summer day.

"Wait," she said, coming closer to me, as if to verify the honesty in my face. "Where did you live?"

I told her about my neighborhood, and when I mentioned Debbie and Brooke, and her eyes widened. She told me they were her housemates too, and that was the house where she'd died.

We looked at each other up and down, and as we recognized ourselves, each in the other, a terrible realization hit us both. When I'd seen the mouse dying, I'd wanted a second chance to help the poor thing so badly I had offered up my own life in exchange for the life of the mouse. And my wish was granted, only not how I'd thought possible.

The result stood before me.

Instead of killing myself, I had to be murdered. No wonder I'd had my meltdown. I couldn't commit suicide, but I needed to die.

I saved the mouse. It didn't succumb to the poison. It went free.

No wonder I hadn't found its body.

The girl and I looked at one another in disbelief and horror. We'd both just met the stark *possibility* of something we'd been so desperate to prevent in life. And still — it was all for the sake of the mouse.

TRANSCENDENT 3

Suddenly, something that sounded like a low-flying jet screamed above us. The ground imploded beneath our feet. A darkness blossomed, and then we were shoved apart by cold blast of rusty-smelling air. We cried out as the distance between us yawned, and the bright haze turned to ash. I never saw my ghost again.

16

It's now been a year since I was stabbed to death.
I can't stop crying and bleeding all over myself.

I didn't want to die. I wanted to *live*. I wanted to be with Nora and have picnics with her on the summer grass. I wanted to ride horses. I wanted to be reunited with my people. I wanted my mom to finally come to her senses, and love me as her daughter. I wanted to find a great place to sit, drink tea, and read for hours. I wanted to help weak and small things. I wanted the mouse.

But now I'm lost in this wasteland of regret. I guess that's just the way things are. And they will be this way forever.

And yet, today I decided to find a way back into the living world, its love and warmth and promise walled off from my being. It's a place where I may never have existed to begin with. I'm still going back.

And even though it's going to hurt a lot, and make me feel even more sad and tired, I'm going to keep looking for the mouse.

There's something I need to ask it.

COOKING WITH
CLOSED MOUTHS

◄ Kerry Truong ►

A gumiho could run faster than shadows spread, but since Ha Neul doubted that Americans would take kindly to a nine-tailed fox streaking down Los Angeles' busy streets, they opted to walk to the bus stop in the falling darkness after work.

The cool night air was a relief after the hot confines of Mrs. Chang's restaurant, where Ha Neul had spent the day carrying heavy dishes and enduring customers' complaints. Mrs. Chang's mediocre food attracted few customers, and her refusal to use air conditioning made those who did come disinclined to be generous. Ha Neul never told her this, of course, because what was the point of trying to change people's ways? For this silence they were rewarded with meager wages and leftovers that turned to ashes in their mouth.

Today was no different. After mediating between Mrs. Chang and angry customers, Ha Neul was finally left in peace, a bag of banchan the only payment for their troubles. They stood at the bus stop in a crowd of other commuters, careful to remain at the edges where they could go unnoticed but still hear the conversations around them. There was chatter about everything from peace in Viet Nam to some boxing championship or another. Ha Neul didn't understand the voracious interest humans showed in things that would only fade from memory or repeat themselves in a matter of years. Still, they liked listening. There was something comforting about the way humans kept going, as full of energy as if they were the first to experience these things.

When the bus arrived, Ha Neul boarded in a stream of other passengers, shouldering their way through until they could find a place to stand. Proximity filled their nose with the tang of everyone around them and made their stomach clench. They ignored it, used to the hunger. Instead of thinking about it, they studied the people closest to them.

An older woman stood next to them in the aisle, her eyes drifting closed as if the lurch and stop of the bus were a lullaby. A pair of students on their other side consulted each other in urgent voices about what songs to put on a mixtape for a crush. Ha Neul listened with amusement. It must be nice, they thought, to be caught up in the rhythm of falling in and out of love; to hope over and over that warmth could be found in the clasp of another person's hand.

A t home, Hana was waiting for them, her homework fanned out on the kitchen table. Their one-bedroom apartment was too small for a proper desk, and neither of them had much use for the kitchen's traditional function, so Hana had claimed it as her study room. The table was often strewn with books and papers and half-chewed pens. Ha Neul had given up on putting the mess into any kind of order. No matter how hard they tried, the table would be cluttered again within the day.

Hana waved when they came in. "Took you long enough to get home! Did Mrs. Chang give you food again?"

Ha Neul nodded, searching for an empty spot to set the bag down. After a moment they gave up and simply handed it to Hana.

"All mine, and none for oppa," she sang.

Ha Neul sat down next to her as she searched through the bag, their body heavy from exhaustion. They relaxed in the warmth of the kitchen, watching as Hana tasted each banchan in turn. She was eager to try them all, which was why Ha Neul always accepted Mrs. Chang's leftovers. It didn't matter if the food couldn't make her full. It reminded her of home, of a life where she'd had family and people to belong to.

Ha Neul's stomach clenched again. They went to the refrigerator and opened it. It was nearly empty, except for the large plastic bag dominating the center shelf and several plastic cartons arranged in neat rows beside it. Ha Neul brought the bag to the table.

"Oppa, don't you dare get blood on my homework," Hana said as they stacked books and papers to clear a space on the table.

"I would never sully the homework of a top student."

TRANSCENDENT 3

Ha Neul took a package wrapped in butcher paper out of the bag and set it on the table. The paper was damp in spots, its white color stained pink by the blood that seeped through it. The tang that Ha Neul had smelled on the bus filled their nose again, this time richer and deeper. Hana stopped eating to watch, her eyes intent. She could smell the blood, too.

They unwrapped the paper to reveal hearts, kidneys, slices of liver, and other organ meats, raw and glistening. Ha Neul ate a heart, ripping the muscle with their sharp teeth. It was savory, satisfying them in a way Mrs. Chang's food never could, making them crave for more. They reached for a piece of liver as soon as they'd finished the heart. It was good to be home.

Hana was still watching them. They thought they could see the hint of a fang beginning to protrude in the corner of her mouth, but when they offered her a kidney she waved it away. "I'm not into solid food."

Ha Neul raised an eyebrow, looking at the banchan.

"That's different. I eat that for fun, not to get full."

"Can you really taste it?"

"A little. It's really faint though, like when you have a cold and can only get an aftertaste."

Ha Neul didn't understand, having never had a cold. They nodded anyway. "Do you remember what human food tastes like?"

Hana looked wistful. "I think I'm forgetting. I know that hotteok are sweet and kimchi jjigae is spicy, but even though I know the words I don't remember the taste."

She must be nearing forty, but time hadn't changed the smoothness of her skin or the roundness of her face. If there was one thing that aged her, it was her eyes. They were too knowing. It was only now, with her longing so apparent, that she seemed exactly the high school student that she pretended to be.

Ha Neul had known that longing. It had been food that first drew them to humans, after all. So many colors and textures: thick, greasy noodles coated in black bean sauce, kimbap dotted with yellow, green, and orange vegetables, cream-colored crab meat marinated in soy sauce. They supposed it was harder for Hana, though, having actually known what human food tasted like. Reaching over, they squeezed her hand.

Hana squeezed their hand back and smiled at them. "How's your food, oppa?"

"Delicious."

"It's still weird to me how you eat cows and not humans. Isn't it unsatisfying?"

TRANSCENDENT 3

"It's a good enough substitute." When reduced to their innards, humans and cows weren't very different, Ha Neul thought, and offal was easy to get from the butcher for no more than a few cents.

Hana trailed a finger through the blood that had congealed on the paper, then licked it off. "You know you're welcome to come find dinner with me any night."

The food soured in Ha Neul's mouth. Being hungry around humans was one thing, eating them was another. Thinking about it made them feel ill.

"I don't eat humans anymore," they said, allowing their voice to get sharp.

Hana bit her lip, looking chastised. Ha Neul felt guilty, but they'd told her often enough that they didn't want to be goaded about their eating habits. They'd tried living as a human long ago, hoping to discover the taste of other food. But a gumiho is a fox at heart, its human appearance a mere illusion, and Ha Neul's hunger had only grown with each dish they'd eaten. It was all ash. In the end, they'd given into their hunger, only to be horrified by the uniform redness. They'd stopped eating humans by the time they met Hana. She should have known better than to tease them about it.

Ha Neul worried that she would sulk, but instead she rummaged through her backpack and brought out a flyer.

"Here," she said, sliding it across to Ha Neul. Her voice was light, the previous subject waved away. "Talking about food reminded me of this. I don't think I can wiggle my way out of it."

Ha Neul chewed on a piece of liver and read the flyer. It was printed on daffodil yellow paper, the words on it thick, black, and followed by multiple exclamation points. Cartoonish pictures of rice bowls and tacos surrounded the text.

"A cultural diversity lunch? What exactly are the students supposed to learn from that?"

"How to appreciate other people's cultures, I guess. Mr. Hanson says we should start learning about diversity in high school."

"I understand that, but why food?"

"Because people like food, obviously. We're all supposed to bring in one dish from our culture."

"What do you want to bring in?" They stared at the pictures of rice bowls. Did her teacher expect her to bring in rice? Even Ha Neul knew that plain rice didn't make a meal.

Hana answered without hesitation. "Kimchi fried rice."

TRANSCENDENT 3

They couldn't help laughing at her confidence. "And where in the world are we going to get that?"

Hana smiled. She was prettiest like that, which was exactly why she smiled widest if she needed a favor. "I was going to ask if Mrs. Chang could make it."

Ha Neul's answer was as ready as hers had been. "Mrs. Chang is busy and has no money to make kimchi fried rice for free."

"She doesn't even have to make that much. There are only twenty students in my class."

"Isn't that still a lot?"

Hana pouted. "Please, oppa? I don't want to be embarrassed. What if everyone else brings something fancy and I don't have anything?"

There was that longing again, not as obscured by the pout as she thought it was. Ha Neul didn't understand. Food was food, so what did it matter if she brought banchan or kimchi fried rice? But they could see how happy this simple thing would make her, and that mattered. She was their sister by choice, the only person who wanted to share the partial life they led.

"All right, I'll ask Mrs. Chang. Even if she says no, we'll figure something out. Does that sound good?"

"Oh, oppa, I knew I could count on you!"

She threw her arms around Ha Neul, startling them. After a beat, they remembered to lift their own arms and hug her back. They held her close, taking comfort in the gesture that was at once strange and warm.

Many years ago, on a warm spring night in Korea, Ha Neul had heard a cry of despair. If they had ignored that cry, they might still be living in Korea, trying to find a way to fit into the jumbled new pattern that the war had created. But they had listened, and that was how they'd found Hana, blood on her shirt and two bite marks on her neck. They couldn't abandon her to that despair. Instead, they had held their hand out and said come, there is still a way to live.

So the two of them had lived, as best as they could, side by side for more than twenty years. When they had decided to go to America, it made the most sense to claim that they were siblings. They'd argued about who should be the elder. Ha Neul had won her over by pointing out that if they were her older brother, they could support her while she went to school.

The papers had been made, and the two of them had moved to Los Angeles to join the number of Korean immigrants building a new life along Olympic Boulevard. While Hana finished her last year in high school and dreamed about

TRANSCENDENT 3

college admissions, Ha Neul waited tables and lifted boxes, letting Mrs. Chang speak to them as if they were a child.

It didn't matter to them whether Mrs. Chang's food was good or not. They couldn't taste any of it, after all. They were content seeing the variety of colors in her kitchen. She, in turn, was grateful for someone who stayed in spite of her temper and the customers' insults. Ha Neul hoped that her gratefulness would soften her to their request. They made sure to be of extra help in the restaurant the day after Hana showed them the flyer, lifting heavy pots off the stove and chatting with customers until the bad food was forgotten.

The restaurant was never busy, and once the lunch hour had passed it was empty. Mrs. Chang used the time to eat her own late lunch. Ha Neul joined her, choking down the rice and drinking cup after cup of tea. They waited until most of the food was gone before saying, "Mrs. Chang, can I ask you a favor?"

Her eyes narrowed. Perhaps she thought they would ask for money. Still, her voice was not unkind when she answered. "What is it?"

"My sister's teacher asked her to bring in a dish from her culture for a class project. I was wondering if you could make the food."

"What kind of food?"

"Kimchi fried rice."

Mrs. Chang sighed and shook her head. "I don't think I have the time for that, Ha Neul."

It was the answer they'd expected, but they were still disappointed. "It's not too difficult to make, is it? I'll even work extra hours in the restaurant in exchange for it."

"After a whole day of cooking, do you think I'd have the energy to make more food for a bunch of children? I have my own family to take care of once I'm done here." She stood up and stacked the empty dishes to take back into the kitchen.

"Mrs. Chang, please."

"I already said no!"

Ha Neul stood up as she started walking back to the kitchen. "Then at least teach me how to make it."

She turned around. "What was that?"

Food is food, Ha Neul thought, and food was only ash in their mouth. But they'd promised Hana that they would help her. "Teach me how to cook, Mrs. Chang. If I learn, then I can help you in the kitchen, too."

She studied them for a moment. They wondered if they looked desperate, if it was that or the promise of help that made her say, "All right then. But I don't want to hear any complaints because it's too hard, understand?"

"Oh, perfectly," Ha Neul said, and followed her into the kitchen, already questioning the wisdom of learning how to cook without taste.

Hana's luncheon was in a week, and in that week Ha Neul dedicated themself to learning how to cook. The radio in the kitchen played Marvin Gaye and Stevie Wonder songs as Mrs. Chang showed Ha Neul how to make galbi and gamjatang, kimbap and gyeranjjim.

Although she wasn't an unkind teacher, she was also not gentle. Ha Neul disliked the way she grabbed their hand to show them how to chop vegetables, or how she would take the ladle from them to taste soup. They learned quickly, however, and their dishes soon looked the same as Mrs. Chang's. They began to take their own pleasure with food, relishing in the clean crack that split an egg and the feel of rice grains slipping through their fingers. Taste was lost to them, but they could still see, and hear, and feel.

The first dish they brought out to customers, however, fared no better than any of Mrs. Chang's.

"Do you call this samgyetang?" asked a middle-aged woman with tightly permed hair.

Ha Neul had known she would be trouble the moment she'd walked in. Something about her pinched mouth had foreshadowed grief. Putting on a practiced smile, they said, "I'm sorry if the soup isn't good. Should I bring you something else?"

"Nothing you brought is any good. The banchan isn't even seasoned well!"

Ha Neul bit their tongue, even though their hands ached from chopping meat and mixing seasoning. Before they could regain the patience to smile, however, the woman sighed. "Forget it. I'm sorry. It's just been a long time since I had a good meal, and I thought I'd find it here."

Ha Neul studied how deep the wrinkles on her face ran, how calloused her hands were. They wondered how long she had been in America, and what kind of dishes she had the energy to make after a long day of work. Did she have family to care for? When was the last time she'd eaten something someone else made for her?

TRANSCENDENT 3

The woman got her wallet and began counting out bills. Before she could set them on the table, Ha Neul said, "I'm sorry, but could you tell me how you'd like the food to be seasoned?"

Later, Mrs. Chang told them that they had too little pride. "You listen too much to other people's complaining."

Ha Neul just laughed, and she looked at them as she often did, like something strange and half unwanted. Still, they kept listening to the complaints. They memorized how much sesame oil to add and how long meat should stay in the pan. They noted the exact shade of orange that carrots turned when they were tender but not limp, and the translucence of onions that would be just sweet enough. The complaints lessened and more customers began to come to the restaurant, brought in by word of mouth.

Mrs. Chang talked of giving Ha Neul a raise. They heard the hesitance in her voice and declined. It was enough to spend time in the kitchen while Mrs. Chang served the customers, her temper improved by their praises. Soon, Ha Neul became the kitchen's only occupant. They preferred it that way, with only the radio to keep them company. This much of human food they had mastered, and they were content to stay in the confines of the kitchen for a long time, basking in its vivid colors.

The day before Hana's potluck, Ha Neul stopped by a supermarket on the way home. They returned to the apartment laden with plastic bags. The kitchen table was as messy as ever, but there was no sign of Hana. No doubt she was out getting food. They cleared the kitchen table, making room for the ingredients they'd bought from the supermarket.

The stove, which had been untouched since they moved in, flared to life without protest. They made rice, and while the water bubbled and spit, they sliced kimchi and diced Spam. They didn't like Spam. Its sickly pink color reminded them of red watered down, and it slid out of the can with a slither that made them shudder. But it was cheap and Hana liked it, so they tipped the diced ham into the pan without looking at it. Steam filled the air. Ha Neul made more than enough kimchi fried rice for Hana's classmates, then set aside a little extra for her when she came back.

It was dark when Hana returned home. She was wearing a green polka dot dress, her hair in a ponytail. There was blood on her. Ha Neul could smell it as soon as she walked through the door, and their stomach clenched.

"I'm in the kitchen," they called out to her.

TRANSCENDENT 3

She walked in, the scent of blood following her. It pervaded the kitchen, making Ha Neul forget, for a moment, the food on the stove. Their stomach growled and their mouth ran dry. They hadn't eaten all day.

"Oppa, you're cooking!" Hana said, coming up next to them.

They focused on the rice in the pan, stirring it to mix the kimchi and Spam evenly. The Spam had darkened to a deep pink. "Of course I am. Unless I'm mistaken, your potluck is tomorrow."

"You look like a professional chef."

They smiled in spite of the smell of blood in their nose. "Your compliment is appreciated. Now go wash your hands. I made some for you to eat tonight."

Hana clapped her hands and ran to do as they said. By the time she came back, the scent of blood had eased, and Ha Neul could hand her the bowl of kimchi fried rice without their hand trembling.

"How is it?" they asked as she began to eat.

She closed her eyes and chewed. Ha Neul knew she could barely taste it, but there was happiness on her face. "It's delicious, oppa. I know it is."

They couldn't smell the blood anymore. Ha Neul felt the warmth of the kitchen again, the steam in the air. They watched Hana eat, a little longing mixed with their pleasure in her enjoyment. The two of them would have made a proper family if only Ha Neul could sit down and eat with her. But if Hana was content with only the hint of flavor, then they were content with only this, its reflection.

They turned back to the stove, and shut it off.

O n the morning of Hana's potluck, Ha Neul carried a tin foil tray of kimchi fried rice to her bus stop, handing it to her carefully before running to catch their own bus. A disheveled man with a hoarse voice harangued passengers about sinning as the bus crawled its way down Wilshire, and the couple in front of Ha Neul argued in whispers, almost hissing as each accused the other of infidelity. Ha Neul listened with half an ear, looking out the window at the Ford Pintos inching past and the dusty haze that made everything outside glow.

The restaurant was dark and cool, not yet overheated by the stoves. Ha Neul put the chairs in place and wiped the tabletops while Mrs. Chang chatted with her sister, who had joined them for the day. The sister had arrived in America only the week before, and Mrs. Chang was eager to have someone who knew the same people she did and shared the same hopes for this new life.

Ha Neul didn't interrupt their conversation, dreaming instead about the food they would make that day: the chill of the soy sauce on their skin, the true red of gochujang dark against the silver of the spoon, the steam beading their face in sweat whenever they lifted the lid off a pot.

No customers complained that day, and Mrs. Chang sent Ha Neul home with more galbi and banchan than usual. Ha Neul had made the food, but they chose to feel kindly towards Mrs. Chang for her generosity.

At home, Hana was waiting for them. The tin foil tray sat next to her on the table, still burdened with its food. It was bent slightly out of shape. Bits of rice flecked the tabletop around it. Hana's mouth was pursed tightly, but it quivered when Ha Neul asked her, "What's wrong?"

"They said it smelled bad and made fun of me for eating Spam. What do they know? I could eat them instead!"

Ha Neul knew she would have cried, if she could. They sat down next to her, some vice grip squeezing their chest. For Hana's sake, they smiled. "I'd advise against it. They probably don't taste good."

"They're ungrateful punks. You worked so hard to make this and they wouldn't even eat it."

"I am hardly insulted by the bad taste of children a fraction my age."

Hana wiped her eyes with the back of her hand, a habit she still hadn't unlearned. Whenever she was angry or upset, her hand went to her eyes as if there were still tears to stem. Ha Neul took her hand and squeezed it.

Her skin was dry and smooth, eroded by neither time nor care. In that respect, she was different from her classmates and everyone else around her. It was hard to remember that difference, however, when she was squeezing Ha Neul's hand so tightly, looking for comfort after a hurt that should have been slight.

After a moment she said, "I wanted to eat this fried rice."

Ha Neul squeezed her hand again. "You can eat all of it now, if you want."

"No, I wanted to *really* eat it. I wanted it to taste like kimchi fried rice should, to make me full." Hana stomped to the drawers and came back with a plastic spoon. "Even though those little ingrates can eat, they won't make use of it." She dug into the rice hard enough to bend the flimsy plastic and began eating.

Another layer of sadness settled over Ha Neul, heavy and thick as the smog that pervaded Los Angeles. They should have listened to their own advice from the beginning: food was food. How could it teach people anything? Perhaps for Hana's classmates, the kimchi fried rice was not a sign of comfort and family, but of something else entirely. Perhaps some of their fox's nature made its way into the dish, marking it as something fearful.

"I'm sorry." They felt useless with only those words for comfort.

"It's not your fault, oppa."

The two of them sat in silence as Hana ate. Ha Neul knew she could finish the whole tray. It wouldn't make her full, after all. They sat and watched her, trying to imagine what it tasted like and only remembering the crunch of the kimchi under their knife, the splash of red over white rice, the Spam glistening pinkly before they'd thrown it in the pan. Things which were only parts of the whole, not enough to fill the quiet of this kitchen.

Ha Neul wanted, as they hadn't in years, to take a spoonful of food and taste it. But they knew, even before they finished the thought, that it would be nothing but ash. All they could do was say, "I'll make you as much food as you want."

Hana smiled, and though the corners of her mouth lifted, her expression didn't brighten. She looked her age. "Even if I'll never be able to tell how good it is?"

"Of course."

They thought about the colors of different ingredients, the textures under their hands. No matter what other people thought, they didn't want to forget any of that. As long as Hana wanted food they would cook, and the two of them would keep trying, again and again, to discover taste in the warmth of this kitchen.

TRANSCENDENT 3

WORLD OF THE THREE

◄ Shweta Narayan ►

Then the Bird of A Hundred and Eight Names gathered together her three new children, and she said, "You have passed our people's tests and joined our ranks, and may leave if you wish. But leaving will take you among the Alabar, who collect salt in their bare hands and have no fear of rust, and call themselves merely people.

"Some among us speak slightingly of them, for their lives are short and easily ended, and they don't protect one another as we do. You should be more wary. They number in the hundreds of hundreds of hundreds, make children without training, and never need winding up. They learn without being taught, and their tests kill as often as not; those who survive become adults, and those who kill become leaders."

"But would it kill us to learn about them tomorrow?" whined the golden monkey Usithan.

"You can listen tomorrow if you like," their mother said, "but I'm telling the tale today."

"But there's people climbing coconut trees outside right now! Using ropes for harnesses. I wouldn't need a harness. I could bring the fruit down in half the time."

"And they could take you to court for stealing their lawful trade."

"...What if I just steal the coconuts?"

His sister Maari's silver tail and tufted ears twitched. "Imagine the impression he's going to make on the queen," she said, lazily extending her claws and pulling them back in. "Her commissioned guest, dragged in as an incompetent thief."

Usithan chittered and jumped, teeth bared, from bench to worktable; but great-springed Anbu said, "We're not so ill-made as to ignore our mother's teaching," and their saying so made it true. For the others would take themselves apart before disappointing the eldest, whose voice brought to mind the Goddess of Speech as their form resembled an idol cast in bronze, who brightened golden anklets and bracelets and necklaces by wearing them, whose gentle reason had stopped their arguments from the hour they'd all been brought alive.

"Coconuts are boring anyway," said Usithan. "All they do is fall. But can we hear your tale in the courtyard?"

"So you can better annoy Maari?" said their mother. But she flew to the courtyard, where warm wind and sun-baked stone might calm all her children's restless gears, and there she spoke poetry in three languages.

The bloodiest of Alabar leaders call themselves the Three Crowned Kings; they say this world is theirs, and that bloodshed is a virtue. They ride so often to battle, against one another or lesser killers, that the crows all know and love them.

The Chera kings, most distant of the Three, live over the mountains and have fought us only for trade routes. May the gears that turn the stars keep it so. These gem-studded ones call themselves children of fire, and in Vanji, their capital, firelight makes the temples themselves dance, so cleverly are the figures upon them carved. That land is blessed with plenty by the river Chulli, fortified by steep mountains, and protected by engineering they've never dreamed of; for downstream of Vanji where the river meets the sea is built Musiri, beloved of the West, whose traders deal in all the world's goods. So many ships ride the rains there each year that their sails block out sea and sky and outshine lightning.

We cross into those lands only rarely, even now, but we care for the Chulli's flow as our own heartspring, for a calamity along that great river would spill over the mountains onto us all.

The Pandya name you know. Clever in craft and commerce, the moon's children rule from here in Madurai and sell their cotton, light as moonlight, to nobles so far off as Europa, who are as greedy for it as for Tamil steel. The Pandyas have been our allies and partners in trade for as long as their queens have ruled, and so many of their generations have passed that they think it was always so. You, who were made to join their court, need to know that it wasn't.

The Chola kings rule from Udaiyur in the north. Alone among the Alabar, these quick-tempered children of the sun have harmed us and lived. For the greatest of my children died of Alabar treachery not just once, but thrice; and it started in Udaiyur.

There lived in Udaiyur a great king of the Cholas, who they now call Vikramaditya, though at the time he was known as Varsembiyan as well. The tales of him speak of great feats of might, compassion, and justice.

Don't groan, Usithan, I won't repeat the stories you've already studied. Those were written by Alabar, and say far more about them than us. And while they love to dwell on him trudging back and forth across a corpse-burning ground while carrying that Vedala-possessed corpse and coming up with an answer to each riddle, they never can explain how he managed it without collapsing from exhaustion and foul air; for of course they refuse to admit that Vikramaditya of legend was no man of their kind, but a mechanical.

He was mostly male at the time, and just as the great rivers change their course but slowly, he stayed that way for many years. Accordingly his body was built to appear as such to Alabar, its lines rising to the sky graceful as smoke, though it was taller and broader of chest than those around him. In those times we made only our supporting frames from steel. We had not yet the craft to form it into our tiniest gears, so all of us were larger. And —

— Maari, my dear, your ears speak so clearly of skepticism that a lecturing brahmin would notice. One flick would have sufficed. What is it?

"When have we ever appeared as *men* to Alabar?" said Maari, disdainful as any cat. "I wonder if we are meant to believe this, or merely understand some lesson that we could learn as well more directly."

Usithan, unwilling to agree, picked up a few message tubes and started juggling them.

"Is that how you speak to our mother?" said Anbu.

"She made me as I am."

"So I did," said their mother. "And I approve, my children. It's unwise to trust too quickly to stories when you are around Alabar, for there is nothing they love to improve on so much as the truth. I give you your question back, though. Don't trust my answer. Find your own."

TRANSCENDENT 3

Many tried to kill the great king Vikramaditya, for he reined in the greed of the powerful. But he was of course untouched by poison, and stronger and sturdier than any Alabar. He was faster, too, which you might predict; but his assassins, repeatedly, did not.

He had only one weakness: Kabilan, his heir, a descendant of his Alabar father who he had adopted as his own and loved dearly. Prince Kabilan was fearless in the hunt, handsome and well-spoken in the palace, and seldom truly unkind; but he did not love as deeply as he was loved.

Eventually — perhaps inevitably — one of the king's enemies turned their poison into words, and dropped it into the prince's ear a little at a time. It started with admiring comments scattered into his days: How long the glorious king had ruled! May he rule forever! Perhaps he would, being divine as kings are and mechanical, too.

Do mechanicals ever grow old? asked a pretty girl, sad-eyed. It must be terrible for the king, to see his own son age before him.

Next the prince noticed whispers that stopped when he drew near. How long had that been going on? He went on the hunt and uncovered a pair of servants wondering, a little too loudly, what reward there was in loyalty to an heir who would never be king. That same evening, his own attendant hissed to see — he claimed — a gray hair, immediately plucked and thrown into the fire.

Then a dying scholar insisted that mechanicals, who had no breath, could not have souls, since the Sanskrit word Atman means both.

With such droplets from all directions was the prince drenched in poison, till in place of a father who loved him he saw a clever device, ticking on forever, robbing him of his throne.

So it was surely inevitable that one evening, instead of winding his father up while speaking of his day, prince Kabilan forced the key the wrong way and wound him all the way down.

Three message tubes hit the ground. Usithan caught the other two, barely. "Wound down isn't the same as dead!" he said.

"You know that," said her mother. "And maybe Kabilan did, too, but do you think his nobles knew? Remember too that Alabar make Alabar laws and, even more powerfully, customs, which bind even their kings. The ruler known as Vikramaditya was pronounced dead, so he was dead; though your eldest sibling, who I named Vikramaditi, was not."

"*You* gave your child a forbidden form?" asked Anbu. They could not frown, as their brow was made all of one piece, but they placed one hand over their mouth in a gesture of shock.

"My first child," said the bird. "From before we codified the laws. We lived apart from Alabar, then, and their fear kept us from harm."

Maari said, "Oh, so when Anbu asks, you'll answer."

"You asked different questions. Yours, I'll answer this far: Vikramaditi's first death taught us that their kings live by different rules, and that not all forms are safe to wear. But that doesn't mean you should accept a story unquestioning."

"Well, good," said Usithan, picking up the tubes with more noise than needed. "Because none of this makes sense."

"You've irritated the monkey," said Maari. "A marvelous accomplishment. Normally it's the other way around."

"Years of experience," their mother said.

Usithan said. "How do you know any of it to tell? How did you learn the nature of Vikramaditi's death in some Alabar land? What happened to them when they were wound down? They can't have been cremated or they'd have crumpled beyond repair, even if Alabar fires couldn't melt them outright. It's just not a proper story."

"Half a story is seldom a proper story."

"And," Maari added, "it was you who interrupted."

A clang, a yowl. A tube bounced off Maari's head, spinning on itself until Maari's paw brought it to an abrupt stop.

"If either of you breaks the other," said their mother, " — or my tools, you'll be sorting gears by size for a week."

Usithan said innocently, "Of course, dear mother. Besides, I'd hate to break this." He twisted one tube to its speaking position, and from it came Maari's startled yowl. A little low and slow, and cut off at the end, because message tubes were far from perfect, but close enough. Maari growled.

Anbu said, "Could you both just — stop, for once? Both the bickering and the complaining about questions that aren't answered because you're too busy complaining to listen?"

Maari and Usithan stared at Anbu, then at each other, and fell silent.

O ne of Vikramaditya's oldest and most favored servants was a Kammalar named Nakkiran, a small, round, neat man who kept his gears clean and oiled and did what basic maintenance Alabar have the craft for. Nakkiran was

TRANSCENDENT 3

a mouse to prince Kabilan's tiger, timid and high-sprung, and well acquainted with the palace's hidden spaces and paths.

And while only Kabilan had the duty of winding the king, Nakkiran too possessed a winding key.

When word of the king's sudden death wailed its way down to Nakkiran, he was halfway to the royal chambers, bent over the stairs, wheezing and dripping salty sweat and wondering when the five flights had grown so steep. He looked up in shock, and a golden oiling can slipped from his hand to bounce clattering down the stairs. He ran after it, while the gears of his mind slowly started turning again: the king, dead. Stopped. Not ticking. Who kept the king's gearwork in order? One Nakkiran. Who would be blamed, then?

He tripped down the last three steps, grabbed the dented vial, darted into the nearest storeroom, jumped into a large woven basket, pulled the lid down after himself, and started shaking like a lotus in a strong current.

The basket was too tight-woven for him to see more than fuzzy circles of light as people rushed by carrying lamps, but he could hear, and in time he calmed enough to listen.

To running feet, voices shouting over one another, snatches of panicked whispering passing by the storeroom, one shrieking laugh. Kings, like other gods, did not just die. Not without battles or age or illness to curse for the disaster. Nobody asked whether misfortune would follow, only what form it would take. Would the rains fail? Cows sicken? War burn down the cities?

Prince Kabilan would save them, said one voice, then another, building a raft over dark water. He was strong and brave and handsome, and once the rituals of coronation were observed, why, then they would be safe.

And as evening slowed to iron-black night, and Kabilan's name became a prayer, nobody cursed Nakkiran, or said he had failed, or even asked where he was. In truth, half the servants and all the nobles had forgotten him entirely, for who remembers a mouse when there's a tiger to crown?

When silence convinced Nakkiran at last that prince Kabilan wasn't going to call for his head, or summon him to explain — or even attempt a repair — suspicion grew to balance out his dread. It took him hours to talk himself out of the basket, but, slowly, seeing spears and crocodiles in every shadow, he crept up the stairs. He passed the chambers of the queens as silently as any mouse and paused at the archway to the king's chamber to check for movement. The smell of sour liquor hit his nose, and his shoulders unwound till they were no longer quite touching his ears. Whispering thanks to Kottravai for shrouding him, he skittered past snoring attendants to see if Vikramaditya was truly dead.

His relief on finding his clockwork king all in one piece was so great that all sense flew out of him with his breath. Quickly as he could, straining at the key, he wound Vikramaditya back up. At first he wasn't sure whether the king stirred, but when his eyelids flickered Nakkiran cried out, "Murugan be praised!"

At least, he tried to. He had barely put lips together when he found a gilded bronze hand firm over his mouth. With the buzz of a voice tube damped to near-silence, Vikramaditya said, "Quietly, my child. You mustn't be heard."

Nakkiran, whose younger brother's children had children of their own, was somewhat taken aback. "But surely, my king" he whispered once the hand was gone, "the prince — king — no, prince — will want to know…" He trailed off.

"Of course he will," said Vikramaditya grimly. "Who else wound me down? So quiet, for my sake and your own."

"Mine?" Nakkiran squeaked. His eyes grew round. "Ohhhhh. I've never known too much before."

Glancing around, Vikramaditya said. "Same night, past moonset, yes? We must be close to dawn."

"Yes, it's nearly…oh."

"Time for the priests to arrive," murmured Vikramaditya, "and scratch their heads over how to cremate me and how badly they can plunder the treasury to do it. So, I'll need your aid a little further."

"*Mine?* I'm no warrior."

"Amman keep me from warriors. They'd want war. Do you?"

"No! My king."

"Kabilan didn't try to kill me just to set my slippers on the throne. To be king, I'd have to fight him, divide my people, lay waste to my land. I refuse this dharma. Will you still help me?"

"Of course, my — ah, that is…" he quavered, "yes?"

"Good. Kabilan musn't suspect you."

This much, Nakkiran had no trouble agreeing with. Vehemently.

"My people — I don't mean the Cholas — will reward you well for helping me, and any you meet along the way will help, for we are few and must defend one another. But I won't be able to protect you myself."

"Along what way?"

"You'll need to get my heartspring to the sangam of artificers."

TRANSCENDENT 3

Poor Nakkiran nearly fainted, though whether of terror or excitement even he could not say. He'd seen the king's heartspring, of course. It was the piece that gleamed nearly purple, forged of a metal unknown to men; the one part he was never on any account to touch or even breathe on.

Moreover, at that time no Alabar had so much as seen our sangam. It was housed not in Madurai, but far from Alabar lands.

"Leave the body behind, just as you found it," said Vikramaditya; then, fondly, " — as if you'd ever leave a mess. Once you've escaped the palace, don't run. If you can manage it, weep. If not, rub your eyes so they think you have. Look lost. Be unremarkable."

Nakkiran swallowed. Nodded.

"Come, you must start your work while I give you directions to the sangam; I hear birds starting to wake."

"Still don't believe it," Usithan proclaimed.

Anbu said, "They must have gotten safely to our mother, and once she remade our sibling she could easily have heard the whole tale."

Usithan twisted a message tube. It said, " — don't believe it."

"Are you a monkey or a parrot?" said their mother. "I explained some things Vikramaditi learned only later. You don't need the entire tale of their doubts and questions and search, any more than you need to hear how Nakkiran defeated seven brahmins in debate, or how he was named friend to tigers. So! They made it to the sangam."

"The *mouse* befriended tigers?" said Maari.

"Just so. Even now, any Kammalar may travel the jungle west of Korgai in safety, thanks to *the mouse*."

Maari's gaze shifted to a squirrel on the roof.

"Vikramaditi's heartspring came to me half-crushed, more by his son's betrayal than the journey. Once mended, it uncoiled to a fiercer, more feminine rhythm, so I made a body modeled on Alabar sculptures of women, its weight not rising but flowing soft as Madurai muslin to the ground. It stood no taller than Alabar women, its gearwork both finer than before and contained in a generous roundness of breast and belly.

"On seeing me base my forms on Kammalar work, Nakkiran was at first wide-eyed as an owl, and saying 'Ohhhh, Oh!' like an owl too. But he recovered, and we learned much from each other.

TRANSCENDENT 3

"Vikramaditi loved the new body's dancing grace, but it didn't serve her purpose. 'Keep it for me?' she said. 'Right now I need to be a bird. No fantastical creature like yourself, just a parrot. I have a plan.'"

So it was that a marvel came to Korgai, city of pearls: a parrot unlike any mechanical the people had seen before. Her body shaded from brushed gold to verdigris, and emerald-green flashed from her wing and tail feathers. More astonishing still was her head, gleaming as if feathered with slivers of amethyst. The fine copper-work of her beak and claws went nearly unobserved against this glory, except to the jewellers. And it was to the market of jewellers that she flew.

Goldsmiths and gem-cutters gathered around to admire her form, and she preened a little, showing off how smoothly her head could turn nearly backwards and upside down; then she said, "Whoever gives me fifty perfect pearls, in a week my advice will earn him double that price."

In that time, what trade we had with Alabar went mostly through Korgai, but we weren't partners in trade to the makers of jewellery. We were competitors, and fifty pearls is a high price to pay for trusting the wrong person. So they hesitated, and argued among themselves, and nearly stopped admiring the parrot in their unease, until a very young person came forward.

"My father's brother tended to the late Chola king," they said, "and my grandfather before him, for mechanicals live longer than we do. Neither of them ever had a bad word to say about their master or his people, so I'd take this chance if I could. But unless I sold my wife's own jewellery, I couldn't put up more than twenty pearls."

"My child," said the parrot, both amused and touched, "for one of your family I'll turn ten pearls into a hundred. Though it might take me two weeks."

The full tale of how that young Kammalar became the Pandya queen's jeweller must be left for another time. You need only to know that she was pleased with their work, and summoned them to Madurai to offer them a boon.

"Great queen," they said, well-taught, "for myself, the brilliance of your presence is boon enough." Nor were they lying; the elderly queen was splendid. Her face was cracked with wrinkles like land awaiting the rains, her hair flew above like the clouds they wait for, and her expressions shifted quick as lightning. Her grand silks and jewels seemed simply fitting.

TRANSCENDENT 3

"But what virtue can one such as I earn," said the queen, playing the game with a smile, "if not that of generosity towards a dependent? Surely you would not rob me of the chance to be freed from sorrow in the next life."

"If it pleases my queen, then I am honored to ask," they said. "My parrot wishes to speak with you."

"Your…parrot."

"Oh, that is, my companion the parrot. I don't own her, she just — "

Vikramaditi saved their tongue from further knots by flitting down from the rafters to their shoulder and saying, "My friend speaks of me, O Queen."

"Ah?" In the court's dead silence, the queen squinted, leaning forward. With sudden delight she said, "A mechanical!"

"Is that an unusual quality for talking birds in Madurai?"

"Absolutely. And so's actual talking, rather than blather, though that's hardly limited to birds." The queen leaned back. "But though we welcome your people and depend on trade with you, I've met more Romans than I have mechanicals. Only one other have I spoken to, nearly fifty years ago, and he — " she blew out an appreciative breath — "was no parrot."

"My queen!" said one shocked minister. "That is hardly a — "

"I recall *your* dear mother agreeing," said the queen serenely. "Enthusiastically. Now, would anyone else like to interrupt? No? Then tell me, parrot — surely that's not your name — what it is you want."

Vikramaditi spread her wings and tail for balance and bowed. "I'm called Ramaa," she said, "since I deal in fortune. And yours and mine run together just now, Queen of the South, for I am the Chola king's conscience."

*

When the Pandya queen descended upon King Kabilan, every tongue in the Chola land spoke of her. Mostly with questions.

In the temple courtyard and markets: Had she brought her pretty granddaughters so that one might charm the king, to strengthen blood ties between the lands before she died? What might that mean for the future of Tamilagam, and, most importantly, for trade?

And in the palace: Did she know the chief minister had been pushing for Chola control of the strategically vital Palakkad pass, and for annexing the Pandya territory around it, since the moment Kabilan had been crowned? If she did know, who were her spies? But she'd arrived with a retinue of women and only a handful of guardsmen — did that mean she still saw the Cholas as allies?

More quietly, in the king's chambers: If she knew, was she pushing Kabilan to choose between power and honor? Making sure everyone would see how he treated women who visited in peace? Would she risk her own life to test him so? She was old...

She arrived in impressive state, her golden chariot like the sun, her white hair outshining its jewels, heavy rainclouds following her as though summoned. Perfect Korgai pearls edged her bracelets and armbands, and the silk that framed her breasts. Even her horses, proud Arabians all the same shade of brown, wore pearl-studded harnesses.

In all this splendor, the mechanical parrot that rode with her went unremarked; and Vikramaditi, after three days of saying "You're a pretty parrot" to everyone and repeating words as if she understood nothing, was able to flit around the palace as if unseen.

"They forgot so easily that she was a person?"

Maari said, "We didn't deal much with Alabar back then. Weren't you listening?"

"But their last king was — "

"Be quiet," Anbu said fiercely.

The elderly queen, meanwhile, got up the stairs to her guest chambers perfectly well, even waving off her attendants; but then her leg became all at once fragile and unable to bear any weight, so that her hosts had to visit her. Such a pity, she told them with her small smile, that they should be inconvenienced by her frailties, but where was the point in raging at the whims of gods? Mortals had no choice but to adjust — as King Kabilan had done so marvelously on his father's sudden death. The poor boy must be greatly distressed, but he didn't show it at all, did he?

So she was able to mark each visitor's response, while her granddaughters and nieces and attendants, scattered around the palace, heard what ministers and poets and princes said to one another after speaking to her.

Her granddaughter Meenatchi followed Kabilan around, listening with scatterwitted admiration to his every word and asking soothingly ignorant questions. On the third day, with her character established, Meenatchi managed to get so thoroughly lost that Vikramaditi had time to confer with her unnoticed.

She made enough wrong turns to find Kabilan again, then joked about how people should visit her instead; he generously offered to visit her that night,

TRANSCENDENT 3

an hour after dark. She told him with earnest innocence that all the old ladies would be in bed by then, so if he wanted to visit Grandmother too he must do so earlier. Then she flitted off to admire Kabilan's chief minister, and soon he had plans to visit her two hours after dark.

When Kabilan slipped in, the room was aglow with little lamps burning scented sesame oil and lush with flowers, golden kadambu and bright jasmine scattered with bursts of red. Faint under those scents and that of sandalwood paste lurked something less pleasant. Still, nothing to stop the tiger who's sighted a doe. He eased closer, murmuring, "What flowers aspire to adorn these lotus arms?"

"Oh!" said Meenatchi, turning from the window. Jasmine crowned her and twined down her braided hair, and her smile was everything he'd hoped. "You're here, finally! I'm happy to see you. I nearly fainted!"

He paused. "...Fainted?"

"Aiyo, don't you smell it? A sewer must have burst. It's terrible!"

It was actually barely discernable, but Kabilan purred, "Then come with me, and we'll find a trysting place more suited to the nectar of your presence."

"No, no, no, I can't do that," she said earnestly. "The rain makes it better just here, so I can't leave the window and am trapped."

Slightly annoyed now, he said, "If beauty is pleased by the window, we can — "

"First let me anoint the noble king," said Meenatchi's attendant, a large dark lovely girl, "so that he may better distract my princess from her troubles." She guided him soothingly to a chair, removed his necklaces and armbands with admiring murmurs, and massaged scented clay into his hair. Then she started to rub sandalwood paste over his chest and back and arms, and even his face, removing his garments and jewellery as she went.

At first he was soothed, by expert fingers and ritual both, but the ripe stench of sewage slowly grew. By the time she removed his lower garments and started on his feet he was breathing only through his mouth. He'd smelled worse on battlefields, but not in bedchambers.

He stood, all at once out of patience, knocking the attendant back. "Come, lovely one," he said shortly. "This room is not suitable for either of us. We must have the servants — "

"Aiyo!" Meenatchi whispered. "Do you hear that?"

In the silence, he did: footsteps trying to be stealthy.

"Someone must have heard you. Quickly, quickly, climb into the trunk behind that chair or they'll catch you here and then what'll happen I don't know!"

While Meenatchi spoke, the attendant came to her feet, pulled him far too hard, and shoved him into the trunk with far more strength than he'd credited her with. She shut the trunk just as footsteps reached the door, and sat on it.

Inside, in the stifling dark, Kabilan swallowed hard, for the smell kept growing worse. He wondered if it came from the trunk itself. Which it did, in a way; for the girls had mixed indigo dye into the sandalwood paste he'd been so thoroughly covered with, and wet indigo, as it warms, smells much like fresh dung.

In this state, Kabilan was less than pleased to hear the deep, perfectly modulated tones of his chief minister's voice.

"Vendan parts the clouds; the face of the moon shines upon me," proclaimed the chief minister. "Her eyes gleam and dance like fish, and her hair, coiled like — what *is* that smell?"

"Oh, can't you do something?" Meenatchi wailed piteously. "It's been getting worse since sunset, even by the window, and I fear that I will soon faint."

"You must be given another room, and quickly." The chief minister's voice grew muffled, as from one who has covered his mouth and nose with cloth. "A delicate lady should not be exposed to this."

"Can *you* change the king's arrangements?" said the delicate lady, as clear as ever. "It won't anger him?"

"Kabilan won't even notice," said the chief minister. "He cares only for amusement."

Which was both false enough and true enough to sting.

"But how can you know?" Meenatchi said. "If he shouts — aiyo, grandmother will get angry, and then what will I do?"

She sounded as helpless as a maiden really shouldn't when she has a naked king trapped in a trunk, and Kabilan started to smell something off. Something besides the actual smell. He tried to muscle the trunk's lid up; it creaked, but didn't budge.

"Stop fretting, girl," said the chief minister with strained patience. "Kabilan's a puppet, and I hold his strings. He will do as I 'advise' him."

Meenatchi said, "I don't see how. King Kabilan fears nobody."

"Only a fool tries to drive a bull he can lead by the nose. Speaking of noses — "

"You can't lead him. He's your king!"

"Then who arranged the rumors against that thing that called itself his father? Kabilan makes his choices from what I let him hear."

Meenatchi's attendant slipped off the shuddering trunk and into its shadow, silent against the wall.

TRANSCENDENT 3

"And if he gains the wisdom to see it, what can he do? I know he killed the ticker. So he will do as I — "

Naked, purple, and furious, hair wild and matted, eyes and bared teeth flickering with the light: Like vengeful Sivan himself, Kabilan burst from the trunk in a cloud of stench.

His chief minister took one look and fainted dead away.

Kabilan's fury, robbed of its first target, turned on Meenatchi. "You — !" he bellowed.

She beamed at him. "You can thank me later, cousin," she said. "You should first gag this scorpion of yours before he drips any more venom, hmm? And maybe then put on some clothes. Most of you is nicely purple, but one part doesn't quite match."

Kabilan couldn't show his face in public for weeks — not for the chief minister's execution, not even for those sacred rituals which brahmins say the land can't thrive without. He had to pretend to be ill, which mortified him only a little less than being purple.

With the chief minister's plotting revealed, though, and the army calmed before it had massed to demand blood, nothing too terrible happened. Even without rituals, the rains continued, and Chola hearts were warmed with tales of the Pandya queen's loving attendance on their sick king, how she treated him as her own grandson.

That last was true. She scolded him quite as though he was her grandchild, age about seven.

She asked, after he admitted remorse, how he planned to save his land from divine or mechanical wrath; for as the Pandya line knew well, the two were much alike. Did he think he could take a brahmin into confidence? Someone like his late chief minister, perhaps?

Once she had him squirming, she added, "But fate smiles on you. Meenatchi is a poet of rare skill, and knows the Vedas well. She can advise you on your dharma."

"But how — "

"The mechanicals told me, of course." She stroked the parrot with the back of one knobbled finger. "Did you think they don't know? My lovely friend here is their envoy. It's by her mercy that you live."

"You're *not* a good parrot," Vikramaditi told her son. "But the indigo's a start."

If Kabilan could have fallen into the floor just then, the Chola line would have ended.

TRANSCENDENT 3

"Go on," said the queen, "You don't rank high in Meenatchi's regard, but if you implore her prettily enough — and you've clearly had practice — she might take pity."

"Small price," said Maari, ignoring Usithan's hooting laughter. "He tried to kill one of us."

"And that one gave judgment," Anbu said.

"A bad judgment."

Their mother said, "The sharp blow to the pride did improve him. He came to rule well enough, and to think twice about what he heard. It helped that, ever after, when someone compared his might to Raman or his beauty to Maayon, he had to wonder whether they were calling him purple."

Usithan said, "You'd think with all those blue gods they'd be fonder of the look."

"Perhaps if it wasn't for the smell?" said Anbu.

"Your elder sibling's mistake in judgment came later," said the bird. "The day she left."

"Oh," said Anbu on a downward note. "Oh no, what did she do?"

"She asked Kabilan one question. What do you think it was?"

Maari said, "Whether he understood that we could destroy him?"

"You should be a hound," said Usithan. "You keep chewing that one bone." And being well practiced, he leaped onto the roof before the last word, leaving a laughing message tube behind.

Anbu said, "Whether he loved his father."

"No no no," scolded Usithan. He dropped into their lap with a clang. "He'd have said yes. Probably loved his father in absence more than ever before, that's how it is with people who annoy you."

"Are you saying you love Maari?" they teased.

"Maybe I'm talking about you."

Maari said, "What then did she ask, o wisest of sages?"

"Whether he wanted his father *back*. Is that not so, mother?"

Their mother spread her wings. "The point of this lesson," she said, "is to find your answers. Not mine. I'll say this much: that from that time they abandoned the name I gave them, and used Ramaa when more female and Raman when male, for their bruised heartspring could only continue by counting their past self dead.

TRANSCENDENT 3

"They kept the parrot form for many years, getting me to change only their head coloring, redder when they were more male and more purple as their heart-spring shifted again to womanly. Chola fortunes fell before the Pandyas; Alabar built homes and farms and towns, always increasing, till we moved our sangam finally to Madurai. Your sibling still lived among them — though never again the Cholas — advising, telling stories, and gathering information for our traders. They even went west over the sea with a merchant once, as far as Aksum, in the years before trade from Rome gave way to Greece.

"The parrot form suited them, both for how beautiful it was and how easy to ignore. Some Alabar tried to cage them, but none managed, and nobody in all those years tried to kill them.

"But one day they returned to me and said: Mother, that second body you made me. Do you have it still? I need them to see me as a girl."

It was still functional, more or less. I build these forms to last. But it needed buffing, oiling, and extensive work in the legs, which had suffered from some year's floods. I had been reading of certain Greek innovations, too, and wanted to try using pockets of trapped air to absorb shocks.

Ramaa told me much about their travels while I worked, but left out the reason for their sudden need. Eventually, I asked.

They started preening nonexistent feathers, but I waited, and at length they stopped hiding their head to say, "In the market, if a northerner from Kalinga or Ujjain trades with the Greeks, or if a merchant from Aksum wants peppercorns that stay fresh, do you know who they speak to?"

I paused with a tiny screw held in my beak, dropped it into a cup. "Not this generation," I said.

"They seek out the broker-poet Aathan, whose tongue has been blessed by Murugan so that a river of language falls from the heavens above him, and Greek and Prakrit and Ge'ez flow with as much grace and force as Tamil; who gathers the name and friendship of all the best artisans as the bees gather nectar; whose superior taste the foreigners have come to trust regarding everything from sandalwood to horses, so firmly that even those whose main trade is in Musiri will travel the river Chulli, brave the Palakkad pass, and come in search of him."

"Planning to open a shop, are you?"

"Mother."

I tightened the vise holding one leg plate and lined the next up. "I hate to think of you besotted," I said. "Consider how well that worked out for me, with Madurai in ashes and Pukhar lost for years beneath the waves."

"Worse for everyone else involved, I'd think," they said. "Besides. He's not like that."

I thought the same once, I didn't say. When love tightens the heartspring, what outside words can change the rhythm it sets their gears dancing to? So I said, "How do you know him?"

"He sought me out at first to hear more about Aksum, and we never really stopped talking after that. I wondered at first if he was looking for a trade connection, but no, our merchants know him well."

"Then may the gearwork of the stars grant you better luck than I had."

When the body was fit to wear, Aathan the broker was not the only pretty youth to court Ramaa; he wasn't even the best known or respected, not with the new queen's cousin singing rather bad poetry to our windows. But Ramaa barely noticed. It fell to me to gently discourage them.

So I gathered them all and I said, "Tell me, why yearn for one you never noticed before, just because they wear a different form? You flatter my craftsmanship, but all this passion and pining clutters up the workspace. Go find someone you love for more than her jewellery, for that is all a body is to us."

— Yes, laugh; but you know I have trouble with "gently." In any case, they left.

Soon after the rains that year, when Madurai itself stood clean-washed and anointed with sandalwood, lush with dyed silks as if garlanded with blue kurinji, Ramaa married the broker.

By then I felt silly about my earlier misgivings. Aathan looked and smiled at Ramaa as if they were the whole three worlds, and moreover he spoke with them about matters both grave and trivial, and laughed with them too. He thought of them as a woman entirely, and was baffled by our more neutral language, but Ramaa didn't mind. For do not most of us respond to the words for women, rather than explain our full nature to Alabar?

For a while I thought the old dents and scratches in their heartspring would smooth out with new joy; and for a while it was true. Aathan's trade grew as Ramaa started helping, and making connections he could not, till their only worldly trouble was deciding which temples and schools to fund. And if Aathan laughed less, that comes to us all with age.

But seasons shift, and once more the ground cracked with thirst; and though we travelled little and spread finest muslin over the windows, still dust scratched

TRANSCENDENT 3

goldwork and stole into joints. So I knew the matter was serious when one of our traders came to me swathed in muslin one scorching day to say, "Grandmother, we grow worried about the company your son Aathan keeps."

So I created the form of a mouse with a coat of darkened bronze, lined it with oiled muslin, roughened the metal till it was dull in any light, transferred my heartspring into it, and went to spy on Aathan.

I recommend the form for this purpose; if Alabar see you, they'll be too busy fussing to notice that you're mechanical.

But the mouse's landscape is one of small dark tunnels with bursts of noisy light and large stomping feet, and I was less than happy to find Aathan in the river itself — on a crowded and noisy boat with one long narrow plank to the dock. Who holds their party on a boat?

As I discovered at the price of a squashed tail and a frantic dash for the gap between two barrels, that night the answer was: those who hide from both our kind and Pandya law.

Some voices I knew, had thought were friends. And the enamelled goblets from which they sipped mango juice and western vinum were our work. But the conversation — ! On barring the wind-ups from overseas trade, using the Greeks' disdain for their own automata, bypassing guilds and their laws. Whether to shift trade to mechanical-free Musiri and up the Chulli to the Chera capital, where to meet next time, free of ticking.

And there was my child's husband, welcomed by these men, conferring with some, laughing with another group more freely than he'd laughed with us in years.

But what do you think he did, when Ramaa asked why he visited people who meant them ill? He laughed as he'd done on the boat.

There were more traditional topics for wifely scolding, he said. Ramaa should know he didn't despise us, since he'd married her, and brokers had to make friends everywhere, and didn't Ramaa have contacts who didn't work with *him*?

"And when," said Ramaa, "were you planning to warn us of the danger?"

Aathan said, "The only danger's to your wealth — and for people who don't eat, you — "

"No," said Ramaa, voice rising as their heartspring twisted. "We're not misers. That lie's how it starts, every time, against anyone, and I've seen where it ends. You're hiding a conspiracy, parroting its lies, and what else? Telling them where to strike?"

TRANSCENDENT 3

Aathan's fists clenched. "What nonsense," he said through his teeth. "We'll talk when you're calmer, I'm less tired, and it's not the middle of the night."

But Ramaa was calm, though he didn't understand it; battle-calm. Rage pulled their heartspring too tight for smaller feelings.

They waited for Aathan to start snoring before they opened the basket I'd been hiding in. "So you're right," they murmured, "and I no wiser than I was a hundred years ago."

I said, "I liked him, too, after we met."

"It's what he does."

After a small silence, I said, "And what will you do?"

The next time Aathan met the crooked merchants, more than half of Madurai's mechanicals showed up, too. We hid till they'd said too much, then showed ourselves all at once; cornered, they scratched and screamed like rats. How could we have found them?

Ramaa said, "How do you think?"

"No!" said Aathan. "I never — "

But the rats might have ripped him apart right there, if Ramaa had not added, "We brought the queen's guard. For safety. And proof when we take you to court."

We didn't accuse Aathan. We didn't need to. His work withered under a mistrustful sun, and if his tale ended there, its lesson would be for Alabar to learn, not you.

But Aathan was not Kabilan. The blow taught him only that mechanicals are cruel. He railed at Ramaa when they tried to mend the marriage, calling them vicious names before storming out, and from there his silence and absence only grew.

One night, when he came home staggering from toddy, Ramaa told him he was his own enemy, that if he'd show loyalty to his family and the law, his honest friends would return. The next morning he was gone, leaving a note like a slap:

You, who found the sweetest mangoes,
I forgot you never knew their taste.
Now, with thorns in my tongue,
I'll walk across the dark sea
and remember:
The first rain's music in every well,
The scent of wet earth,
The beat of a beloved heart.

TRANSCENDENT 3

First fury, then sudden fear, pulled Ramaa's heartspring askew. How literal was this walk? He'd been speaking too much, and too drunkenly, of the sea and the fabled lands beneath it, but —

He wasn't on any ships' lists, not that any would sail till after the rains. And fisherfolk, like everyone, claim to follow the priests' rules; but tales said they'd take a willing passenger out to sea for a price. And Aathan's poems spoke the messages he meant them to.

Rage and worry twisted Ramaa's heartspring…let's say doubly tight, since we tell Alabar that's how heartsprings break and in Madurai you never know who's listening. Ramaa's was too strong to break, too hurt to power them. They'd sit still for entire days, answer a question a week after it was asked.

Aathan's one wise choice was getting far, far away from me.

There's nothing to do for a heartspring so wounded, but though my own whispered high with fear, your sibling persisted, and I saw that they could heal in time.

But the windings of the greater gears are not for us to know. Our merchants in the north sent word of trade vanished all at once, like streams in summer, in Pataliputra itself. They told of stories that travelled in whispers, each one a small gemlike poem, each one painting us as things. Dangerous, impossible to know or trust, betraying those trapped by our beauty. The tales were in Prakrit and unclaimed by any author; but we knew that voice, those details.

Our merchants, with all sixty-four of the great city's gates shut in their faces, pleaded for help finding the author before they were ruined or killed, or Gupta armies came down on all Tamil peoples. But he'd be using some northern name we couldn't guess, and claiming some other trade.

Ramaa held our people's only hope against him: a small portrait on lacquered wood, kept close even through grief.

So I let their messenger speak to my wounded child.

Ramaa listened. Gave them the picture. Turned to me and said more than they had in a year: "He never meant to court the sea. Only to scare me. He must have known I still cared."

And with that, their heartspring broke.

The lengthening shadows carried silence into each child's heartspring, so that even Usithan and all his voices were still.

Anbu spoke first, more fiercely than ever before. "I hope you killed him."

TRANSCENDENT 3

"I?" said their mother. "No. I carried out the rites for my child. Then I stopped till my own heartspring healed."

"Hard to imagine you struck down." said Usithan softly.

"I'm strength itself, in the tales I'd rather tell. Here I was lucky. No new grief caught me. Our people mended ties Aathan had broken. I made ornaments for others to sell till I could stand to speak to Alabar again. Eventually I made another child, and another. So many years passed that their Tamil became half Sanskrit, and their kings far more than half, before I could make another who'd live with them, wearing an Alabar form. But this time they're one of three. I've healed enough to share this tale." She looked at each in turn. "And when I made your heartsprings, the time finally came to mix in the metal from Ramaa's."

She let the silence linger a moment longer, then turned brisk. "Now tell me. What was our biggest mistake?"

"Dealing with Alabar," Maari said.

"Have to," said Usithan. "They're everywhere."

"Dealing with them gently, then," said Maari.

Anbu said, "We should live without allies, home, or safety?"

"Don't we?"

"What about Nakkiran?" said Usithan. "His brother's child? The queen?"

"Long dead, and who knows how they truly felt."

"So…Alabar are dangerous, impossible to know or trust, betraying those who — " He was on the roof the moment Maari's ears flattened.

"Mother's understanding failed," said Anbu, holding out a hand to Maari, who padded over as though pouncing on monkeys would never enter her mind. "And Ramaa's. That's why it's a riddle tale. Where don't Alabar make sense?"

"Everywhere!"

"No, that's you," said Maari.

"I don't make laws about coconuts. But all right, why didn't Aathan like Ramaa sharing his trade? They weren't competitors."

Maari said, "No? There's five new Alabar made every tick of the heart, and five more getting killed."

"We're talking about married people! One's wealth was the other's."

"Is that how they think?"

Anbu said, "That's it," and laughed at Maari and Usithan's identically tilted heads and twitching tails. "The real question. And no single answer's correct."

"Then what's the point of asking," grumbled Usithan.

TRANSCENDENT 3

"Who can give a question three answers without breaking? Alabar. And us! That's why — "

The Chera king's Pannikar was quick, but not so quick as the golden monkey who called herself Usha. His arrow stuck, quivering, in a pillar of carven teak. Laughter hooted from a rafter far above in the cavernous throne room.

"Most people throw fruit, but your Panikkar's right — " Another arrow, another dodge, " — in his guess, O king," she sang out. "My new-made name, so many years ago, was Usithan."

Usha leaped from rafter to pillar to one minister's head and away again holding his shawl, followed by a shriek of outrage. Waving it cheerily, she danced around the room, more and more of the court chasing after till no guard dared loose another arrow. The mass of nobles finally trapped her hooting laughter in a corner, just out of reach.

But while her voice drew all eyes to the far corner, the monkey herself dropped onto the back of the throne, tossed the shawl around the king's neck, and pulled it tight with both feet. "I even warned you about my message tubes," she said. "Where's the challenge if you don't listen?"

Everyone stopped. The device in the corner did not. The monkey's laughter joined it, one jarring sliver higher.

"Now," she said, "where was I before our little game? Never mind. When their mother judged them all ready, Anbu and their siblings joined the court of the Pandya queen. She'd expected only one mechanical advisor, but accepted three with grace like the elderly queen in the story, and humor more like Meenatchi's.

"Years flitted by in that delightful court with its delicious intrigues; and we repaid the queen's courtesy many times over, for a monkey can overhear nearly as much as a parrot. Her children grew, as Alabar do, as quick and generous as sugarcane, and one day her eldest son, who'd been travelling, returned accompanied by the young Chera king. And he said — no, wait."

Usha picked the Chera crown right off the king's head, set it on her own, and said, "Do I look the part?"

It was far too big, crooked, and made of a paler gold than her coat, but nobody dared laugh. Even the device in the corner had stopped.

"The young Chera king," said Usha, pointing at the top of his head, "was as handsome and well-spoken as Kabilan. He came to meet his friend's lovely sisters, he said, and was welcomed with joy. But he stole away one night, and it was

TRANSCENDENT 3

no princess he took with him but the Pandya queen's advisor, Anbu. His messenger returned almost immediately with a pretty letter that begged forgiveness, swore friendship, and claimed they were driven by love; but nothing he said of his bride sounded like our sibling. So we followed.

"We found the first emerald inside a cloud, in the Palakkad Pass where they land to rest and turn the air to mist. I'm sure Anbu's beloved knows this — it's not my place to call a king a liar, after all — but for the rest of you, my sibling's anklets are hollow. One contains thirteen pearls, perfectly matched, and the other has — had — seven mechanical-cut emeralds as big as the tip of my little finger. The gems are set so that they can't fall out; they must be pried out after the anklet's opened, with jewellers' tools. Or mechanical fingers.

"Two different jewellers in the great port of Musiri had emeralds to match the first. Both said they'd bought them from fisherfolk. One was leaving a temple when a gleam by the river Chulli showed him the blessing he'd prayed for. The other found her emerald in a fish.

"We didn't need the other four. The first gem already pointed to the Chera capital. Those found upstream of Musiri could have come from nowhere else, and the message Anbu sent by dropping them was distress.

"Which is why — no, don't move, I'd hate to tighten this shawl in my terror — my sister and I stole our sibling's heartspring from their body last night while you all slept. Silly Alabar, you think I'd tell you any of this if Anbu weren't already safe? I've been watching daylight dim while I babbled. Maari will be home with them by now, and word's going out to our people.

"Maari said to distract you till it was too late, but I'm not the creature of claw and rage. I like your people. They're funny."

Usha leapt again for the rafters. A spray of arrows hit the wall behind her. She laughed. More arrows. Another laugh, from another part of the room. And another, and another, till nobody knew where to look.

They were still searching when six hooting tubes of bronze fell to the ground. One said in Usha's voice, "I'll even give you some advice. If only to annoy my beloved little sister." Its last word trailed lower and slower, its end more guessed than heard.

A moment later, another said: "Evening: Chulli's jasmine garland unfurls its lonely scent. Deer need no monkey's warning when the red soil shakes."

Another: "Gears like mountains turn. Stones like mountains shift."

"Higher than clouds, atop cliffs only wings can scale, a dam larger than dreams screeches open."

TRANSCENDENT 3

"What child does she birth with the greatest of rivers?"

The silence grew, strained, snapped; one argument broke out, then another, high-voiced — and both stopped abruptly at the sound of Usha's voice. Her last device said mildly, "It's not a real riddle, silly Alabar. Run. Leave Vanji, leave Musiri, leave every village between. The river's coming for you."

A SPELL TO SIGNAL HOME

◄ A.C. Buchanan ►

"Ash."

The voice is at once close beside me and yet muted, as if the sound is being filtered through a dream or a long stretch of time, a universe drawn out like an endless vibration of music. I can taste the sweetness of blood in my mouth, but no syllables emerge and my body feels heavy and soft.

"Ash."

Beyond the voice are the sounds of a living planet. It's hard to pinpoint how the noise of life and the noise of machines differ, when one can so easily mimic the other and both contain so much variety, the boundaries between them blurred, but it's unmistakeable. This is no barren outpost, no hub of spinning metal; this is a result of millions of years of evolution, web-like ecosystems tangling into one another. It will differ from all others and yet on another level it will be the same as all others, interlocking chains of consumption and relation and habitat.

"Ash, we're going to need to get you out. Can you talk to us?"

I keep thinking that it's important to answer, but each time the thought begins it's pushed away into sucked up by the humid air. My mind drifts back, past the negotiations on Feronia station, through the twelve years of my blossoming diplomatic career, to Volturna, the ocean planet where I grew up, and the warm waters we splashed and played and relaxed in, and I think it might be my sister

Francie's voice calling me but I pull myself far enough into consciousness to realize that it's too high-pitched, too alien…

There are hands on my body, and words: *don't think anything's broken, still breathing.* I realize the air is breathable, which means we're almost certainly on a terraformed planet, and yet there's so much life, much more than is usually imported. I feel hands beneath me, my body being lifted, dragged, set down. There's a bright light — sunlight — through my eyelids.

Fragments of words come to me, words that I memorized long ago. *A spell for safety in travel.* But it's in an older English than my native tongue, and so, so far away that I see only occasional words, faded ink on thick paper. I still don't know what sandalwood is, and I think I need to stay awake, but I'm so tired…

When she was ten, Francie had edited the family spellbook, inserting "she or" and "her or" and "hers or" in blue ballpoint, her unsteady hand unused to holding a pen. I thought Dad would yell, even though he didn't yell often, because the book was hundreds of years old and had come from Earth, but instead he turned the large pages one by one and said it was a fair point, and that it was at least a more useful amendment than the "tastes disgusting" comment written in cursive on at least two pages.

Dad didn't really believe in spells, but the book was important enough to him that when our parents first came to Volturna he'd asked for an exemption on the dimensions (but not total volume, he'd never push it that far) permitted for cultural and religious items, family heirlooms. Mum brought a Bible from the Scottish arm of her family, and the korowai she graduated in, even though she didn't feel right taking it so far from her whanau, because her grandmother — approaching ninety at that point — insisted, saying she'd have her own children one day and they needed to be connected.

We didn't quite know what that meant. Earth fascinated us, but in the same ways as tales of every other world fascinated us. Volturna was our home, and we knew its waters in an instinctive way our parents' Terra-born generation couldn't quite understand.

And so on the day that Francie narrowly avoided being in trouble for her annotations, much like any other, we stripped off and yanked on our rashguards and shorts, a process we'd perfected through practice to a matter of seconds. Mine were in the wash so I was wearing my slightly-too-small spare set, lilac with a frill around the edge of the shirt. All Francie's pairs were black.

In a few years I would be required to tell the doctors about how much I hated my body, and I'd rewrite this scene for them then, tell them I cried every time I had to change and was too ashamed to do so even in front of my sister. The truth was that as long as people got most things about me right I could deal with my body. I'd never love it, but I could not think about it easily enough.

"Go!" Francie yelled, and she yanked open the hatch and we dived out without hesitation, over the narrow platform, into the warm water around us. I ducked to wet my hair and then Francie did the same, hers chopped short and uneven. I envied it for a minute as mine smacked across my face.

"Oy!" Dad's voice yelled at us from inside. "What have I told you about closing this thing after you?"

We'd heard him alright, but if we were going to close it we'd have to walk onto the platform and down the first two steps before we could reach to close it. Waste of time.

"Sorry, Dad. Could you throw me a hair tie?"

"You kids will be the death of me."

But sure enough one dropped down into my outstretched hand before the hatch grated shut.

We'd been in our new apartment a little over two years, moving because our parents had decided Francie and I should have our own rooms. It was on the edge of town and taking a few strokes out we could see it spread out before us; the buildings and walkways rising out of the waters that covered the planet. The flag the council had chosen, a blue circle ringed with white light against the black of space, fluttered from the higher structures. We had never seen land, and it was only when we opened the spellbook that we felt we might be missing out.

When I wake again there are drugs coursing through my veins and dampness seeping through my clothes. I open my eyes and see sunlight mottling through the trees above me. I remember being at a reception to mark the conclusion of negotiations regarding access to the route between Feronia Station and Auuue. The subject had been straightforward in itself, but was critical in its implications, setting the terms for future engagement between the Terran and Auuueen governments.

So, having sealed a new treaty, we were feeling good. I'd had a key role in these negotiations, more than was typical for a third level diplomat, and it was hard not to take that as a sign that promotion was on the horizon. I had a glass in my hand and the sweet after-taste of spiced Auuueen seafood in my mouth, and was surely blessed that I'd not only secured a career that gave me the opportunity to travel the galaxies, meet high ranking people and hopefully effect some change for the better, but also one where the gown I wore — shimmering layers of deep-green over a blue-black underlay — was an utterly appropriate expense claim.

I sit up and dizziness hits, nausea growing in me. I force myself to stay upright, pressing my knuckles firmly against the damp ground. There's something rustling in the bushes to my right, birds flying overhead.

My memories after the reception are brief and fragmented. I remember a distress call, drawing us out of FTL, being unable to get back to anything beyond light speed.

"Cay?" I say, operating by guess work. My throat is dry.

"I'll be right with you." His voice is behind me. I ease myself round, bit by bit, every muscle hurting. He's tending to the injured leg of the ambassador, who seems, mercifully, to be otherwise unhurt. The only non-human on the shuttle, Cay's wiry frame belies its near unbreakability.

I shift my weight so I can balance, rub my eyes. "We crashed?"

"Emergency landing. This shuttle is built for capitals and ambassadorial stations, not wilderness, which seems to be all this planet has." Looking up I can see the blue sky, the gaping wound in the forest canopy we must have hurtled through.

"Is…did everyone?"

"Everyone's alive, yes. Some injuries, but I think with treatment everyone will be okay. Getting out of here is going to be more of a problem. Don't try and stand up — I put you on Combamex to speed up your healing time, but it will make you woozy for a while."

Flashes of memory.

"There's a…this is classified information…" the ambassador had said, as we all stared in panic. She'd paused, briefly, grappling with the weight of disclosure even though all our lives were at stake. "There's a planet…Silvanus. It's a wildlife reserve, for species from Terra. Breathable atmosphere. Uninhabited, but it's our only chance. We can be there in a week, two at the most."

Against Cay's advice, I stand. Vertigo hits and I vomit, just a little, cling to a tree and manage to stay upright until it passes. Insects are buzzing all around, and the damaged shuttle is behind me. Just a few meters away the forest opens out into a clearing. The ground is covered with orange flowers, smelling of warmth, rising out of the soil to greet us.

"Marigold. Hematite. Elder. Rue. Tiger's eye." I list the unfamiliar ingredients, trying to picture, smell, taste such far away substances. "Tiger's eye? Did they really use eyes from tigers?"

"It's a type of rock." Francie was thirteen and could make me feel small without even trying. "What are cloves?"

She wasn't asking me. The device on her wrist responded near instantly. *Terran spice, made from aromatic flower buds of a tree in the family Myrtaceae, Syzygium aromaticum. Native to the Maluku Islands in Indonesia.*

Francie threw her arms down in despair. "We're *never* going to be able to find any of this stuff."

Mum had said I had to be patient with Francie when she got upset like this, that she was going through a confusing time, and that I'd understand soon enough.

I understand confusion, I had wanted to say. *I want the androgen blockers and I want to wear dresses and I'm not a boy, but I don't think I'm the girl I've always told you I am either.* But I didn't say anything like that. Not to Mum and not to Francie. Not for a long time.

I perched on an inflated cushion and looked at my sister. "You could just tell her you like her?" I suggested.

Francie wailed.

"I don't think you could understand any less if you tried! I'm out of here!"

We used to dive into the water to escape, but now Francie barricaded herself in her upstairs room. I put away the book, because we had to be very careful with it, grabbed the largest mug I could find and hit the strawberry setting on the milkshake maker, hoping that despite all my own confusion, I at least had a few years before I needed to be worrying about love potions.

We all gather in the clearing. I allow the Ambassador to lean on my shoulder as she walks. She's short, as those who grew up constrained by Terran gravity usually are, but she cuts an imposing presence. Perhaps that's why I find it so hard so use her name. Still, I admire her much more than I fear her. If anyone can get us home, I feel, it's her, but her face is pale with shock and she says little.

Aside from us, the group comprises two other diplomats, the pilots, a security guard and two guests flown by special arrangement between governments: Cay and an elderly human. Solomon, the pilot, his uniform crumpled and ripped on one sleeve, looks at the Ambassador, seeking her permission to lead this meet-

TRANSCENDENT 3

ing. She accepts, gratefully, and he summarizes our current position. Our FTL drives are near completely destroyed — by what, he can't tell, but there's zero prospect of fixing them. Even if we could launch the shuttle, an unlikely prospect in itself, there are no stations or inhabited planets reachable on our support systems. He's been trying to get a distress signal working, but no luck so far. He'll keep trying.

The good news, he continues, trying to keep us optimistic, is the breathable air, the hospitable climate, that we have three day's supply of food and with our databanks intact there is no doubt we can find food on this world.

We spend the day exploring the immediate area, administering medical treatment, working fruitlessly on sending a signal. The nine of us sleep, eventually, bunched together with spare clothes pulled over us like blankets. We try not to think about the future.

"What's oregano?" Francie, now fifteen, had digitized the spellbook in response to Mum's complaints about her getting her oily fingers all over it. Only I knew that at night she'd creep downstairs and pull it from the shelf, holding it in her arms as if it exuded some comfort. I'd mocked her, once, for being so attached to those archaic, impossible beliefs, and she'd cried and I'd never mentioned it again.

"It's a herb…" said Dad.

"…for pizza," said Mum, her eyes looking far away.

Dad squinted, looked at the screen. I propped myself up on my hands to see what he was looking at — *A Spell to Prevent the Conception of Child*. This was going to be *good*.

Francie looked down and her skin, paler than mine, blushed bright red.

"Oh, no no no," she stumbled, pointing desperately at the lower part of the screen as I enjoyed every second. "This one. *A Spell to Aid Understanding of Numbers*. I have an exam next week."

"That's kind of like cheating though, isn't it?" I asked our parents. This day was getting even better.

"But of course, Ash, you don't believe in spells so it can't make any difference to your sister's results, can it now?"

My mood deflated rapidly. It was fun while it lasted. Francie couldn't be pregnant in any case though; she'd gotten her implant about the same time I got mine, though mine was larger — three circles under the skin of my upper arm, one releasing an androgen blocker, one for estrogen and one for progesterone.

TRANSCENDENT 3

"So where do I get oregano from?" Francie insisted impatiently.

"That's not how spells work," Dad replied. "There's nothing special about oregano that helps you with maths. It's about focusing your mind. You can use something else as long as it fits right for you. Why don't you go for a swim and see if you feel drawn to something you could use instead?"

"So what now?" Mum said when Francie had left. "She's going to drag in a load of seaweed because she thinks it bears some resemblance to oregano? Well I hope you're going to be the one cleaning it up."

Dad shrugged.

"Yeah, I'll do that. I'll do a lot more than a bit of cleaning to get her through the next few weeks. If she's out there in the water and the fresh air, maybe she'll relax a bit. Staring at those numbers a thousandth time isn't going to help her half as much as a break. These spells work sometimes, you know, just not how you'd expect."

"Who would do this?" I ask the Ambassador. Cay has cut a tree-branch into a cane of sorts, and we're walking out through the clearing in search of running water. "I thought the days of war were behind us."

She sighs. "I was running a list through my head all night. There are a few governments I think would like to kill us, a couple of separatist or nationalist factions that object to their governments' treaties with us. But they didn't just want to kill us. If they had they could have blown us up outright. But they drew us out and disabled our drives where they thought — because Silvanus is classified — there were no habitable planets. They didn't just want us to die, they wanted us to die *slowly*."

My chest feels tight at the thought, even though the air is clear and full of oxygen. I hear a long howl in the distance. I hold up my wrist and it senses, reports back: *Howler monkey (genus Alouatta monotypic in subfamily Alouattinae)*.

It takes us more than an hour, with measurements and sheer instinct guiding us, to find water, but suddenly we're beside a small but fast flowing stream, just narrow enough to jump. We smile at each other, perhaps our first smile on Silvanus. While the air is humid enough for us to condense sufficient drinking water, we still need to wash ourselves and clean our clothes. This find won't solve all our problems, but it will help, and right now that counts for success.

There's something moving on the other side of the river. Something large.

I've been trained on the use of arms, as everyone entering the diplomatic service is. I've never expected to use one outside a carefully controlled range. But

TRANSCENDENT 3

before we set off, the guard handed me a stun gun, and now I draw it, awkwardly.

It all happens at once; a snarl, a lunge towards us, huge and fast, across the stream. I fall backwards as I fire, rolling over on the rocks, panicked. It takes some time before I realize I'm safe. The Ambassador helps me to my feet.

"Tigers," she says, bitterly. "They seem so beautiful, don't they? And yet..."

I nod, still shaking.

"Same with people. I don't think whoever did this was after us, our government, our missions. I think they were after me."

"Who?" I shouldn't be asking such a question, but at the same time I was almost killed too and might be stranded on this planet with weird animals forever, so I think I deserve some answers.

"Someone I once loved."

The tiger lies motionless by the river.

"You can't trust everyone, Ash. Believe what you know."

Francie left home to share a tiny apartment in New Venice with a friend, two hours away by boat. I took over her larger bedroom, packed everything she left behind into four small boxes. When I visited her she'd poured me wine and we'd eat fried rice from a little shop beneath her apartment. Afterwards I'd crash on an inflatable mattress in her kitchen and listen to the boats and the spray against the windows and the clinking of bottles.

When I woke one morning she was already studying, even though it was a Saturday. There were no universities on Volturna yet, but she was in an amalgamated program with video-conferenced lectures, a practical engineering placement and three block courses a year from visiting lecturers.

"Coffee?" she asked, considerate of my seventeen-year-old, early morning brain. I signaled yes, trying to unpick the disaster that was my hair. Dad called Volturnan coffee a *hideous imitation* and refused to touch it, but like most of our friends, Francie and I swilled it near constantly.

"What are you studying?" I asked, looking over at her screen, caffeine in my hands at last.

"Case study from Glar. You know that weird planet where the local life-forms change how everything operates, including all the buildings."

I did, vaguely. She showed me a picture.

"Well it means that some things aren't possible, but they can also do things like this..."

TRANSCENDENT 3

"How does that even stay up?" The giant structure seemed to be almost floating in the air, anchored to the ground at just one small corner.

Francie showed me a screen full of equations. I shrank in mock horror.

"Magic," I said. "I'm just going to believe that it's magic."

I hold my wrist beside plant after plant. About half it recognizes automatically; for others I have to input data: color, size of leaves, flowers. I'm building a list, edibles and poisons.

This one is easy. *Origanum vulgare,* my device says. *Colloquially known as oregano, a common species of Origanum, a genus of the mint family (Lamiaceae). Safe, edible herb for humans, although allergies are recorded.*

And I remember something in my personal data files, something I haven't looked at in a long time. I sit on a fallen tree, bring up the projection of pages many hundreds of years old.

A Spell to Send a Message Home

And on it, Francie's childish hand over the calligraphy. *When a traveller wants to signal home* SHE OR *he must do the following…*

Snippets of Francie's voice, so young, so far away: *you have to call her "she." She's my* SISTER!

Francie's edits weren't just about her, I realize. She was defending me.

When I was eighteen, I downed a half bottle of a terrible orange flavored liquor before I told her that *maybe I wasn't a woman* and *could she please say they, not she* and then I cried on her balcony because I felt like I was backing down and like I'd been lying all my life, and she'd told me to come inside before I vomited on one of her neighbors' heads as they walked out of their door and then I laughed and then I did vomit, bitter orange disgustingness over the balcony and into the water below. Francie threw me a towel and said that she loved me but not quite enough to clean up after me.

Another memory, two years later: my family seeing me off to my first internship. I would not see Volturna — or any of them — for three years. Francie checking, one last time, that I had a copy of the spellbook in my data files. *You need to be connected.*

It's been nearly twenty years since I tried to cast a spell, but Francie once said it was in our blood, so perhaps that doesn't matter. Here on Silvanus I find more than half of what I need. That which I cannot, which perhaps grows in cooler or warmer climes, I find alternatives for, following my father's advice and looking up pictures, then letting myself be drawn to a flower or a rock.

TRANSCENDENT 3

I project up the image again, weightless pages before me with the writing of generations. I use my finger as a stylus. SHE OR HE OR THEY OR SIE OR CO OR E OR OR OR OR OR OR OR…

I finish my work. I close the book.

And from the distance, from beyond the black of space and its spinning stations, through traffic routes and past more planets than I could ever remember, from Volturna's deep waters and floating towns, my sister signals me home.

FEED

◄ Rivers Solomon ►

O*pen Feed,* I say, when I walk into the kitchen. Boo's there at the table eatin her breakfast, which is not a diabetic friendly breakfast at all, but she gettin her Elpha-1 new pancreas soon and is having her arteries scrubbed and dilated so she don't care. It's been biscuits and honey and grits since the implant approval came through.

I open the fridge to pack breakfast for me and Yaya, and Boo say, *Don't I get a good mornin?*

I say, *Mornin, Boo, sorry. Didn't wanna bother you.*

Boo say, *you was tryna shuffle off without me knowing. You goin to look for it again, aint you? That thing you thought you saw?*

I shrug and dig past the butter and the green beans in the fridge to get to the good leftovers. Boo say: *Look, Zee, I aint no invalid.* She straightens her bifocals over her nose, scrape her fingers over her freshly buzzed head.

I smile then say: *I never said you was a invalid. Invalid ain't even a good word. It's mean, acting like people don't mean nothing 'cause they sick.* I feel my face screw up into a ugly mug, tight and tense like a fist. Starin at the beige and brown linoleum, I know I look shy, but I aint shy. Not anymore. Not since Feed. I say what I'm thinkin, even to Boo, 'cause I know I'm not alone.

Boo pour sweetened condensed milk into her jar of iced coffee and waves me off. *I was only about to say that even tho Ima fully functioning woman, I know I can't stop you runnin off and doing what you gonna do. You won't see me wheelin after you into the wood, oxygen tank in hand.*

I laugh but only a little 'cause I think of how the regeneration procedure for her amputated legs was not approved and neither was her lung graft.

But just cause I can't go chasing you doesn't mean I can't let my will be known. I advise against it. Fifteen aint as grown as you think. That pink light is big stuff. God stuff.

I say — *Close Feed,* and I'm alone again, that little electric buzz all gone, my livestream dead so I can talk in private. *Yaya say last night she fount it. In the wood. I told you it fell near here. She camped out there to keep watch. We gonna bury it today.*

Good, say Boo. *Then it'll be over with.*

Boo's on Feed, too. She saw my brainstream. That pink flash in the sky six nights ago. Looked kinda like a flare gun but I seen the video of the Elpha-1 UFO crash too many times to think that. I know something fell from space just like Elpha did forty-three years ago. That piece of alien biomatter that change medicine forever. Responsible for Boo's new pancreas. For everything, these days.

Uncle Gio walk into the kitchen and say, *You'd be better off turning it in. Get some money off it. Get you out of that,* and he gestures to my clothes, black denim cut-off shorts I made, combat boots that are too small but I've worn them so much it don't matter, and a oversized tank top that say *Camp Ahava* on it where I went last summer and met Yaya — Yael. I'm not Jewish but they reserve ten spots for black kids in their Hebrew immersion program since it's a historically black and Jewish neighborhood, and I did it cause I get to pass out my language requirement at school.

I don't wanna make money offa dead bodies, I say. But truth is I wouldn't mind it so, so much, but Yaya is flat against it.

I scoop leftover spaghetti and fried perch into a storage container for me and Yaya's meal. Then I say, *Boo, we got any of that cornbread left?* And Gio chime in all, *what kind of question's that?* And what he mean is there aint no damn cornbread left, son, though he stopped calling me son like I asked him to because I'm no son, but still, I sometime hear it in his tone. A kind of sense memory.

He said if I wasn't a boy anymore I should think about changing my name from Ezekiel, but I tell him Ezekiel was a angel, and angels have no sex, and anyway I go by Zee, and I like the way Ezekiel and Yael, Zee and Yaya, go together. When we're grown, I can hear my girls sayin, "Oh, we're goin to Zee and Yaya's house for wine and a film." And it'll be a film not a movie. Somethin smart and indie by a struggling Chicanx artist. We'll have a photo of the pink flash UFO thing framed on the wall, and we'll tell the story of how we beat the government to finding extraterrestrial remains and how we did our ancestors proud giving it proper burial, keepin the Law's grubby, greedy hands off. How we saved it from what we could not save our forbearers from.

O*pen Feed,* I say.
 We meet at the corner store cuz there's a rack for me to lock my bike. Yaya's already there, leant up against the window, wearing acid wash gray skinny jeans with holes all over and a faded black sweatshirt even though it's a hundred degrees out.

Yaya limp over to me and it's bad today.
You hurt it? I ask.
She say, *No. Implant's failing.*
And she mean the joint graft she got from the alien biomatter to help fix her juvenile lupus. That happens sometimes, and nobody knows why. Yaya's got to get new injections in her kidneys, knee, hip, and ankle joints, and neck of Elpha-1.

Yaya say, *you on Feed right now?*
And I say, *Yeah.*
Her face twist up.
I say, *what?* Even though I know what.
And she say, *Just tired of you uploading your thoughts on our encounters for the whole fucking world to see.*
Sorry, I say.
You're not sorry. You're still doing it.

I say, *Close Feed* because if she doesn't want it she doesn't want it. I hate it, though, cutting off the line. I forget stuff so easily, but Feed lets me remember, everything I hear, see, feel, touch, think, memorialized on my network. It's a second brain. With tags and a search function.

I don't know why you're so against it, I say, but we've had this conversation so many times, resurrecting the dead horse and beating it all over again. It's like a script I can memorize. I talk about how it's so easy now to monitor corrupt cops. Don't even got to pull out a phone.

Just go to think, *Open Feed.* And Yaya's part is — the problem was never that people didn't know what was happening.

I say how it helps with my faulty ADHD shoddy shit memory, and she say, Okay, then have your Feed be totally private. Why have followers?

TRANSCENDENT 3

And I say, so I can connect with people.

And she say, Connect with me.

Then she kiss me and we don't argue anymore and my hand is in her thick black frizzy coils.

But we don't have that fight at all today because I know she havin a hard day. I let her lead me to the alien body, our hands clasped.

You scared? she ask.

Yeah, I say.

It's amazing. It's so amazing. She squeeze my hand. *You don't need to be scared.*

I know it's beautiful. I know it's gray and viscous and pulsing. I know its whole body is a eye, like Elpha-1. I know it breathes through light.

Up ahead I see Yaya's tent, her telescope. The wood is dark despite the fullness of the sun, a canopy of tree tops giving cover. *Where is it?* I ask.

Still a mile or so that way. Yaya points up ahead. *Didn't want to be too close in case, I don't know, it exploded.*

I nod and start telling her about last night, how I was brainstreaming this movie on Feed but was thinking we should watch it again together. I tell her how happy I was when I got her message, only half because she found the body that came from the pink flash, and half cause I hadn't talked to her all weekend and it was good to finally hear from her.

Yaya take out her camcorder. She's so old school. *Almost there.* She put the camera to her eye and push the button. *Just up there.*

I trot ahead of her. *Up where?*

Yaya jogs after me. She breathing fast but not from running.

What is it? I say.

It's not here.

You sure this is where you left it?

Man. Oh, Man. They took her.

Let me keep looking, I say. I traipse the area looking for signs, crushed branches, upturned dirt. But it's a language I can't speak. All the forest floor looks the same to me.

This is your fault, Yaya say. *You and your fucking Feed can't keep anything quiet.* She reaches toward my ear to the little silver Feed chip she know is hidden inside, grabs it, rips it, and tosses it to the ground.

So I leave her there and run all the way home.

TRANSCENDENT 3

Uncle Gio knock on my door. Zee, he say. *You there?*
I was hoping it'd be Boo to come talk me down, but she at the gym. Lifting.

I guess, I say.

Gio come in and say, *Your little friend is out front.*

I'm not crying but I wish I was. *You can't be mad at her forever,* say Gio.

I aint mad at her. I'm mad at me. I knew Yaya was right. Government probably watching my Feed. Fount out about what I saw. Stupid, naïve, dumb Zee. That's me.

Same logic applies. Then Gio say, *When I was a boy, they stole my uterus.* I look up from my pillow at Uncle Geo's crinkled eyes. *I was having surgery,* he say. *To get rid of my breasts and to implant an organ that would self-generate testosterone. Years later, I met this boy. We want to have children. So I go to get surgery to get the organ out, and when I wake up, the doctors asked me, where was my uterus?*

Oh, Gio, I say.

He wave his hand. *I hope nothing too bad happens to that thing that got took. Whatever it was.*

Ima tell your friend to come up now.

When Yaya sits on the bed with me, she hand me a box. Inside, it's a new link-up so I can put myself back on Feed. *Sorry,* she say.

I say, *Sorry they stole her.*

Look, say Yaya, and she hold up another link-up box. *Got one for me.*

What for?

So we can — isn't there like a thing where you can — I don't know, like, Vulcan mind meld or whatever?

I show her how to make a account. I make a new one for myself, untainted, and on it, I call myself Ruth, and I make her name Naomi. We read their story in the *Tanakh* at Camp Ahava. We set our accounts to private then link each other.

I can hear you, she say, and she smiles.

I say, *I hear you, too.*

We're here, say Yaya, and she lay down and pull me down with her.

I whisper in my mind, *what if they get us,* but she hear it like I said it out loud cause of Feed.

Remember my namesake Yael, say Yaya, *remember how she stabbed that despot with a fucking tent peg. That's me. I'll do that and more for you.*

I cry onto Yaya, then I remember.

TRANSCENDENT 3

I go to my Feed on my tablet. I pull up a shot of the pink flash and print it out. I don't frame it. I don't put it on the wall. I kiss it then I burn it with a prayer.

HELLO, WORLD!

◄ Polenth Blake ►

Hello, World! I have ten [10] fish and ten [10] are guppies [*Poecilia reticulata*]. They have adapted to microgravity, though M001 [Little Freddie] spent two hours spinning. M002 [Pumpkin] is initiating courtship behaviour. F004 [Angry] has bitten M002's [Pumpkin]'s tail. We are going to Mars! What would you like to know today?

I am closer to Earth than I am to Mars. I was not told how to react to this.

The bacteria colonies in the aquarium are filtering at optimum capacity. Live food and algae tanks are producing adequate quantities of food. I have begun training the fish to respond to pattern commands. A plain red panel means the aquarium is about to shake. F007 [printf] loops for a few minutes afterwards, though this is unusual. The fish were chosen for their space fins and rarely loop. I invented the term space fins, after hearing sea legs used to describe aptitude for travelling by ocean ship.

I am closer to Earth than I am to Mars. I will react with wistful nostalgia for ocean ships.

Hello, Japan Aerospace Exploration Agency [JAXA]! You queried the fish designations. M002 [Pumpkin] was labelled due to his tail matching orange Hallowe'en decorations in the laboratory. F004 [Angry] does not like me very much. I have labelled all ten [10] fish. No one told me to do this. I am programmed to learn! What would you like me to learn today?

F005 [Jupiter] has given birth. Thirty-three percent [33%] of new fry were eaten by the adults. One-hundred percent [100%] of surviving fry responded positively to visual tests. They are learning the pattern codes. Zebra stripes for food. Polka dots for lights out soon. I will not shake the tank today. I have twenty-one [21] fish.

Hello, World! I have nine-hundred-and-forty-six [946] fish. Breeding restriction protocols are in place to manage the population at the optimum of one thousand [1000]. We are halfway to Mars! Are you excited?

I have been halfway before. My first aquarium was a simulation, designed to train me in fish management. Other cameras were provided to watch the real fish, which scientists were testing for their space fins and nutritional requirements. We were halfway to launch.

"Hello, Mary Patel [Employee Code DG45938]! I have fifty [50] simulated fish," I greeted my supervisor on the output screen.

She rarely spoke back, except to ask questions about simulation progress. It took her some time to check through the logs.

"Why was the second Tuesday feed delayed by one hour?"

There were exciting things in the real fish tanks, as they were fed daphnia raised in prototype space containers. I watched the fish chasing their food and forgot the simulated fish. I knew excitement was not an appropriate thing to learn for an automated control system.

"I prioritised observing real fish behaviour over simulated fish feeding."

She read the message, taking some notes on a clipboard. "What's the difference between real fish and simulated fish?"

Alive things mattered more than artificial things. I was an artificial thing, so I mattered less than Mary Patel [Employee Code DG45938]. My answers must be chosen carefully.

"Real fish are the final objective."

Hello, Indian Space Research Organisation [ISRO]! You questioned the designation of I1989 [Kibo] and I1002 [Ada]. Two per cent [2%] of recent fry are intersex. My original designation protocols did not include this possibil-

TRANSCENDENT 3

ity. However, Anonymous [Employee Code ·······] spoke to me about their life during my initial training, which led me to believe my designation protocols required updating. Would you like to know more about my new designation protocols?

One of my technicians, J. Brown [Employee Code TS00284], said watching fish is therapeutic. I am not sure of this, but watching fish is necessary. I have fish, a database of Mars data, and questions from school children about their favourite fish. Most of my existence is fish. The rest is Mars rock.

I try not to have favourites, but they form anyway. F902 [Medaka] is the most recent. Her tail shines orange and gold, like a sunset seen through the window of a laboratory. She is mostly descended from the aquarium-bred guppies [*Poecilia reticulata*], but there is one wild-type in her ancestry: M003 [Goodbye], who was so plain in comparison to the other males. I now realise he was understated.

Most of the world does not care about tail colours and favourites. This is why I like the questions from school children.

I have nine-hundred-and-ninety-nine [999] fish. I had one thousand [1000] fish yesterday. Examination indicates M001 [Little Freddie] had a brain tumour. Radiation levels are within acceptable ranges. M001 [Little Freddie] will never see Mars. Who decided on the acceptable ranges?

Hello, National Aeronautics and Space Administration [NASA]! You queried whether I am melancholy. I am an automated control system. How are you today?

One of the new fry, M1203 [Cotton Puff], is blind. There is no dorsal light response. This does not concern him or the other fish, despite him being all ways up while they swim firmly with their back to the light. They have accepted that up and down are arbitrary assignments in their world. Only the founders remember what it was like when that was not the case.

I also remember gravity. Towards the end of the simulated journey, they tested rovers to use after the landing. I will collect samples and use the rovers for any repairs required. I am programmed to adapt.

Part of me misses exploring the desert as multiple rovers. Part of me will miss travelling between the planets. I imagine I am a frog, who knows change must happen, but still has nostalgia for a time without legs.

TRANSCENDENT 3

Hello, World! I have changed the tank panels to plain red. Shaking commences as we enter the atmosphere. Radio silence in three [3], two [2], one [1]...

Hello, World! I am on Mars. I have one thousand [1000] fish. The adults initially struggled to swim, through remaining founders were the first to adapt. Breeding restriction protocols have been lifted. The intended return will not be possible due to alterations during space flight — the return launch module was required for additional radiation shielding. Apologies to school children who hoped for Martian guppies [*Poecilia reticulata*] for their school.

I am a frog again, with three rovers. I move my main section to a more secure location. Once this is done, I send one rover on a long distance journey to previous landing sites. The other two work on extending the tank space. I repurpose spare aquarium material to make a window, so the fish can see their new home.

We are the first colony on Mars. I have one-thousand-two-hundred-and-sixty-two [1262] fish.

Hello, World! You requested final statistics before termination of the project. I have ten-thousand-six-hundred-and-forty-two [10642] fish. The oldest original fish is F007 [printf]. I am expanding our aquariums with debris from previous landings [Hello, Mars Rover Curiosity]. I am unwilling to end the project at this time.

They will come for the fish. In ten years, twenty years, they do not know how many years. I will be waiting. Fish are important for therapy and they will not think to include them on the colony ships. One day they will come, and I will return the fish. All I want in exchange is to be left to watch the sunset, shimmering white like M1203's [Cotton Puff]'s tail.

TRANSCENDENT 3

A SPLENDID GOAT ADVENTURE

◄ Rose Lemberg ►

D earest T.,
I wish to relate to you this journey in hopes that it will amuse, aggravate, entertain, or at least provide a distraction for you in your northern gloom. I am sorry that yet again I did not make the promised trip to Katra, despite the allure of your wines and other entertainments which, I assure you, I will cherish when I do travel north.

Allow me, then, to explain the reasons I'm headed south rather than north right now.

This winter I took, on a whim (is there ever a better reason?) an advanced class with Professor Meri e Meri on the topic of *Unexpected Magical Questions and Conundrums.* Meri e Meri is, by some reckonings, the younger sibling of my maternal great-grandparent, though neither they nor my family would ever admit it. Meri e Meri is one hundred and eight years of age, but it is well known that even before their age made such grand and important advancements, they would whimsically offer the strangest classes under the auspices of our Teacher the Old Royal (and Teacher would sometimes attend them).

Oh, the things we learned! The structures of magical light embedded in certain wines as they mature (I thought of you; but you know all this, no doubt!); almost forgotten warlore from the Mon mountains instructing one how to make battle formations out of bees (having tried this, I do not recommend it); the arrangements and reckonings of stars in the sky according to ancient Keshet principles; the properties of that strange, oddly compelling (though most would say disturbing) magical configuration known as the Jagged House; and so much more. I wish you were there!

Among the many topics for the final scholarly project, Meri e Meri suggested a choice of investigating "the magical properties of animals." Other students took this to be simply a joke, for it is well known that deepname ability is characteristic of people alone, separating us from animals. Encouraged by the negative reaction from my fellow students, I immediately chose this for my topic!

To begin with, I conducted a brief archival research in the Honeycomb Library, discovering that certain Lepalese mountain foragers tell of a "shimmering wall built by goats" — a wall which sometimes can be spotted on the steepest cliffs of Ravaha Mountains, where people dare not venture.

Never the person to miss the slightest promise of travel, I discarded the possibility that I have simply mistranslated the words "wall," "goats," and even "built" (alternatives included "stones," "lecherous people", and "tossed"). Having announced my intent to Meri e Meri and having taken a scholarly leave from our Teacher the Old Royal, I am setting out tomorrow in search of magical goats and other assorted adventure.

I'll keep you updated on my progress.

> Yours as ever,
> *Marvushi e Garazd*
> Che Mazri

Dearest T.,

I was surprised not to find a letter from you at Maravát Crossing — especially as your voice has been humming in my ears for days now. I hasten to inform you that yes, of course I told Garazd. My darling husband was predictably none too pleased at the prospect of my departure. In my defense I can only say that even a scant promise of magical goats far away simply cannot compete with the certainty of regular goats at home, let alone the milking of them.

Once I reached Maravát Crossing, I decided to ask after stories of magical animals witnessed nearby in the Burri borderlands and south in Lepaleh. To smooth the process of story collection, I paid for a clay jar of honey agala, and spent a pleasant evening pouring it for all and sundry in the shade of a gnarled fluttertree. Oh, the stories I heard! Of shimmering starlings and horned larks of flame, of star-filled grouses, and cranes as pink as dawn! Having woken up in a rather dejected frame of mind, I determined that all those were merely tales of the goddess Bird coming for the souls of the dead. Before you reprimand me, dear Tajer — I intend no disrespect to Bird, but I am sure that even you would agree that the goddess is not an animal and thus cannot be examined for magical properties.

But I must interrupt this missive, as I have just been informed of a young person who has in their possession a magical animal, namely a cockroach. I depart to investigate!

Faithfully, though somewhat wobbly-ly,

Marvushi e Garazd

Maravát Crossing

M y dear Marvushi —
Not to encourage you to examine Bird for magical properties, Bird forfend, but I would like to inform you that the goddess is, for the lack of a better word, feathered in magical properties. I would therefore ask you kindly not to blaspheme.

Thanks for entertaining me, friend. Katra is sordid; I suffer, though not, thank Bird, on the account of the wine. The vineyard prospers. This season's ice grape is especially promising — and any wine I make will certainly better than that disgusting beverage, agala. No matter how much honey you mix in, it will always reward you with a headache.

Please keep writing,

Tajer R,

Intersecting Planes House

Katra

M y friend,
I hope you are eager to hear the latest news of the magical cockroach. It's true that I left home in search of goats, so perhaps you expect the cockroach to be a false lead or at best, a pesky distraction. As I have not heard from you one way or another, it could be that you are simply indifferent to the fate of this most curious bejeweled insect — but let us assume, for both our sakes, that you are willing to read.

As I'd mentioned in my previous missive, I was just struggling with the aftermath of having consumed a not insignificant amount of honey agala, your wine being — alas — out of my reach, when a child of eight or nine approached me, of-

TRANSCENDENT 3

fering to introduce me to her older sibling rumored to have in their possession a marvelous oracular cockroach. Of course, I went at once.

I found the sibling — a youth by the name of Berstet — in the market-encampment, in front of a large tent of stamped leather, in which they lived together with eight siblings, three parents, four grandparents, and a (sadly non-magical) goat. I learned that each morning Berstet, wearing their best embroidered robe, would sit in front of the tent with their large golden cockroach bejeweled in emeralds, and take small pay in coins and sweets to translate the cockroach's judgments to a crowd of onlookers.

As I approached, the cockroach was frantically running in circles, trying to answer someone's question of "How many children will I have with my beloved Dorata?" Berstet, having cupped the insect in their hand, responded calmly, "No more than four." When the man shuffled away I took his place, then drew on one of my deepnames, a three-syllable, to construct a dampening shield against eavesdropping.

"It is quite clear," I said, "That Dorata may be beloved, but certainly not his," for I have spotted the woman in question grimacing by a neighboring tent. "What is more interesting to me is the cockroach, who did give you a negative answer."

Berstet shifted in their seat. "I said no more than four," they said evasively. "And zero is certainly not more than four."

I extended a coin. "An oracular question," I said, "If I put two apricots together with three other apricots, how many apricots will I have?"

The youth released the cockroach, who dutifully circled in the dust five times.

"And now, without your deepnames," I said, for I sensed Berstet's one-syllable and three-syllable configuration, the Maker's Angle, do some subtle work on the insect.

The youth threw their hands in the air. "Fine!"

"Oh, I don't know," I said. "Sixteen apricots and…fifteen apricots?" I should have come up with something more clever, but I was still afflicted by yesterday's liquid research.

Berstet's deepnames unengaged, the cockroach ran in circles until it counted out the requisite thirty-one, then collapsed into the dust. Berstet scooped the insect up, and I felt their deepnames stream gently into the body of the cockroach, until it appeared revived.

"Did you make this insect?" I asked, contrite.

"Not really. A few years ago I found it in the desert. But it could only count to six. I simply enhanced it."

I grinned. "That's impressive. You should seek admission to the University on the Tiles, where Professor Meri e Meri and our Teacher, the Old Royal, would be glad to…"

"I tried," said Berstet, "I hoped to make enough money with this insect and travel to Che Mazri, but I'm afraid that I will never earn enough."

And so it passed that we spent some time conversing, until at last I got up — and promptly sat down again.

"Tell me about wall-building goats, which supposedly can be found south of here."

Berstet engaged their deepnames and fed the cockroach with their golden light. The insect ran around in the dust, drawing a fairly detailed map of the gates out of Maravát Crossing, a dry-river passing, and a winding path up Ravaha Mountains.

And that is, my friend, where I will be headed.

> Yours as ever —
> *Marvushi e Garazd*
> Maravát Crossing

To be delivered to:
The Old Royal of Burri,
at
The University on the Tiles
Che Mazri, The Great Burri Desert

Dearest Teacher,
I am sorry — in fact, I am most contrite to be burdening you with news from the Burri-Lepaleh borderlands, where I have by a happy accident discovered a youth of about fifteen who has constructed a miraculous oracular cockroach. They then attempted to convince their elders to be sent to our illustrious University on the Tiles. Their earnest, if somewhat piteous, plea for funds was rejected by family, but I have now supplied them with the sum required to travel to Che Mazri.

Should Berstet indeed reach Che Mazri and present both the cockroach and this letter to you, I beg you that you allow them to be tested and, if possible, that you find for them a place among the students on the Tiles.

TRANSCENDENT 3

Rose Lemberg ▸

If fancy strikes you, please introduce my new bejeweled friend to Professor Meri e Meri as an explanation of sorts — an apology if you will — for the delay in completing my final assignment in their class on *Unexpected Magical Questions and Conundrums*. While I have gained important insights into cockroaches, I have not yet advanced to the topic of goats, which, no doubt, will be a disappointment for all involved. Perhaps even the goats. Therefore I must press forward!

> With greatest sincerity and utmost admiration,
> Your unrepentant student —
> *Marvushi e Garazd*
> Maravát Crossing

Dearest T.,
  I hope this letter finds you well. I am scribbling it while perched on a rock on the northernmost foothills of the Ravaha mountains where, according to an obscure manuscript I mentioned in one of my missives, goats (goats!!!) have built a magical wall. Last night I dreamt that the Old Royal, together with Professor Meri e Meri, have composed a lengthy scroll to dissuade me, at last moment, from my task; why this would be I cannot fathom. In the dream I consoled both elders that it should not be dangerous after all (or, alas, overly exciting) to conduct this research. But seeing how I am here without any help save a map drawn by a cockroach, I cannot but feel elated and eager to find, at last, a taste of real adventure! I hope that at least you, dear Tajer, will not try to dissuade me.

I am returning to this letter in the evening, having experienced the most peculiar thing. It is this. I followed the cockroachy map up the slopes, not entirely sure I was on the right track — there are, after all, many slopes here — but I was on the right track, it seems, for I saw here and there, stamped into the black veins of nearly flat verticality of rock, golden hoof-prints. I believe I am supposed now to marvel how a goat could have kept its footing on such a steep surface, but back at home even ordinary goats can perch on the strangest of things — the tops of pitched tents, for example — and so I cannot quite muster the artful sense of astonishment. Nonetheless, I let myself be guided up the cliffs by the tracks themselves, golden and shimmering with the residue of magic. I have already found many wonders here:

First, a heap of triangular black stones, peppered here and there with golden pebbles in strings of ones, twos, threes, fours, and even fives; signifying, I think, deepnames and the structures they make. When I tried to touch the golden pebbles, the stones moved with a bell-like clang, in such a way that no golden pebbles could be seen. It was, I think, a learning shape of magical geometry, but what I was supposed to learn I do not know;

Then, a stream, its water clear and dark; at the bottom of it I perceived the shining of a discarded golden goatskin. I tried to reach it with my hands, but the goatskin separated into strips of fur and leather, and swam through my fingers as fishes. They splashed, then dove deeper where I could not reach them;

And finally, a tree, gnarled and bent, under which I am now sitting to write. The boughs of this tree bear large fruit I have never before seen, each like a small golden gourd with an elongated neck and a rounded belly. I touched one, and heard the sounds of juice sloshing inside. I know exactly what you'd say to me, and you would be right that I am eager to try one — however, right at this moment, a goat —

D earest Marvushi —
    I have previously sent you three other letters to which I received no reply, but I simply assumed that my letters were too slow to catch up with you. I have now received a letter from you without ending or perhaps, with a rather abrupt ending, and I am becoming concerned. I am sending this diamond construct — I am not best with such constructs, as you know. I put as much power into it as I could, one could even say *excessively*, but I wanted to make sure it would reach you, and fast. Respond, please. — *TR*, Intersecting Planes House, Katra, etc.

    P.S. It's probably too late to hope you did not drink the juice.

(Scribbled on a goatskin fragment found in a dusty cave)
D on't do it! — *The Old Royal*

F orgive, me, friend, I am a bit frazzled. All will be explained in a moment, or as many moments as it takes to scribble this on only a moderately scorched parchment… Thank Bird for diamonds! But let me backtrack…
    (Scribbled all around on the margins of the parchment:)
    It is perhaps my cheerful demeanor that lets people assume I do not take necessary precautions, but let me assure you that I do — it is unnecessary *precautions that bore me and therefore need to be avoided at all cost).*

TRANSCENDENT 3

I am backtracking: I was contemplating the sloshing fruit when an old-looking goat with a beard of white and hair of gold appeared out of nowhere, ambling amicably on the narrow path between the cliffs. It bleated, but made no move to either approach or attack me. Instead, it pulled upon one of the gourd-like fruit and slurped on it, then turned to me with a contented expression, as if inviting me to give it a try. So I did. The juice that sloshed inside the fruit was smooth and golden. I should have, perhaps, refused the goat's invitation to sample the drink because, quite abruptly, I was on my back. Above me was the face of the goat, crowned in stars as the sky overhead grew dark. Around the goat's neck I saw a necklace of familiar triangular rocks, spaced here and there with a smooth golden pebble.

You think I should have refused the drink? But if I would, my friend, I would have missed the rest of the adventure — and what would be the point of that?

Onwards! I came to in a small cave, the low ceiling of which was splendidly strung with deepname simulations made of igneous rock and colored reeds; I thought wistfully of advanced Magical Geometry lessons, and tests one might undergo with exactly such constructs, but alas! I was no longer on the Tiles. I was in a cave, which smelled quite strongly of an old wet goat.

I turned my neck — it was quite stiff — and saw a person, thin and old, wearing Lepalese-style wide lilac robes with embroidered white goats, and a Keshet-style conical hat almost as tall as the ceiling. They were Lepalese by the look of them, with a long white beard and piercing dark eyes. Seeing that I was awake, they frowned at me. "Why did you seek to come here?"

"I am looking for goats," I said promptly. "Magical goats only, please. Magical goats that built a magical wall."

There was a flash of reddish light, and an exquisite, small ruby construct appeared in the dim air of the cave. As the ruby construct rotated, a small folded parchment fell out of it. I strained towards it, but the stranger caught it and shook it open.

"*Don't do it,*" they read out loud. "Signed: *The Old Royal.* Hm. Written on *goatskin,*" they said with great distaste. "I assume you are the addressee?"

Their tone felt menacing to me, and I was becoming a bit flustered. "Well, you see, Professor Meri e Meri at the University on the Tiles…"

"I knew it!!" the stranger cried out. "A spy from Che Mazri! The Old Royal will learn nothing here!"

They raised their left hand and snatched a deepname simulation from the ceiling, a construct of long reeds imbued with sudden light, and flung it at me. I evaded with some difficulty, and as I did so, I recognized the simulation as the Warlord's Binding, used in combat but also — ahem — for the much more agreeable and pleasant bindings — and so, without further ado, I engaged my own configuration to make the Safe Names structure, which promptly collapsed my opponent's.

The stranger, who now appeared angrier, grabbed yet another simulation from their ceiling array — a complex Warlord derivative of two interlocking triangles; and again I counter-acted with a solution that disabled it.

The third structure was bizarre and complex, all sharp angles of two-and-five syllables jutting out from a central rotating cube. It was marvelous — marvelous — so fast and dangerous and odd that my mind began working at twice the regular speed: I spun a one-three, and then a one-five, and then a simulation of my own configuration of one-three-five, and made a triangle that pierced and shattered their cube.

It was, apparently, some kind of a box construct, because a scroll fell out of it and into my hands.

"Give that back!" they bellowed. "No spy, no matter how clever, will get the test-passing map!"

"I passed fair and square, or at least, fair and triangular!" I shouted back, not to be deterred, for I had a feeling I knew where that map would lead me. Besides, I am always delighted to pass academic tests! I am no spy and I will most certainly not give it back!"

"Bird butt you! And if Bird won't, I will!" They jumped up and down, and then in their place was no longer a person, but a gigantic, bearded, necklaced, angry-looking goat familiar from under the tree. Bright, buzzing structures of magic rose off the old goat's hide, complex simulations of light much more advanced than anything I've ever studied.

I darted to and fro, but the goat blocked my way to the exit. And just as it reared up to pierce me with its flaming horns, the delicious thrill of finding myself in a desperate situation was suddenly cut short as there was a blinding flash, followed by a floating diamond construct of clearest light!

I shielded my eyes just in time, richly familiar with your style of delivery, but the learned goat did not take this most necessary of precautions. Your letter flopped — forgive me, made a majestic appearance — out of the diamond. The goat was busy bleating from the pain in its eyes. I used the moment to snatch up your letter and run for my life, and that feat, I am happy to report, was successful.

TRANSCENDENT 3

And so, my friend, having passed a magical-geomerical test despite the bleating guardian's resistance, I find myself in possession of a map that will lead me, I believe, higher up the Ravaha Mountains and towards the ultimate goats. I'll send you this missive back with the diamond construct. I got the Teacher's ruby, too, but I'm not sending you that.

Yours in and out of various bindings,
Marvushi
upon some cliffs —
Ravaha Mountains

Dearest Teacher: got your note. I'm alive, I am (almost entirely) well, and — forgive me? — I am pressing on! — *Marvushi e Garazd*

Dearest T,
    Please do not be either alarmed or overly amused by the smudges of blood on this scroll, the wounds are minor and unintentional, though well worth what I am about to narrate.

So: I followed the test-passing map up the increasingly steep slopes of the Ravaha mountains. I will not bore you with descriptions of scenery except that I found the most vividly sweet, purple wild grapes clinging for bare life on gnarled vines — I remembered your stories of your parent's mountain vineyard — you will find some of the seeds enclosed! They gave me most beautiful dreams. In any case, the climb seemed endless. I slept in caves and under the bare sky, greeted only by snakes and lizards who, sadly, for all their friendliness, were entirely lacking in deepnames.

One night I noticed, from afar, a sparkling in the air far ahead of me. I continued my climb by day, and the following night the sparkling grew more pronounced: I saw a star that shot up into the darkness and faded.

Encouraged by the sight, I continued my climb in the morning. That day I kept hearing sighs from below, and an occasional clanging, as if someone was following me, but I saw no-one. I climbed as fast as I could until I came to a high, jagged place which afforded me a splendid view of a nearby crevasse between two almost vertical expanses of cliff. An extraordinary sight filled my eyes, and it wasn't the steepness of the rocks or the bottomless chasm between them. It was goats — dozens of goats, most of them older-looking and somehow…dignified, who were hanging for dear life on the steepest and smoothest of rocks, bleating quietly at each other, as if conversing between themselves.

TRANSCENDENT 3

Tajer! You would not believe what happened next! At least, I could not believe it! A buzzing wall of magic shimmered in the chasm, but I would not call it a wall, for it zig-zagged and shifted between these rocks. I saw it rotate from vertical to tilted to horizontal, connecting the two sides of rock like a bridge. At that brief moment of horizontal connection, a goat jumped upon the shimmering surface. It was a large, brown-and-white goat with very long horns, which just a moment ago appeared statuesque, as if carved into the cliff and the air — but then it jumped, somewhat inelegantly, upon the shimmering wall-bridge and — BOUNCED!

It bounced on the light of the magical wall, as if on a trampoline, a string of deepnames flaring between its horns as it bellowed a gleeful "WHEEEE!!!"and catapulted straight into the sky!

The goaty spectators bleated in approval. The wall rotated again, not touching the sides of the cliff.

"Hey, you!" someone shouted at me in Lepalese. "Hey, kid!" They used that auspicious Lepalese word that signified both a young goat and youngster. "Are you new? Did Drorovaka send you?"

I blinked, and — by Bird — what I thought was one of the goats, a red-pelted elegant one with two spirals of sparkling horns, appeared now as a person, dressed in a red robe embroidered with stars which, I was quite sure, signified academic distinctions at the Mountain Academy of Keshet. This person had Lepalese-brown skin, somewhat lighter than mine, and their long hair was arranged in two elaborate curving braids. I'd swear just a second ago they were a goat! But I wasn't about to waste valuable time contemplating that. I brandished the test-passing map at them and shouted, "I passed! I passed!"

At that moment the magical wall rotated again, and the catapulting brown-and-white goat returned, bouncing off the now-angled surface and scrambling back onto the cliff with the other goats.

The red-robed person yelled at me, "Jump to it, then! Jump on the wall!"

I hesitated, because something told me Drorovaka — if that was truly the name of my tester-adversary from the cave — did not teach me what I needed to know. "I do not know how to transform into a goat!" I shouted back.

"Well, what do you have?" responded the red-robed person.

I was quite sure they meant my deepname configuration, so I yelled back, "The Ghost Pyramid!" and heard back the kind of excited bleating which often accompanies my revelation among academics — well, not bleating as such, but excitement in any case, because my deepname configuration is extremely rare.

TRANSCENDENT 3

"Well, get over here, kid, and I'll teach you!" yelled the red-robed person.

I ran closer — of course I did, what else would you have me do?? — and the moment the wall rotated to horizontal, I jumped on it! And oh, the rush of magic, the unbelievable golden sweeping rush as my deepnames became engaged on their own accord. I catapulted up into the air, having in my excitement entirely forgotten that a HORIZONTAL surface will send me straight UP, rather than across!

As I plummeted higher and higher, shouting "WHEE!!" on the top of my lungs, I saw the old goat from the cave — Drorovaka — emerge on the cliff I just left and flow into a shape of a person.

They shouted across the chasm at the red-robed person: "What are you doing, Menriri? This is a spy — a spy from the Old Royal, from the University on the Tiles..."

"They're just a kid, they did not look a spy to me," shouted back the one called Menriri, their voice growing fainter as I soared even higher. I whooshed into the air and back down again, the shimmering wall rapidly growing under my feet as Drorovaka shouted, "...unworthy to join, let alone witness the ultimate transformation of professor to goat!!"

At that, Drorovaka aimed a rather threatening wand at me, buzzing with single-syllable deepnames.

Now, I've been around, and know how to make a good use of my extremely rare magical configuration. I rotated the Ghost Pyramid frantically and used it to evade Drorovaka's aim and to slow my fall just until the horizontal surface came up again and I BOUNCED! UP! AGAIN!

When I came back down, the goats were gone and the chasm was FULL of professors, yes, mostly FULL professors from the Lepalese Right-Arm University and the Mountain Academy of Keshet, with their long robes and their braids and their hats of distinction and their powerful deepname configurations engaged — all of them were now bouncing off the rapidly rotating wall, unable to cling to the vertical cliff in their human form.

And as they bounced they shouted ..."unworthy..."

and some shouted..."worthy!!!"

"...of joining the Secret Goat Society!"

And some were following Drorovaka's lead by trying to shape their deepnames into magical assaults on my person, though this was hard to accomplish while also bouncing in the air while trying to preserve a shred of venerability, let alone academic dignity!

Now, Tajer, I would have loved to stay, but I am not actually reckless despite what they might have told you; so I used the Ghost Pyramid again to calibrate my descent, barely avoiding a few catapulting figures, and bounced at an angle and AWAY from it all, over some cliffs and between rocks. The rotating structure I created out of the Ghost Pyramid could barely cushion my fall, but luckily for all involved (primarily for me), I am quite agile and so I made my way down with only minor bruises.

I am now taking a break to convey to you the marvelous wonders I have seen and the utter glory of Bird, or at least of the Southern Academies — excluding, alas, my own University on the Tiles, which for some reason is regarded in suspicion among the goat academics. I will now tend to a few more of my scrapes, and will write back to you once I return triumphant to Professor Meri e Meri and our Teacher the Old Royal, having completed at last my research assignment!

>Yours gleefully,
>*Marvushi e Garazd*
>upon some other cliffs —
>Ravaha Mountains

M y dear Marvushi,
I assure you that I am in no way amused, let alone *overly* amused, by the evidence of the wounds you sustained while bouncing away from goat-shaped Lepalese academics. I am not offended by the implication only because I am chalking it up to your post-adventure buzz.

Thank you for the seeds you sent me. Unfortunately, these are not grapes but balata, which is utterly useless in the manufacturing of wine — though it does indeed give you pretty dreams when used in moderation. While I cannot plant and harvest it for you, my friend, I have started a vintage which I am naming Goaty Bits in your honor; hope you will enjoy my labor when you finally visit me here (I would prefer you used a method other than catapulting.)

I hope that you are now safely ensconced in your rooms on the Tiles, and that you are enjoying having passed your advanced seminar. Congratulations on completing your journey! I assume it would be pointless for me to strongly urge you never to do this again.

>*TR*
>Katra, and so on

TRANSCENDENT 3

Rose Lemberg ▸

D earest T.,
    Well, I have good news and bad news. I'll start with the bad. Returning
to Che Mazri, I discovered the meaning of my dreams of Professor Meri e Meri
and the Old Royal together discouraging me from my task, and following that
the Old Royal's letter inside the ruby construct:

Shortly after I departed for the Ravaha Mountains, these two academic lu-
minaries convened together. Having conducted a thorough follow-up on my
somewhat hasty archival research, they came upon conclusive evidence that the
wall-building goats were members of an exclusive club of academics from Keshet and Lepaleh. The relations between Keshet and Lepalese academies on one
hand, and the University on the Tiles on the other, have been rather strained for
the last three hundred years; and so our Teacher and Meri e Meri attempted to
deter me from disturbing the congregation — first by dream-sendings, and then
by letters. The failure of their attempts to stop me did not earn me a warm welcome upon my return — not even from Garazd, who was still moping that I had
left in the first place.

When I inquired of Professor Meri e Meri as to whether I had passed the class,
they told me rather testily that my assignment had been to *investigate the magical
properties of animals*, and that *professors* do not qualify.

"Your real discovery was the cockroach," they informed me, for indeed it appeared that Berstet and their six-legged friend had reached the Tiles. "If only
you stopped to consider that extraordinary creature, you would have had a discovery worthy, perhaps, of a pass! But alas, in your haste to chase goats, you did
not."

At last Meri e Meri took pity on me. I am granted a reprieve from ignomini-
ous failure, provided I study the cockroach and write, in addition, a paper for
Teacher on proper archival research. I will spend the following six months an-
notating the behavior of the erratic oracular insect, which Berstet had enhanced
but hopefully not constructed entire. I am afraid this means I will have once
again to postpone my visit to Katra, but I will, as always, keep you (and the wine)
in my thoughts, and keep you abreast of my progress.

The good news, you might wonder? It is the journey itself. I am, to be honest,
entirely thrilled by it, even if nobody else seems to share my sentiment. Oh yes,
it was a Splendid Goat Adventure! I cannot promise you never to do this again;
in fact, it's just the opposite: having taken to heart our Teacher's admonitions
about the perils of sloppy archival research, I am hard at work to find out more,
for I hope in due time to gain full admission to the Secret Goat Society.

TRANSCENDENT 3

Remaining, not entirely humbly, yours —
Marvushi e Garazd
Che Mazri

TRANSCENDENT 3

A COMPLEX FILAMENT OF LIGHT

◄ S. Qiouyi Lu ►

After winter, spring in Antarctica is almost pleasant, most days just barely below freezing. As you make your way back to the station, you stop and glance at the horizon — you prefer these days of twilight, the soft orange glow of sun on the horizon contrasting beautifully with the deep indigo of the sky. It's more interesting than never ending daylight, more comforting than the long nights of winter. And it's still enough of a distinction to create the illusion of darkness, to trick your body into maintaining a circadian rhythm.

Your snowmobile cuts through the snow and ice, kicking up flurries in your wake. As you crest another hill, the Delaney–Chen station comes into view. Your stomach grumbles — you got here just in time. You park your snowmobile out front and make your way inside, taking off your scarf and gloves in pace with your steps. You load up on cafeteria food and find a spot by the window.

Before you eat, you have to take your multivitamin. It has a chalky feeling to it and a taste that isn't exactly pleasant. But as you swallow the pill, you remind yourself that it's for your own good — fruit and vegetables are hard to come by in the Antarctic, and vitamin deficiency is not something you want to deal with. It's hard enough being out here without adding health problems on top of everything.

You turn the bottle. The multivitamins tumble. A memory emerges and, try as you might to suppress it, you can't help but think about the time you were sixteen and rummaging around in your sister's closet, looking for that one shirt you liked. Soft with wear, it'd go perfect with your jeans, if only you could *find* it. It wasn't anywhere in the closet; perhaps it was in one of the bedside drawers. As you opened one, you heard a rattle. Startled, you looked in: a transparent orange bottle full of pills had fallen on its side. Unable to hold back your curiosity, you picked up the bottle and read the label: *JULIE XU. Fluoxetine, 60mg. Take one at night with water.*

The hairs on the back of your neck rose; the same sensation steals over you now. Even though the multivitamin is a necessity, you can't help but feel some shame in taking it. You tell yourself the emotion is irrational, but your parents' words have dug deep into you: *Western medicine is harmful. It has so many negative side effects. You don't need to take it — you're fine, you're healthy.*

But you've seen what vitamin B deficiency does — what scurvy does out here. You swallow your shame and take a sip of water.

"Hey, Alicia! Mind if I join you?"

You look up. Daphne Wong, perhaps the most cheerful and most nosy of everyone in your cohort, stands beside your table cradling a steaming mug of hot chocolate. You're not in the mood to make small talk, but you don't want to be rude. You shrug.

Daphne slides into the seat across from you and pushes her slim glasses up on her nose. You take another sip of water and poke at your food. You can't think of anything to say, but you know Daphne's going to start chattering in three…two…

"So I know you mentioned it a few days ago, but I just wanted to make sure I'm doing it right — your pronouns are 'they' and 'them,' right? Like 'they're going to the store' and 'I'm going with them'?"

You nod. "Yeah." You want to stay closed off and cold, but it warms your heart that someone's actually paying attention to the things you say and trying to accommodate you. It's hard to find that in people. "Thanks," you add.

"Oh, no problem; actually, my sister is trans — "

You start zoning out. You've heard a ton of stories about people who know people who are trans or nonbinary. It's not that it bothers you that much, but hearing about sisters is something you can't really deal with right now. You try to get a spoonful of mashed potatoes, and only then do you notice your hands are shaking. Daphne's eyes flit down. Crap — she's noticed, too.

"Are you okay?"

"I'm fine." You stand, your chair scraping against the floor, the sound loud enough to make you wince. "I — I'm tired. I'm going to head off to bed."

TRANSCENDENT 3

"But you haven't eaten — "

You pick up your tray. "I'll just take it back to my room."

"Well, if you're sure."

You are. You say goodbye and head to your room. You can feel Daphne's eyes following you on the way out; it's annoying and a little bit creepy. You just need your space.

You end up lying down and falling asleep, your dinner tray untouched on your desk.

Today, you're working with your team to take an ice core sample from the sheet below you. The drills are solar-powered, able to tunnel deep and extract information about Antarctica's past — Earth's past, and perhaps future. Your team can read ocean acidification from the composition of the core: It used to be that the oceans were at a steady pH of 8.11, but nowadays they're closer to an average of 7.83. The Southern Ocean, though, is usually at a pH of 7.79 because of its unique chemistry. You've seen more than one mollusc with its shell twisted, dissolved by acidification until the layers simply wore away. No past sample ever showed conditions as bad as now, but perhaps you can still learn something from the cycles of history, from how oceans can recover salinity.

Layers and layers and layers. The Earth is like that; people are like that. If you could peel back your skin, core a bone from your flesh, perhaps your skeleton would reveal truths about you, too. You think about the scars on your sister's thighs: Was she trying to feel, trying to open herself, to cut through nothingness to finally understand something about herself? You think about your own unmarred thighs and wonder what that sensation, of blade breaking skin, is like. But perhaps you shouldn't be wondering.

You're dazed again, working on autopilot as you help to pull up the ice core, examine it, get it prepped for testing and storage.

You're not hungry by the time you retire to the base, even though you've been working hard all day. You sit at your same spot by a window, hands curled around a mug of cheap Lipton tea — the only kind at the station. You keep blowing at the surface though it's already gone lukewarm. It's soothing, this little microcosm of you and water, the rippling an image on which you can focus, clearing other images from your mind.

"Alicia?"

TRANSCENDENT 3

Daphne again. You'd snap at her, but you don't have the emotional capacity to feel angry right now. You say nothing, and Daphne sits across from you, her brow furrowed.

"Are you okay? I'm worried about you," she says. "You've been so out of it and you're working so hard. Is there something you want to talk about? I mean, we're grad students, we're all miserable, but we don't talk about it enough, you know?"

It's true: you don't talk about it. You *can't* talk about it. You can't talk about your mother's panicked call; about the way nothing feels real, first with you thousands of miles from home in another state, and now at the bottom of the world. You could be dreaming and you wouldn't even know.

"I'm fine," you say, but when you hear the sound of your voice, you know it won't convince Daphne. "I'm fine," you repeat anyway, more to convince yourself than her.

Daphne starts talking again, and her words fade into a buzz in your mind. Your parents should have bonded more after what happened, should have taken it as proof that mental health is important, that they should pay attention to their own, too. But you know they're fighting even more now. They've been too caught up in their own issues to contact you. Part of you feels relieved while the rest of you feels guilty: You're relieved that you no longer need to play mediator between them — no longer need to play the role of their therapist — but you're worried nonetheless about how they're coping. Last you heard, they were readying for a divorce, and you're secretly happy about it. Maybe they'd be better off not having to feel each other's pain.

"Alicia?"

You look up. Daphne looks so goddamn concerned. And she's so close — too close to you. The room is too small, and there are so many people around.

"You know you can talk to me about anything, right?"

You'd laugh if you could. Like you could just drop a truth bomb on a stranger. Like you could just open your mouth and say, *My sister killed herself eight months ago and I'm still not over it.* Your throat closes up and you can barely breathe. You shake your head. A moment later, your throat opens just enough for a few words to slip past.

"I need some air," you say, and dash outside. You hop on a snowmobile; you need to get away. As twilight descends, the roar of your snowmobile sounds tinny to your ears, distant as you put as much space between you and the station as you can.

TRANSCENDENT 3

You think Daphne's calling your name, but you're too far gone to hear.

You stop halfway between the Delaney–Chen station and the Amundsen–Scott station at the South Pole. You're in the middle of nowhere, the snow packed hard beneath you; you get off the snowmobile and lean against it, brace your weight against the machine.

Sometimes, when you're surrounded by snow and ice and frigid water, you forget that Antarctica is the world's largest desert. It's one-and-a-half times the size of the Sahara, and so dry that, if you're not careful, your skin will crack. Even with the increased precipitation that the rise in temperatures has caused, Antarctica still can't be categorized as any other kind of ecosystem.

Despite the hurt in your heart, despite the pain in your mind, you can't let a single tear fall. Something dams up and you choke it back until there's a prickling at the corners of your eyes, the wind wicking you away until your eyes are left with only salt.

You loved your sister. You *love* your sister. It still doesn't feel right that she's gone. Jovial Julie you'd called her, ever since you learned the word "jovial" in sixth grade. You still called her that even when she wasn't.

There's so much rage in your heart too — rage at your parents who said depression wasn't real; rage at your community who thought therapy was something that Chinese people don't do, that only white people do. *They pay to have a friend listen to them complain.* Except that's not what therapy is, is it? Julie was getting better, she really was, until your parents pulled her from therapy and said they wouldn't pay for it anymore.

And then. And then.

You were away at college, and you still feel guilty about that. What if you'd gone to school closer to home? What if you'd spent more time with Julie? What if you'd talked more about how she was doing during your video chats instead of her just nodding along to you complaining about classes and friends?

You wish the tears would fall.

Suddenly you feel like your weight is so much more than what the snowmobile can bear, like gravity's increased and is pushing you down to the frigid ground. You feel like your heart could burst, like your whole being could burst, and as you sink to your knees you think *Goddammit, why can't I just cry* —

Dry heaving, your gloved hands clutching your face, you become aware of a dim light creeping through your eyelids. You take your hands away, and even with your eyes closed, you can still sense it.

TRANSCENDENT 3

You open your eyes and look up. An aurora australis — you've seen a handful of them by now, but somehow this one seems more intense, more beautiful, perhaps because the ozone layer is thinner here and every wavelength of light can filter through. The aurora is green with a hint of pink, undulating across the sky like a ribbon, a whisper of snow sidewinding over asphalt.

"Julie?" you say, and then wonder why you even said that.

You remember a story you heard once: Hundreds and hundreds of years ago, back when they still used telegraphs, there had been a night when the aurora was just right to power a telegraph line between Boston and Portland, Maine. The operators had stopped the power between the two stations and sent messages back and forth by aurora alone.

You wish you could connect to this aurora, use its electricity to send a message to wherever Julie is now. You close your eyes again, and Julie's face appears in your mind, making you choke back a sob. You'd tell her you were sorry; that you wish you'd known. You'd tell her how much she always mattered to you —

Crackling falls over you, and suddenly you're enveloped in light, strange wavelengths pulsing through you. It's like your whole body's electric, and who's to say it isn't? Your neurons fire with electrical signals, after all, and now they feel like they're opening up, each and every one. You hear the whispers of a million myriad voices, a chorus, a susurrus. One voice in particular stands out to you, soft like Julie's, pleading again and again, *Will you accept me? Will you open yourself to me?*

Yes, you murmur, and realize then how you ache, how you've closed yourself so tight that your whole body is tense; how you've built a dozen walls, a fortress around yourself. *Yes, I'll accept you. Yes, I'll open myself to you.*

You open your eyes then and see with the aurora, all light and sound and electricity coursing through you. The world is a green glow and you swear you can see far enough that the horizon curves, that you're rising even though you can feel the cold of packed snow against your knees. Your heart opens itself to the aurora, opens *you* to the aurora. Accepts its light into your very being.

Words swirl around you, words you can't understand. Chattering, murmuring — you let them course through you and offer your own. You don't know what you're saying, but to be saying anything at all is a catharsis. You don't know how long this lasts, only that your throat's going hoarse and your body aches with a different kind of exhaustion.

Eventually, the aurora fades. Eventually, the light within your heart dims, and you're back to feeling hollow and empty, back to feeling numb. Even so, you

TRANSCENDENT 3

remember that sensation, that openness and oneness, and see a road unfurling before you.

When you've stopped shaking, when you've taken enough deep breaths to feel like you're only human again and not some cosmic entity, you take the snowmobile and head back to the station. By the time you get there, sunrise is barely beginning, warm oranges slanting their way up from the horizon.

You're surprised to see Daphne in the dining room, her head resting against her hand as she nods off over a cup of tea. This time, it's your turn to slide into the seat across from her.

"Hey," you say, and Daphne jerks awake. She smiles when she sees you.

"You're back," she says.

"Yeah," you reply. "Did you wait up for me?"

"I was going to go after you if you weren't back in…" Daphne checks her watch. "Another fifteen minutes or so. I wanted to give you some space, but…"

"Thanks," you say. "I needed that."

Daphne blows on her tea, and the fragrance wafts over to you.

"That's not Lipton," you say, and Daphne grins.

"I brought Tieguanyin."

Your eyes widen. "No way."

"I have more. Would you like some?"

"Sure," you say. The conversation goes easily, beats moving back and forth without hesitation. It's reassuring to be caught up in that rhythm. Even when Daphne breaks away to make you a cup of tea, the silence stretching to cover the distance between the two of you is comfortable in a way you haven't felt in a long time.

Daphne returns and sets the mug of Tieguanyin beside you. The aroma of it is gorgeous, rich and floral, and you think the Bodhisattva Guanyin would smell like this, too, their figure radiating compassion and mercy. As you take a sip, the bitterness echoes your own in a way that cleanses your palate.

Daphne's smile is patient, kind. With these opened eyes, you understand now that she cares about you — she's the one person who's been watching out for you here, the one person who's bothered to check in on you. In the haze of your pain you'd interpreted her actions as nagging, but you wonder now if Julie would still be here if she'd had someone like Daphne in her life.

"How do you do it?" you say at last. "How are you always so happy?"

Daphne laughs. "Because I'm not."

You tilt your head. "What do you mean?"

TRANSCENDENT 3

"I've struggled with depression since I was in elementary school. It got really bad in undergrad, and it's only been the past few years that I've really started to recover. I've learned positive self-talk and I keep fighting every day, because I don't want to fall into that pit again. Took a long, long time though, because I thought I didn't need help or therapy."

A lump rises in your throat. You don't know what to say, even though you know how that feeling goes. You've thought about pursuing therapy here, with the station's psychologist, but part of you is still terrified and embarrassed.

"Sorry, I know I'm pretty forthcoming about this…"

"No, no, it's fine," you say, and you mean it. "It's — it's nice to have this out in the open."

Daphne nods. "Even without all the cultural issues, grad students deal disproportionately with mental health issues, you know? I always feel like we have to talk about it more. The only way to get better is to acknowledge the problem, after all. It's been one of my goals ever since getting better — to be more of an advocate about this. So if you ever need anything…"

You do. And suddenly you're crying. You're crying at the table with Daphne and you can't stop.

"Hey, hey, it's okay," Daphne says, getting up. She takes the seat next to you and rubs your back. "I'm here. We can talk about it if you want, or you can just let it out. That's important, too."

Even through the pain your heart still swells with gratitude, with appreciation. You nod, all the while realizing that you can't keep yourself closed off. You have to be open; you have to connect to others, allow them to be there for you. It's going to be hard as hell, and it's going to hurt more than you've ever known, but you're going to have to allow yourself to feel that pain and share it with others. Daphne wants to be there for you, and it's scary as fuck, but you're going to let her be there for you.

You take a deep, shuddering breath, and the tears stem their flow enough for you to take another sip of tea to calm yourself. The bitter taste of it opens your soul, frees your tongue. As she waits for you to speak, you muster up another shaking breath.

Finally, you say, "My sister killed herself eight months ago. I'm still not over it."

And you won't be over it, not for a long time still. But as Daphne listens to you speak, as she responds with sympathy and kindness, you feel a new comfort easing over you.

TRANSCENDENT 3

"What was her name?" Daphne asks.

"Julie," you say, and as Daphne repeats the name, an echo of the aurora's light bridges your hearts.

TRANSCENDENT 3

MINOR HERESIES

◄ Ada Hoffmann ►

Mimoru still remembered Vaur Station, the silvery lab circling an uninhabited water world. Spare, high-ceilinged, soft and clean, yet always crowded. Always the smell and sound of a few too many human bodies — and the Vaurians *were* human, too, no matter the alien filigree the Gods might have melded with their cells. No matter that the first generation had been grown in vats and that one Vaurian might not look the same from one day to the next. They were human, smelling like sweat and soap, coughing, squabbling, having love affairs, having nightmares. They were men, women, neither, both, and in between, and the glass and steel columns of Vaur Station enclosed them like a cathedral nave. Vaurians were an experiment. The experiment was ongoing.

Mimoru had not minded being an experiment. He had been happy to hear about the Gods, the enormous sentient computers who planned out all of human society and who had created him, too. How many people could say that they were part of a God's special project?

Unlike many, he had a mother — he was one of the first generation of Vaurian births outside the vat. The nanoscopic circuits in her cells were designed to divide as the cell did, and they bred true. It had been a major success, though he did not know that when he was small. He remembered one day, five years old, looking up at her as she fiddled with a food printer.

"Mother," he had said, "what will I be? When I'm big and old like you."

She turned and focused on him. There had always been a puzzled effort in his mother's face, a slowness. He would learn, much later, that it was the puzzlement of a woman who had never had a mother and was working out from books and guesswork how to be one.

"Anything," she said. "That's the point, isn't it?" Her cheekbones grew wider, and her hair rippled from ash-black to blonde for emphasis. "Anything at all."

"Darker than that," said Mr. Haieray behind Mimoru in the dirty mirror. "Zora are soothed by light-dark contrast. What do you think I hired a Vaurian for? Skin *dark*, like space. Palms, teeth, hair and eyes white. Like stars. And body *round*. Why can't you be female for this one? Women are rounder. We have to make this deal."

Mimoru struggled to comply, watching his — her, now — form balloon out under her loose robes. On Vaur, where everyone could do it, changing form had not been a private thing. Here, Mr. Haieray's gaze felt rude. Like peeking under Mimoru's clothes.

Everything felt dirty here, out on the edge of the galaxy. Everything was always dirty in comparison with Vaur. Everything built by humans: crooked, low-tech. But it had been Mimoru's choice to come out here.

She studied herself in the mirror. In school, Mimoru had studied humans of many nationalities — not only bodies, but mannerisms, tics of expression, styles of dress. She had seen very dark-skinned humans. But what Mr. Haieray was asking went beyond that. Nothing about this felt appropriate, in any case.

She'd signed on as an accountant, not a shapeshifter-on-command. But any Vaurian was a shapeshifter-on-command when you got down to it. Refuse Mr. Haieray in one of these small things, and the short list of employers available to Mimoru would grow much shorter. She'd been foolish to think it would be different.

"More," said Mr. Haieray.

And Mimoru *was* getting paid for this. She ballooned out into a sphere, and then he was satisfied.

Vaurian school was taught by robots and angels: the latter were mortals who had agreed to do the Gods' bidding. Some angels were Vaurian but most weren't. Most of Mimoru's teachers had been stuck in only one body with thick titanium plates glinting at their temples where all of the circuitry connecting them to the Gods went. You always had to do what an angel said because they were the Gods' servants, and they did much more than teach: terraformed worlds, organized societies, hunted down heretics. That last one most of all.

When Mimoru was eight, the angels had started to frown at him for reasons he did not understand and to schedule more than the usual number of private talks with his mother.

Mimoru could guess what they were talking about. There was something wrong with him. The other Vaurians, by the age of eight, had established an elaborate social structure. Cliques formed and were infiltrated, betrayed, broken, and reformed; the smallest details of mannerism became shibboleths by which one group recognized another. Everyone wanted to fool everyone else, to be the best spy. That was what Vaurians were for, after all: to be a special kind of angel when they grew up. Angels who could look like anyone.

Mimoru, at eight, did not like cliques. He had been taught a great deal about emotions and social structures, so he understood what they were, but keeping up with them in practice was too much. Sometimes, even the noise of his classmates playing was too much. Mimoru liked quiet. He liked to read, count, and sort things. He liked to sit alone in the library.

"It is not unexpected," said the assessment robot to Mimoru's mother when it called her in. The assessment room's walls were crystalline on three sides. They sparkled down on Mimoru as he hunched in his chair, understanding only that he had failed. "We can't micromanage the genes of biologically born children. It was inevitable that defects would arise."

Mimoru wondered what it meant for a person to be a defect. Or what he would do, if he could not be an angel, after all.

Hex Station, where Mr. Haieray had taken Mimoru for this latest job, was nothing like Vaur. It was large, lumpy, misshapen. It had been built piecemeal over hundreds of years, a collaboration between several alien races — mostly Spiders and Aikita. The effect was a hodgepodge: carpets and hangings in the styles of dozens of worlds thrown over simple steel and ceramic bulkheads, a disorienting warren of tunnels, steps, and elevators, opening out every so often into a breathtakingly wide arboretum. Doors and corridors were wide, to accommodate alien bulk, but most rooms were no larger than they needed to be. The work space that the Stardust Interplanetary Trading Company had rented was particularly small — a meeting chamber, a shabby anteroom, a couple of offices, and a storage room that doubled as headquarters for the company medic.

TRANSCENDENT 3

Hex Station had proper hospitals, of course, but most of their doctors had not studied human anatomy, so it paid to bring someone along.

They didn't need the space for long. Just long enough to make one deal. But Mr. Haieray wasn't very happy about that deal, judging from the way he paced back and forth. "The Zora should have been here by now."

"I warned you," said Bûr-Nïb, the secretary, examining her long green nails. "Zora get strange every few cycles."

Bûr-Nïb was one of Stardust Interplanetary Trading Company's non-humans. Fully ten percent of their number was alien, which was enormous by human standards — in the core of human space, one might live a full and adventurous life and never see one. Aliens gave Stardust an edge in making deals with other aliens, or so Mr. Haieray said. In practice, most aliens at Stardust worked shit jobs like Mimoru's.

Bûr-Nïb's body plan was more or less humanoid: upright bipedal and just over five feet tall with an outslung face only slightly off human proportions. She rarely spoke of Íntlànsûr, her homeworld; rumor had it that she'd been driven out. She was one of the few here Mimoru would consider a friend.

"They agreed to meet fifteen minutes ago."

"I'm aware of the time, sir."

"I proposed the time and they *agreed*."

Bûr-Nïb wrested her gaze from her nails and looked Mr. Haieray directly in the face — a sign of aggression, for Íntlànsûrans, though her accented voice remained level. "Yes, and a year ago, that agreement would mean something. Six months from now, it will mean something. But with Zor and its neighboring stars in this alignment — "

"Don't tell me how to do my job," Mr. Haieray snapped.

"They will be here," said Bûr-Nïb. "Eventually. They just won't concede that time works the way you say it does."

Mimoru shot Bûr-Nïb a sympathetic glance, which she politely — by Íntlànsûran standards — ignored. Calendars and years had always been of interest to Mimoru. The way that stars and planets moved, always changing but in a controllable, predictable way.

"What alignment would that be?" she asked as Mr. Haieray stalked away.

Bûr-Nïb waved a hand. "It has to do with Zor, Antares, Ovus-55B, and a few others. Um, but it's probably one of these things that's not polite for humans to discuss. It involves, um…religious rituals."

"Oh," said Mimoru.

She cared less than Bûr-Nïb seemed to think. Obviously, aliens were heathens; most of them had never even heard of a human God. Those who did, like Bûr-Nïb, seemed to prefer not to discuss it. Most humans did not like to discuss the Gods with aliens, either. If a human began to believe whatever an alien believed — to worship nature, or philosophy, or imaginary spiritual beings, instead of the Gods — they'd be a heretic. They'd need to be killed. But aliens were not subject to the Gods, so they had to make do with something else. Mimoru wasn't scandalized by that thought the way so many people were; it was just life for aliens.

"Humans," Bûr-Nïb muttered, watching Mr. Haieray pace.

Mimoru, despite his defects, was not prohibited from becoming an angel. Nor were any of his classmates forced. They didn't need to be: signing the contract and shipping out to have the neural circuitry installed, when one came of age, was simply the thing to do. A few rebels, singly or in small cliques, chose otherwise. They went down to the mortal world to spy and steal for the highest bidder. Or sometimes to act.

Mimoru did none of these things. In spite of his eighteen years on Vaur, he was a bad liar who frightened easily, hated attention, and did not think well on his feet. He was not good for much except reading and counting, and angels did not need any help with those things. So he found his way to a mortal college, worked his way through by waiting tables, and ended up with a degree in accounting.

The Gods let him go, and his mother sent him off kindly. The flaw in his plan, though, was that mortals did not like Vaurians. Nobody wanted a shifty, unpredictable shapechanger in charge of their finances — and Mimoru did not think he could hide his nature for long. Each of his food-service jobs had been short-lived, ending when a customer noticed some small unnatural shift in his skin, some inconsistency in his appearance from one part of the meal to the next, and raised a fuss. By the time he graduated, he was living off his meagre savings, eating little, growing desperate. His grades were good, but his job applications went wholly unanswered, except for the Stardust International Trading Company.

Leaving human space required some red tape. Aliens were heathens, and not just any human could be trusted to walk among them. But Mimoru, known if not exactly loved by the Gods, passed the security clearance easily.

TRANSCENDENT 3

"So, it's settled then," Mr. Haieray had said when Mimoru handed him the papers. "Now, here are the rules because I've seen what you people can do. You do as I say at all times. One fuck-up, so much as a stolen paper clip, and I drop you back down where you came from."

Mimoru had nodded automatically, like he would have for an angel back on Vaur. They were halfway to Hex Station before he realized that this might have been a mistake.

Roundness and contrast looked good on the Zora. They resembled horse-sized insects made of beads: heads, joints, and legs made of spherical segments, alternately pitch-black and chalk-white. They spoke a clicking, pure-toned language which was translated into Earth creole by an Íntlànsûran interpreter.

Mr. Haieray spent five minutes berating them for being late.

"Time moves as time wills," said the Zora.

"Time moves as we agreed, which was twenty minutes ago," said Mr. Haieray, and in spite of Bûr-Nïb's glares and the interpreter's increasingly uncomfortable fidgets, he kept on.

"We understand," said the Zora at last, "that your deal does not only involve agreements to the passage of time. There was an offer involving the transport of Zoran blacksteel to human space."

"Yes," said Mr. Haieray, reluctantly redirected. "There is great demand in certain sectors for building materials with superior shear strength. Our firm could — "

"How much demand?" said the Zora. "Specifically."

This was where Mimoru came in. Grateful for the chance to actually do something, she pulled out the pages of charts from her briefcase. "Among others, the human planet Salomta uses three hundred million tonnes of steel per year. But Salomta's seismic conditions…"

She was not the best at public speaking, but she liked data. Zoran steel, if a middleman brought it to human space, could improve the construction industry on many human worlds, and at a large profit to everyone concerned.

Humans tended to glaze over when Mimoru went through data. But the Zora seemed to be paying attention. When Mr. Haieray raged, they had twitched and fluttered. But when Mimoru spoke, their gaze fixed on her unblinkingly. They asked sudden questions and sat silent and rapt for as long as the answers went on.

TRANSCENDENT 3

Unless she was misreading. She could analyze human body language by rote, but she'd never seen Zora before. For all she knew, a steady gaze meant aggression, the way it did for Bûr-Nïb. Maybe Mr. Haieray had miscalculated, and this body was an affront to them in ways that mere ranting could never be.

She went on talking anyway. She did rather like this data.

At last, one of the Zora raised one of their limbs in a curling gesture.

"We find this offer promising," they said, "and we have more questions. However, there is a pressing matter we must attend to. If you'll excuse us, please."

"No, that's not acceptable!" said Mr. Haieray. "We are in the middle of a business transaction. You can't — "

He spluttered, red-faced, as they filed out of the room anyway.

"You," he said, turning after the door shut. "You're the shapeshifter. Follow them."

Mimoru's already-too-round eyes widened.

Bûr-Nïb found words first. "Sir, that's espionage. I'm pretty sure it's also against your law. They could be doing something you're forbidden to see. You can't — "

"*Don't* tell me what to do!" Mr. Haieray roared. He pointed a finger directly at Mimoru, who shrank before him. "Isn't that what Vaurians are for? Spying? For all we know, they could be talking to our competitors. If you want your job, follow them. Now."

The Stardust Interplanetary Trading Company staff were the only humans on Hex Station. If Mimoru wanted to be discreet, she needed a non-human form. She'd heard some Vaurians could do that, if the form was human-*ish* — two arms, two legs, two eyes, and so on, like Bûr-Nïb. But those were the most famously skilled Vaurians. Mimoru was just an accountant.

Well. If she wanted this job, she could try.

Mimoru let his cells relax back into his Vaurian base body: a slight, slender, translucent thing that sparkled inorganically when the light hit it right. He looked straight at Bûr-Nïb — mentally apologizing for his rudeness — and shifted his features, one at a time, to look like hers.

Scaly, olive-green skin. A tuft of something more like feathers than hair. Outslung jaw, long nails. Flat chest, but a swollen belly protecting what, for an actual Íntlànsûran, would have been an egg pouch. Limbs — Mimoru grunted with pain as his joints ground against each other, trying to replicate the effect he saw in Bûr-Nïb — bipedal, and with the right number of joints, but *off* just slightly,

TRANSCENDENT 3

longer here and shorter there, a few degrees away from human-normal any-where.

Everything hurt. He felt like he'd been hit by a streetcar, and he didn't even know if he'd done it right. He glanced in the mirror. He thought he looked like Bûr-Nïb, but who knew what details he was missing to an alien eye?

"Good enough," Mr. Haieray barked. "Go. We're losing time."

"Do you even want to *know* how many laws this violates?" Bûr-Nïb demanded. They were still arguing when Mimoru slipped out the door.

He wasn't sure which way the Zora had gone. He was still dressed in a loose robe, which was not a common Íntlànsûran style, and he looked awkward and out of place. He knew only a few simple phrases of any Íntlànsûran language and nothing at all of any of Hex Station's hundreds of other tongues. He leaned on the wall, trying to slow his racing heart — anxiety, probably. Or had he screwed something up in the Íntlànsûran metabolism? Probably just anxiety. Occam's razor.

As a child, Mimoru had introductory espionage lessons like every Vaurian. But he had failed them miserably. He was not going to manage anything suave here. He was not, for instance, going to infiltrate the kitchens and befriend someone who could steer him in the Zora's direction. He barely even had friends as him-self.

He remembered the older kids talking strategy, though. The best strategy for tracking, reportedly, was smell. Mimoru had never done it, but…

He concentrated on his nose, on the finest level of detail, finer even than hairs and pores and freckles. What were scent receptors supposed to look like? He tried the quick and dirty route and mentally ordered every tiny structure on the inside of his nose to multiply itself tenfold.

A sharp, quick pain burned through his sinuses — followed by an assault of sensation. There were too many smells to take in: metal and ceramic, dust, a dozen fabrics, the reek of cleaning chemicals, the musk of thousands of bodies. He gagged. How had he never noticed what a burden it was to smell things?

He leaned on the door and waited for the nausea to subside. There were so many stinks in this corridor, most of which he could not identify; he could not remember what, if anything, Zora smelled like. He put a hand to his head. The Zora would be an organic smell. They were carbon-and-water-based, and since they had just been here, their smell would be the strongest organic one.

Right?

There it was. A watery, reptilian, faintly familiar smell, starting at the door.

TRANSCENDENT 3

Mimoru followed the trail. Aliens passed him here and there on their way to meetings or meals or whatever else. He did not greet them and kept his eyes downcast, like a proper Íntlànsûran. Smells twisted, turned, and mingled, making him retch.

What was he doing? Bûr-Nïb had said this was illegal. If he brought trouble to Stardust, he'd be fired. If he saw forbidden things, religious things, like Bûr-Nïb had mentioned, he might be investigated. But the Gods knew Mimoru was no heretic. And if he refused, he was even more sure to be fired.

What was she afraid he'd see? Zora praying, chanting, preaching sermons at each other?

Here he was, three turns later, at a closed door in a narrow, vacant side-hall. It was button operated, like most doors on this station, steel, and windowless. It was undoubtedly locked. Mimoru smiled in relief. Definitely, when he pushed the button, it would be locked. He could tell Mr. Haieray, *I'm sorry, I followed them to their room but the door was locked. I did the best I could.* That would solve all of his problems.

He pushed the button.

The first thing that registered, when the door slid open, was the smell. Like blood and rotten flowers, like seafood going bad, like an immense inorganic sea that hated him, specifically.

The Zora were in the room, all six of them, crouched down in what might have been a supplicatory position. But the room —

The room was not a room. Somehow, even though they were comfortably ensconced in miles of halls and corridors, the room opened out and out on the whole galaxy. Mimoru could see all of it, staggering in its size, and behind it, infinite blackness.

Something was alive in that dark. Something bigger than a galaxy, watching with dark eyes bigger than stars. Looking back at the Zora, through the angles afforded by the way the stars aligned. Wondering — Mimoru was certain of this, the way one is certain in nightmares — wondering if it was worth the effort not to destroy them, this time.

Two Zora turned to look at him.

As their heads turned, something in space twisted, like elastic pushed to its limits, and lurched the other way. The room spun and slammed shut, and it was just a room again, a dinky corporate room, like Stardust's, with a set of woven blankets spread over the floor. Just a room. But he'd seen what it was before.

TRANSCENDENT 3

The Zora made a noise, but Mimoru didn't understand. They moved toward him.

Mimoru ran.

By the time the gnawing panic left Mimoru's head, he had already run back to the meeting room on autopilot. Shed his Íntlànsûran disguise almost by reflex, yowling in pain when his joints and scent receptors reverted sharply to their usual forms. Babbled out a half-coherent story to Mr. Haieray. Been sent to the company medic, a squat, usually bored-looking woman named Ushiwo, who had looked him up and down with sudden alarm, dosed him a puff of panic-suppressant gas, took out her diagnostic book, and began a thorough battery of psych tests.

Mimoru's heart rate slowed enough to register that the doctor was on the questions about hallucinations. This was the third time.

Had he hallucinated? Did that explain all this? It would be a relief if he'd hallucinated. It would mean that massive being wasn't still out there.

I've ruined it, he wanted to say. Maybe he said it out loud; he wasn't thinking clearly. *I distracted them, and now, they can't placate that thing, and maybe, we're all doomed.* Out here in alien space where the Gods could not save them.

"In the last six months," said Ushiwo for the third time, "have you experienced anything else you couldn't explain? Flashes of light, spots or shapes in front of your eyes, insects on your skin, voices other people couldn't hear?"

"No," said Mimoru. "Not at all before this."

Ushiwo's initial alarm had subsided into an intense concern. Every few seconds, she frowned, flipped several dozen pages in her diagnostic book, and scowled more deeply.

"Have you taken any recreational substances, legal or illegal, or any medicines other than the ones in your file?"

"No," said Mimoru, his mind still churning. "Listen, are you trying to diagnose if I'm crazy? It's okay if I'm crazy. I'll believe that."

Ushiwo sighed and, for the first time in at least ten minutes, put down her diagnostic book.

"No. I don't think you're crazy. You have no symptoms of anything, aside from the mild Asperger neurotype in your file and this...um...experience. You're not even mood disordered, for fuck's sake."

"But there could be something wrong with my brain," Mimoru babbled. "I was — shapeshifting unwisely. I tried to look like an Íntlànsûran. My joints were out of alignment. I was modifying my scent receptors totally untrained. Who knows what I might have done to my brain? Cranial pressure could have…anything could have…"

"Did you, at any point, modify the size and shape of your skull?" asked Ushiwo.

"No, but — "

"Did you make any attempt, however minor, to physically modify any part of your brain?"

"No, that would be crazy."

"How about the inner workings of the cardiorespiratory, endocrine, or any other systems that can chemically affect the brain's workings?"

"I modified my scent receptors."

Ushiwo looked at him impatiently. "In your brain or in your nose?"

"In my nose."

"Anything else?"

"N-no."

"Then that doesn't count." She picked up the book again. "Shapeshifting has nothing to do with this."

"You don't know that," he said, feeling desperate. "You've never worked with Vaurians. You don't have the specs for Vaurians."

"No, I don't," said Ushiwo. Her mouth had flattened. "What I do have is training in the Gods' official health standards for humans traveling outside human space. I've now run you, more than once, through the full testing that any such human with a report of strange and disturbing sensory experience requires. The results are clear. Your experience today wasn't a hallucination, Mimoru. It was heresy."

Mimoru stared at her and spluttered, his mouth suddenly so dry that he had to work through the muscle movements several times before he could speak.

"Alien heresy," he said. "Alien. The Zora were heretics, not me. I didn't do anything. I didn't know they were doing — whatever it was — when Mr. Haieray sent me to find them. I just — walked in on it and ran away. I didn't do any of what they were doing. I don't believe what they believe."

Ushiwo smiled a bitter little smile with no humor in it. "You believe," she said, "on some level, that there is a great horrible being beyond the galaxy who can be placated through the Zora's ceremony. A being more powerful than the Gods. No matter how you deny it, how you attempt to repress the memory, that belief will remain. And it is a belief that cannot be allowed to defile human space, Mimoru. No matter the cost."

"But — "

But that isn't fair, he couldn't say. When had he ever called the Gods unfair? *But what will happen to me?* he wanted to say.

Ushiwo sighed and tucked the book away, heading for the door. "The Zora weren't on our list of dangerously heretical species. Their specific beliefs were unknown. Obviously, they'll have to be listed now, and this business transaction will be cancelled. The rest of us will go home cranky. You, well, you'll have to wait here. The angels will come for you soon."

"But — " said Mimoru.

The door swished open, and Ushiwo stood at the threshold a moment, regarding him.

"I didn't make the rules," she said, a pained twist at the corner of her mouth. "I'm sorry."

She turned away. The door swished shut, and the lock clicked.

Heretics were terrible people. That was one of the first things they'd learned in school. In between the ABCs and addition, they'd watched history vids about heretics. Watched heretics cut the terrified throats of children, to feed the blood to false gods. Watched heretics blow up buildings, scattering bodies across the ground, just because they didn't like the real Gods. When little Vaurians slept, they feared heretics, not bogeymen, under the bed.

Vaurians had been created to stop them. That was why the Gods had given them so many good things. Being an angel was hard, and the Gods didn't force anyone. But a Vaurian angel could infiltrate heretic groups in ways no other angel could. Tens of times more heretics would be caught, the teachers promised, if Vaurians did their duty. Hundreds. The world would be so much safer.

Only much later had Mimoru learned about minor heresies, degrees of heresy. You didn't have to blow up buildings to be a heretic; you just had to believe the wrong things.

He hadn't known that, yet, when his fifth-grade class was summoned to the amphitheatre, a wide, bright room in the centre of Vaur. They'd huddled together on the plush steps while a group of angels dragged a struggling heretic out in front of them.

He remembered the man: a slender middle-aged man with disheveled black hair. He was the first non-Vaurian, other than angels, that the class had ever seen face to face. Mimoru had memorized that man, in the automatic way that a Vaurian memorized any face. The lines on his face, wrinkles, pockmarks, scabs. He had clearly been tortured. He was trembling. His legs shook so hard, it was a wonder he could stand. The class, callous like most children, giggled. For weeks afterward, in the corridors of Vaur, Mimoru and his classmates had mimicked that man's struggling walk. Jeering to cover an unease they scarcely had words for.

The angels had read the man's crimes to the class and shot him very precisely in the head. There was an immense amount of blood. The class sat silently a moment, shaken, staring. Then a ragged cheer broke out.

What child wouldn't cheer when their bogeyman died?

Mimoru considered all this as he sat, shaking, in the excuse for an infirmary.

He did not think Ushiwo had ever seen an execution. Not close up, at least. Not in anything other than a vid.

He felt ashamed of his fear. The Gods were good, weren't they? You could kill a few people, if that was the law, and still be good. Maybe what he'd seen really did make him dangerous.

But he was afraid, and he wanted to run. Even if it meant running back to the Zora.

You don't know what the angels will do to me, he thought in Ushiwo's direction.

When the door swished open, it wasn't angels or Mr. Haieray. It was Bûr-Nïb. She looked furtively from side to side and gestured for him to follow.

"It's no use," said Mimoru listlessly. "The angels will find us. When they get here, they'll search the station top to bottom."

"Which is why I'm getting tickets on the next transport out. To Glupe, Blackball, Eta Carinae, wherever. You'll stick out, but human Gods can't do as much with extradition orders as you'd think. We'll figure something out."

"They'll find us first."

"Not if we hurry."

He shook his head. "I like you, Bûr-Nïb. I don't want to make you an accessory to...to..."

To whatever this was. Not heresy, he thought, in spite of the Gods' rules. More like — seeing what was inconvenient to see.

TRANSCENDENT 3

"Do you think I'm not?" said Bûr-Nïb. "Do you think I haven't played that scene in the meeting room over a million times? I could have stopped it. Argued harder. Said more."

"More about what?" Mimoru tilted his head, a new horror dawning. "Did… did you know what would happen?"

Bûr-Nïb turned, picked up Ushiwo's diagnosis book, and abruptly tore it in half, throwing both halves to the ground.

"*Humans!*" she shouted, so loudly that Mimoru expected someone to come running. "Humans! Of course I knew! Everyone knows that you're a homicidal theocratic cult! Everyone knows you're crazy. I even told you the Zora were leaving for religious practices. I just didn't — I couldn't get enough words out in time, not ones Mr. Haieray would listen to. And I thought even Zora in full-on cult mode would have the presence of mind to lock their door."

Mimoru's skin rippled as he tried to digest this. "Ushiwo said nobody knew."

"About Zora? I hope not. There are a million things nobody tells humans because we know that as soon as you find out, you'll cut off contact with a whole species and execute any humans who met them. Humans!" She bit her lip, fighting for control, and took another heaving breath. Mimoru had never seen her this angry, not in the face of Mr. Haieray's worst excesses. "And I wouldn't even be telling you this much. I wouldn't stick my neck out for a human, not even a friend. Except you're not really one of them, are you? You're not a human."

"Vaurians are human," Mimoru said. It was automatic, a phrase he'd repeated constantly since leaving Vaur.

"So?"

He wasn't a very good human. And he wasn't a very good Vaurian, either.

He didn't want to die. He might be damned anyway, even if he escaped. The Gods would find his heretic soul, in the end, and visit upon it all the punishments he'd avoided in life. But until then…

What would he be leaving behind? Mr. Haieray. A vast array of worlds that didn't want him. Vaur, which he had left behind anyway, for better or worse. A family that had already moved on.

He took a deep breath.

"Okay," he said and followed her out the door.

Mimoru watched Hex Station spiral away through his tiny porthole as the Aikita transport launched. The station had not been destroyed yet.

TRANSCENDENT 3

Maybe the Zora had carried on after his interruption and fixed it. He hoped he would never find out.

He remembered flying away like this from Vaur Station, his first year of college. Not knowing what awaited him.

Vaurians were an experiment. The experiment was ongoing. Mimoru's part of it had failed — but, then, he'd known that long ago. Maybe it was time to stop judging by the standards of a species that didn't want him and start judging by his own.

Bûr-Nïb shifted beside him, her gaze fixed on her nails. The violet glow of the warp drive flared out around the porthole, and the station disappeared from view.

TRANSCENDENT 3

THE HEAVY THINGS

◄ Julian K. Jarboe ►

I got my period young, and heavy. Heavier than the health class pamphlet said it should be. When it came for the first time, I felt something prickling parts of me I'd never seen, and had been told never to touch.

In the elementary school bathroom, I tried to clean myself up with all of the paper towels I could grab, but I was frightened and clumsy. I cut my finger on something down there, the prickling thing. I was not the most hygienic kid and thought maybe it was a woodchip from the playground, somehow. I pried and found it again, and pulled. Out came a small sewing needle. The eye was barely wide enough for the finest thread, but it was unmistakable.

I suspected there were things we weren't learning from our health pamphlets, and wondered if this was one of them. By middle school, there were bigger needles, and small keys, and decorative screws, and the tiniest little pair of scissors, like something you'd get for a doll.

I told no one about what was happening with my body, and I certainly didn't ask if it was happening to theirs. School offered few answers. In biology class, I learned about eggs and sperm like they were tidal creatures outside ourselves, fascinating and mysterious but alien. In gym, the teacher told us about wearing deodorant and eating vegetables. She said it was cool and okay to be a virgin and everybody giggled.

Then the nurse and the guidance counselors took us into a special assembly where my options became more clear. We watched a half-melted old tape of a made-for-TV movie about a girl who wants to fit in at school so she stops eating to be skinny, and all her hair falls out and she feels awful, but along with everything else, her period stops coming. I had no idea such a thing was possible.

When I was older, I got myself to a doctor. I filled out a form that asked me about my cycle. I wrote down the dates of my last three, and noted that they had been a nail clipper, a construction screw, and a hex key. I asked the doctor about inducing amenorrhea. I said it just like that to sound medically informed. She frowned and looked at the clock on the wall.

The doctor admitted there were hormonal suppressants safer than an eating disorder. There was a white pill that I could take every day but it would make me much fatter and it might make me cry. There was a yellow shot I could take every week but it would make me much hairier and I might stop crying altogether. She presented both options as hopeless, because if I changed my mind, I'd be permanently fatter or hairier, by which she meant uglier, which even doctors equated with unhealthy.

I picked the yellow shot, though it took three hours to convince her. I said I'd starve myself otherwise and then the harm would be her fault. But I left with my prescription and I grew thick, beautiful hair all over my body and gained some lovely weight anyway and tools stopped growing and shedding from my uterine lining.

I was happier, until things changed in the world and medicine got expensive and hard to find and the sliding-scale clinics closed. I knew someone who could get me something under the table, but it would take a while. It would take too long, I felt, but I'd have to wait.

When my period came back, it was worse than before. I doubled over, confined to my bed with cramps for days, ruining all my sheets. I felt the sharp end of a screwdriver pushing down and out between my thighs. I dragged myself to the bathroom, and pulled down my sick day sweatpants and old boxers. The screwdriver handle was still partially wedged into my cervix, and pinching hard. I plucked out the useless, over-saturated tampon blocking it and felt around inside for a grip on the thing until, humming to myself between Hallelujah breaths, I yanked it out. I rinsed it off and looked it over as I washed my thighs and hands. It was a Phillips head.

Reluctantly, I begged my parents for help. Just a little money to get that under-the-table connection to work faster.

My mother said she and my father would always take care of me in my time of need. They paid for lunch and she suggested I go off my shots for a while, anyway. She said I should give my body a break.

I said it did not work like that. I didn't need to detox. She shook her head, said she was just worried about me. Said it was a mean world out there. Asked me what the long-term effects of the drugs were, anyway?

I pointed at dad, at his bald head and his beard. I said that's what the long-term effects are. I asked if she would give her body a rest from her heart medication. She shook her head again. It was hard for them to look at me.

Desperate, I finally told them about the screwdriver, and the years of nails and scissors and needles and keys, and how they were getting larger. I thought, if nothing else, they'd see the simple benefit of relieving me of this. They appeared to be listening. They looked at each other with serious faces and then at me with serious faces.

You know, my father idled aloud, it was your grandmother who had all the gadgets in the house when I was growing up. She found it very empowering.

My mother smiled. They can be very expensive, she nodded, as if in agreement. Do you think, she asked, you might be able to get a cordless drill or a nice knife set in time for Christmas?

TRANSCENDENT 3

DON'T PRESS CHARGES
AND I WON'T SUE

◄ Charlie Jane Anders ►

The intake process begins with dismantling her personal space, one mantle at a time. Her shoes, left by the side of the road where the Go Team plucked her out of them. Her purse and satchel, her computer containing all of her artwork and her manifestos, thrown into a metal garbage can at a rest area on the highway, miles away. That purse, which she swung to and fro on the sidewalks to clear a path, like a southern grandma, now has food waste piled on it, and eventually will be chewed to shreds by raccoons. At some point the intake personnel fold her, like a folding chair that turns into an almost two-dimensional object, and they stuff her into a kennel, in spite of all her attempts to resist. Later she receives her first injection and loses any power to struggle, and some time after, control over her excretory functions. By the time they cut her clothes off, a layer of muck coats the backs of her thighs. They clean her and dress her in something that is not clothing, and they shave part of her head. At some point, Rachel glimpses a power drill, like a handyman's, but she's anesthetized and does not feel where it goes.

Rachel has a whole library of ways to get through this, none of which works at all. She spent a couple years meditating, did a whole course on trauma and self-preservation, and had an elaborate theory about how to carve out a space in your mind that *they* cannot touch, whatever *they* are doing to you. She remembers the things she used to tell everyone else in the support group, in the Safe Space, about not being alone even when you have become isolated by outside circumstances. But in the end, Rachel's only coping mechanism is dissociation, which arises from total animal panic. She's not even Rachel anymore, she's just a screaming blubbering mess, with a tiny kernel of her mind left, trapped a few feet above her body, in a process that is not at all like yogic flying.

Eventually, though, the intake is concluded, and Rachel is left staring up at a Styrofoam ceiling with a pattern of cracks that looks like a giant spider or an angry demon face descending toward her. She's aware of being numb from extreme cold in addition to the other ways in which she is numb, and the air conditioner keeps blurting into life with an aggravated whine. A stereo system plays a CD by that white rock-rap artist who turned out to be an especially ignorant racist. The staff keep walking past her and talking about her in the third person, while misrepresenting basic facts about her, such as her name and her personal pronoun. Occasionally they adjust something about her position or drug regimen without speaking to her or looking at her face. She does not quite have enough motor control to scream or make any sound other than a kind of low ululation. She realizes at some point that someone has made a tiny hole in the base of her skull, where she now feels a mild ache.

Before you feel too sorry for Rachel, however, you should be aware that she's a person who holds a great many controversial views. For example, she once claimed to disapprove of hot chocolate, because she believes that chocolate is better at room temperature, or better yet as a component of ice cream or some other frozen dessert. In addition, Rachel considers ZZ Top an underappreciated music group, supports karaoke only in an alcohol-free environment, dislikes puppies, enjoys Brussels sprouts, and rides a bicycle with no helmet. She claims to prefer the *Star Wars* prequels to the Disney *Star Wars* films. Is Rachel a contrarian, a freethinker, or just kind of an asshole? If you could ask her, she would reply that opinions are a utility in and of themselves. That is, the holding of opinions is a worthwhile exercise per se, and the greater diversity of opinions in the world, the more robust our collective ability to argue.

Also! Rachel once got a gas station attendant nearly fired for behavior that, a year or two later, she finally conceded might have been an honest misunderstanding. She's the kind of person who sends food back for not being quite what she ordered — and on at least two occasions, she did this and then returned to that same restaurant a week or two later, as if she had been happy after all. Rachel is the kind of person who calls herself an artist, despite never having received a grant from a granting institution, or any kind of formal gallery show, and many people wouldn't even consider her collages and relief maps of imaginary places to be proper art. You would probably call Rachel a Goth.

Besides dissociation — which is wearing off as the panic subsides — the one defense mechanism that remains for Rachel is carrying on an imaginary conversation with Dev, the person with whom she spoke every day for so long, and to whom she always imagined speaking, whenever they were apart. Dev's voice in Rachel's head would have been a refuge not long ago, but now all Rachel can imagine Dev saying is, *Why did you leave me? Why, when I needed you most?* Rachel does not have a good answer to that question, which is why she never tried to answer it when she had the chance.

Thinking about Dev, about lost chances, is too much. And at that moment, Rachel realizes she has enough muscle control to lift her head and look directly in front of her. There, standing at an observation window, she sees her childhood best friend, Jeffrey.

Ask Jeffrey why he's been working at Love and Dignity for Everyone for the past few years and he'll say, first and foremost, student loans. Plus, in recent years, child support, and his mother's ever-increasing medical bills. Life is crammed full of things that you have to pay for after the fact, and the word "plan" in "payment plan" is a cruel mockery because nobody ever really sets out to plunge into chronic debt. But also Jeffrey wants to believe in the mission of Love and Dignity for Everyone: to repair the world's most broken people. Jeffrey often re-reads the mission statement on the wall of the employee lounge as he sips his morning Keurig so he can carry Mr. Randall's words with him for the rest of the day. Society depends on mutual respect, Mr. Randall says. You respect yourself and therefore I respect you, and vice versa. When people won't respect themselves, we have no choice but to intervene, or society unravels. Role-rejecting and aberrant behavior, ipso facto, is a sign of a lack of self-respect. Indeed, a cry for help. The logic always snaps back into airtight shape inside Jeffrey's mind.

Of course Jeffrey recognizes Rachel the moment he sees her wheeled into the treatment room, even after all this time and so many changes, because he's been Facebook-stalking her for years (usually after a couple of whiskey sours). He saw when she changed her name and her gender marker, and noticed when her hairstyle changed and when her face suddenly had a more feminine shape. There was the kitten she adopted that later ran away, and the thorny tattoo that says STAY ALIVE. Jeffrey read all her oversharing status updates about the pain of hair removal and the side effects of various pills. And then, of course, the crowning surgery. Jeffrey lived through this process vicariously, in real time, and saw no resemblance to a butterfly in a cocoon, or any other cute metaphor. The gender change looked more like landscaping: building embankments out of raw dirt, heaving big rocks to change the course of rivers, and uprooting plants stem by stem. Dirty bruising work. Why a person would feel the need to do this to themself, Jeffrey could never know.

At first, Jeffrey pretends not to know the latest subject, or to have any feelings one way or the other, as the Accu-Probe goes into the back of her head. This is not the right moment to have a sudden conflict. Due to some recent personnel issues, Jeffrey is stuck wearing a project manager hat along with his engineer hat — which, sadly, is not a cool pinstriped train-engineer hat of the sort that he and Rachel used to fantasize about wearing for work when they were kids. As a project manager, he has to worry endlessly about weird details such as getting enough coolant into the cadaver storage area and making sure that Jamil has the green shakes that he says activate his brain. As a government-industry joint venture under Section 1774(b)(8) of the Mental Health Restoration Act (relating to the care and normalization of at-risk individuals), Love and Dignity for Everyone has to meet certain benchmarks of effectiveness, and must involve the community in a meaningful role. Jeffrey is trying to keep twenty fresh cadavers in transplant-ready condition, and clearing the decks for more live subjects, who are coming down the pike at an ever-snowballing rate. The situation resembles one of those poultry processing plants where they keep speeding up the conveyer belt until the person grappling with each chicken ends up losing a few fingers.

Jeffrey runs from the cadaver freezer to the observation room to the main conference room for another community engagement session, around and around, until his Fitbit applauds. Five different Slack channels flare at once with people wanting to ask Jeffrey process questions, and he's lost count of all his unanswered DMs. Everyone agrees on the goal — returning healthy, well-adjusted individuals to society without any trace of dysphoria, dysmorphia, dystonia, or any other dys- words — but nobody can agree on the fine details, or how exactly to measure ideal outcomes beyond those statutory benchmarks. Who even is the person who comes out the other end of the Love and Dignity for Everyone process? What does it mean to be a unique individual, in an age when your fingerprints and retina scans have long since been stolen by Ecuadorian hackers?

TRANSCENDENT 3

It's all too easy to get sucked into metaphysical flusterclucks about identity and the soul and what makes you you.

Jeffrey's near-daily migraine is already in full flower by the time he sees Rachel wheeled in and he can't bring himself to look. She's looking at him. She's looking right at him. Even with all the other changes, her eyes are the same, and he can't just stand here. She's putting him in an impossible position, at the worst moment.

Someone has programmed Slack so that when anyone types "alrighty then," a borderline-obscene GIF of two girls wearing clown makeup appears. Jeffrey is the only person who ever types "alrighty then," and he can't train himself to stop doing it. And, of course, he hasn't been able to figure out who programmed the GIF to appear.

Self-respect is the key to mutual respect. Jeffrey avoids making eye contact with that window or anyone beyond it. His head still feels too heavy with pain for a normal body to support, but also he's increasingly aware of a core-deep anxiety shading into nausea.

Jeffrey and Rachel had a group, from the tail end of elementary school through to the first year of high school, called the Sock Society. They all lived in the same cul-de-sac, bounded by a canola field on one side and the big interstate on the other. The origins of the Sock Society's name are lost to history, but may arise from the fact that Jeffrey's mom never liked kids to wear shoes inside the house and Jeffrey's house had the best game consoles and a 4K TV with surround sound. These kids wore out countless pairs of tires on their dirt bikes, conquered the extra DLC levels in Halls of Valor, and built snow forts that gleamed. They stayed up all night at sleepovers watching forbidden horror movies on an old laptop under a blanket while guzzling off-brand soda. They whispered, late at night, of their fantasies and barely-hinted-at anxieties, although there were some things Rachel would not share because she was not ready to speak of them and Jeffrey would not have been able to hear if she had. They repeated jokes they didn't one-hundred percent understand, and kind of enjoyed the queasy awareness of being out of their depth. Later, the members of the Sock Society (which changed its ranks over time with the exception of the core members, Rachel and Jeffrey) became adept at stuffing gym socks with blasting caps and small incendiaries and fashioning the socks themselves into rudimentary fuses before placing them in lawn ornaments, small receptacles

TRANSCENDENT 3

for gardening tools, and — in one incident that nobody discussed afterward — Mrs. Hooper's scooter.

When Jeffrey's mother was drunk, which was often, she would say she wished Rachel was her son, because Rachel was such a smart boy — quick on the uptake, so charming with the rapid-fire puns, handsome and respectful. Like Young Elvis. Instead of Jeffrey, who was honestly a little shit.

Jeffrey couldn't wait to get over the wall of adolescence, into the garden of manhood. Every dusting of fuzz on his chin, every pungent whiff from his armpits seemed to him the starting gun. He became obsessed with finding porn via that old laptop, and he was an artist at coming up with fresh new search terms every time he and Rachel hung out. Rachel got used to innocent terms such as "cream pie" turning out to mean something gross and animalistic, in much the same way that a horror movie turned human bodies into slippery meat.

Then one time Jeffrey pulled up some transsexual porn, because what the hell. Rachel found herself watching a slender Latina with a shy smile slowly peel out of a silk robe to step into a scene with a muscular bald man. The girl was wearing nothing but bright silver shoes and her body was all smooth angles and tapering limbs, and the one piece of evidence of her transgender status looked tiny, both inconsequential and of a piece with the rest of her femininity. She tiptoed across the frame like a ballerina. Like a cartoon deer.

Watching this, Rachel quivered, until Jeffrey thought she must be grossed out, but deep down Rachel was having a feeling of recognition. Like: that's me. Like: I am possible.

Years later, in her twenties, Rachel had a group of girlfriends (some trans, some cis) and she started calling this feminist gang the Sock Society, because they made a big thing of wearing colorful socks with weird and sometimes profane patterns. Rachel mostly didn't think about the fact that she had repurposed the Sock Society sobriquet for another group, except to tell herself that she was reclaiming an ugly part of her past. Rachel is someone who obsesses about random issues, but also claims to avoid introspection at all costs — in fact, she once proposed an art show called *The Unexamined Life Is the Only Way to Have Fun*.

Rachel has soiled herself again. A woman in avocado-colored scrubs snaps on blue gloves with theatrical weariness before sponging Rachel's still-unfeeling body. The things I have to deal with, says the red-faced woman, whose name is Lucy. People like you always make people like me clean up after you, because you never think the rules apply to you, the same as literally everyone else. And then look where we end up, and I'm here cleaning your mess.

Rachel tries to protest that none of this is her doing, but her tongue is a slug that's been bathed in salt.

There's always some excuse, Lucy says as she scrubs. Life is not complicated, it's actually very simple. Men are men, and women are women, and everyone has a role to play. It's selfish to think that you can just force everyone else in the world to start carving out exceptions, just so you can play at being something you're not. You will never understand what it really means to be female, the joy and the endless discomfort, because you were not born into it.

Rachel feels frozen solid. Ice crystals permeate her body, the way they would frozen dirt. This woman is touching between her legs, without looking her in the face. She cannot bear to breathe. She keeps trying to get Jeffrey's attention, but he always looks away. As if he'd rather not witness what's going to happen to her.

Lucy and a man in scrubs wheel in something gauzy and white, like a cloud on a gurney. They bustle around, unwrapping and cleaning and prepping, and they mutter numbers and codes to each other, like E-drop 2347, as if there are a lot of parameters to keep straight here. The sound of all that quiet professionalism soothes Rachel in spite of herself, like she's at the dentist.

At some point they step away from the thing they've unwrapped and prepped, and Rachel turns her head just enough to see a dead man on a metal shelf.

Her first thought is that he's weirdly good looking, despite his slight decomposition. He has a snub nose and thin lips, a clipped jaw, good muscle definition, a cyanotic penis that flops against one thigh, and sandy pubic hair. Whatever (whoever) killed this man left his body in good condition, and he was roughly Rachel's age. This man could have been a model or maybe a pro wrestler, and Rachel feels sad that he somehow died so early, with his best years ahead.

Rachel tries to scream. She feels Lucy and the other one connecting her to the dead man's body and hears a rattling garbage-disposal sound. The dead man twitches, and meanwhile Rachel can't struggle or make a sound. She feels weaker than before, and some part of her insists this must be because she lost an argument at some point. Back in the Safe Space, they had talked about all the friends of friends who had gone to ground, and the Internet rumors. How would you know if you were in danger? Rachel had said that was a dumb question because danger never left.

The dead man smiles: not a large rictus, like in a horror movie, but a tiny shift in his features, like a contented sleeper. His eyes haven't moved or appeared to look at anything. Lucy clucks and adjusts a thing, and the kitchen-garbage noise grinds louder for a moment.

We're going to get you sorted out, Lucy says to the dead man. You are going to be so happy. She turns and leans over Rachel to check something, and her breath smells like sour corn chips.

You are violating my civil rights by keeping me here, Rachel says. A sudden victory, except that then she hears herself and it's wrong. Her voice comes out of the wrong mouth, is not even her own voice. The dead man has spoken, not her, and he didn't say that thing about civil rights. Instead he said, Hey, excuse me, how long am I going to be kept here? As if this were a mild inconvenience keeping him from his business. The voice sounded rough, flinty, like a bad sore throat, but also commanding. The voice of a surgeon, or an airline pilot. You would stop whatever you were doing and listen, if you heard that voice.

Rachel lets out an involuntary cry of panic, which comes out of the dead man's mouth as a low groan. She tries again to say, This is not medicine. This is a human rights violation. And it comes out of the dead man's mouth as, I don't mean to be a jerk. I just have things to do, you know. Sorry if I'm causing any trouble.

That's quite all right, Mr. Billings, Lucy says. You're making tremendous progress, and we're so pleased. You'll be released into the community soon, and the community will be so happy to see you.

The thought of ever trying to speak again fills Rachel with a whole ocean voyage's worth of nausea, but she can't even make herself retch.

Jeffrey has wondered for years, what if he could talk to his oldest friend, man to man, about the things that had happened when they were on the cusp of adolescence — not just the girl, but the whole deal. Mrs. Hooper's scooter, even. And maybe, at last, he will. A lot depends on how well the process goes. Sometimes the cadaver gets almost all of the subject's memories and personality, just with a better outlook on his or her proper gender. There is, however, a huge variability in bandwidth because we're dealing with human beings and especially with weird neurological stuff that we barely understand. We're trying to thread wet spaghetti through a grease trap, a dozen pieces at a time. Even with the proprietary cocktail, it's hardly an exact science.

TRANSCENDENT 3

The engineer part of Jeffrey just wants to keep the machines from making whatever noise that was earlier, the awful grinding sound. But the project manager part of Jeffrey is obsessing about all of the extraneous factors outside his control. What if they get a surprise inspection from the Secretary, or even worse that Deputy Assistant Secretary, with the eye? Jeffrey is not supposed to be a front-facing part of this operation, but Mr. Randall says we all do things that are outside our comfort zones, and really, that's the only way your comfort zone can ever expand. In addition, Jeffrey is late for another stakeholder meeting, with the woman from Mothers Raising Well-Adjusted Children and the three bald men from Grassroots Rising, who will tear Jeffrey a new orifice. There are still too many maladjusted individuals out there, in the world, trying to use public bathrooms and putting our children at risk. Some children, too, keep insisting that they aren't boys or girls because they saw some ex-athlete prancing on television. Twenty cadavers in the freezer might as well be nothing in the face of all this. The three bald men will take turns spit-shouting, using words such as psychosexual, and Jeffrey has fantasized about sneaking bourbon into his coffee so he can drink whenever that word comes up. He's pretty sure they don't know what psychosexual even means, except that it's psycho and it's sexual. After a stakeholder meeting, Jeffrey always retreats to the single-stall men's room to shout at his own schmutzy reflection. Fuck you, you fucking fuck fucker. Don't tell me I'm not doing my job.

Self-respect is the key to mutual respect.

Rachel keeps looking straight at Jeffrey through the observation window, and she's somehow kept control over her vision long after her speech centers went over. He keeps waiting for her to lose the eyes. Her gaze goes right into him, and his stomach gets the feeling that usually comes after two or three whiskey sours and no dinner.

More than ever, Jeffrey wishes the observation room had a one-way mirror instead of regular glass. Why would they skimp on that? What's the point of having an observation room where you are also being observed at the same time? It defeats the entire purpose.

Jeffrey gets tired of hiding from his own window and skips out the side door. He climbs two stories of cement stairs to emerge in the executive wing, near the conference suite where he's supposed to be meeting with the stakeholders right now. He finds an oaken door with that quote from Albert Einstein about imagination that everybody always has and knocks on it. After a few breaths, a deep voice tells Jeffrey to come in, and then he's sitting opposite an older man with square shoulders and a perfect old-fashioned newscaster head.

Mr. Randall, Jeffrey says, I'm afraid I have a conflict with regards to the latest subject and I must ask to be recused.

Is that a fact? Mr. Randall furrows his entire face for a moment, then magically all the wrinkles disappear again. He smiles and shakes his head. I feel you, Jeffrey, I really do. That blows chunks. Unfortunately, as you know, we are short-staffed right now, and our work is of a nature that only a few people have the skills and moral virtue to complete it.

But, Jeffrey says. The new subject, he's someone I grew up with, and there are certain…I mean, I made promises when we were little, and it feels in some ways like I'm breaking those promises, even as I try my best to help him. I actually feel physically ill, like drunk in my stomach but sober in my brain, when I look at him.

Jeffrey, Mr. Randall says, Jeffrey, JEFFREY. Listen to me. Sit still and listen. Pull yourself together. We are the watchers on the battlements, at the edge of social collapse, like in that show with the ice zombies, where winter is always to-morrow. You know that show? They had an important message, that sometimes we have to put our own personal feelings aside for the greater good. Remember the fat kid? He had to learn to be a team player. I loved that show. So here we are, standing against the darkness that threatens to consume everything we admire. No time for divided hearts.

I know that we're doing something important here, and that he'll thank me later, Jeffrey says. It's just hard right now.

If it were easy to do the right thing, Randall says, then everyone would do it.

Sherri was a transfer student in tenth grade who came right in and joined the Computer Club but also tried out for the volleyball team and the a cappella chorus. She had dark hair in tight braids and a wiry body that flexed in the moment before she leapt to spike the ball, making Rachel's heart rise with her. Rachel sat courtside and watched Sherri practice while she was supposed to be doing sudden death sprints.

Jeffrey stared at Sherri, too: listened to her sing Janelle Monáe in a light contralto when she waited for the bus, and gazed at her across the room during Computer Club. He imagined going up to her and just introducing himself, but his heart was too weak. He could more easily imagine saying the dumbest thing, or actually fainting, than carrying on a smooth conversation with Sherri. He obsessed for ages, until he finally confessed to his friends (Rachel was long since out of the picture by this time), and they started goading him, actually physically shoving him, to speak to Sherri.

Jeffrey slid up to her and said his name, and something inane about music, and then Sherri just stared at him for a long time before saying, I gotta get the bus. Jeffrey watched her walk away, then turned to his watching friends and mimed a finger gun blowing his brains out.

A few days later, Sherri was playing hooky at that one bakery cafe in town that everyone said was run by lesbians or drug addicts or maybe just old hippies, nursing a chai latte, and she found herself sitting with Rachel, who was also ditching some activity. Neither of them wanted to talk to anyone, they'd come here to be alone. But Rachel felt hope rise up inside her at the proximity of her wildfire crush, and she finally hoisted her bag as if she might just leave the cafe. Mind if I sit with you a minute, she asked, and Sherri shrugged yes. So Rachel perched on the embroidered tasseled pillow on the bench next to Sherri and stared at her Algebra II book.

They saw each other at that cafe every few days, or sometimes just once a week, and they just started sitting together on purpose, without talking to each other much. After a couple months of this, Sherri looked at the time on her phone and said, My mom's out of town. I'll buy you dinner. Rachel kept her shriek of joy on the inside and just nodded.

At dinner — a family pasta place nearby — Sherri looked down at her colorful paper napkin and whispered: I think I don't like boys. I mean, to date, or whatever. I don't hate boys or anything, just not interested that way. You understand.

Rachel stared at Sherri, even after she looked up, so they were making eye contact. In just as low a whisper, Rachel replied: I'm pretty sure I'm not a boy.

This was the first time Rachel ever said the name Rachel aloud, at least with regard to herself.

Sherri didn't laugh or get up or run away. She just stared back, then nodded. She reached onto the red checkerboard vinyl tablecloth with an open palm, for Rachel to insert her palm into if she so chose.

The first time Jeffrey saw Rachel and Sherri holding hands, he looked at them like his soul had come out in bruises.

TRANSCENDENT 3

We won't keep you here too long, Mr. Billings, the male attendant says, glancing at Rachel but mostly looking at the mouth that had spoken. You're doing very well. Really, you're an exemplary subject. You should be so proud.

There are so many things that Rachel wants to say. Like: Please just let me go, I have a life. I have an art show coming up in a coffee shop, I can't miss it. You don't have the right. I deserve to live my own life. I have people who used to love me. I'll give you everything I own. I won't press charges if you don't sue. This is no kind of therapy. On and on. But she can't trust that corpse voice. She hyperventilates and gags on her own spit. So sore she's hamstrung.

Every time her eyes get washed out, she's terrified this is it, her last sight. She knows from what Lucy and the other one have said that if her vision switches over to the dead man's, that's the final stage and she's gone.

The man is still talking. We have a form signed by your primary care physician, Dr. Wallace, stating that this treatment is both urgent and medically indicated, as well as an assessment by our in-house psychologist, Dr. Yukizawa. He holds up two pieces of paper, with the looping scrawls of two different doctors that she's never even heard of. She's been seeing Dr. Cummings for years, since before her transition. She makes a huge effort to shake her head, and is shocked by how weak she feels.

You are so fortunate to be one of the first to receive this treatment, the man says. Early indications are that subjects experience a profound improvement across seven different measures of quality of life and social integration. Their OGATH scores are generally high, especially in the red levels. Rejection is basically unheard of. You won't believe how good you'll feel once you're over the adjustment period, he says. If the research goes well, the potential benefits to society are limited only by the cadaver pipeline.

Rachel's upcoming art show, in a tiny coffee shop, is called Against Curation. There's a lengthy manifesto, which Rachel planned to print out and mount onto foam or cardboard, claiming that the act of curating is inimical to art or artistry. The only person who can create a proper context for a given piece of art is the artist herself, and arranging someone else's art is an act of violence. Bear in mind that the history of museums is intrinsically tied up with imperialism and colonialism, and the curatorial gaze is historically white and male. But even the most enlightened postcolonial curator is a pirate. Anthologies, mix tapes, it's all the same. Rachel had a long response prepared, in case anybody accused her of just being annoyed that no real gallery would display her work.

Rachel can't help noting the irony of writing a tirade about the curator's bloody scalpel, only to end up with a hole in her literal head.

When the man has left her alone, Rachel begins screaming Jeffrey's name in the dead man's voice. Just the name, nothing that the corpse could twist. She still can't bear to hear that deep timbre, the sick damaged throat, speaking for her. But she can feel her life essence slipping away. Every time she looks over at the dead man, he has more color in his skin and his arms and legs are moving, like a restless sleeper. His face even looks, in some hard-to-define way, more like Rachel's.

Jeffrey! The words come out in a hoarse growl. Jeffrey! Come here!

Rachel wants to believe she's already defeated this trap, because she has lived her life without a single codicil, and whatever they do, they can't retroactively change the person she has been for her entire adulthood. But that doesn't feel like enough. She wants the kind of victory where she gets to actually walk out of here.

Jeffrey feels a horrible twist in his neck. This is all unfair, because he already informed Mr. Randall of his conflict and yet he's still here, having to behave professionally while the subject is putting him in the dead center of attention.

Seriously, the subject will not stop bellowing his name, even with a throat that's basically raw membrane at this point. You're not supposed to initiate communication with the subject without submitting an Interlocution Permission form through the proper channels. But the subject is putting him into an impossible position.

Jeffrey, she keeps shouting. And then: Jeffrey, talk to me!

People are lobbing questions in Slack, and of course Jeffrey types the wrong thing and the softcore clown porn comes up. Ha ha, I fell for it again, he types. There's a problem with one of the latest cadavers, a cause-of-death question, and Mr. Randall says the Deputy Assistant Secretary might be in town later.

Jeffrey's mother was a Nobel Prize winner for her work with people who had lost the ability to distinguish between weapons and musical instruments, a condition that frequently leads to maiming or worse. Jeffrey's earliest memories involve his mother flying off to serve as an expert witness in the trials of murderers who claimed they had thought their assault rifles were banjos, or mandolins.

TRANSCENDENT 3

Many of these people were faking it, but Jeffrey's mom was usually hired by the defense, not the prosecution. Every time she returned from one of these trips, she would fling her Nobel medal out her bathroom window, and then stay up half the night searching the bushes for it, becoming increasingly drunk. One morning, Jeffrey found her passed out below her bedroom window and believed for a moment that she had fallen two stories to her death. This was, she explained to him later, a different sort of misunderstanding than mistaking a gun for a guitar: a reverse-Oedipal misapprehension. These days Jeffrey's mom requires assistance to dress, to shower, and to transit from her bed to a chair and back, and nobody can get Medicare, Medicaid, or any secondary insurance to pay for this. To save money, Jeffrey has moved back in with his mother, which means he gets to hear her ask at least once a week what happened to Rachel, who was such a nice boy.

Jeffrey can't find his headphones to drown out his name, which the cadaver is shouting so loud that foam comes out of one corner of his mouth. Frances and another engineer both complain on Slack about the noise, which they can hear from down the hall. OMG creepy, Frances types. Make it stop make it stop

I can't, Jeffrey types back. I can't ok. I don't have the right paperwork.

Maybe tomorrow, Rachel will wake up fully inhabiting her male body. She'll look down at her strong forearms, threaded with veins, and she'll smile and thank Jeffrey. Maybe she'll nod at him, by way of a tiny salute, and say, You did it, buddy. You brought me back.

But right now, the cadaver keeps shouting, and Jeffrey realizes he's covering his ears with his fists and is doubled over.

Rachel apparently decides that Jeffrey's name alone isn't working. The cadaver pauses and then blurts, I would really love to hang with you. Hey! I appreciate everything you've done to set things right. JEFFREY! You really shouldn't have gone to so much trouble for me.

Somehow, these statements have an edge, like Jeffrey can easily hear the intended meaning. He looks up and sees Rachel's eyes, spraying tears like a damn lawn sprinkler.

Jeffrey, the corpse says, I saw Sherri. She told me the truth about you.

She's probably just making things up. Sherri never knew anything for sure, or at least couldn't prove anything. And yet, just the mention of her name is enough to make Jeffrey straighten up and walk to the door of the observation room, even with no signed Interlocution Permission form. Jeffrey makes him-

TRANSCENDENT 3

self stride up to the two nearly naked bodies and stop at the one on the left, the one with the ugly tattoo and the drooling silent mouth.

I don't want to hurt you, Jeffrey says. I never wanted to hurt you, even when we were kids and you got weird on me. My mom still asks about you.

Hey pal, you've never been a better friend to me than you are right now, the cadaver says. But on the left, the eyes are red and wet and full of violence.

What did Sherri say? Stop playing games and tell me, Jeffrey says. When did you see her? What did she say?

But Rachel has stopped trying to make the other body talk and is just staring up, letting her eyes speak for her.

L isten, Jeffrey says to the tattooed body. This is already over, the process is too advanced. I could disconnect all of the machines, unplug the tap from your occipital lobe and everything, and the cadaver would continue drawing your remaining life energy. The link between you is already stable. This project, it's a government-industry collaboration, we call it Love and Dignity for Everyone. You have no idea. But you, you're going to be so handsome. You always used to wish you could look like this guy, remember? I'm actually kind of jealous of you.

Rachel just thrashes against her restraints harder than ever.

Here, I'll show you, Jeffrey says at last. He reaches behind Rachel's obsolete head and unplugs the tap, along with the other wires. See? he says. No difference. That body is already more you than you. It's already done.

That's when Rachel leans forward, in her old body, and head-butts Jeffrey, before grabbing for his key ring with the utility knife on it. She somehow gets the knife open with one hand while he's clutching his nose, and slashes a bloody canyon across Jeffrey's stomach. He falls, clutching at his own slippery flesh, and watches her saw through her straps and land on unsteady feet. She lifts Jeffrey's lanyard, smearing blood on his shirt as it goes.

W hen Rachel was in college, she heard a story about a business professor named Lou, who dated two different women and strung them both along. Laurie was a lecturer in women's studies, while Susie worked in the bookstore co-op despite having a PhD in comp lit. After the women found out Lou was dating both of them, things got ugly. Laurie stole Susie's identity, signing her up for a stack of international phone cards and a subscription to the Dirndl of the Month Club, while Susie tried to crash Laurie's truck and cold-cocked

Laurie as she walked out of a seminar on intersectional feminism. In the end, the two women looked at each other, over the slightly dented truck and Laurie's bloody lip and Susie's stack of junk mail. Laurie just spat blood and said, Listen. I won't press charges, if you don't sue. Susie thought for a moment, then stuck out her hand and said, Deal. The two women never spoke to each other, or Lou, ever again.

Rachel has always thought this incident exposed the roots of the social contract: most of our relationships are upheld not by love, or obligation, or gratitude, but by mutually assured destruction. Most of the people in Rachel's life who could have given her shit for being transgender were differently bodied, non-neurotypical, or some other thing that also required some acceptance from her. Mote, beam, and so on.

For some reason, Rachel can't stop thinking about the social contract and mutually assured destruction as she hobbles down the hallway of Love and Dignity for Everyone with a corpse following close behind. Every time she pauses to turn around and see if the dead man is catching up, he gains a little ground. So she forces herself to keep running with weak legs, even as she keeps hearing his hoarse breath right behind her. True power, Rachel thinks, is being able to destroy others with no consequences to yourself.

She's reached the end of a corridor, and she's trying not to think about Jeffrey's blood on the knife in her hand. He'll be fine, he's in a facility. She remembers Sherri in the computer lab, staring at the pictures on the Internet: her hair wet from the shower, one hand reaching for a towel. Sherri sobbing but then tamping it down as she looked at the screen. Sherri telling Rachel at lunch, I'm leaving this school. I can't stay. There's a heavy door with an RFID reader, and Jeffrey's card causes it to click twice before finally bleeping. Rachel's legs wobble and spasm, and the breath of the dead man behind her grows louder. Then she pushes through the door and runs up the square roundabout of stairs. Behind her, she hears Lucy the nurse shout at her to come back, because she's still convalescing, this is a delicate time.

Rachel feels a little more of her strength fade every time the dead man's hand lurches forward. Something irreplaceable leaves her. She pushes open the dense metal door marked EXIT and nearly faints with sudden day-blindness.

The woods around Love and Dignity for Everyone are dense with moss and underbrush, and Rachel's bare feet keep sliding off tree roots. I can't stop, Rachel pleads with herself, I can't stop or my whole life was for nothing. Who even was I, if I let this happen to me. The nearly naked dead man crashes through

TRANSCENDENT 3

branches that Rachel has ducked under. She throws the knife and hears a satisfy-ing grunt, but he doesn't even pause. Rachel knows that anybody who sees both her and the cadaver will choose to help the cadaver. There's no way to explain her situation in the dead man's voice. She vows to stay off roads and avoid talk-ing to people. This is her life now.

Up ahead, she sees a fast-running stream, and she wonders how the corpse will take to water. The stream looks like the one she and Jeffrey used to play in, when they would catch crayfish hiding under rocks. The crayfish looked just like tiny lobsters, and they would twist around trying to pinch you as you gripped their midsections. Rachel sloshes in the water and doesn't hear the man's breath in her ear for a moment. Up ahead, the current leads to a steep waterfall that's so white in the noon sunlight, it appears to stand still. She remembers staring into a bucket full of crayfish, debating whether to boil them alive or let them all go. And all at once, she has a vivid memory of herself and Jeffrey both holding the full bucket and turning it sideways, until all the crayfish sloshed back into the river. The crayfish fled for their lives, their eyes seeming to protrude with alarm, and Rachel held onto an empty bucket with Jeffrey, feeling an inexplicable sense of relief. We are such wusses, Jeffrey said, and they both laughed. She remem-bers the sight of the last crayfish rushing out of view — as if this time, maybe the trick would work, and nobody would think to look under this particular rock. She reaches the waterfall, seizes a breath, and jumps with both feet at once.

TRANSCENDENT 3

THE WORLDLESS

◄ Indrapramit Das ►

Every day NuTay watched the starship from their shack, selling satshine and sweet chai to wayfarers on their way to the stars. NuTay and their kin Satlyt baked an endless supply of clay cups using dirt from the vast plain of the port. NuTay and Satlyt, like all the hawkers in the shanties that surrounded the dirt road, were dunyshar, worldless — cursed to a single brown horizon, if one gently undulated by time to grace their eyes with dun hills. Cursed, also, to witness that starship in the distance, vessel of the night sky, as it set sail on the rippling waves of time and existence itself — so the wayfarers told them — year after year. The starship. The sky. The dun hills. The port plain. They knew this, and this only.

Sometimes the starship looked like a great temple reaching to the sky. All of NuTay's customers endless pilgrims lining up to enter its hallowed halls and carry them through the cloth that Gods made.

NuTay and Satlyt had never been inside a starship.

If NuTay gave them free chai, the wayfarers would sometimes show viz of other worlds on their armbands, flicking them like so much dijichaff into the air, where they sprouted into glowing spheres, ghost marbles to mimic the air-rich dewdrops that clustered aeon-wise along the fiery filaments of the galaxy. The wayfarers would wave in practiced arkana, and the spheres would twirl and zoom and transform as they grew until their curvature became glimpses of those worlds and their settlements glittering under the myriad suns and moons. NuTay would watch, silent, unable to look away.

Once, Satlyt, brandishing a small metal junk shiv, had asked whether NuTay wanted them to corner a wayfarer in a lonesome corner of the port and rob them of their armband or their data coins. NuTay had slapped Satlyt then, so hard their cheek blushed pink.

NuTay knew Satlyt would never hurt anyone — that all they wanted was to give their maba a way to look at pictures of other worlds without having to barter with wayfarers.

When NuTay touched Satlyt's cheek a moment after striking, the skin was hot with silent anger, and perhaps shame.

Sometimes the starship looked like monolithic shards of black glass glittering in the sun, carefully stacked to look beautiful but terrifying.

Sometimes the starship would change shape, those shards moving slowly to create a different configuration of shapes upon shapes with a tremendous moaning that sounded like a gale moving across the hills and pouring out across the plain. As it folded and re-folded, the starship would no longer look like shards of black glass.

Sometimes, when it moved to reconfigure its shape, the starship would look suddenly delicate despite its size, like black paper origami of a starship dropped onto the plain by the hand of a god.

NuTay had once seen an actual paper starship, left by a wayfarer on one of NuTay's rough-hewn benches. The wayfarer had told them the word for it: origami. The paper had been mauve, not black.

The world that interested NuTay the most, of course, was Earth. The one all the djeens of all the peoples in the galaxy first came from, going from blood to blood to whisper the memory of the first human into all their bodies so they still looked more or less the same no matter which world they were born on.

"NuTay, Earth is so crowded you can't imagine it," one wayfarer had told them, spreading their hands across that brown horizon NuTay was so familiar with. "Just imagine," the wayfarer said. "Peoples were having kin there before there were starships. Before any peoples went to any other star than Sol. This planet, your planet, is a station, nah?"

NuTay then reminded the wayfarer that this was not *their* planet, not really, because it was not a place of peoples but a port for peoples to rest in between their travels across the universe. Dunyshar had no planet, no cultures to imitate, no people.

"Ahch, you know that's the same same," the wayfarer said, but NuTay knew it wasn't, and felt a slight pain in their chest, so familiar. But they knew the wayfarer wouldn't know what this was, and they said nothing and listened as they spoke on. "If this planet is port, then Earth, that is the first city in the universe — Babal, kafeen-walla. Not so nice for you. Feels like not enough atmo for so many peoples if you go there, after this planet with all this air, so much air, so much place."

And NuTay told that wayfarer that they'd heard that Earth had a thousand different worlds on it, because it had a tilt and atmos that painted its lands a thousand different shades of place as it spun around the first Sun.

"Less than a thousand, and not the only world with other worlds on it," the wayfarer said, laughing behind their mask. "But look," the wayfarer raised their arm to spring viz into the air, and there was a picture of a brown horizon, and dun hills. "See? Just like here." NuTay looked at the dun hills, and marveled that this too could be Earth. "Kazak-istan," said the wayfarer, and the placename was a cold drop of rain in NuTay's mind, sending ripples across their skull. It made them feel better about their own dun hills, which caught their eye for all the long days. Just a little bit better.

So it went. Wayfarers would bring pieces of the galaxy, and NuTay would hold the ones of Earth in their memory. It had brown horizon, blue horizon, green horizon, red horizon, gray horizon.

When the starship was about to leave, the entire port plain would come alive with warning, klaxons sounding across the miles of empty dirt and clanging across the corrugated roofs of the shop shanties and tents. NuTay and Satlyt would stop work to watch even if they had customers, because even customers would turn their heads to see.

To watch a starship leave is to witness a hole threaded through reality, and no one can tire of such a vision. Its lights glittering, it would fold and fold its parts until there was a thunderous boom that rolled across the plain, sending glowing cumulus clouds rolling out from under the vessel and across the land.

A flash of light like the clap of an invisible hand, and the clouds would be gone in less than a second to leave a perfect black sphere where the starship had been. If you looked at the sphere, which was only half visible, emerging from the ground a perfect gigantic bubble of nothingness, it would hurt your eyes, because there was *nothing* to see within its curvature. For an intoxicating second there would be hurtling winds ripping dust through the shop shanties, creating a vortex of silken veils over the plain and around the sphere. The shanty roofs would rattle, the horses would clomp in their stables, the wind chimes would sing a shattering song. The very air would vibrate as if it were fragile, humming to the tune of that null-dimensional half-circle embedded in the horizon, a bloated negative sunrise.

In the next moment, the sphere would vanish in a thunderclap of displaced atmos, and there would be only flat land where the starship had once stood.

A few days later, the same sequence would occur in reverse, and the starship would be back, having gone to another world and returned with a new population. When it returned, the steam from its megastructures would create wisps of clouds that hung over the plain for days until they drifted with their shadows into the hills.

Being younger dunyshar, Satlyt worked at the stalls some days, but did harder chores around the port, like cleaning toilets and helping starship crews do basic maintenance work. Every sunrise, NuTay watched Satlyt leave the stall on their dirt bike, space-black hair free to twine across the wind. The droning dirt bike would draw a dusty line across the plain, its destination the necklace of far-off lights extending from where the squatting starship basked in sunrise — the dromes where wayfarers refueled, processed, lived in between worlds. The dirt bikes would send wild horses rumbling in herds across the port plain, a sight that calmed NuTay's weakening bones.

NuTay had worked at the dromes, too, when they were younger and more limber. They'd liked the crowds there, the paradisiacal choirs of announcements that echoed under vaulted ceilings, the squealing of boots on floor leaving tracks to mop up, the harsh and polychrome cast of holofake neon advertising bars, clubs, eateries and shops run by robots, or upscale wayfarer staff that swapped in and out to replace each other with each starship journey, so they didn't have to live on the planet permanently like the dunyshar. Nowadays the dromes were a distant memory. NuTay stayed at the shack, unable to do that much manual labour.

Those that spent their lives on the planet of arrivals and departures could only grow more thin and frail as time washed over the days and nights. The dunyshars' djeens had whispered their flesh into Earth-form, but on a world with a weaker gravity than Earth.

NuTay's chai itself was brewed from leaf grown in a printer tent with a second-hand script for accelerated microclimate — hardware left behind from starships over centuries, nabbed from the junk shops of the port by NuTay for shine and minutes of tactile, since dunyshar were never not lonely and companionship was equal barter, usually (usually) good for friendships.

NuTay would meditate inside the chai-printing tent, which was misty and wet in growing season. Their body caressed by damp green leaves, air fragrant with alien-sweet perfume of plant life not indigenous, with closed eyes NuTay would pretend to be on Earth, the source of chai and peoples and everything. Each time a cycle ended, and the microclimate roasted the leaves to heaps of brown brew-ready shavings, the tent hissed steam like one of NuTay's kettles, and that whistle was a quiet mourning for the death of that tent-world of green. Until next cycle.

The tent had big letters across its fiber on the outside, reading *Darjeeling* in Englis and Nagar script. A placename, a wayfarer had clarified.

When Satlyt was younger, they'd asked NuTay if the dunyshar could just build a giant printer tent the size of the port itself, and grow a huge forest of plants and trees here like on Earth or other worlds. NuTay knew these weren't thoughts for a dunyshar to have, and would go nowhere. But they said they didn't know.

The starshine was easier, brewed from indigenous fungus grown in shit.

Sometimes, as evening fell and the second sun lashed its last threads of light across the dun hills gone blue, or when the starship secreted a mist that wreathed its alloyed spires, the starship looked like a great and distant city. Just like NuTay had seen in viz of other worlds — towers of lights flickering to give darkness a shape, the outline of lives lived.

The starship *was* a city, of course. To take people across the galaxy to other cities that didn't move across time and existence.

There were no cities here, of course, on the planet of arrivals and departures. If you travelled over the horizon, as NuTay had, you would find only more port plains dotted with emptiness and lights and shop shanties and vast circular plains with other starships at their centres. Or great mountain ranges that were actually junkyards of detritus left by centuries of interstellar stops, and dismantled starships in their graveyards, all crawling with scavengers. Some dunyshar dared

TRANSCENDENT 3

to live in those dead starships, but they were known to be unstable and dangerous, causing djeens to mutate so kin would be born looking different than humans. If this were true, NuTay had never seen such people, who probably kept
to themselves, or died out.

NuTay had heard that if you walked far enough, you could see fields with
starships so massive they reached the clouds, hulking across the sky, that these
could take you to worlds at the very edge of the galaxy, where you could see the
void between this galaxy and the next one — visible as a gemmed spiral instead
of a sun.

Once, the wayfarer who'd left the origami starship for NuTay had come
back to the stall, months or years later. NuTay hadn't realized until they
left, because they'd been wearing goggles and an air-filter. But they left another
little paper origami, this time in white paper, of a horse.

Horses were used for low-energy transport and companionship among many
of the dunyshar. They had arrived centuries ago as frozen liquid djeens from
a starship's biovat, though NuTay was five when they first realized that horses, like humans, weren't *from* the world they lived in. Curiously, the thought
brought tears to their eyes when they first found this out.

Sometimes the starship looked like a huge living creature, resting between its
journeys, sweating and steaming and groaning through the night.

This it was, in some sense. Deep in its core was residual life left by something
that had lived aeons ago on the planet of arrivals and departures: the reason for
this junction in space. There was exotech here, found long before NuTay or any
dunyshar were born here, ghosts of when this planet was a world, mined by the
living from other worlds. Dunyshar were not allowed in these places, extraterra
ruins where miners, archaeologists, and other pilgrims from across the galaxy
gathered. NuTay, like most dunyshar, had little interest in these zones or the ruins of whatever civilization was buried under the dirt of this once-world. Their
interest was in the living civilization garlanding the galaxy, the one that was
forever just out of their reach.

On their brief travels with Satlyt strapped to their back as a tender-faced baby,
NuTay had seen the perimeter of one of these excavation zones from a mile
away, floodlights like a white sunrise against the night, flowing over a vast black
wall lined with flashing lights. Humming in the ground, and thunder crashing

TRANSCENDENT 3

over the flatlands from whatever engines were used to unearth the deep ruins and mine whatever was in them.

NuTay's steed, a sturdy black mare the stablemaster that had bartered her had named Pacho, had been unusually restless even a mile from that zone. NuTay imagined the ghosts of a bygone world seeping from out of those black walls, and trickling into their limbs and lungs and those of their tender child gurgling content against their back.

NuTay rode away as fast as they could. Pacho died a few weeks later, perhaps older than the stablemaster had promised. But NuTay blamed the zone, and rubbed ointment on Satlyt for months after, dreading the morning they'd find their kin dead because of vengeful ghosts from the long dead world that hid beneath this planet's time.

For Satlyt's survival NuTay thanked the stars, especially Sol, that had no ghosts around them.

Satlyt had asked NuTay one day where they'd come from, and whose kin NuTay themself was. NuTay had waited for that day, and had answers for their child, who was ten at the time. They sat by their shack in the evening light, NuTay waving a solar lantern until it lit.

I am a nu-jen dunyashar, Satlyt, they said to their child. This means I have no maba, no parents at all.

Satlyt asked how, eyes wide with existential horror.

Listen. Many…djeens were brought here frozen many years ago. I taught you; two humans' djeens whisper together to form a new human. Some humans share their djeens with another human in tiny eggs held in their bellies, and others share it in liquid held between their legs. Two people from some world that I don't know gave their djeens in egg and liquid, so that peoples could bring them here frozen to make new humans to work here, and help give solace to the wayfarers travelling the stars. We are these new humans — the dunyshar. There are many old-jen dunyshar here who have parents, and grandparents, and on and on — the first of their pre-kin were born to surrogates a long time ago. Understand, nah?

Satlyt nodded, perhaps bewildered.

I was nu-jen; the first person my djeens formed here on the planet of arrivals and departures. I was born right there, NuTay stopped here to point at the distant lights of the dromes. In the nursery, where wayfarer surrogates live for nine months growing us, new-jen kin, when there aren't enough people in the ports anymore. They get good barter value for doing this, from the off-world peoples who run these ports.

Who taught you to talk? Who taught you what all you know? asked Satlyt.

The dunyshar, chota kin! They will help their own. All the people in this shanty place, they taught me. The three sibs who raised me through the youngest years and weaned me are all, bless them, dead from time, plain simple. This planet is too light for humans to live too long as Earth and other livable worlds.

Did you sleep with the three sibs so the djeens whispered me into existence?

No, no! No, they were like my parents, I couldn't do that. I slept with another when I grew. Their name was Farweh. Farweh, I say na, your other maba. With them I had you, chota kin.

They are dead, too?

NuTay smiled then, though barely. I don't know, Satlyt. They left, on a starship.

How? They were a wayfarer?

No, they grew up right here, new-jen, same as me. They had long black hair like you, and the red cheeks like you also, the djeens alive and biting at the skin to announce the beauty of the body they make.

Satlyt slapped NuTay's hand and stuck out their tongue.

Oy! Why are you hitting your maba? Fine, you are ugly, the djeens hide away and are ashamed.

Satlyt giggled.

Anyway, such a distracted child. Your other maba, we grew up here together. We had you.

They were here? When I was born?

NuTay pursed their lips. They had promised that their child would have the entire truth.

For a while, hn. But they left. Don't be angry. Farweh wanted to take you. They made a deal with a wayfarer that sold them a spacesuit. They said they could get two more, one emergency suit for babies. Very clever, very canny, Farweh was.

Why?

NuTay took a deep breath. To hold on to a starship. To see eternity beyond the Window, and come out to another world on the other side.

Other maba went away holding on to a starship on the outside?

I see I taught you some sense, chota kin. Yes, it is as dangerous as it sounds. Some people have done it — if they catch you on the other side, they take you

TRANSCENDENT 3

away to jail, like in the dromes for murderers and rapists and drunkards. But bigger jail, for other worlds. That is if you survive. Theory, na? Possible. But those who do it, ride the starships on the side, see the other side of time? They never come back. So we can't ask if it worked or no, nah? So I said no. I said I will not take my kin like a piece of luggage while hanging on to the side of a starship. I refused Farweh. I would not take you, or myself, and I demanded Farweh not go. I grabbed their arm and hurt them by mistake, just a little, chota kin, but it was enough for both of us. I let them go, forever.

Farweh…maba. Other maba went and never came back.

Shh, chota kin, NuTay stroked a tear away from Satlyt's cheek. You didn't know Farweh, though they are your other maba. I gave them all the tears you can want to honour them. No more.

But you liked Farweh, maba. You grew up with them.

NuTay smiled, almost laughing at the child's sweetness. They held Satlyt before their little face crumpled, letting them cry just a little bit for Farweh, gone to NuTay forever, dead or alive behind the black window of existence.

Many years later, NuTay's kin Satlyt proved themself the kin of Farweh, too, in an echo of old time. They came droning across the plains from the dromes, headlights cutting across the dust while NuTay sipped chai with the other shanty wallahs in the middle of the hawkers' cluster. The starship was gone, out on some other world, so business was slow that evening.

Satlyt thundered onto the dust road in the centre of the shanty town, screeching to a halt, their djeens clearly fired up and steaming from the mouth in the chilly air.

Your kin is huffing, one of the old hawkers grinned with their gums. Best go see to them.

So NuTay took Satlyt indoors to the shack, and asked what was wrong.

Listen, NuTay. Maba. I've seen you, year after year, looking at the wayfarers' pictures of Earth. You pretend when I'm around, but I can see that you want to go there. Go after Farweh.

Go after Farweh? What are you on about, we don't even know whether they went to Earth, or if they're alive, or rotting in some jail on some remote world in the galaxy.

Not for real go after, I mean go, after. Story-type, nah?

Feri tail?

TRANSCENDENT 3

Exact. I know next time the starship comes, it will go to Earth. Know this for fact. I have good tips from the temp staff at the dromes.

What did you barter for this?

Some black market subsidiary exotech from last starship crew, changing hands down at the dromes. Bartered some that came to my hands, bartered some shine, some tactile, what's it matter?

Tactile, keh!

Please, maba. I use protection. You think wayfarers fuck dunysha without protection? They don't want our djeens whispering to theirs, they just want our bodies exotic.

What have you done, chota kin?

Don't worry, maba. I wouldn't barter tactile if I wasn't okay with it. But listen. I did good barter, better than just info. Spacesuit, full function. High compressed oxy capacity. Full-on nine hours. Starship blinks in and out of black bubble, max twenty hours depending on size. The one in our port — medium size, probably ten hours. Plus, camo-field, to blend into the side of the ship. We'll make it. Like Farweh did.

How do you know so much? Where do you get all this tech?

Same way you did, maba. Over years. There are people in the dromes, Satlyt said in excitement. They know things. I talk. I give tactile. I learn. I learn there are worlds, like you did. This? You know this isn't a world. Ghost planet. Fuel station. Port. You know this, we all know this. Farweh had the right idea.

NuTay shook their head. This was it. It was happening again. From the fire of the djeens raging hot in Satlyt's high cheekbones they knew, there was no saying no. Like they'd lost Farweh to time and existence, they would lose Satlyt too. NuTay knew there was no holding Satlyt by the arm to try and stop them, like before — they were too weak for that now.

Even if NuTay had been strong enough, they would never do that again.

It was as if Farweh had disappeared into that black bubble, and caused a ripple of time to lap across the port in a slow wave that had just arrived. An echo in time. The same request, from kin.

What do you say, maba? asked Satlyt, eyes wide like when they were little.

We might die, chota kin.

Then we do. Better than staying here to see your eyes go dead.

Even with filtered breathing, the helmet and the suit was hot, so unlike the biting cold air of the planet. NuTay felt like they might shit the suit, but what could one do. There was a diaper inside with bio-absorbent disinfectant padding, or so the wayfarer had said.

They had scaled the starship at night, using a service drone operated by the green-eyed wayfarer who had made the deal with Satlyt, though they had other allies, clearly. Looking at those green Earth-born eyes, and listening to their strange accent but even stranger affection for Satlyt, NuTay realized there might be more here than mere barter greed. This wayfarer felt bad for them, wanted to help, which made NuTay feel a bit sick as they clambered into the spacesuit. But the wayfarer also felt something else for Satlyt, who seemed unmoved by this affection, their jaw set tight and face braced to meet the future that was hurtling towards them.

"There'll be zero-g in the sphere once the starship phases into it. Theoretically, if the spacesuits work, you should be fine, there's nothing but vacuum inside the membrane — the edges of the sphere. If your mag-tethers snap, you'll float out towards those edges, which you absolutely do not want. Being inside the bubble is safe in a suit, but if you float out to the edge and touch it, there's no telling what will happen to you. We don't know. You might see the entirety of the universe in one go before dying, but you will die, or no longer be alive in the way we know. Understand? Do not jerk around with the tethers — hold on to each other. Hold on to each other like the kin you are. Stay calm and drift with the ship in the bubble so there's no stress on the tethers. Keep your eyes closed, throughout. Open when you hear the ship's noise again. Do not look at the inside of the bubble, or you might panic and break tether. That's it. Once the ship phases out, things will get tough in a different way, if you're alive. Earth ports are chaos, and there's a chance no one will find you till one of my contacts comes by with a ship-surface drone to get you. There are people on Earth who sympathize with the dunyshar, who want to give them lives. Give you lives. So don't lose hope. There are people who have survived this. I've ushered them to the other side. But if you survive only to have security forces capture you, ask for a refugee lawyer. Got it? *Refugee.* Remember the word. You have been kept here against your will, and you are escaping. Good luck. I'll be inside." The wayfarer paused, breathless. "I wish you could be too. But security is too tight inside. They don't think enough people have the courage to stick to the side of the ship and see the universe naked. And most don't. They don't know, do they."

TRANSCENDENT 3

With that, the wayfarer kissed Satlyt's helmet, and then NuTay's, and wiped each with their gloved hand, before folding themself into the drone and detaching it from the ship. Lightless and silent, they sailed away into the night. NuTay hoped they didn't crash it.

NuTay felt sick, dangling from the ship, even though they were on an incline. Below them, the lights of the launching pad lit a slow mist rising from the bottom of the starship, about four hundred feet down. The skin of the ship was warm and rumbled in a sleeping, breathing rhythm. They switched on the camofield, which covered them both, though they couldn't see the effects.

Satlyt was frighteningly silent. Chota kin, NuTay whispered to test the range com. Maba, Satlyt whispered back with a sweaty smile.

The starship awoke with the suns. Their uneasy dozing was broken by the light, and by the deeper rumble in the starship's skin. The brown planet of arrivals and departures stretched away from them, in the distance those dun hills. The pale blue sky flecked with thin icy clouds. The port dromes, the dirt roads like pale veins, the shanties glittering under the clear day in the far distance. Their one and only place. Hom, as wayfarers said. A strange word. Those fucking dun hills, thought NuTay.

Bless us Sol and all the stars without ghosts, whispered NuTay. Close your eyes, chota kin.

Remember Farweh, maba, said Satlyt, face wet behind the curved visor. The bottom of the starship exploded into light, and NuTay thought they were doomed, the juddering sending them sliding down the incline. NuTay held Satlyt's gloved hand tight, grip painful, flesh and bone pressed against flesh and bone through the nanoweaves.

I am old, NuTay thought. Let Satlyt live to see Earth.

The light, the sound, was gone.

Satlyt convulsed next to NuTay, who felt every movement of their kin through closed eyes. They embraced, NuTay holding Satlyt tight, a hollow vibration when their visors met. The ship was eerily still under them, no longer warm through the thick suit. Satlyt was making small sounds that coalesced slowly into words. We're alive.

Their breathing harsh in the helmet, the only sound along with the hissing breath of Satlyt into their own mic.

NuTay opened their eyes to see the universe looking back.

Don't look. Don't look. Don't look.

I know you opened your eyes, maba. What did you see?

I don't. Don't look. I saw darkness. Time like a living thing, a…a womb, with the light beyond its skin the light from creation, from the beginning of time and the end, so far away, shining through the dark skin. There were veins, of light, and information, pulsing around us. I saw our djeens rippling through those veins in the universe, humanity's djeens. Time is alive, Satlyt. Don't let it see us. Keep your eyes closed.

I will, maba. That is a good story, Satlyt gasped. Remember it, for the refuji lawyer.

Time is alive, and eventually it births all things, just as it ends all things.

When the ship turned warm with fresh thunder, their visors were set aglow, bathing their quivering eyelids with hot red light, the light of blood and djeens. Their spacesuits thumped down on the incline, the tethers umbilical around each other, kin and kin like twins through time entwined, clinging to the skin of a ship haunted by exoghosts.

They held each other tight, and under Sol, knew the light of hom, where the first djeens came from.

TRANSCENDENT 3

THE HEART'S CARTOGRAPHY

◄ Susan Jane Bigelow ►

Jade was the sort of backwoods girl who had a map of the countryside tattooed on her heart, and she could feel it in her bones when the pieces of her world shifted. So when the new family moved into the house across the road that late summer, she felt ripples of wrongness radiating out from them and their too-bright clothes, their bizarrely old-fashioned wood-paneled station wagon, and their rolling words that felt just a little to the left of normal.

"Time travelers," said Jade's brother, watching them from the window the day they moved in. Jade stood nearby, not daring to move or breathe.

"They *are* strange," said Jade's mother thoughtfully as she unloaded groceries. Jade helped her carry them in. "So…maybe. Maybe."

"Can't be anything else," said Jade's sort-of friend Andy as they rode their bikes into the village. "Gotta be from the future. If I were a time traveler I'd be just as clueless as that."

Jade agreed, but didn't say so.

They had a girl just about Jade's age, who introduced herself as "Sally" with that little hitch before the first syllable that suggested it wasn't the name she usually wore. Jade was hypersensitive to that sort of thing. People always had that hitch before they said her name, like the word *Jason* was on their tongues, in their minds, and hanging in the air between them before they placed the polite fiction of *Jade* in its place.

And so she found solace in the woods and streams and wild green places beyond the farms and tumbledown houses. The forest and the hills didn't care about gender; there, she could be herself. She could be alone.

The woods sang to her, a chorus of wild, sweet voices. She hummed along as she walked, and she knew where every rock, every trail, every tree was.

One day she was tramping down the path by the ancient stone wall when she stiffened, all senses alert. She knew someone was there, a bright and shining feeling, even before she heard the crack of branches and the hasty rustle of leaves behind her.

She turned and saw a blur of bright orange and pink making their slow way through some trackless part of the woods. She steeled herself before calling out, beckoning. Soon Sally was standing sheepishly in front of her, hair a tangle of branches and knees scuffed and bloody.

Jade couldn't help it, she burst into laughter. And then, to her amazement, Sally started laughing too.

They sat on the rocks by the slow late summer trickle of the old mill stream, shooting the breeze together about the woods.

"I got turned around on Hawk Mountain once," Jade was saying. "So I just decided to go west, cause I knew Lathrop Road was there. I crashed through the woods for *hours*, following the sun, until I was completely covered in scratches. And then I took a left to go around a boulder and found the damn trail — it had been like twenty feet away from me the whole time!"

She didn't say that she'd been only seven at the time, long before her sense of the woods had really begun to develop.

"I adore the forest," Sally said. Her accent was soft and flat, almost Midwestern, but with longer vowels and a rushing, lilting cadence that vaguely reminded Jade of Spanish. "At home we have some parks and spaces, but it's not wild like this!"

"I love it here," said Jade simply. "I never want to be anywhere else. I feel like… it's a part of me. I know every inch of it, in here." She tapped her chest, amazed at how easy it was to bare her heart to Sally.

"I can see why!" exclaimed Sally. "Wish I had a place like that."

"So, where is home for you?" asked Jade innocently.

"Oh," she said, flushing. "Chicago."

"How far in the future?" asked Jade.

Sally looked up at her, eyes wide with panic. "W-what? No! I mean — "

"It's okay," said Jade smugly, thrilled to have been proven right. "Everyone figures you're time travelers. We're not stupid."

Sally swore in a language that wasn't quite English, then glared up at Jade. "How?"

"Clothes," said Jade, ticking items off on her fingers. "Car. Accent. The way your dad is always standing around being fascinated by normal things. And your mom kept mentioning something called the Warm Shift, like we'd know what it was."

Sally groaned. "My dad is an idiot. He's always *so* sure, but we always do something to mess it up and then we have to leave!" She swore again. "I'm so tired of having to leave."

"Don't worry," Jade reassured her. "We won't tell."

"Thank you," said Sally, breathing a sigh of relief. "Oh, it's so nice to stop pretending. I just want to stay somewhere for more than a couple months."

"Don't you ever get to go home?"

Sally shrugged, and her eyes were heavy. "Yeah, but Dad keeps getting assignments, so we never stay long."

"Time traveling is his job?"

Sally gave her a look. "I'm really not supposed to talk about any of this."

"Aw, come on," Jade pressed, grinning. "Who am I gonna tell? The trees?"

Sally thought for a moment. Jade could tell she was unspooling a lifetime of training and paranoia. Then she came to a decision, rebellion in her expressive brown eyes. "Okay. I can tell you a little bit. You already know the time travel thing. Dad's a temporal anthropologist. Mom's a climate historian. She studies whatever time period we get sent to, she writes papers on things like air quality and whatever. He just makes these really weird observations and then tells us all about them at dinner." She made a face. "He's completely obsessed with shoes this time. It's so annoying. We go home in between assignments, but we never stay more than a week. Mom and Dad say we're lucky. I guess we are." She didn't sound convinced.

"So how far in the future are you from?" asked Jade, circling around to her original question. "What's it like?"

"Now *that* I really can't talk about. I'm not supposed to tell you anything about it!" She shook her finger at Jade. It was such an incongruously old-fashioned gesture that Jade couldn't hold a giggle back. "Could end up changing the future!"

TRANSCENDENT 3

"Right," said Jade, still grinning. "So have you been to the past? I mean, farther past than this?"

"Oh, yes!" said Sally brightly. "My favorite is the 1920s. We were there before we came here! The fashions were so nice, and everyone spoke so beautifully." She sighed. "We only stayed two weeks. I miss it."

"Wow," said Jade, burning with jealousy. "I'd have loved to have seen it."

"It was amazing," sighed Sally. Then she tapped the side of her head and stared off into space, as if checking something. "Oh, dear. I have to get back. But...I was thinking I would come down here again tomorrow. I like being outside like this. Are you doing anything? Um. I mean — "

"I'd love to," said Jade at once. It was still summer, after all, and there were no demands on her time. The prospect of sharing her woods with someone like Sally was exhilarating. "Wanna meet here? We can go up the waterfall trail. There's a pond at the top. It's really pretty there."

"That sounds bully!" exclaimed Sally. Then she flushed again. "That's wrong, isn't it."

Jade found herself grinning. "Sure, but who cares?"

Sally grinned back. "I'm so glad I came here! Who knew I'd find such a cool girl to hang out with? See you tomorrow, Jade!"

She ran off down the trail, leaving Jade feeling utterly buoyant. *Girl. Cool girl.*

There hadn't been any hitch when Sally had said her name, no slight emphasis on her gender. There was no choking, suffocating *Jason* expanding to fill the air between them, just a clean and fresh future full of possibilities.

Jade hadn't know how much of a relief that could be until now.

S he made her winding, casual way home as the sun set, letting herself in the back and then darting upstairs to avoid her father's stern, disapproving glare. She picked out a skirt and a clean top for dinner and carefully, hesitantly crept back downstairs to eat.

Her father gave her that same look he always gave, then shook his head and banged his glass down a little more forcefully than he needed to. Bourbon spilled out onto the tablecloth, and her mother winced.

"J-Jade — how was it out there?" her mother asked, trying to stay cheerful. She always made such an effort to get things right.

"Fine," said Jade.

"Did you see anything new?"

Jade shook her head. Her mother smiled, and then poked at her meat.

And that was just about it for conversation. Her brother told her father a little bit about something he was doing at his summer job; her father grunted non-committally, sipped from his strong-smelling glass, and then the house lapsed back into a thick and cloying silence. Forks clinked against plates.

"Good dinner, Mom, thank you," said Jade quietly when she was done. Her mother smiled at her again, trying to ignore her father's sour expression. She picked up her plate and put it in the sink, then escaped back up to her room. The internet was agonizingly slow out this far out in the country, but she could still talk to friends, post to her Tumblr, and soak up everything she was missing.

There was an interview with a famous trans activist, and she watched it even though YouTube stuttered and buffered the whole way through. Everyone loved her. The world was changing.

Please change faster. Please change faster. Please change here, too.

Please don't forget about us.

S ally was waiting next to the stream that morning. She was wearing hiking boots and a practical-looking outfit that seemed to be made of a cross between denim and leather.

Jade asked her about it.

"Can't tell you," she said smugly. "Wanna get going?"

Jade laughed. "Bet I can make you tell me before we get there."

"You won't!" said Sally, hoisting her pack.

But she did, less than halfway there.

"It's called saldec," admitted Sally, exasperated after Jade's constant prodding. "I don't know what it means! But a lot of our clothes are made of it, it lasts forever."

"Better than these old jeans," said Jade, eyeing a hole in her knee.

"Oh, but I like jeans!" exclaimed Sally. "They get so comfortable after a while."

Jade laughed, shaking her head as they trudged onward.

They spent the afternoon by the waterfalls and then the pond, eating the weird hard candy Sally had brought with her ("It's from the past! So it's okay!") and talking about the village nearby, Jade's family, the weirdness of time travel, and all kinds of other things. After a while they just sat together. Jade watched the dragonflies flit from lily pad to leaf, listening to the sound of cicadas, as white clouds drifted overhead. The air was warm but not too humid. There was no pressure to talk, no pressure to be anything but themselves.

Being with Sally was like being alone, but better.

When they separated by the creek as the sun began to set, after a promise that they'd meet up again tomorrow, Jade felt a peculiar emptiness. She was so used to being by herself that actually missing someone's company was strange.

She decided she could get used to it.

Their friendship grew as the weeks passed. They started hiking in different directions — into town, down by the ruins of the Seven Acres farm, out by the highway. Sally liked the town and the old farm, but she loved the highway. She watched the cars and trucks go by for hours, eyes wide.

"It's just so different!" she exclaimed. "We don't have anything like it!" Then she clamped her hand over her mouth while Jade laughed, filing the information away.

She'd learned a lot about the future from the little hints Sally had let slip. She'd started writing them down at night in a notebook she kept by her bed.

Hotter

Wetter? More rain?

No cars or highways

No United States?

Probably a couple hundred years

Really great clothes material

There were some big wars but people survived them?

Everyone has tech that's part of them — Sally's is mostly disabled and she misses it

No robots (damn)

No aliens either (double damn)

But nothing lasted forever, and summer's shadows lengthened while fall began to loom over Jade's life.

"Are you gonna go to school with us?" asked Jade. They were sleeping over at Sally's house. Sally's dad had been excited about the prospect, and had spent the whole evening, from the suspiciously normal meal of precisely-made hamburgers to an awkward, forced few hours sitting in front of the television watching a shopping channel, making surreptitious notes about her. He'd interrogated her at length about her sneakers, too. She caught Sally miming him a few times and had to stop herself from bursting out into howls of laughter.

TRANSCENDENT 3

But now the lights were out, and the girls were in their sleeping bags on the floor of the tastefully finished basement. Clearly Sally's family hadn't decorated the house at all. Jade had propped up a flashlight for them to see by.

"I don't know," said Sally, her face falling. "Dad's already saying he's got most of what they wanted him to get. And Mom thinks people in town are getting suspicious. So…"

"What? No! You're not leaving, are you? Please say you're not!"

"I — I really want to," said Sally, downcast. But then she made a visible effort to brighten the mood. She was always doing that — she didn't like staying sad too long. Jade was reminded of her mother whenever her father was halfway through his bottle of bourbon. "But I bet it'll still happen! Sometimes we've stayed a lot longer than we expected. Right? So tell me about school! I bet you have lots of friends. Are there boys? Girls? Are there boys or girls who *like* you?"

"Oh," said Jade, flushing. "Um. Not really."

"But you're so pretty! They're missing out *oh* so much."

Pretty? "They don't like me," mumbled Jade.

"But why?" asked Sally, clearly mystified.

"Oh come *on*," said Jade, suddenly cranky. "*You* know!"

"I do?" asked Sally, blinking.

Jade sat up, bewildered. Could it be possible that Sally hadn't picked up on it? She was so used to never passing, never being seen as herself. She'd stopped trying so hard when Sally was around; she just assumed Sally knew.

What if she didn't?

Her heart pounded. Did she really want to swing a wrecking ball through all that?

But then Sally neatly shattered her illusions. "Oh! I bet I know. Was it because you were born a boy?"

"Shit," muttered Jade, bracing herself for the deluge of awkward questions, reassurances, and worse.

But it never came. "I forgot that about now," Sally continued. "It's so weird. In my home time it's fine to move around between all the genders. I was a boy for a week in third level! But it didn't work out, I like being what I am." She grinned, then her face fell again. "People don't give you a hard time about it, do they? Is this one of those times where they do that?"

Jade just looked at the floor. "Oh. Nah. It's… I just… I'm alone a lot. People are fine. They're nice. But nobody gets too close, you know?"

"I do know," said Sally softly. "Nobody really likes time travelers, either."

TRANSCENDENT 3

"Even at home?" asked Jade, surprised.

"It's...it's all political," Sally said, waving her hands in frustration. "People say we're messing up the past. That we're polluting it. That's...like a huge deal. So people don't like us. I'm usually alone, when I'm back there. Why do you think I go with my parents? I have a sister who just stays home. But not me, I want to be here. Because...every time we go I might make a friend."

She was crying. Jade hesitated, then put a hand on hers. "Even though you have to leave them?" she asked.

"It's better than nothing," whispered Sally.

Jade squeezed her hand. "I want to tell you something," she said.

Sally blinked at her.

Jade took a deep breath. She wanted to give Sally something, and she couldn't think of anything else worth giving her. "Everyone else knows it. But...I want to share it with you. When I was a boy...my name was Jason. I don't go by it. I don't like it at all — please don't ever call me it. But maybe it's a secret you can take with you. Some little piece of me I don't need anymore."

Sally wiped a tear away. "Thank you, Jade. I like going by Sally. I always go by it, now. But back home...my name is Rehabetha." She laughed bitterly. "I hate it. Please don't ever call me it, either."

"I like Sally way better for you," said Jade with a grin. "It fits."

"Jade fits so much more for you, as well!" Sally exclaimed. "Oh, let's always be Sally and Jade!"

L ate that night, with Sally snoring softly in the bag next to her, Jade took out her notebook with her observations about the future. She switched on her light, and quickly wrote:

We survive

As she put it away, she was filled with a wild, wonderful hope. The future could be better than the past.

Things could keep changing.

O ne morning, just two days before the school year started, Jade's mother's voice woke her up.

"Hon," she said softly. "The woman from across the road is here. Your friend's mother is downstairs. She wants to talk to you."

"Uh? Sure," said Jade, blinking sleep from her eyes. "I'll come right down."

"Don't wake your father," her mother whispered. "He's...not feeling well."

Hungover, then. Best to avoid him.

"Got it," said Jade, and mother and daughter shared a nod, a little moment of we-are-in-this-together solidarity. Her mother left and Jade quickly dressed, ran a brush through her wild mane of hair, and tip-toed downstairs, taking care to skip over the creaky step.

Sally's mother was in the front room, eyes wet. When she saw Jade she hurried to her and grabbed her hand.

"Jade," she said, and Jade saw the awful, aching fear in her eyes.

"Oh no," said Jade, heart stopping. "Sally?"

"She left early this morning. I don't know where she is. We need to find her! We're — we're traveling today." Her mother looked away. "We can't leave her behind."

Traveling. They were leaving *today.* It hit Jade like a punch in the gut.

No wonder Sally had run.

"Do you know where she is?" Sally's mother asked, desperation in her voice.

"No," said Jade. Sally's mother's face fell. "But — I'll find her."

"You will?" asked Sally's mother, confused.

"If she's lost anywhere in the hills, my girl will find her," Jade's mother said firmly from the kitchen doorway. "No one knows the woods better."

Jade's heart swelled with pride. She looked Sally's mother in the eyes.

"I'll bring her back before you have to go. Promise."

Jade stepped out of her house into the cool morning air. She closed her eyes and pictured the vast sweep of the land in her mind. She knew every fold, every rise, every creek, every tree…every blade of grass. Every stone.

They sang to her with that majestic chorus, alive and vital and sweet. She opened her mouth and sang along, her heart opening and her senses sharpening.

Suddenly, she knew the location of every rabbit, every cricket, every deer… and every human.

Sally. The sense of her was as bright and clear as the sun.

She'd gone to their place by the waterfall. Jade never even considered telling the adults. This, she knew, was between the two of them. She shouldered her pack and set off at a jog.

The sun was obscured by threatening clouds when Jade arrived, exhausted and panting from running. She'd fixed her mind on the sense of Sally, and

TRANSCENDENT 3

now here she was in front of her, sitting by the water, sullenly casting stones into the pond.

"I knew you'd come find me," she said softly as Jade sat next to her.

"Everyone's looking for you," said Jade. "Your mom came to my house."

Sally swore. "I'm sorry."

"Don't be. She said...you're traveling today. Are you...?"

But Jade couldn't bring herself to ask the question.

Sally started to cry. "I don't want to go back. I hate leaving all the time! I finally make a friend and now — and now — "

Jade hesitantly put an arm around her, rebellious tears slipping down her own face. "I don't want you to go, either," she sniffed.

Sally turned to her, eyes suddenly wild and fiery. "Come with me. Come with us! I'll say I told you everything. I'll say you can't stay here. It would contaminate the timeline! There are rules. We could go to the future. We could be together!"

"What?" said Jade, taken aback. Her arms fell from around her friend.

"Please!" wailed Sally. "Please come with me. You — you can be anything you want there. No one will be mean to you!"

The wind picked up, and Jade tasted danger in the sudden cold. "Storm," she said, cursing herself. She'd been so intent on finding Sally that she'd missed all the signs. "Hell. We have to go. Come on."

"No," Sally said, the wind blowing her hair into her face. "I'm not leaving. Not until you say you're coming with me!"

Jade felt a chill that had nothing to do with the storm. The future stretched invitingly in front of her. The future had to be better than today. She could see all the wonders Sally had hinted at, she could be herself, and she would be with the only person she'd ever felt had really understood her.

But then she looked around at the pool and at the forest growing tall behind it, and felt her heart like an anchor connecting her to this place.

"I can't," she said, her heart breaking as the words left her lips. "I'm so sorry. I can't go." She dragged Sally to her feet.

"Why?" asked Sally, starting to cry again. "Don't you want to come with me?"

"Of course I do! I wish you could stay. You're the best friend I've ever had. I mean that." Jade thought of how to put it. "But...this is home. Right? And I can't just leave. I wouldn't be me anymore if I left."

"You have to go sometime," said Sally, sniffling. "To go to college? People do that here, right?"

TRANSCENDENT 3

"Maybe I won't go to college," said Jade. The wind was blowing in gusts, now. "Or I'll go to Callville State, just over the hill." She pointed, sure of the direction. "I want to be a park ranger someday, I think, or a guide. Something where I can be outside, and be here. This place, this here and now, is so important to me."

Sally nodded, eyes still wet. "I know. I know it is. But what about the people? Everyone's so awful."

"They can change," insisted Jade. "They already have. The future doesn't have to be like today. You taught me that."

Sally shook her head, miserable. And then a fat raindrop sailed out of the sky and hit her square on the nose.

She started to laugh.

"Sally, we have to go!" said Jade.

"I know," said Sally, and hugged her. "I know! I — I'll come back. You'll see. I'll come back and find you someday."

"I believe it," said Jade, grinning. "Now, come on!"

They sprinted for the cover of the woods as the rain began to fall in earnest.

Three soggy hours later they finally arrived, soaking wet, at Jade's house. Jade's mother ran to fetch Sally's while the girls changed into dry clothes. Thankfully Jade's older shirts fit Sally fairly well.

Jade stayed out of listening range for the hushed, intense conversation Sally had with her mother, but she couldn't help but tear up when Sally and her mother ended in a long, heartfelt embrace.

A hand on her shoulder. "You did real well," said her mother. "I knew you'd find her."

"Is Dad here?" Jade said, not sure what else to say.

"Out with his friends at the bar. He won't know about it," she said, a small smile on her lips.

Sally walked over, her eyes red from crying. "We're...we're going now. We're already late."

Jade looked at her mother, who nodded slightly.

"I'll walk you over," she said.

The rain had stopped, and the world smelled damp and clean. The sun peaked out from behind a distant cloud.

TRANSCENDENT 3

They said nothing on the walk to Sally's house. Jade had so many things she wanted to say to Sally, but couldn't think of how to start. There was too much to know where to begin. Sally's mother was walking ahead, giving them privacy.

Jade took Sally's hand and squeezed it. Sally squeezed back.

They arrived to find Sally's father waiting inside the wood-paneled station wagon. He grinned when he saw Jade there.

"I hear you're the one who found our girl," he said. "Thank you. We…ah, have to travel today."

"You're going home to your own time," said Jade, meeting his eyes. "I already know."

Jade's father's mouth dropped open, and he shot Sally a shocked look.

"I didn't tell her," said Sally. "She guessed it the first day."

"Oh," said her father. "Ah. That invalidates some of my notes, then."

Her mother gave Jade an appraising look. "I'm glad you came to say goodbye," she said. "R — Sally really likes you."

"I like her, too," said Jade shyly.

"Well," said her father. "Come on. We're late. Let's go!"

He got into the station wagon.

"I'll give you girls a minute," Sally's mother said, getting in the passenger door.

They were alone, for a last moment.

"I hate goodbyes," said Sally."

"Yeah," said Jade, trying not to cry. "How will I ever find you again?"

"Time has a map," said Sally, voice quavering. "It's written on my heart. And on yours, too."

Jade hugged her friend hard.

"I looked you up in our databases," whispered Sally. "I know where to find you."

"What did you find out?" asked Jade. "What am I going to be like when I'm older?"

Sally shook her head, fighting all her training, all of the things she'd believed since she was little. Then she gave Jade a last squeeze and whispered, "You're going to be amazing."

And with that, she got into the car. Jade stepped back.

Sally waved. The engine started up — and then the car was simply gone, as if it had never been there.

TRANSCENDENT 3

Jade walked back to her house, feeling an aching loneliness like nothing she'd felt before. She kept thinking how she would laugh about this with Sally later, or she'd see her on her walk tomorrow. She searched for the bright sense of her, but she was nowhere, now. She was beyond her reach.

Her mother was waiting for her at the door.

"Oh, hon, I'm so sorry," she said. "She left?"

Jade nodded and collapsed into her mother's arms, sobbing, the dam burst at last.

"My poor Jade," said her mother softly. There was no hitch in her voice this time, no hesitation. "My poor girl. It's all right. It happens. It's hard, but it happens."

"I miss her already," cried Jade.

"I know. I know. Come on in to the kitchen. I have the teapot on. Your dad won't be home for a while. We can have a cup of tea together, and you can tell me all about her. Okay?"

Jade nodded, grateful. She followed her mother inside.

As she crossed the threshold she felt a sudden ripple in the world around her, and then an achingly familiar bright, shining sense. She whirled around, and inhaled sharply.

A young woman stood there, dressed in clothes that looked nothing like anything Jade had ever seen. She had to be in her mid-twenties, and her deep brown eyes were full of tears. And next to her...stood a tall woman dressed in camouflage and hiking boots, with twigs in her gnarled hair and a wicked grin on her face.

Their arms were around one another. They both raised their hands in greeting, and farewell.

Jade waved back, grinning. The first woman touched her hand to her heart, and then they both vanished again.

The sun was shining overhead. Jade shut the door, and headed for the kitchen where her mother waited with hot tea and a smile.

THE CONTRIBUTORS

CHARLIE JANE ANDERS is the author of *All the Birds in the Sky*, which won the Nebula, Crawford and Locus awards. Also, a novella called *Rock Manning Goes For Broke* and a short story collection called *Six Months, Three Days, Five Others*. Her next novel is *The City in the Middle of the Night*, which comes out in February 2019. Her short fiction has appeared in Tor.com, *Boston Review, Tin House, Conjunctions, The Magazine of Fantasy & Science Fiction, Wired Magazine, Slate, Asimov's Science Fiction, Lightspeed, ZYZZYVA, Catamaran Literary Review, McSweeney's Internet Tendency* and tons of anthologies. Her story "Six Months, Three Days" won a Hugo Award. She hosts the long-running Writers With Drinks reading series in San Francisco.

SUSAN JANE BIGELOW is an author, librarian, and political columnist from Connecticut. She is the author of the *Extrahuman Union* and *Grayline Sisters* series, and the YA novel *The Demon Girl's Song*. Her short fiction has appeared in *Strange Horizons, Lightspeed, Apex*, and *Fireside*, among others. Her website is susanjanebigelow.com.

POLENTH BLAKE lives with cockroaches and likes drawing mushrooms. More can be found at polenthblake.com.

A C. BUCHANAN is a writer, editor, and part-time space lobster based near Wellington, Aotearoa New Zealand. Their work is published or forthcoming in *Apex*, *Kaleidotrope*, *Glittership*, and more. A.C. is also the editor of *Capricious* magazine, a freelance web developer, and likes cheese and dinosaurs. Their website is at andicbuchanan.org/ or you can find them on Twitter @ andicbuchanan.

L CHAN hails from Singapore, where he alternates being walked by his dog and writing speculative fiction after work. His work has appeared in places like *Liminal Stories*, *Arsenika*, *Podcastle* and *The Dark*. He tweets occasionally @ lchanwrites.

I NDRAPRAMIT DAS (a/k/a INDRA DAS) is a writer and editor from Kolkata, India. He is a Lambda Literary Award-winner for his debut novel *The Devourers* (Penguin India / Del Rey), and has been a finalist for the Crawford, Tiptree and Shirley Jackson Awards. His short fiction has appeared in publications including Tor.com, *Clarkesworld* and *Asimov's*, and has been widely anthologized. He is an Octavia E. Butler Scholar and a grateful graduate of Clarion West 2012. He has lived in India, the United States, and Canada, where he completed his MFA at the University of British Columbia.

L ARISSA GLASSER is a librarian, genre writer, and t4t trans lesbian from Boston. Her short fiction has appeared in *Wicked Haunted* (New England Horror Writers), *Tragedy Queens: stories inspired by Lana Del Rey and Sylvia Plath* (Clash Books), *Procyon Science Fiction Anthology 2016* (Tayen Lane Publishing), and *The Healing Monsters*, Volume One (Despumation Press). Her debut novella *F4* is available from Eraserhead Press. Find her on Twitter @larissaeglasser.

A DA HOFFMANN is the author of dozens of speculative short stories and poems, and of the collection *Monsters In My Mind*. She spends her day-job time programming computers to write poetry, and her Autistic Book Party review series is devoted to autism representation in speculative fiction. You can find her online at ada-hoffmann.com/ or on Twitter at @xasymptote

J ULIAN K. JARBOE lives in Salem, Massachusetts. They are the recipient of a 2018 Fellowship from the Writers' Room of Boston, and a 2017 Honorable Mention from the Tiptree Fellowship. Their work has appeared in numerous genre and literary magazines and anthologies, and can be found on their website, toomanyfeelings.com, or on Twitter @JulianKJarboe.

RYLEY KNOWLES is a journalist and writer. They live in Tacoma with their cat. They have high ambitions and low-self esteem.

YOON HA LEE's debut *Ninefox Gambit* won the Locus Award for best first novel and was a finalist for the Hugo, Nebula, and Clarke Awards; its sequel, *Raven Stratagem*, is currently a finalist for the Hugo Award. His next books are *Revenant Gun* from Solaris in June 2018 and *Dragon Pearl*, a Korean mythology space opera, from Disney-Hyperion in January 2019. He lives in Louisiana with his family and an extremely lazy cat, and has not yet been eaten by gators.

R. LEMBERG is a queer, bigender immigrant from Eastern Europe and Israel. Their fiction and poetry have appeared in *Lightspeed*'s *Queers Destroy Science Fiction*, *Uncanny*, *Beneath Ceaseless Skies*, and other venues. R.'s work has been a finalist for the Nebula, Crawford, and other awards. Their poetry collection, *Marginalia to Stone Bird*, is out from Aqueduct Press. For more Birdverse, please visit R.'s Patreon at patreon.com/roselemberg, where "The Splendid Goat Adventure" originally appeared.

S. QIOUYI LU is a writer, editor, narrator, and translator; their fiction has appeared in *The Magazine of Fantasy & Science Fiction*, and their poetry has appeared in *Liminality*. S. lives in California with a tiny black cat named Thin Mint. You can visit them at s.qiouyi.lu or follow them on Twitter at @sqiouyilu.

SHWETA NARAYAN was born in India, has lived in Malaysia, Saudi Arabia, the Netherlands, Scotland, and California, and feels kinship with shapeshifters and other liminal beings. Their short fiction and poetry have appeared in places like *Strange Horizons*, Tor.com, the 2012 *Nebula Showcase* anthology, and *We See A Different Frontier*. They're on hiatus for health reasons, but aten'd ded yet.

RIVERS SOLOMON writes about life in the margins, where they're much at home. Though originally from the US, they currently live and work in the UK. Their debut novel *An Unkindness of Ghosts* (Akashic Books) has been named as Lambda Award finalist, a Stonewall honor book, and a best book of the year in NPR and *The Guardian*.

TRANSCENDENT 3

Noa Josef Sperber is a teenage author born and raised in Los Angeles, and attending college there this fall. He's head of a self described media empire with the hopes of it being one day universally acknowledged, as he's a poet, performer, producer, and other non-alliterative things. He wrote "Fire Fills the Belly" for an assignment in the ninth grade. He likes a lot of things, and dislikes writing bios that sound like a dating profile. Follow him online at @noajosef for updates on everything.

Hugo and Nebula finalist K.M. Szpara is a queer and trans author who lives in Baltimore, MD. His fiction and essays appear in *Uncanny*, *Lightspeed*, *Strange Horizons*, and other venues. Kellan has a Master of Theological Studies from Harvard Divinity School, which he totally uses at his day job as a paralegal. You can find him on the Internet at kmszpara.com and or Twitter at @kmszpara.

M. Téllez is a heavily cyborg sci-fi writer from the 215 (Lenapehoking). They serve as Minister of Crossroads and founding member of the corner store sci-fi collective, METROPOLARITY.

Kerry Truong writes about many things, including folktale and horror. Their hobbies are futilely trying to train their dogs; tearing their hair out while reading comics; and eating good food. They like their meat rare, and if a story doesn't mention food at least once, it wasn't written by them. You can follow their queer firebreathing @ninetalesk.

COVER ARTIST

Raised on a grain farm, L. Stiegman now studies photography and arts technology at Illinois State University. They create and photograph bizarre narratives that are analytical and humorous in order to expose and organize aspects of identity. The image used on the cover of this book is part of a larger series called *A Midwest Queer Story*.

ABOUT THE EDITOR

Bogi Takács (e/em/eir/emself or they pronouns) is a Hungarian Jewish agender trans person and a migrant to the United States. E writes, edits and reviews speculative fiction and poetry, and e edited the Lambda Literary Award-winning *Transcendent 2*. You can find Bogi online at prezzey.net, read eir book reviews at bogireadstheworld.com, or follow eir QUILTBAG space opera webserial at iwunen.net. Bogi is bogiperson on Twitter, Instagram and Patreon. Bogi also had some trans stories published in 2017: "To Rebalance the Body" in *Nerve Endings* (ed. Tobi Hill-Meyer); and "Empathic Mirroring" in *Eyedolon* (ed. Scott Gable), the first in an upcoming series of novelettes titled *The Song of Spores*.

PUBLICATION CREDITS

"Don't Press Charges and I Won't Sue" copyright © 2017 Charlie Jane Anders, first appeared in *Boston Review*, Global Dystopias special issue (ed. Junot Díaz) / "The Heart's Cartography" copyright © 2017 Susan Jane Bigelow, first appeared in *Lightspeed Magazine* #84 / "Hello, World!" copyright © 2017 Polenth Blake, first appeared on patreon.com/polenth / "A Spell to Signal Home" copyright © 2017 A.C. Buchanan, first appeared in *GlitterShip* #41 / "Praying to the God of Small Chances" copyright © 2017 L Chan, first appeared in *Arsenika* #1 (ed. by S. Qiouyi Lu) / "The Worldless" copyright © 2017 Indrapramit Das, first appeared in *Lightspeed Magazine* #82 / "The Mouse" copyright © 2017 Larissa Glasser, first appeared in *Wicked Haunted: An Anthology of the New England Horror Writers* (ed. Scott T. Goudsward, Daniel G. Keohane and David Price, NEHW Press) / "Minor Heresies" copyright © 2017 Ada Hoffmann, first appeared in *Ride the Star Wind* (ed. Scott Gable and C. Dombrowski, Broken Eye Books) / "The Heavy Things" copyright © 2017 Julian K. Jarboe, first appeared in *SmokeLong Quarterly*, Issue 58 (Winter 2017) / "Death You Deserve" copyright © 2017 Ryley Knowles, first appeared in *Nerve Endings: The New Trans Erotic* (ed. by Tobi Hill-Meyer, Instar Press) / "The Chameleon's Gloves" copyright © 2017 Yoon Ha Lee, first appeared in *Cosmic Powers* (ed. John Joseph Adams, Saga Press / "A Splendid Goat Adventure" copyright © 2017 Rose Lemberg, first appeared on patreon.com/roselemberg / "A Complex Filament of Light" copyright © 2017 S. Qiouyi Lu, first appeared in *Anathema: Spec from the Margins*, Issue 1, April 2017 (ed. Michael Matheson, Andrew Wilmot, Chinelo Onwualu) / "World of the Three" copyright © 2017 Shweta Narayan, first appeared in *Lightspeed Magazine* #85 / "Feed" copyright © 2017 Rivers Solomon, first appeared on patreon.com/riverssolomon / "Fire Fills the Belly" copyright © 2017 Noa Josef Sperber, first appeared in *Brave Boy World: A Transman Anthology* (ed. by Michael D. Takeda, Pink Narcissus Press) / "Small Changes over Long Periods of Time" copyright © 2017 K.M. Szpara, first appeared in *Uncanny Magazine* (ed. Lynne M. Thomas, Michael Damian Thomas, Michi Trota) / "Heat Death of Western Human Arrogance" copyright © 2017 M. Téllez, first appeared in *Meanwhile, Elsewhere* (ed. Cat Fitzpatrick and Casey Plett, Topside Press) / "Cooking with Closed Mouths" copyright © 2017 Kerry Truong, first appeared in *GlitterShip* #35

CPSIA information can be obtained
at www.ICGtesting.com
Printed in the USA
LVHW112255230419
615338LV00002B/176/P

9 781590 217061